The Two Dea

Nick Louth is a million-selling thriller writer and an award-winning financial journalist. He self-published his first novel, *Bite*, which was a No 1 UK bestseller on Kindle in 2014. He was a Reuters correspondent for twelve years, and wrote regularly for the *Financial Times*, *Investors Chronicle*, *Money Observer* and MSN. He is married and lives in Lincolnshire.

Also by Nick Louth

Bite
Heartbreaker
Mirror Mirror
Trapped

DCI Craig Gillard Crime Thrillers

The Body in the Marsh
The Body on the Shore
The Body in the Mist
The Body in the Snow
The Body Under the Bridge
The Body on the Island
The Bodies at Westgrave Hall
The Body on the Moor
The Body Beneath the Willows
The Body in the Stairwell
The Body in the Shadows
The Body in Nightingale Park

Detective Jan Talantire

The Two Deaths of Ruth Lyle

THE TWO DEATHS OF RUTH LYLE

NICK LOUTH

First published in the United Kingdom in 2024 by

Canelo
Unit 9, 5th Floor
Cargo Works, 1–2 Hatfields
London SE1 9PG
United Kingdom

A CIP catalogue record for this book is available from the British Library.

Print ISBN 978 1 80436 717 9
Ebook ISBN 978 1 80436 718 6

Cover design by Dan Mogford

Cover images © Alamy

Look for more great books at www.canelo.co

Printed and bound in Great Britain by Clays Ltd, Elcograf S.p.A.

1

For Louise, as always

Chapter 1

Saturday, seven p.m. Good, bang on time. The suspect's car, a dark BMW estate, slid into the car park of the Royal Oak. It was a carefully chosen rendezvous. A village ten minutes south of Barnstaple, where she wouldn't be recognised. Detective Inspector Jan Talantire watched from her own darkened vehicle, in the shadow of the pub's gable. Ignition off, no lights. She was just thirty yards away, but able to scribble down the registration number in her pad. Six years old, one rear brake light not working. The BMW came to rest in the position she had expected, opposite the lounge, nose towards the pub so the driver could see in. The suspect was silhouetted in the glare of the pub window, broad-shouldered, hair short at the sides, shaped above, and a neat beard. Her electronic intel looked correct, so far. She waited as he emerged from the car. Tall, tight trousers that gripped at thigh and calf, some kind of formal jacket. He made his way round to the rear of the vehicle, and opened the boot. Bent over whatever was inside, both hands busy. Smiling, and apparently talking to himself.

Interesting.

The suspect locked the vehicle, then made his way, empty-handed, into the pub, wiped his feet carefully, and could soon be seen through the front window. He took a seat within view of his vehicle. Clearly wary, no drink as yet. A bit nervy, perhaps. Good; he appeared to think the stakes were high. So did she. Things had gone on long enough. Weeks of research, swiping through mugshots, chasing down leads. The inevitable disappointments when a promising line of enquiry came to nought. She had just ten minutes to wait, her decision. A policy. She risked the interior light, which she was pretty sure could not be seen from inside the pub, and took a final glance in the mirror at her disguise. Long, indulgently dangly earrings, chestnut hair, highlighted just yesterday, full-bodied, down at her shoulders, the work ponytail banished. Eye make-up, fairly extensive eyeshadow, eyeliner underneath to emphasise her big blue eyes. And lipstick; not the full crimson, but a softer shade, which she reapplied quickly. A small handbag, containing both work and personal phones. She took a quick glance at each, then switched them off. It was something she rarely did. But this time it was essential not to be disturbed.

She smoothed down her black zip-up skirt. It was a shortish number, which she rarely wore and which now didn't seem a great idea. She checked her lap for crumbs from the cereal bar she had gulped down as a precaution against a rushed exit, then slid down the sleeves of her white blouse, and added a bracelet. Nothing flashy, but smart. She pulled off her flat work shoes, and slid on the royal blue high heels she had kept in the passenger footwell. That would add a couple of inches to her height, making her five-ten. She saw the suspect check his watch. Two minutes to go. Okay, time to make her move. She slid out of the door into the April chill, walked gingerly round the puddles and made her way to the pub entrance. The warmth of the place slid over her as she turned to the table. She was within five yards before he looked up. A cautious smile.

'Hi, you must be Jan,' he said, standing up and offering his hand. Nice smile, great teeth. His profile said over six feet, but he was barely taller than she was. Five-eleven at most. A lie, but maybe a forgiveable one. He hadn't lied about his age, though. That looked spot on.

'Glad to meet you, Adam. I'm sorry I'm a bit late.' It was deliberate, a calibrated time to build expectations.

'I hadn't noticed.' *Liar. But a nice liar.* 'Glass of wine?' he asked, getting ready to head to the bar. *Imposing expectations, not so good.*

2

'I see they have an oatmeal stout, so I'll go for a half of that.' Her first challenge. He hid his surprise well. She sat and looked down at the menu, but with a sidelong glance checked him out as he headed to the bar. Yes, the trousers were tight, but at least properly belted. Firm bum. Clearly fit. Some kind of stain near the vent of his jacket. She told herself to turn it off, she wasn't at work now, despite the meticulous preparation. But still she saw him looking back at her reflection in the bar mirror. A good sign.

Back with the drinks, he sat down, looked through the menu and asked: 'Did you say you were a vegetarian?'

She laughed. 'No, no, not at all. You must be mixing me up with someone else.' He probably had a few dates on the go, but right there was a beginner's mistake.

'Sorry.' He laughed, and flexed his eyebrows in acknowledgement. That attractive smile again. She found herself grinning back at him. *Steady on, Jan. This is date one, five minutes in.*

'The pan-fried pork chop with garlic mash is very good here,' she said.

'Garlic?' he asked, leaving the rest unspoken. Flirtatious.

'Or there's the home-made pasta vongole. If you like seafood.'

'I love seafood,' he said.

She began to relax, embracing the conversation rather than assessing Adam from afar as if he was a habitual liar just dragged out of the cells. Lowering her defences never came easy, even more so now. The trouble was, it had been so long since Jon. Comfortable, taciturn, self-contained Jon had slipped from her life to go back to London. She'd had no hint that he'd even been unhappy. Never a cross word, but then hardly a word at all. She had taken shocked months on her own before she realised she never even knew the man with whom she had shared her life and her body for two years.

The conversation flowed. Until the inevitable question.

'So Jan, your profile said you worked with social services?'
Oh God, here we go. 'That's basically right.'

'So with adults or kids?'

'A bit of both really. Of course I spend my day like most of us do, behind the computer terminal bashing away on a keyboard. A bit boring, really.' This was a line she had polished with all the previous dates. She wasn't going to tell him what she really did. Good God, no. Kiss of death on the first date, surely.

'Yeah, tell me about it,' he said. 'I'm a freelance web designer, so I know all about that. So what about this kid that disappeared? Is that one of your responsibilities?' he asked.

She didn't want to go there. 'I'm hoping that case doesn't fall to me.'

Alice Watkins, aged seven, had disappeared a day and a half ago. One minute she was playing near a static caravan where her parents were on holiday. Gone the next. It had made the papers already, but was at this stage still primarily a uniform job. Door-to-door, trawling the entire holiday park, where most cabins were at this time of year empty. Appeals for witnesses. But the anxiety had spread through the entire Barnstaple office, amongst not only all the officers but the receptionists too, and right through to the man who fixed the photocopier.

'Fingers crossed she's found,' Adam said, as he called the waitress over.

'Yes. So I suppose you work from home?'

'I used to, but it was driving me mad, so I rented a shared office. I found it was important to be able to relax when I was at home, knowing I wasn't at work. Different headspaces, know what I mean?' That smile again.

They talked about music, and found Latin jazz in common. He was impressed to hear that she ran, and even more impressed by the distances. 'You regularly run ten to fifteen k?' he said.

'It's not so far, with practice. I'm a member of the Black Bull Harriers.'

'I used to run a bit, and go to the gym. Bit more of a fair-weather exerciser. A jogger, not a runner, I suppose.'

They ordered and the food came quickly; she didn't even notice what she was eating.

'Presumably you're not always stuck in the office, client visits, tough council estates and so on?' he asked.

This was good, and a nice change. The dating websites were crammed with conversational broadcasters, who didn't listen but simply waited for the next opportunity to talk. There was Brian, who had droned on and on about investment and pension strategies, and Aaron, who while describing his software sales business had stared almost without interruption at her peach-coloured jumper, as if he'd been gifted X-ray vision.

'Yes. I managed to get out yesterday, to sunny Woolacombe,' she said. 'Can't tell you about the case, you know, data protection.' What had actually happened was that she'd been called to a vermin-infested house where an elderly man had died, sitting on the toilet with his trousers round his ankles. There were signs of a break-in, but it wasn't clear whether it was related to the death.

He smiled and nodded. 'I spent yesterday trying to get images I'd been sent to configure correctly. Three worked perfectly, and the fourth kept overlapping the text. Took all day to figure out why. Sorry, it sounds so boring.'

'No, not at all.' She excused herself, and headed to the bathroom. She felt his eyes on her as she walked away, her unpractised ankles trying not to fall off the heels. Maddy had persuaded her to wear the skirt to show off 'those long shapely legs', but Talantire realised now that on a first date it was better idea not to distract his gaze. She wanted his eyes firmly on her face. Still, too late now.

Once she was inside, she switched on her work phone out of pure workaholic habit.

Shit.

Three text messages and a voicemail from DC Stephen Dowling, who was on duty covering Barnstaple and Ilfracombe tonight. Dowling was just twenty-two, a probationer within

CID, and had been on one of her situational judgement training courses. He was a laggard, so she had mentored him informally for the first few months. But this was now getting a bit out of hand; she was on a date, for heaven's sake. With a sigh she checked the voicemail.

'Sorry to bother you when you're off duty, ma'am, but I'd appreciate a bit of help. I've got one uniform here and a dead body.'

She rang him. 'Ma'am, thanks for calling back.' His voice was high pitched, squeaky almost, as he gabbled away. 'We've got a big crime scene here in Ilfracombe, and I mean massive. I'm a bit out of my depth. DI Lockhart is the duty DI but he's stuck out in Snozzle and told me to get on with it.'

St Austell, locally known as Snozzle, was down into Cornwall, two hours' drive from Ilfracombe.

'What's happened?'

'We've got an elderly lady in a holiday home. She's been stabbed, in the kitchen. Blood everywhere.'

She looked into the bathroom mirror, seeing tiny creases in her brow. The arrival of work mode. In the harsh light of the bathroom her eyeshadow made her look like a panda, and at this rate just as likely to get a mate.

'Okay, don't touch anything—'

'Well, sorry ma'am, I've been sick.'

'Please tell me, Stephen, not on the crime scene.'

'I got out as far as the hall. It's down me jacket though.'

She rolled her eyes. 'Let me speak to the senior uniform.'

'There's only me and PC Moody at the moment.'

That was worse news. Philip Moody was even more junior than Dowling, and notoriously dim with it. Talantire stared into the washbasin, seeing her date spiralling down the plughole.

'What about CSI?' she asked.

'Ah, now they can't get here until morning. The main crew is in Exeter, because there's been a hit and run with two injuries, and the second crew's still in Penzance.' That was three hours away from the crime scene. So, it was to be another ruined Saturday night. The curse of Devon and Cornwall Police: a huge rural policing area, not a single motorway west of Exeter, and never enough officers.

'All right, Stephen. I'll be there in half an hour.'

'Thank you so much, ma'am, it means a lot to me.'

'I'm not doing it to help you, Stephen, I'm doing it because it needs doing right, and if we get it done right now that saves an awful lot of fuss and paperwork tomorrow. Is the crime scene secure?'

'Yes. It's taped off. We called a locksmith to get a padlock, he'll be along directly.'

'Good. Have you rung the duty forensic pathologist?'

'Yes. I'm waiting for confirmation whether he can come.'

'Have you taken some photos?'

'Yeah, but we've got no evidence markers.'

'But I take it you do have booties and gloves?'

'Gloves, yeah, but I got puke on the first pair and I s'pose that's got my DNA, and we didn't know we needed booties when we first went in, so there's footprints and that.'

Jan could only imagine what mess the crime scene might be in. Thank God she had only drunk half of her beer. She didn't like anyone smelling alcohol on her breath. She splashed water on her face, and then with rapid and practised movements used some cream and make-up removal pads to tone down the slap. She looked at the lipstick marks left on the tissues and wondered if she would ever see Adam again. She hoped so.

Heading back into the restaurant, she saw him playing with his phone. He looked up and smiled, then did a double-take at her emerging workaday face.

'I'm really sorry, Adam. Something's come up at work. I have to go.'

'Really?' He clearly didn't believe her and looked a little downcast. 'Is it the little girl?' he asked, staring at his hands. It was almost as if he wanted it to be the case, something definitely serious enough to justify abandoning the date. Anything as long as it wasn't about him.

'Look. I like you, and I think we should meet again. But I have some secrets I can't share with you right now.' She pulled out enough cash to cover what they'd eaten so far.

'No, it's fine. I'll get it,' he said.

'No, you won't. I insist. I'll message you later in the week.' As she left, she felt his eyes on her. Not assessing her figure this time, but wondering whether she had told him the truth. That it clearly mattered to him was a good sign. Maybe not all was lost.

Chapter 2

Ilfracombe was a sleepy Victorian coastal resort of around ten thousand people, twenty minutes north of Barnstaple on a winding road. During its heyday, dozens of trains would arrive each day, disgorging thousands of holidaymakers from the Midlands and the North, eager to walk its cliffs and headlands and dip into the chilly waters. But by the 1960s, the European package holidays boom had begun. Like so many British seaside towns, Ilfracombe couldn't compete with the lure of Spanish and Greek beaches and their guaranteed warmth. The station closed in 1970, leaving the town a much more difficult place to get to.

She used the hands-free phone to ring in to the control room in Exeter, to find out the state of play. The male call handler summarised what they knew so far: 'Female, mid-sixties, found stabbed in a rental property in Mercer Lane, in the town centre. The alarm was raised by a neighbour who had heard a violent argument on Thursday afternoon—'

'Two *days* ago!'

'Yes. And hadn't seen the lady emerge from the house. He knocked on the door this morning, and again this afternoon, and finally rang us on the non-emergency number shortly after five. Our first officer, PC Moody, arrived at 8:15 p.m. and shortly after effected an entry.'

'And the rest, as they say, is histrionics.' Talantire thanked him, rang off and checked the time. The initial call was nearly four hours ago. Not an outrageously slow response for a non-emergency call. In some parts of the country they were not

9

answered at all. Fortunately, she always kept a go-bag of forensic coveralls, booties and gloves in her own car as well as in her official unmarked vehicle. Next to it in the boot was a holdall containing wellies, torch, DNA swabbing kit, yellow plastic evidence markers and fingerprint lift gel strips.

She raced out on the B3230, keeping to the speed limit, and within twenty minutes got her first sight of Ilfracombe from the hilltops above. She pulled over in a lay-by to unzip her skirt and wriggle into the pair of jeans she'd left on the back seat. She placed her high heels in the rear footwell, and slid on her trainers. As she did so, she took in the harbour lights twinkling in the dusk against a gunmetal sea, the town wedged between steep cliffs that resembled stacks of dark books, sliding obliquely into the water.

It took only another five minutes to get to the crime scene. Mercer Lane was a very steep and narrow residential street in the town centre leading up from Wilder Road towards the High Street, to which it was connected by an alleyway. Parking was difficult, and the two squad cars already there were blocking the road right up at the top. She left her vehicle behind them and made her way up through the sizeable crowd of rubberneckers to the crime tape. Five uniformed officers were visible. Amongst them she recognised the looming presence of Inspector T. P. Carnegie, and heaved a sigh of relief. Known universally as Wigwam because of his first two initials, Carnegie was six foot two, mid-fifties and bespectacled, with thinning hair. He was operationally a safe pair of hands, if only he would keep them to himself in the office. Never turn your back on Wigwam, was one of the first pieces of advice she was offered when she had started at Barnstaple five years ago. To be fair, Wigwam was much better behaved these days after her robust deputy, Detective Sergeant Maddy Moran, had 'had words' with him a year ago, but a reputation like that once earned wasn't easily lost.

Carnegie was talking to Dowling and Moody, gathered right at the top of the cul-de-sac around the entrance to a substantial stone-built cottage with a steep wooden gable, tucked in behind a three-storey Victorian building on the High Street above. It was Bluebird Cottage, according to the glazed tile sign outside, and incorporated a much older, narrow building, recessed to the right, whose arched wooden door stood slightly ajar.

'Very kind of you to turn up on your evening off, Jan,' Carnegie said.

'That's all right, I wasn't doing anything much.'

'We're a bit stretched here.'

'Retched, I heard.'

Carnegie rolled his eyes in agreement. The smell of vomit by the doorway was overpowering. She glanced at Dowling, who looked decidedly sheepish. His borrowed stab vest didn't completely conceal the damp zip-up fleece jacket that still bore some traces.

'Who's been inside?' she asked him.

'Just us two,' Dowling said.

'Show me your holiday snaps, then.'

'It's pretty ghastly,' Dowling said, passing across his phone. She swiped through half a dozen images. A blood-drenched woman was lying spreadeagled but fully dressed on a kitchen table, with six inches of a crude iron crucifix protruding from her chest.

She blinked away her shock. 'Right. I'll go and suit up.'

'I'll sign you in then, ma'am,' said PC Moody, shrugging a clipboard. 'The tent should be here in half an hour.'

'The sooner the better,' she said.

Five minutes later, now wearing her Tyvek coveralls, gloves and booties, and armed with packs of fingerprint gel lifts and swabs, Jan made her way back through the growing crowd, past the uniformed officers and up the step. She eased the old wooden door open, and it creaked like something from a Hammer film. It was an unusual cottage, that was for sure. A short hallway, with a kitchen off left, but her eye was drawn to the long lounge with a high vaulted ceiling, and tall narrow ecclesiastical windows at the far end. It looked like a converted church. To the right, a spiral metal staircase led up to a galleried bedroom with a balcony looking out over the hallway and lounge. The flagstone floor was marked with bloody footprints, from what might well be constabulary boots, as well as the spattered remains of Dowling's lunch. Before moving in, she took a gel lift from the light switch by the door, and followed it with a DNA swab. She didn't have any stepping plates, but carefully placed her feet around the right-hand edge of the hallway. There were two women's coats on the coat rack, and she took fibre lifts from the collars. She moved forward methodically, taking samples as she went, finishing with the round brass handle of the door to the kitchen from where the bloody footprints originated.

Only then did she allow herself to ease open the door and take in the horror and stench of the crime scene. As she stepped inside, a couple of metallic green flies buzzed away to the ceiling, fat and lazy, well fed. The poor woman had been gagged with a pair of tights and her eyes were slightly open, only the whites visible. There was evidence she had lost control of her bowels in her final moments of life. The crude metal of the cross looked like it may have pinned the victim to the table, leaving her limbs dangling. Her fingers were bloody, as if in death she had desperately tried to reverse her impalement. Images of a dozen vampire films flitted like shadows through Talantire's mind, adolescent fears urging her to flee. Others had opposite impulses; the wound, small, blood-dark and sticky, drew back a fly, which crawled on it, then meticulously rubbed its forelimbs one around the other, as thorough as a surgeon soaping up for an operation. The urge to swat the creature away, out of some misplaced sense of hygiene, was almost irresistible.

Jan set down plastic evidence markers, then concentrated on taking pictures, more than a hundred images for this room alone. She crouched for low angles, and stood on tiptoe for top-down perspectives, swallowing back bile that tried to force its way into her throat. Under the table she spotted a handbag, and retrieved it, putting it into a plastic evidence bag. She wondered what evidence could be secured that might deteriorate before CSI's eventual arrival. There was one crucial element.

Time of death.

The longer the delay, the harder it can be to establish exactly when the victim has died. Though there are standard count-down calculators of time against body temperature, these can be thrown by environmental factors. If the ambient temperature changes – say the central heating comes on – a body may retain heat for longer. She looked around the kitchen. A rather swish newly installed set of cupboards, worktops and drawers. Hardwood. A well-equipped rental, with lots of money spent. Loads of pans hanging from ceiling hooks, Brabantia utensils on a wall rack. Knives, lots of 'em. This wasn't just domestic envy, it gave her an idea. She did fingerprint lifts of the two principal drawers before sliding them open. Bingo! She was right.

A meat thermometer. This was a brand-new digital device with a steel probe the size of a darning needle. She turned it on, then noted the room temperature: 16 °C. Carefully she approached the body, hoping that she wasn't going to get into trouble with the forensic pathologist for making a fresh hole in the victim. Still, without a probe that only a CSI team would have, this was the only way to get this vital information. With her gloved hand, she lifted a section of unbloodied blouse, exposing the woman's waist. She rested a thumb against the pale skin. Cool, but not cold. Flexible, so presumably beyond rigor mortis. She took a photograph of the unblemished skin, before pressing in the long probe to its full depth. She waited while the digital readout temperature climbed. Then when it had stabilised, she photographed the display. It showed 19.2 °C, about half a living body temperature. She'd have to look it up precisely, but it didn't seem out of kilter with the witness statement reporting hearing the noise of an argument two days ago. That could well have been when she died.

She was just wondering what else she could do when the phone rang. Detective Superintendent Michael Wells, her boss.

'Hello, Jan, thank you for giving up your Saturday night to help us out here.'

'I'd like not to make a habit of it,' she said, looking at the impaled body in front of her. 'I'd rather be sitting at home watching *Strictly*.'

'Well, as you are aware, we are having a resourcing crisis.'

'That's been true for as long as I've been in the police service, sir. With all due respect, I think it's high time that the police and crime commissioner managed to get us some more resources. Half the time we've got one overnight duty DI covering the entire region. It's not enough.'

'I hear what you're saying, Jan. DC Nuttall is coming in to take over from midnight, so you're off the hook until tomorrow. Now, about this body. I was getting garbled reports about a crucifix of all things.'

'Well, whatever else was garbled, it wasn't that. Sir, this is the clearest case of murder I've ever seen. We need CSI here as soon as you can possibly get them, along with the duty forensic pathologist.'

'Well, we've got a couple of crime scene investigators on their way now. I understand Dr Piers Holcombe will be there by eight a.m. It sounds like we need to keep the body in situ until he arrives. And Jan, I'd like you to be SIO. Nuttall, Carnegie and the uniforms will hold the fort overnight but I'd like you to be in charge by the time Dr Holcombe arrives.'

'All right, sir.' She had been due the whole weekend off, but had accepted from the first moment she started removing her make-up in the Royal Oak that she was going to be hard at work until her scheduled duties resumed on Monday.

Talantire looked around to ensure she hadn't brought anything into the crime scene apart from the evidence markers. She then carefully retraced her steps. Emerging outside into the narrow street, she was blinded by the flashguns of the press.

Though kept back a good twenty yards by the crime tape, they were using their long-lens cameras to good effect. What they really needed was a good crime scene tent, so they could work around the cottage entrance unobserved. As things stood, residents were staring out of upstairs windows opposite, and could see exactly who came and went. There were a dozen uniformed constables present now, along with Inspector Carnegie.

She called him over. 'We're going to need to have the houses opposite cleared. We can't have all these people gawking down at us. And seeing how cramped the street is, we won't be able to get the mobile incident room down here.'

'I've already made arrangements for tomorrow,' Carnegie said, pointing up the alleyway. 'We're taking over the Stag and Hounds Hotel on the High Street. I've notified the pub company.'

Jan remembered a good night in the Stag, well over a decade ago, when she and fellow trainee Caroline had gone, off duty, to see some heavy metal band, and got very drunk with the locals. They only narrowly escaped being arrested when the police arrived after a window got broken outside.

'That should be perfect. Refreshment on tap,' she said.

'Sorry to disappoint, it's closed for refurbishment, though they haven't yet started on it. There's no booze on the premises.'

'Spoilsports,' she said.

'It'll be ready first thing, and it's only fifty yards from the scene.'

'Great. I'll ring Nuttall to brief him, then I'm heading off home for a bit of shut-eye.'

'Thanks for coming in, Jan. Much appreciated.' He pointed to a bin bag by the side of a patrol car. 'Stick your overalls in there.'

She passed him the evidence bag containing the handbag. 'I hope there is some ID in there. We need to find out who she is.'

'The landlady's emailing me the rental contract. Tenant wasn't a local, apparently. Been here seven or eight months.' He

15

shrugged the bag. 'I've appointed one of the PCSOs as evidence officer until tomorrow. He only did the course last week.'

As Jan walked away towards her car she reflected how few experienced officers there were around. Everyone seemed to be straight off a training course. It's all very well getting to use the latest gizmos, but there is no substitute for experience.

When she was inside the vehicle, she checked her personal phone for messages on the dating app. Nothing from Adam. Oh well, probably the end of that. They hadn't even swapped surnames, so at least her cover was intact. She drove home, and got in about a quarter to eleven. She was just cleaning her teeth when her phone buzzed. A message through the dating app from Adam.

> Hi. Hope work wasn't too onerous. Meet up again next week?

She grinned into the mirror, a little beard of white foam dripping from her chin.

Chapter 3

It was shortly before eight on Sunday morning, and Ilfracombe High Street looked like the epicentre of a localised recession. Apart from the Lidl, there were no national names, not even a Boots. Just a run-down nightclub, a couple of tatty convenience stores, some charity shops, and one brave bookshop. This was the rotting heart of an otherwise pretty and apparently prosperous seaside town. But the gap between well-heeled holiday home owners and the struggling locals was obvious. Oxford Grove, a steep street leading up to Princess Avenue police station, was a perfect case in point. Wonderful Victorian architecture, now utterly neglected, with piles of rubbish outside each of the front doors. She had sometimes been here on drugs raids.

Talantire parked at the bottom of Oxford Grove, opposite the Stag and Hounds. As she got out of the car she saw the rest of her team arrive. Detective Sergeant Maddy Moran and DC Dave Nuttall, both from the Barnstaple team, along with a new officer, wearing a trouser suit and a fawn hijab, emerged from the unmarked Ford.

'Jan, this is Primrose Chen, she's the new digital evidence officer,' Maddy said. 'Joining us from the Met, no less.' Maddy was stockily built, with her dark hair cut in a bob that framed her heart-shaped face. She was thirty-six, a couple of years younger than her boss.

'Welcome, Primrose,' Talantire said. 'You've caught us on a very busy day, so you'll be straight into the action.' Talantire had been notified of Primrose's appointment, but wasn't expecting

17

her for another week or so because of training. The young DEO had only served six months in London, and had previously worked in the U.S.

'That's perfectly fine,' she said, with a slight American accent. 'I like to be busy.'

'Then you'll love CID,' said Nuttall. His trademark leather jacket was unzipped to reveal a denim shirt that matched his ripped jeans. He was as usual chewing gum. He was late forties, with thick-framed glasses, dyed dark hair slicked back, like a superannuated Teddy boy.

'Where's Wigwam?' Jan asked Maddy.

'He's going to join us later on.' Seeing the puzzled expression on Primrose's face Maddy explained how the uniformed inspector had gained his nickname. 'What you'll find, Primrose, is that it's best not to use nicknames to people's faces.'

'Especially if your nickname is wanker,' Nuttall interjected.

Maddy and Jan shared a glance. Primrose's face had coloured slightly as she glanced towards Nuttall.

'Don't worry, he's just trying to be funny,' Jan said.

'Of course, we'd never use that as a nickname, Primrose,' Maddy whispered, leaning towards her. 'The reason being that there are no end of wankers in Devon and Cornwall Police, and we wouldn't know who you were talking about.'

They all laughed.

'Right, let's get this show on the road,' Jan said. Nuttall had the keys, and let them into the pub through the side door, and it all came flooding back to her: the smell of stale beer, the sticky carpet with its paisley pattern designed to hide the stains. The hand pumps and the taps, this week's guest ale or cider sensation. Above them a nicotine-stained ceiling with its exposed mock beams. The round tables with curlicue cast-iron legs, perfect for smashing your shins on and far too heavy to throw. The jukebox was gone, replaced by a quiz machine. There was no sign of the pool table either.

Maddy went to the windows and drew the curtains, while Nuttall and Primrose brought in whiteboards, magnets, paper and marker pens from the car outside. Jan set up a laptop and projector screen, and in ten minutes they were ready to run.

'Right, I can confirm that Dr Holcombe is there now,' Jan said, looking at her phone, where a text message was displayed. She opened an envelope and pulled out a sheaf of photo enlargements, fixing them to the whiteboard with magnets. Right at the centre she put a shocking image of the poor woman impaled by the crucifix, gagged and drenched in blood.

'It's like something from a horror film,' Nuttall said.

Talantire agreed. 'Maybe there were ritual elements.' She hoped not. Lurid press reportage always followed anything with satanic overtones.

'That crucifix looks pretty crude,' Maddy said. 'Two massive iron nails, and a load of blobby solder.'

'Those blobs are probably bronze or lead,' Nuttall said. 'Is it intended to be Christ?'

'Presumably,' Talantire said, pinning up a close-up image of the murder weapon. 'Those runnels could be arms on the cross, and the biggest blob could be a head.'

'The legs are quite convincing, if you squint a bit,' Maddy said. 'For a year five metalwork project, anyway.'

For all the dark humour, Talantire knew not one of the team, not her, probably not even the most experienced officers in the entire force, had ever seen anything like this. The juxtaposition of the most holy symbol in Christianity with an unspeakable act of brutality. For a few moments, they all just stared, taking it in.

Breaking the spell, Talantire exhaled and laid out half a dozen clear plastic evidence bags. 'Mobile phone, purse with bank cards, passport. All the usual stuff, but no driving licence. She is Mrs Ruth Lyle, aged sixty-six, formerly of 106 Alexandra Terrace, Exeter. According to the landlady she'd been living here since June last year.'

'I'll do a financial check,' Maddy said, 'and follow up all the ID information.'

'Good. Primrose, I need to get inside that phone and find out who had been messaging her, any images or videos and of course the movements of that phone in the last fourteen days.'

'Okay,' Primrose said. 'I'm told that you now have a data kiosk in Barnstaple. Otherwise I'll have to send it to Exeter.'

'Yes, we got a spanking new Aceso Dual, although hardly anybody knows how to use it yet.'

'Wow, that's a cool device. It can be used in the field as well as a desktop. I'm quite familiar with it.'

'Good,' Talantire said. 'Dave, I want you to liaise with the uniforms – your immediate task is finding next of kin. I also want you to find out everything you can about the building: who had access, where the keys were kept, and run a criminal background check on the landlady, plus an elimination DNA sample.'

'Right, boss, I'm on it,' he said.

'Finally, we need to find any CCTV in the area. The assailant could only have come from two directions, and there must be some coverage. I'll be asking Inspector Carnegie to coordinate that... ah, speak of the devil.'

Carnegie arrived in his usual baggy uniform, his dark tie so badly knotted it didn't lie flat on his shirt. 'I'm sorry I'm late, Jan. It's taken a while to persuade the neighbours opposite the crime scene to vacate their house.' He glanced at the whiteboard, the photographs and the name of the victim now written up in marker pen.

'Ruth Lyle? That's a bit of a coincidence.'

'Why?'

'It's the same name as a young girl who was murdered in the town half a century ago.'

Nuttall snorted with derision, and began to chuckle.

Carnegie fixed him with a stare. 'Have you not heard of the famous case, Nuttall? I would have thought a sharp sleuth like you would be aware of some of the criminal history of this county.'

Nuttall shrugged and continued chewing. 'Well, it's hardly the same person, is it?'

'Obviously not. But I was brought up here in Ilfracombe and my father was the coroner at that time, and I can tell you that the crucifix murder was a pretty big deal in 1973.'

'Did you say crucifix?' Talantire asked. She removed one of the enlargements on the whiteboard, and handed it to the inspector. 'Our victim was impaled with this, which to me looks like a crucifix.'

'Good Lord,' Carnegie said, and grabbed a seat-back to steady himself. 'Dowling said she was stabbed with a big nail. Good God.' He went pale.

'Hold on a second,' said Maddy Moran, typing at her laptop. 'Yes, there it is. In the *Devon Argus* newspaper database. Head-lined "The Devon vampire murder". It says Ruth Lyle was sixteen when she was found dead on April Fool's Day 1973 with a crucifix in her heart—'

'Hang on, that's exactly fifty years last Thursday,' Talantire said.

Maddy continued: '—"The crime was unsolved for two months until a youth by the name of Gawain Entwistle confessed to the killing. Entwistle, a neighbour of the victim, was considered retarded"—'

Nuttall sucked his teeth. 'You can't say that nowadays.'

'Learning difficulties,' Talantire said.

'—"and was sentenced to life imprisonment",' Maddy continued.

They were all staring at Carnegie, who looked like he was in shock. 'Are you all right?' Talantire asked.

'I just cannot believe this,' he muttered. 'That case devastated Ilfracombe, the entire community was in shock. And now, fifty years later...' He stared back at the whiteboard, his eyes glazed.

'It would be a very long time for a copycat killer to wait,' Nuttall said.

'True,' Talantire said. Nuttall might be annoying, but there was nothing wrong with his detective antennae.

Carnegie was holding the photograph and his hands were shaking. 'I just can't believe this. I was only six when it happened, but my mother told me that this case almost destroyed their marriage.'

'Listen to this,' Maddy said. '"The original killing took place in the Dimpsy Chapel." Where is that?' She turned to Carnegie.

'I've heard of it, but I don't think it exists now,' Wigwam said. 'Probably demolished after the killing.'

Primrose was busy at her laptop. 'I've found a record online from the Ilfracombe Civic Society. The Dimpsy Chapel was originally known as St James Without.' She looked up. 'Such crazy names in this country.'

'Without what?' Nuttall asked.

'It probably means St James without St Philip,' Carnegie said. 'The reason being there is another church near the Promenade, called St Philip and St James – or, as it is known locally, Pip and Jim's.'

'Dimpsy is Devon slang for shaded or dusky,' Talantire said.

Maddy was busy on her laptop as they were talking. 'St James Without is on a map from the local antiquarians. I just found it.' She squinted at the screen. 'You can't zoom in much, but it's also on Mercer Lane, number four, so it must be very close to Bluebird Cottage, which is number eight.'

'I found some press pictures from the time,' Nuttall said, pointing to his laptop screen. 'Two or three of the buildings in the lane have been demolished, but this is the same wrought-iron lamp sticking out of the wall.'

Talantire looked over his shoulder. The picture showed a press of helmeted police around an arched doorway into a narrow stone wall. There was a number by the door, and by zooming in Nuttall identified it as a four. 'Okay, so it was number four Mercer Lane. It doesn't look like a historic church. All right, there is one easy way to sort this out.' She grabbed her coat, which had been lying on the bar behind the whiteboard. 'Come on everyone. School trip.'

One minute later the assembled detectives made their way out of the incident room into the High Street, carefully locking the door behind them. They made their way right, and then down the alleyway into Mercer Lane. A female PC guarded the lane, closed off by an arc of blue crime tape. Ten yards beyond it was a CSI van, behind which a white tent was connected to the front of the cottage. A few passers-by were taking selfies.

'Has Dr Holcombe been?' Talantire asked the PC.

'The forensic pathologist? Yes, he just left a few minutes ago. The body has been removed, but there are two CSI staff still inside.'

Someone called from the tape barrier, a good-looking young man in a bomber jacket and jeans. 'Hi, Detective? I'm Tim Harvey, *North Devon News*. Can you tell me what happened here?'

'No comment,' Nuttall muttered back.

'Is it true there's been a murder?'

The detectives ignored him and ducked under the tape, then made their way along the lane until they were opposite Bluebird Cottage. The historic Victorian-style lamp protruded from the wall high up to the left of the door. Nuttall, who now had the 1973 photograph on his phone, held it up to show Talantire.

'Looks like the same place,' he said.

Talantire almost felt faint at the revelation.

'This just cannot be true. A girl called Ruth Lyle was killed here in 1973, and then fifty years later, almost to the day, a woman of the same name is killed with a similar murder weapon at the same location.'

Chapter 4

'It's a curious object and no mistake,' CSI evidence technician Pavel Kaminski said to Jan Talantire, as he led her from Barnstaple Criminal Investigation Department on the first floor, through the CSI office and into the adjacent evidence room, where items from current investigations were stored. Kaminski unlocked the knife cabinet, and pulled open the metal door. This cupboard held three rows of knives, perhaps fifty in total, some bloodied, some clean, each in a screwtop plastic tube. Each weapon had been seized from an individual, discovered at a crime scene, or removed from a body – dead or alive. They included a shelf with a samurai-style sword seized from a recently released psychiatric patient in Woolacombe, a wicked-looking multi-bladed zombie knife used in a playground altercation over a vaping kit in Plymouth, and a sharpened machete found during a drug raid in Torbay.

Here were the tools of dispute in twenty-first-century Britain. Amongst this rack of ruination, the crucifix seemed incongruous, and almost innocent. The width of the crossbar meant it was in the widest available container, and Pavel needed two hands to lift it from the shelf.

'With the square cross-section, and the raised square heads, these look to me like medieval nails. I don't think it's actually intended to be a crucifix, it just happens to look curiously like a Christ figure because of the way the blobs of molten lead cooled and ran down the larger nail.' Kaminski, a balding man with gingery stubble, stood the tube on a desk, unscrewed the

24

top and in nitrile-gloved hands lifted it out and under his desk inspection lamp.

'So it's not home-made?'

'Well, not recently, I would say. It's certainly grimy.'

'Inspector Carnegie reckoned that the one used in the original murder was the prized possession of St James Without,' she said. 'Some local dignitary apparently brought it back from the Crusades.'

Kaminski peered closer, using a magnifying glass. 'I doubt it. If it was really a thousand years old, there presumably would be corrosion.'

The dazzling light clearly showed three inches of dried blood at the bottom end of the foot-long vertical iron nail. 'I took three or four swabs of the blood when it was still wet,' Kaminski continued, 'and a couple on the shaft, plus two on the cross-beam where you would expect someone to hold it if using it as a weapon. If there is any DNA on there, we will find it. Then we used gel lifters for fingerprints, but couldn't find anything.'

'What other tests could we do on it?' Talantire asked.

Kaminski scratched his head. 'I'm sure the historians would love us to do a proper metallurgical analysis, an X-ray and even a carbon dating test. I'm sure that's never been done, seeing as it was out of circulation after the original murder.'

'Pavel, let's be clear. From a criminal forensic point of view, we don't much care whether it was brought back from the Crusades or hammered together in 1970 by a schoolboy in a garage in Torbay. The only relevant question is whether it's the same one used to kill Ruth Lyle in 1973; the same one that should from then onwards have been kept in police custody.'

'True,' Kaminski said.

'Personally, I think I'd prefer if it was a home-made one,' Talantire said. 'Then we won't have to explain quite how the police managed to lose it from a secure evidence store.'

'Well, we'd best look after it, eh?' he said, replacing it and screwing the plastic lid on the container. 'I'm the evidence officer, so I think it should stay in the cutlery cupboard, with the other weapons.'

--

Talantire had left a message with Dr Holcombe asking for some initial impressions. He rang back as she was driving back from Barnstaple to Ilfracombe, and she took the call on the hands-free.

'Morning, Dr Holcombe.'

'Good morning, Detective Inspector.' His voice was pure Home Counties, honeyed with self-confidence.

'A bit of an unpleasant scene, wasn't it, Piers?'

'Well, there's not too many pleasant ones in my line of work but yes, it was a tad grisly. I removed the crucifix and gave it to your CSI team to take samples from. The victim seems to have been killed in the same position she was found, with a single thirty-eight-millimetre penetration wound that looked to have pierced the left ventricle of the heart. This all is of course subject to confirmation at post-mortem, which I won't be able to do until Tuesday afternoon, I'm afraid.'

'I'm sure we'll cope with that,' Talantire said. Holcombe was relatively young, new in the area, but had been qualified for six years. Based on previous dealings with him, she trusted his judgement. Still, two days was a long time to wait.

'By the way, thank you for the temperature reading. That's extremely helpful for the time of death, which does accord with Thursday afternoon. I understand you took it with a meat thermometer?'

'Yes. Necessity is the mother of invention.'

'That's very resourceful. Now, how are you doing on the identification?' he asked.

'We've got a name, and plenty of confirmation documents, but the thing is…'

'Yes, I'm guessing that you are alluding to the historic crime. Same name, same type of murder weapon, one of your CSI officers told me. That's going to automatically make it more high profile, I assume.'

'No doubt,' Talantire replied. 'We're not revealing the fact she has the same name. Still, handling the PR is above my pay grade.'

'Definitely above mine,' Holcombe said.

'I've got a call in to Middlemoor to find out where the original paperwork for the 1973 killing would be. Once we can see exactly what happened then, we can see if there's any connection.' Middlemoor was the headquarters of the Devon and Cornwall Police in Exeter.

'Good luck with that. In any case you won't have any DNA records back then. However, if you are fortunate enough to locate the original evidence bags, then it would be possible to test the contents using today's technology.'

'Yes, I've been thinking about that,' Talantire said. 'Still, the first priority is to find out who our current victim is.'

Talantire ended the call as she arrived at the Stag and Hounds. Once inside, Nuttall called her over to his screen. 'I've just had a PCSO go round to the victim's former address in Exeter. It's a rental place, bit basic apparently. The landlord says Mrs Lyle had the place for a couple of years. The neighbours are students and most of them haven't been there very long.'

'Okay,' said Talantire, 'let's go round there tomorrow morning, see what we can discover. But first, let's meet the landlady of Bluebird Cottage.'

—

'How long have you owned Bluebird Cottage, Mrs Lee?' Talantire asked. She and DC Maddy Moran were sitting in the comfortable lounge of the owner. Wendy Lee, whose real name was Yuan Ying Li, was a tiny little bright-eyed bird of a woman in her seventies.

'About four year. My husband die, and we close takeaway, sell all.' She glanced out of the window of her home, which gave

27

a good view over the harbour and the late-afternoon light. She was clearly contemplating happier times. 'We put the money in property, two places in this town. Set up with Airbnb. My son help.'

'Is he here?'

'Brittle.' Talantire initially thought she was referring to his mental health, but then realised she had given him a location. Bristol.

'So just to be clear, Bluebird Cottage was already modernised when you bought it?'

'Yes.'

'But according to the Land Registry it was number four Mercer Lane when you bought it, and now it's number eight,' Maddy said.

'Number four is very unlucky. Number eight is lucky. The number still in sequence, and on correct side of road, so no problem. Original number six and eight were knock-down, and made into garages.'

'Did you know about the crime, in 1973?' Talantire asked.

'Of course. Everyone know. My husband come to Britain from Hong Kong two year before, and open restaurant one month before killing.'

'So, March 1973?'

'Yes.'

'Years later, when property for sale, four years ago, we remind vendor about murder. We got it cheap, very cheap.' She made it sound like chip. Cheap as chips.

'So what did you know about Mrs Lyle?'

'The lady is good tenant. She offer to take cottage for two year if we lower rent. It seem good deal, as last year it always empty in winter. She pay three month deposit. And she no trouble. No party. No damage, no dog or cat. Perfect lady, very nice.'

And very dead, thought Talantire. 'Did she tell you why she had come to the area?'

'No.'

'There's only a short-term previous address on the lease,' Maddy said. 'Why did you accept that?'

'Because she pay cash up front. Beside, she know Ilfracombe, and she know my restaurant on Hillsborough Road.'

'She knew it? Was that Dragon House?' Talantire asked.

'Yes. My husband little joke,' she said smiling. 'Me the dragon lady. New owner change. It now Gate of Asia. Indian, Thai and Chinese.' She laughed. 'I say: make up your mind!'

'When did you open first, and when was it sold?' Talantire asked.

'Open on auspicious day, Monday March five. Year of Ox. Good for grand opening, for prayer for good luck.' Mrs Lee suddenly snapped her fingers, a surprisingly loud noise. 'Ah! She said she been student. I forgot. She said she know my restaurant when she was student.'

'Studying where?' Maddy asked.

'I don't know.'

Over the next ten minutes, two detectives gleaned no more information about the mysterious Mrs Ruth Lyle, but a great deal more about the trials of opening a Chinese takeaway in the high-inflation days of 1973. Talantire was beginning to see why Mrs Lee's husband thought her a fiery woman.

'You know what?' she said, leaning forward and glowering. 'The day that girl killed was April Fool Day. Very evil day.'

'Not auspicious?' Maddy suggested.

'No, first day Britain start VAT. Include charge on all hot food takeaway. A dagger in my heart! And I still angry.'

-

Back at the incident room half an hour later, Talantire and Maddy found the details of the financial order had come through on Mrs Lyle's bank account. At first glance there was nothing out of the ordinary. The monthly rent on Bluebird Cottage, separate payments for gas and electricity, which also went to Mrs Lee, and then various purchases both online and locally, using contactless and cash in equal proportion. The only money coming in was a couple of pensions, the larger being in the name of a former husband, James Arthur Quince, for which she got a widow's benefit. It was paid by insurance company Aviva on behalf of an employer Talantire hadn't heard of. It was a solid sum, certainly enough for a comfortable lifestyle.

'We can get the National Insurance numbers from the pension company,' Talantire said. 'Then we'll know everywhere she's ever worked.'

'There are no benefit payments,' Maddy said, flicking through various screens. 'They only gave us six months of data, but I can ask for more. There's nothing under Ruth Quince.'

'Yes, do so, though I imagine this side of things can go on the back burner for a while,' Talantire said. She then turned to Dave Nuttall, who was standing behind the pub bar, hunched over his screen. 'Dave, how have you been getting on with the CCTV?'

He waggled his hand from side to side and sucked his teeth. 'There are three cameras on the High Street at the end of the alleyway from Mercer Lane, but nothing at the bottom end. If we are assuming the lady got stabbed on Thursday, when the witness heard the scream, that is an awful lot of people passing the end of the lane. But like I say, if I was going to stab somebody at Bluebird Cottage, I'd definitely nip in the other way, off Wilder Road where there's no cameras.'

'Then let's put out an appeal for dashcams and doorbell cameras, we might get something,' Talantire said. She herself was reading through a news report from the original case.

Schoolboy monster caged for life in Devon
crucifix killing

An Old Bailey judge today sentenced fifteen-year-old Gawain Entwistle to detention for life for the brutal murder of sixteen-year-old schoolgirl Ruth

Lyle. The pretty ginger-haired teenager was found dead on April 1st last year, impaled with a metal crucifix, naked and bound on the altar of the disused church of St James Without, in the picturesque North Devon town of Ilfracombe.

The judge, His Honour Charles Kingley, described Entwistle as the 'epitome of evil'. In his summing-up he said the accused had inflicted a despicable, protracted and grotesque assault on a young woman whose sole crime had been her innocent offer of friendship, and a kindness in attempting to help the boy to learn to read.

The prosecution described how Entwistle's fingerprints had been found not only on the murder weapon, but on the lock and keys to the church, which were the responsibility of his father, Arthur Entwistle, who was the verger. Detectives originally accepted the testimony of Mr Entwistle senior, who insisted that the boy's fingerprints could be explained by his role as a cleaner in the church, which has not been open for public worship since 1939. However, an alibi offered by the accused's mother was eventually discounted.

In sentencing the accused, the judge said: 'I am satisfied that despite your mental backwardness, you are underneath a cunning deviant, from whom the good citizens of our country should forever be protected. In sentencing you to be detained at Her Majesty's Pleasure, it rather saddens me to see the passing from the judicial repertoire of the ultimate sanction, which in times gone by would have been appropriate punishment for monsters such as you, whereupon your maker could have consigned your soul to hell.'

The accused's mother burst into tears from the public gallery as her son was led away.

The four-week trial has transfixed the country, offering a harrowing view into the dark under-belly of the pretty seaside resort. Two local men, who had originally been accused, had their names cleared.

'I've put in requests for all the available historic case files,' Talantire said.

'Good luck with that,' Maddy said. 'I wouldn't be surprised if they were all dumped in a skip somewhere in the 1990s.'

'We could start with the local records,' Talantire said. 'But let's take an eye-break. I've been talking to the local parish priest, and have arranged a quick trip to see the grave of our original victim.'

—

Ilfracombe's Marlborough Road Cemetery was a pleasantly landscaped graveyard, spaciously laid out on a hilltop above the town. The view was classic Devon: green hills, a patchwork of small fields and woodland, and in the distance a glimpse of pewter sea. Reverend Neal Vaizey, rector of St Philip and St James, accompanied Talantire and Maddy and led them along to the section of graves that had been dug in the 1970s. There, at the back, was a simple engraved granite headstone.

Ruth Lyle 9th February 1957 to 1st April 1973.

'Our dear daughter, torn from us, lies now in heaven.'

The grave was adorned with fresh flowers, as well as aged plastic ones. It was also marked with the name of her father, William Lyle, who died within three years of his daughter's death.

'Is the mother still alive?' Talantire asked the priest.

'Yes, her name is Gwendoline. She's very frail. She lives in a care home, but regularly comes to services along with a carer. These fresh flowers are undoubtedly from her.'

Maddy crouched down and retrieved a small card in a cellophane sleeve from underneath the white lilies. She slipped the card from its holder, and showed it to Talantire.

> *Lilies are for the memory of you my lost angel. May you*
> *rest in peace. Love Mum.*

Around the grave, the soil had been freshly dug, and cleared of weeds. Even the headstone itself had been recently cleaned of algae and moss, unlike many of the others nearby. 'I've seen her being helped from her wheelchair, to kneel down and scrub the grave,' Vaizey said. 'Most Sundays.'

The Chestnuts Care Home stood in prominent position on Anglesey Avenue, about a mile from the town centre and less than ten minutes' walk from the cemetery. Talantire and Maddy were shown into a large and comfortable reception area, where the heat was simply unbearable. Maddy had only been sitting for five minutes when she began fanning her face with one of the sales leaflets. One of the care staff, a fresh-faced young man, came down to fetch them and escorted them, in quite the slowest lift Talantire had ever experienced, up to Mrs Lyle's room on the second floor.

'Gwen is a lovely lady, quite with it really,' said the carer, just before opening the door. 'Considering she is ninety-three.'

Mrs Gwen Lyle was a tiny shrunken lady with white hair and spectacles, sitting in a comfortable high-backed chair close by her bed. She looked to be wearing her best pearls and matching earrings for this hurriedly arranged visit. 'It's a long time since the police came to see me,' she said in the faintest of whispers.

While the carer fetched tea and biscuits, Maddy gently closed the door behind them. All around the room, on the dressing table and on the walls, in both colour and black and white, were photographs of her daughter. Dotted amongst them were more modern family portraits, of a young man whose age photographically progressed, through to adulthood, until his own children began to appear, and then his grandchildren. A future denied to Ruth.

'Is this your son?' Maddy asked, pointing to one of the pictures.

'Yes, that's Alan. He's a chartered surveyor. And there are all my great-grandchildren.'

'And this is your late daughter?' Talantire asked, pointing to a school portrait, blown up to A4 size. Pretty, as the newspapers had reported, rather understated the truth. Ruth was a dazzling redhead, absolutely bursting with personality. She had dimples in her cheeks and laughing blue eyes. Eyes that could never have known how dreadfully cut short her life was to be.

Mrs Lyle nodded, and the barest sibilance hinted at a yes.

'She's beautiful, bless her,' said Maddy.

'You've come about her, haven't you?' Mrs Lyle asked.

'We have,' Talantire said.

'You'd not be here to discuss the weather, would you?' she said, with a chuckle, then glanced towards the picture. 'I think about her every day, when I'm waking up, and before I go to sleep. She's always with me.'

The two detectives glanced at each other. Time to state their business.

'You may have heard there has been another murder, at the same address where Ruth was killed,' Talantire said.

'At the Dimpsy?'

'Yes, though it isn't a church any more. It's a rental cottage.'

She looked bewildered. 'Who'd want to stay there?'

'Well, quite. The victim was a middle-aged lady with the same name as your daughter.'

'She was called Ruth?'

'Yes, Ruth Lyle. It's not an incredibly rare name,' Maddy said. 'But it's quite a coincidence.'

'Yes it is. Fifty years on,' Mrs Lyle said.

'The thing is, Mrs Lyle, we want to know if anyone has been talking to you about your daughter,' Talantire said.

She blinked and looked away.

'Did someone come and see you?' Getting no reply, Maddy showed her a picture blown up from the dead woman's passport. 'Do you know this woman?'

Her eyes widened, and one hand waved in the air. She seemed to slump sideways in her chair.

'Mrs Lyle?'

She turned back to them, and said nothing. Her mouth was down-turned at one side. Only a sibilant rasp came from her mouth, and saliva began to spill down her chin.

'Mrs Lyle?' Talantire repeated. 'Gwen, speak to me.' She knelt down next to the woman, held her arms and looked into her eyes. 'Maddy, she's having a stroke.'

'I'll call it in,' Maddy said, tapping three nines on her phone.

'I'll go and get someone,' the carer said, turning away.

'Hold on, do you have Activase here?' Talantire asked him.

'I'm sorry?'

'Activase, a clot-buster drug. Also known generically as alteplase.'

'I don't know.'

'You should have it. I saw the sticker – this care home is part of the NHS anti-stroke pilot project in Devon.'

'I didn't know.'

'My mother's a GP, and helped set it up, that's the reason I know.'

'I'm sorry, I'm not sure… I better fetch someone.'

'Yes, I need your most experienced colleague, right away please,' Talantire said. She knew this elderly woman had vital information to give. Quick action was essential, not only to save her life but to solve a killing.

Maddy was already on to the emergency services. While she gave the location, Talantire asked Mrs Lyle to raise her arms, but, though she continued to look at her, there was no movement. It was only a minute later when a middle-aged woman arrived, looking flustered.

'Is Mrs Lyle all right?' she asked.

'No. Do you have the clot-buster Activase here?'

'We do, yes, but I'm not qualified to administer.'

'Someone here should be,' Talantire said. 'Okay, show me your dispensary.'

'It's in the main admin office,' the woman said, leading her out towards the lift.

'Ground floor?' Talantire asked, knowing how slow the lift was. She was already running down the stairs before the woman replied in the affirmative. She jumped the last three steps to the landing below, grabbed the newel post and pivoted to race down the next flight. At the bottom of the stairs, in equatorial heat, she sprinted the fifty yards towards the main entrance, skipped round a carer pushing a wheelchair-bound patient, and burst into a door marked *administration*. Three alarmed female faces looked up from screens simultaneously. One of them, matronly, with spectacles balanced on her fair hair, said: 'What do you think—?'

'Mrs Lyle's having a stroke, where's your drug cupboard?'

'Now hold on. Who the hell—?'

'Detective Inspector Jan Talantire.' She tore off her lanyard and lobbed her warrant card onto the woman's desk.

'We're in the middle of an important Teams call,' said a dark-haired woman, and indeed Talantire could see at least two other startled faces on the screens, mouths hung open. Maybe they were each having a stroke.

'I don't give a monkey's if you're rehearsing for the last ever show of *Jesus Christ Superstar*,' Talantire said. 'I need Activase and a sterile syringe.'

'Yes, we have them,' said a young woman with purple and silver hair, looking towards a secure metal cupboard. 'But our phlebotomist isn't here, he's in town. It's not just an ordinary jab, you know. You have to know—'

'I've seen it administered,' Talantire said, then tried the handle. 'It's locked.' She turned back to the group. 'Keys?'

'I've got them,' said the matronly woman, and started rifling through her handbag. The conference call, at least eight participants, mutely goggling at the drama, watched the woman emptying out her purse, more spectacles and perfume, tissues, eyeshadow, lipstick, before finding a bunch of keys. 'Here,' she said. 'It's one of the silver ones.' She fumbled on the desk for her spectacles.

'They're on your head, Delia,' dark hair said.

'It's the security key,' called purple hair. 'With the dimpled shaft.'

'I know, I know,' Delia answered, squinting, all fingers and thumbs. The specs fell off her head, the keys dropping to the floor.

'Sorry, but this is urgent.' Talantire snatched the keys up, found the correct one and unlocked the cupboard. Opening it, she scanned the bewildering contents.

Purple hair, by her side, pointed out the correct shelf and found the box. 'There's everything you need in there,' she said. 'I'll come with you.'

Talantire ran to the stairs, and purple hair kept pace until they began the ascent, two stairs at a time. When she burst into the bedroom, Maddy was on the phone to the control room. Mrs Lyle was staring at her, mouth sagging. She was making a noise like radio static.

'What's the ambulance ETA?' Talantire asked.

Maddy muted the call and replied. 'Twenty minutes, five minutes ago.'

'Right, can't wait for that, let's get going.' She undid the box and took out a small plastic bottle of sterile water, two plastic syringe cases and two large-bore needles in sterile packaging. She then unfurled a long instruction sheet, written in a font suitable for a microscope.

'I should have nicked her glasses as well as the keys,' she muttered. Talantire's mother, who had devoted four years to

37

setting up the project, had said all first responders should know how to use the drug. Although Talantire was rarely first on the scene, her mother had shown her. But that was two years ago. Now it was a question of remembering how to do it.

The younger woman arrived and, between them, over the course of the next five minutes they set up the needles. 'Right, first bolus in straight away,' she said, reading the instructions as Talantire tried to find a vein in the elderly woman's arm. 'My judgement, for the record, is that she's unable to give consent,' she added. Ideally, the drug would have to be added gradually over a number of hours with an intravenous drip, but the first part of the injection was the crucial one. Not just the difference between life and death, but also between recovering speech and other faculties and failing to do so.

The first part of the injection was successfully administered and then, just as Talantire was asking about getting the rest set up in a drip, the care home's phlebotomist arrived, a young man, along with Delia, the senior administrator, with glasses back on her head.

'Hello, Gwen,' he said, crouching down. 'Now what have you been up to, eh?'

'She's lost speech,' Maddy said, 'But Jan gave her an injection.'

He looked at the open packet, and then took over.

Talantire stood up, and turned to Delia. 'Sorry to ruin your teleconference.'

'Don't worry about it,' the woman said, handing Talantire back her lanyard and warrant card. 'Sorry I was rude. You just caught us on the hop.'

'Who was it with?'

'The Care Quality Commission, unfortunately.'

Chapter 5

'Do you think she'll recover then?' Maddy asked. They were in the car on the way back to Barnstaple police station.

'I don't know, I don't think anybody will for a few days,' Talantire replied. 'But she knows something, about our Mrs Ruth Lyle. Did you see her face when you showed her the mugshot?'

'I did, it was recognition, definitely. But how did she meet her?'

'It's a good question,' Talantire said. 'If Mrs Lyle has only been in town since summer last year the only way they would have met was if our murder victim had sought her out. Gwen Lyle has been in the care home for two years and hardly goes gallivanting around the town. It couldn't have been a random encounter.'

'Gwen Lyle's son might know,' Maddy said.

'Alan Lyle, chartered surveyor. The care home gave me his number. His mum would surely have mentioned it if her dead daughter had apparently come back from the grave fifty years on.'

They crossed the Taw Bridge, with the town on their left and the new industrial estate on their right. The police station was only a couple of years old, a big dark grey industrial shed, with tinted windows, backing onto the Travis Perkins builders' yard. 'Ah, home sweet home,' Maddy said, as Talantire parked the vehicle next to a riot van, in whose windscreen cowl drain fragments of broken bottle glass still winked in the light.

No one missed the old concrete police station, next to the magistrates' court. It had only been closed for three months when the graffiti artists began to use it to make a mockery of the force.

–

'You can sit there opposite me. If you get tired of my face, and I can understand that, there's a view of the builders' yard over the back, and in the other direction you can see the river,' Maddy said.

Primrose Chen had been given the desk next to the cubicle from which Talantire worked on the first floor. Inevitably, two of the male uniforms from downstairs had come up to take a look at the new exotic female officer. A Muslim in Devon, good grief! 'So where are you from, love?' asked Ken Venables, the desk sergeant, running his eyes over her.

'I live in Plymouth now, with my mom,' she replied, quietly.

'No, *actually* from.'

'Leave it out, Ken,' Talantire said. 'It's her first day.'

'I'm a British citizen,' Primrose said. 'My dad worked for the Royal Navy for twenty years. I've been in London for six months—'

'Right, but what I'm asking is—'

'What you're asking is overly intrusive,' Maddy muttered.

'I'm ethnically Malay, my family was originally from Sarawak,' Primrose said. Despite the make-up, she was flushed – whether with anger or embarrassment, Talantire couldn't tell. 'Do you know where that is, sir?'

'Nah,' he said, folding his arms, looking at PC Moody, who was beside him, every inch the sorcerer's apprentice.

'So, sir, where are you from?' Primrose responded.

'Barnstaple,' he said. 'Born and bred.'

'So you know the place well?'

'Absolutely.'

'Is there a mosque here?' she asked him.

'Search me,' he said, his face tightening.

Talantire intervened. 'Ken, bugger off and stop harassing my staff members.' She turned to Primrose. 'There's the North Devon Islamic Centre on Vicarage Road.'

Venables was leaving, but still had a parting shot. 'Mecca's that way,' he said, pointing out of the window, towards the eponymous bingo hall. 'And if you want to bend over and stick your arse in the air, the Locarno used to be over there.'

'Oi, enough!' Talantire yelled.

PC Moody, who was leaving too, sniggered.

Once they had gone, Maddy said: 'And there in a nutshell is why we don't use the nickname wanker.'

'Are they all like this?' Primrose asked Talantire.

'No, thank God. Ken is the worst, well, the least subtle,' Talantire said. 'You don't have to take it.'

Primrose shook her head. 'I'm used to racism.'

'He reckons he's not racist,' Maddy said. 'Calls it "banter", a bit of fun. He claims to hate almost everyone, irrespective of race, creed, colour, ethnicity and sexual orientation. He's not really happy with anyone born east of Exeter, but he reserves his ire for grockles.'

Primrose held up a finger. 'Ah yes, I know this one: grockles are incomers and holidaymakers, right?'

'You got it in one,' Maddy said.

'We've got witnesses,' Talantire persisted. 'You can complain.'

'Not on my first day,' Primrose said.

'I'm minded to make a complaint myself, if you won't,' Talantire said. 'We all have to put up with this, and it's got to stop.'

'Please don't, ma'am. They'll just call me a moaner,' Primrose said. 'That's why I left the Met. I want to be known for the quality of my work, not for being someone who can't take a joke.'

41

'Victim blaming,' Maddy said. 'That's what I got when I complained about Wigwam groping me. He said it was an accident. I mean, he leaned forward from behind and grabbed 'em. How is that an accident? I went through all the complaints process, months of it, and a final disciplinary meeting of four senior male officers, half of whom were – if you can believe this – actually staring at my boobs' – she leaned forward and mimicked an eye-popping expression – 'during the bloody meeting. Then one asked if I had considered wearing looser tops. Wigwam just got a reprimand.'

'That's awful,' Primrose said.

'That was six years ago, things are better now,' Talantire said to Primrose, though she felt far from certain.

'Well, Jan, two out of the four panellists are still in post,' Maddy responded. 'And Venables has friends in high places. He's the brother-in-law of Assistant Chief Constable Jeremy Noone, so he feels immortal.'

Primrose shrugged at Talantire, as if to ask: *what can I do?*

'I took a more direct approach,' Maddy said. 'I took Wigwam aside and threatened to tell his wife if there was ever a repeat. I know her, she manages the Ilfracombe lifeboat station and she'd drown him like a rat.'

Talantire realised Maddy and Primrose were staring at her. Her rising anger must have been obvious. 'Jan wants to put the world to rights,' Maddy said to Primrose. 'Preferably all in one go.'

'Why the hell else are we in the police?' Talantire said.

Maddy turned away and said, lightly: 'Now Primrose, have you been introduced to Dr Crippen yet?'

'The poisoner?' Primrose gasped. 'Isn't he dead?'

'Yes, and no.' Maddy hauled herself out of her seat and led Primrose and Talantire out through the double doors, along the corridor opposite the CSI team office. She pointed to a drinks machine the size of an industrial fridge. 'This is Dr Crippen. You can't drink the soup, the tea is like dust floating on boiling water, and most of the coffee is just plain undrinkable.'

'Isn't it really old?' Primrose said, looking at the faded plastic display.

'Ah, it's been reconditioned, you see. One of the numerous unplanned and unwanted brainchildren of our police and crime commissioner, to try to save money. Don't buy new stuff, recycle.'

'Well, I suppose it is green,' Primrose said.

'Ah, you must be referring to the tomato soup,' Maddy said. 'Course there is the one other thing you must never, ever try.'

'What's that?'

Maddy punched out three buttons, and the machine began to whirr, then click. A flimsy plastic cup dropped from a sleeve onto the drip-mesh. Finally, with a hiss, a scalding-hot jet of fluid shot into it. It gasped, then gurgled and finally stopped.

'No, don't touch it!' Maddy said as Primrose reached forward to grasp the cup. She found a grey plastic cup-holder on top of the machine, and a stained cloth, with which she carefully manoeuvred the cup into the holder. 'Touch that with your bare flesh, and it would burn your hand right off.'

'Ugh. It smells like stale gravy,' Primrose said.

Maddy smiled: 'It's a Crippechino.'

Still steaming about the treatment of Primrose, Talantire volunteered to get proper coffees just to get out of the office. She scooped up the refillable cups, and headed out. She'd had her own run-ins with male officers, particularly during the first year out of training, when they were assessing which of the new female recruits would and which wouldn't. She made sure the word got out pretty quickly that she was the latter type.

The Italian Place closed at six on a Sunday but she might just be able to get there in time. She took her own car, and drove briskly out of the yard, past the closed gates of Travis Perkins and up to the roundabout and the lorry park where the Portakabin stood. The blinds were half down, and she knew she was cutting it fine. Still, they knew her there, so she was prepared to try it on. She parked right outside, and opened the door.

The proprietor greeted her warmly. 'How are you, Jan?' he asked. Azad affected an Italian air, but was actually a Kurdish refugee, and only five foot three tall. 'Caught any crims today?' Police business was important to him, and the on-call firearms unit seemed to be permanently stationed there, along with a couple of motorcycle cops. Not this afternoon, though.

'The ones I've dealt with today are mainly inside CID, but they need locking up just the same,' Jan said.

He tutted and shook his head. 'The usual? No sugar?' he asked.

'One macchiato, plus two cappuccinos and one hot chocolate, please.'

Azad turned to his Gaggia machine, working with practised speed. The man made a mean macchiato, but the coffee he made for himself was Turkish-style, thick enough to resurface the many potholes outside.

While she was waiting, leaning on the counter, her phone beeped. Primrose had forwarded a message to her, and a video, recovered from the victim's phone. Talantire turned away and hit play. The screen showed the front of Bluebird Cottage, and a soft, feminine voice. 'And this is where I was killed fifty years ago. An awful crime that should never have happened.' Shocked, Talantire replayed it. On the second viewing, she noticed that the shadow of the phone and its user could be seen against the wall of the cottage. A slim woman with shoulder-length wavy hair. Flowers could be seen in bloom in window boxes on the cottage.

A woman describing another's death as if it was her own death. Totally bizarre.

'Somebody died?' Azad said, as he passed across a tray of drinks.

44

She had forgotten how well mobile phone audio carried. 'Yes.' There was no point denying what he had plainly heard. 'Thanks for these,' she said, picking up the coffees.

'My condolences,' Azad said, his face full of concern.

'It's all right. We weren't close.'

After racing back to the police HQ, Talantire had only just distributed the hot drinks when a trim man in a grey suit pushed open the door to CID. Detective Superintendent Michael Wells was an owlish individual with bushy grey eyebrows over his horn-rimmed spectacles.

'How is it going, Jan?'

'Not too bad, sir.'

'And you must be Primrose,' he said. 'I've heard terrific reports about you. You'll find you're in a good team here, and your skills will be respected.'

'Thank you,' she said, quietly.

Wells had been appointed at senior rank because of his case handling skills, originally honed in social services in Southampton. That was easily enough to earn him the contempt of many of the front-rank uniforms, who were on the coalface dealing with the great British public, and had to work their way up. Rumour was that Wells had never seen a dead body, or got blood on his hands, or made an arrest, despite already being close to retirement age. However, as far as Talantire was concerned he was a good boss, able to delegate but had supported her when she needed it. Coming from a social services background, he was definitely new school. Given how many old-school coppers were still about, it made a nice change.

He turned back. 'Jan, at some stage we have to organise a press conference on the killing. The press office is already being peppered with calls. Do we have a clear line of enquiry yet?'

'No, sir. We haven't even established who our victim really is.'

'How about an appeal for information? Get the great British public working for us.' He rubbed his hands together with relish.

'I'd rather make more basic progress first.'

'As you wish,' he said. 'Don't have much leeway over resources, so give me a shout as early as possible and I'll see what I can do. Right, off to a meeting now!' He waved a genial hand and disappeared down the stairs.

'Now, he is definitely all right,' Maddy said, now that there were just the three of them. 'You are ever getting any grief from the gorillas downstairs, Primrose, he's a man you should speak to. He'll support you.'

'Of course, we will too,' Talantire said. 'We've got to stick together.'

Primrose nodded.

Maddy was peering between the slats of the venetian blinds into the car park. 'Ooh look, here comes the Prince of Darkness.'

Primrose stood up and joined Talantire and Maddy at the window as a tall, dark-haired, athletic man emerged from an unmarked BMW and made his way towards the building.

'Wow, he's *so* good-looking,' Primrose said softly.

Maddy laughed. 'DI Richard Lockhart is the heart-throb of the office. Thirty-seven, with lovely brown eyes, and a delicious Welsh lilt to his voice, I don't mind saying that he would tempt me to rip his shirt right off—'

'—if it wasn't for his complicated domestic arrangements,' Talantire interrupted.

'Why is he called the Prince of Darkness?' Primrose asked.

'Because he's on a near-permanent nightshift,' Talantire said. 'It's his own choice. He is twice divorced, with three kids that he is devoted to, and because of various frictions with his exes the only chance he really gets to spend time with them is dropping them off or picking them up from school. But that only fits well with the nightshift.'

They stopped talking as they heard his feet ascending. Then Lockhart burst through the double doors at the top of the stairs, and immediately spotted Primrose.

'Hello and welcome,' he said. Talantire watched as Primrose averted her eyes and muttered her own hello.

'What have you got for me for tonight, Jan?' Lockhart asked.

Talantire passed him the printout of that day's crimes compiled by the control room, plus the stapled list of those from the preceding week that had yet to be investigated.

Lockhart flicked through the list. 'No one visited the Okehampton burglary?'

'We've been tied up full-time on the Mercer Lane stabbing,' Talantire responded.

'Ah, yes, the copycat killing,' he responded.

'It's not just a copycat,' Talantire said. 'Anyway you've no need to worry about it. We've got two uniforms posted there in eight-hour shifts, and half of Mercer Lane is still sealed off. There are so many bloody rubberneckers.'

Lockhart looked up, his deep brown eyes quizzical. 'Is her name really Ruth Lyle?'

'Seems to be,' Talantire said.

Lockhart glanced at the clock, which ruled his life with a rod of iron. 'All right. I'm picking Meghan up from violin tuition and then once my shift starts I'll head off to Okehampton.'

'What are you cooking her tonight?' Maddy asked.

'Singapore noodles with prawns. From M&S. And then it's mental arithmetic homework with her for an hour in the car while I drive her home.' He scooped up his files, shared an arc of perfect white teeth with them, and burst out through the doors, leaving a silent glow behind.

'He seems a good father,' Primrose said.

Maddy nodded. 'His first ex moved to Snozzle with Laura and Henry, which is a pig of a journey from here. And his second ex moved to Newton Abbot with Meghan, which is in the opposite direction and hardly any easier. With that and work, he reckons he drives a thousand miles a week.'

'Of course there is his girlfriend who lives in Liskeard,' Talantire said. 'And she's got a little one, not his.'

'It all makes the case of the crucifix murder seem quite simple by comparison, dunnit?' Maddy said.

–

Primrose had only been working on the kiosk for twenty minutes when she announced: 'Ma'am, I've now got all the data from the victim's phone going back six months.'

'Great,' said Talantire, coming round to look at the screen. 'Is there much?'

'There are six more videos and about fifty pictures, plus lots of metadata,' she replied.

'Let's start with the other videos.'

'This is the most interesting,' Primrose said, hitting the button. Talantire recognised the view immediately as the cemetery they had visited earlier that day. The same voice could be heard as she walked with the camera towards the familiar gravestone. 'This is where I was buried. Now I am risen like Lazarus.' At this point the camera was raised to the sky until the sunlight whited out the image.

'This is very strange,' Primrose said, shaking her head.

'You're not kidding,' Maddy said. 'Why would a woman pretend to be a particular dead person?'

'Maybe she was obsessed with the original crime,' Primrose said.

'Or she might have known the victim, gone to school with her, best friends maybe. She seems the right age,' Talantire said.

'We can check that,' Nuttall said. 'Get a list of the school friends of the original victim. Shouldn't be too hard.'

For the next hour they combed through the photographs, which showed various seaside views in and around Ilfracombe, and a couple of selfies, one of them with the landlady Wendy Lee, and a couple inside a pub. There were a few shots of moorland that might have been Dartmoor, and then some in Exeter.

'That's the university,' Talantire said. 'Streatham Campus. Where I took my own degree.'

'Criminology?' asked Primrose.

'No, environmental sciences.'

Nuttall laughed. 'Bugs, moths and meadow plants.'

'I'll check to see if any Lyles went to Exeter Uni,' Maddy said. 'What do we reckon, date wise?'

'Our victim was born in 1957, so for undergraduate she couldn't be in much before 1975,' Talantire said. 'Let's try admission up to 1980 for a start.'

'What about the recent phone contacts?' Nuttall asked.

'Primrose, can you send them to Dave?' Talantire said.

Talantire and Maddy continued to look through the photos. Nuttall soon had some progress on the phone numbers. 'Six calls in the last two weeks to and from the same landline number. Keane Wale Harbyttle solicitors, here in Barnstaple. I tried ringing them, but it's a Sunday and of course there's no reply. There is no out-of-hours number, so I settled for leaving a message and banging off a couple of emails to various partners.'

Maddy snorted. 'Seeing as it's urgent, we'll probably hear by a week next Wednesday. Judging by most of the solicitors that I know.'

'I'll try to find some home numbers for the partners,' Talantire said.

'There are four Harbyttles in the unlisted phone book,' Nuttall said. 'I'll ring round.'

By eight o'clock on Sunday evening, Talantire and Maddy were in Westward Ho! sitting in the grand detached home of Roger

Keane, managing partner of Keane Wale Harbyttle. He was an imposing seventyish man of florid complexion, with a swathe of iron-grey hair. He showed them into a large reception room full of heavy dark furniture, a big bookcase and a large grandfather clock. They sat in deep leather armchairs, and were offered coffee and almond slices by his wife, a slender woman, greying hair and pale-skinned, who seemed to slip silently around her husband like a wraith.

'Yes, I had a number of conversations with Mrs Lyle,' Keane said, munching a cake. 'She introduced herself as Sue, not Ruth, so I never got the connection with the dead girl.'

'What was it she wanted?' Talantire asked.

'She was interested in buying property in the area. As you know, we are one of the biggest conveyancing firms in North Devon.'

'Did you meet her?' Talantire asked.

'I did, actually. She came into the office two weeks ago, I think. It will be in the office diary. I'll get Naomi to look it up for you.'

'We're really having quite a lot of trouble tracing her background,' Talantire said. 'Did she give you any documents? Perhaps an address from outside this area?'

'I'm not aware of any. I think she used the Bluebird Cottage address.'

'Did she confide in you at all?' Maddy asked. 'Was she worried or concerned about something? Did she mention any threats made to her?'

Keane chuckled. 'We're not the kind of solicitors that people who fear for their lives would come to. We just undertake conveyancing and probate, we don't even do divorce any more. I'm really sorry I can't be more help.'

'She must have had a property in mind,' Talantire said.

'If she did, I never got the address or details,' he said.

'Did she make much impression on you?' Talantire asked. 'What kind of person was she?'

He blew a big sigh and leaned to cup his hands behind his head. 'She just seemed a very ordinary retired lady, the mainstay of our work, I suppose.' He looked at his watch and said: 'I wish I had more to tell you.'

As they left, and headed down the garden path towards the car, Talantire said: 'Seems quite a lot of calls exchanged, for so little information.'

'Exactly what I thought,' Maddy replied. 'In all my experience of solicitors, you call them. Then sod all happens for a fortnight, then after you call them again you might get a letter. But I've never been called back by one.'

'Of course, it might have been a receptionist or clerk called her back,' Talantire said.

'Maybe,' Maddy said. 'But I think something more was going on there. Our victim had some legal work she needed doing, something interesting enough to get his attention.'

–

It was nine o'clock and Talantire was missing her run. She'd normally get in a couple of miles near her home on a Sunday evening, all part of getting mentally and physically ready for the working week. Instead, she was alone in the CID office going through the various documents that had been recovered from the murder victim's handbag.

Wearing blue nitrile gloves, she carefully sorted various items of make-up, keys, pens and pencils. Passport, bank credit and debit cards, a couple of loyalty cards. These could all help trace the victim's movements; but if as seemed likely she had spent most of the last six months actually in Ilfracombe, much of the data prior to that might no longer exist.

She opened the passport, which was an old-style EU magenta version. The woman had certainly travelled, with visits to India, Singapore, Hong Kong and Australia in the last five years, along with visits to Estonia and Hungary since the requirement for passport stamps within the EU had been reinstituted.

She then looked again at the picture page of the passport. Something she hadn't noticed before. Place of birth: Ilfracombe. The date of birth was 9 February 1957. She took out her phone, and flicked through the photographs she had taken at the cemetery. There it was. The headstone of Ruth Lyle: 9 February 1957 to 1 April 1973. The same date of birth.

That was beyond coincidence. All right, she could have changed her name to that of the victim, but a false passport? That was a whole order of magnitude more effort. And to what end? Talantire looked through Nuttall's work in progress, chasing down all the possibilities of this name. Thirty-seven Ruth Lyles on Facebook, about the same number again in the UK phone book including non-listed numbers, and a dozen or so on each of the various other social media platforms including TikTok, LinkedIn and Instagram. Getting addresses that way, beyond the one they already had in Exeter, would take time, and there were always easier routes.

One of them was lying on the floor. A series of large clear plastic sacks, within which was almost everything that CSI had found in Bluebird Cottage. One contained clothing: a series of smart tunics, jackets and blouses and skirts. Generally classics, some M&S, but a few designer names. The evidence label said that DNA and fingerprint lifts had been taken, along with hair samples. She'd leave that for later. Next there was a sack of paperwork. She'd already asked Nuttall to start classifying it tomorrow. He was the perfect man for the job. He was proud of the huge collection of jazz he had on vinyl, all carefully sorted and cross-referenced. Duke Ellington, Miles Davis, John Coltrane and many lesser-known artists.

One collection of paperwork had already been separated out, in an A4 document wallet. Talantire flipped open the file and slipped out a thick wodge of correspondence. They were mainly old airmail letters addressed to the victim, received while overseas. There was an address in India, another in Singapore, and one in Estonia. She set these aside while she searched for any that had come to a domestic UK address, one where the trail of who this woman was might restart. Progress on the husband had come easier. There was an order of service for his funeral in March 1999 at Croydon Crematorium.

Were they formally married? If so, she had never taken his name.

Then, she made a startling discovery amongst the paperwork Nuttall hadn't yet got to. One envelope, quite old and faded, contained a piece of paper, carefully folded and printed in red on a faded pink wavy-lined background. It was a certificate for the birth on 9 February 1957 of Ruth Susan Lyle, and was signed by the registrar on the eighteenth of the same month. The perforations were intact where it had been removed from the register, and so was the watermark on the paper. Talantire knew that anyone with the right information could get a certificated copy of a birth certificate, but the certification date, pertaining to the day the request was granted, was the giveaway. This was *the* original copy. It should have been with the family of the dead girl soon after she was born. What on earth was it doing with the new murder victim?

Her head whirled, and she could do no more work that night. After driving home and taking a small brandy as a nightcap, she went to bed. She had a disciplined mind, and could normally file away work and then sleep well, ready to resume the next day. But this case was different, and the cascade of possibilities tumbled through her mind, keeping her awake into the small hours. A woman, Ruth Lyle, both long dead and, until recently, alive. If the newly dead woman had all the documentation to prove who she was, who was 1973's dead girl? Exactly who was in her grave?

Chapter 6

By eight a.m. on Monday, Jan Talantire was back in the CID office at Barnstaple police station, hard at work. She had already assembled all the documentary proof of Mrs Lyle's identity and existence, and it seemed flawless. She was just writing it up when she saw Primrose Chen arrive. Her shift didn't start for another hour. That was impressive devotion to work, considering the digital evidence officer lived in Plymouth, sixty miles and a good two-hour drive away. Talantire left the phones to her while she ploughed on looking through emails and the latest evidence file. It wasn't long before Primrose called across, with a phone receiver in her hand.

'It's the Reverend Vaizey,' she said. 'He's asking if he could see the murder weapon.'

'No, of course not,' Talantire said, rolling her eyes.

'That's what I told him. He says he can help identify whether it is the original. He is part of a local history group that has been trying to get a peek at it since the original murder. It's supposedly historic.'

Talantire rubbed a hand across her face. 'We could show him some photographs, I suppose. I'll have to speak to the chief. We can't risk anyone going to the press, saying, "I've seen the murder weapon and it's the original.". I'd get hung, drawn and quartered. We have to go through official channels for any analysis.'

Primrose shrugged and pointed to the receiver.

'Yes, all right, I'll speak to him.'

Primrose patched the call through, and Talantire greeted him. The rector was good at small talk, which presumably came with the territory, and he managed to extract from Talantire the information that Gwen Lyle had suffered a stroke.

'I do hope she's all right,' he said. 'I'll pray for her.'

'I think she's on the mend. She's a tough one, after all she's been through. Now, about this crucifix. We really can't go putting the thing on display.'

'Good gracious, I'm not asking you to. I know that you must be wondering whether it is the original one used to kill Ruth Lyle in 1973, and we do have some photographs in the archives with which to compare it.'

'Would you be able to send them to me?'

'We could scan them in I suppose, but it would be really rather more illuminating to see the artefact itself.'

Talantire rubbed her hand over her forehead. 'I appreciate that you must be quite enthusiastic about getting your hands on the crucifix, but if you show a little patience I would have thought that once the trial has taken place, it might be released for wider study.'

Vaizey chuckled. 'One of our more long-standing members recalls exactly the same being said after the original murder in 1973. The Ilfracombe Historical Society was promised a look at it, by Detective Chief Superintendent George Hogley no less. But despite our entreaties over several years, it was never released. We even applied again in 1992 after Mr Hogley's death, but were refused.'

This gave Talantire a reason to pause. 'Do you have a letter to that effect?'

'I'm sure we have it somewhere. After all, if there's one thing we're good at in the society, it's carefully hanging on to old papers.'

Talantire laughed. 'All right, let's leave it like this: if you send me the images you have, the letter of refusal and something of the historical context for this object, I will do my damnedest to intercede with the powers that be for your society to get a look. Once the perpetrators are caught and after the investigation is closed.'

'That could take years.'

'Yes it could.'

Vaizey sighed, clearly far from happy. 'I will do my best, Detective Inspector. May God bless you.' He hung up.

Talantire stared down the receiver.

'Any progress?' Primrose asked.

'There could be some. There's a bunch of people in the Ilfracombe Historical Society who've spent the last fifty years trying to get their hands on this thing. And apparently, back in 1992 someone wrote to them and said "no". If I can get a copy of that letter, it might at least give us a handle on who had control over the evidence from the first murder.'

Vaizey emailed the black-and-white photographs within half an hour. They showed the crucifix, from a distance of ten feet or so, in situ on a stone wall, behind a group of elderly-looking clergy. 'This cross is of huge historic importance,' Vaizey wrote. The caption beneath identified the church as St James Without in Ilfracombe on Easter Sunday 1923. It was accompanied by a scan of a historical pamphlet about the siege of Acre in 1291, written by an Oxford professor, and cited contemporary sources.

> 'For on the morrow, did the Mamluks deploy their thunderous catapults, from their substantial artillery train. The two largest named Furious and Victorious hurled stones the size of ponies, which smote the walls of the Accursed Tower, and destroyed the roof of the Tower of Flies. The mangonels known as Black Bulls followed, raining Greek fire above the walls onto the shattered

timbers, causing a liquid conflagration that ran like the blood of Etna and could not be extinguished. Amalric, brother of Henry II of Cyprus, held fast while the remaining factions of the Genovese, fearing defeat, departed. On the Montmusard walls, Lazarists remained while the Templars and Hospitallers made a failed attempt to retake the Accursed Tower. In so doing, Sir Robert de Lisle spotted one of the Lazarists impaled by flaming metal fragments from the roof above. He quenched the burning iron in water, and plucked from the dead man's chest a wonder to behold. The Greek fire had rendered the iron nails in the form of a cross, held fast by lead, reformed by the glory of God into an effigy of our Lord at Golgotha, a symbol of hope. Holding the crucifix in a cloth, he held it to the sky and prayed for victory by His Divine Grace. Thus inspired, Sir Robert led a sally charge from the open gate, which succeeded in killing nine score unbelievers and damaging two mangonels, but on his retreat was pierced by a quarrel beneath the eye. The crossbowman who fired it was quickly dispatched, but Sir Robert succumbed to the grievous wound. His body was lain on a catafalque of shields of the fallen, the crucifix upon his chest, and reclaimed for the host of our Lord.'

This was the first mention of the de Lisle crucifix for 500 years, though it may well have been the so-called Accursed Tower Enkolpion recovered when the Crusader ship Gloria foundered in a storm near Malta in 1292, with the loss of 'four score knights and their retinue'. As an Enkolpion is a flattish crucifix intended to be worn on a chain around the neck of an Eastern

Orthodox Archbishop, the recovery of such an item from the Accursed Tower is considered unlikely.

We can with more certainty substantiate that the crucifix appeared in a stained glass window at the Norman castle of Restormel in Cornwall 1459. It was being held aloft by Sir Robert de Lisle in a depiction of the siege of Acre. The work was attributed to the acclaimed British glazier John Prudde, and this great window in the chapel was the last piece completed before his death in 1461. The window itself was lost when the Royalist forces occupied and ruined the castle in the Cornish uprising of 1497. The next evidence for the location of the actual crucifix came in February 1646 in the English Civil War, when it was seen in the hands of Sir William de Lisle. Sir William, leading the Cornish pikemen, and wounded in battle, retreated to Torrington church, which was being used as a Royalist armoury. The church was destroyed when a stray spark ignited the dozens of barrels of gunpowder stored there. Sir William died, along with dozens of prisoners. The crucifix survived, was hidden from the Roundheads and appeared again in the mid 19th century at St James Without in Ilfracombe, probably brought there by Edward de Lisle, in whose parish it dwelt.

Talantire's jaw sagged at the name that emerged again and again in the narrative. De Lisle. It sounded quite plausibly connected to Lyle. Googling the historic name, she found a heraldic website giving the coat of arms of the de Lisle family, which may originally have hailed from Languedoc in France, and come to England at the time of the Norman Conquest.

She looked up and saw Maddy was staring at her.

'Breakthrough?'

'Well, the pictures are not that clear. I certainly couldn't tell if it's the original or a replica, but the origin of the thing is amazing. Found at the siege of Acre, in the Crusades in the thirteenth century, by a knight with the name of Robert de Lisle.'

'Ancestor of the girl?' Maddy asked.

'Maybe. Take a look.' She forwarded the email to Maddy and waited while her colleague scanned through the contents, eyes flashing down the text.

'Well, I tell you one thing for sure,' Maddy said finally. 'That bloody crucifix is cursed. It killed the bloke that found it, it sank in a ship off Malta, was the last thing painted by that glassworker before he died, was on a stained glass window that got smashed, and was in a church that blew up at the Battle of Torrington in the civil war. And now, in the last fifty years, two people have been stabbed to death with it. I'm surprised anyone wants it on the premises.'

Talantire's eyes flicked to the CSI office. 'Well, right now it's in there.' She gazed at Maddy. 'Are you superstitious?'

'Am I, bollocks. But, if enough other people want hold of it, it's trouble. And you say Vaizey wants to get his hands on it?'

'Yes. I'll get Kaminski to put it in the safe before we head off to Exeter, and leave a note for the others. It has to be kept under lock and key.'

'Based on its history, that might not be enough,' Maddy said.

–

Alexandra Terrace, Exeter was a narrow road with a mixture of homes, some double-fronted Victorian villas divided into flats, small cottages and a couple of low-rise blocks of flats. Number eighty-six was a double-fronted, rather in need of some TLC with untrimmed grass and a number of wheelie bins scattered about. A child's plastic ride-on bus, faded to pale pink, lay on its side in a flowerbed.

The landlord, a small intense-looking man named Martin Trevithick, was waiting for them in the hallway. 'Mrs Lyle was on the second floor, flat F,' he said as he led them up the staircase. 'There's a couple of students in there now.' He gave a perfunctory knock, before getting out his own key and opening the door. Talantire was surprised how tidy the flat was. No discarded clothing, empty pizza boxes or dirty crockery. No traffic cones, no 'interesting' pot plants. Mature students, Talantire concluded. Female, almost certainly.

'Tell us what you know about Mrs Lyle?' Maddy asked.

Trevithick smiled. 'I've got fourteen flats in three buildings and the people I get to know best are the troublemakers. Mrs Lyle wasn't one of those. I'm not even sure what she looked like, but the paperwork shows she was a good tenant, paid the rent on time, no complaints, didn't leave any mess in the hallways, no noisy parties, and that's all I know.'

'Let's see your paperwork then,' Talantire said.

They sat down on the settee side by side and he opened a ring binder. In it was a brown envelope, with utility bills and ID that Mrs Lyle had produced at the start of the tenancy.

'Did she have a car?' Maddy asked.

'She didn't make a request for a garage,' he said, looking down at a sheet of paper. 'And she never mentioned it on the tenancy agreement.'

Talantire looked at the utility bills. 'These are foreign,' she said.

'Yes, I accepted them because the lady had lived abroad and her passport details checked out. I wasn't concerned about her falling behind with the rent. She had evidence of a decent pension.'

The pension document he showed them was a photocopy from a company called Lamprey Offshore Equipment Ltd. It was the same firm mentioned on the Aviva pension deposit on the victim's bank statements.

'Can we have all this?' Maddy asked of the pile of documents.

'I suppose so. The other officer said you are investigating some kind of crime. Can I ask what it is?'

The two detectives looked at each other. 'You'll get to hear about it soon enough,' Talantire said.

'Is she dead, then?'

'We're not at liberty to tell you anything,' Maddy said.

'Who killed her?' he asked.

'Thank you for your help, Mr Trevithick,' Talantire said, 'we'll be in touch if we need any more details.'

'Was she the one found stabbed in that Airbnb in Ilfracombe?'

The landlord was still asking questions from the doorway of the flat as the detectives made their way out onto the staircase. Talantire got her phone out, and began to check emails as they descended.

'Ah, we've got the first DNA results back,' she said, once she was certain Trevithick couldn't overhear. With a frisson of excitement, she clicked open the email and scanned the contents. 'We've got four DNA traces on the murder weapon, one of them the victim, obviously, but another one of them is a match with the database.'

'Brilliant,' Maddie said. 'Who is it?'

Talantire almost stumbled down the final flight of stairs when she read the next line. 'It's bloody Gawain Entwistle. The original murderer.'

'I imagined he was dead,' Maddy said.

'No, he was two years younger than Ruth Lyle, so he'd only be sixty-four or sixty-five. I'll have to see if he's been released.' She squinted at the phone, hardly able to believe what she was reading.

'But why is his DNA even on the system?' Maddy asked. 'He went away in 1974, a year after the crime, and DNA wasn't even used until the eighties, was it?'

'Maybe he was suspected of involvement in another crime. If there was a cold case, being looked at after the 1980s, they might have asked for an elimination sample, which would now be on file.'

'So let me get this right,' Maddy said. 'Not only do we have the same person killed in the same place by the same weapon as happened exactly fifty years ago to the day, but according to the DNA it was done by the same perpetrator.'

'That's what it says.'

'It's like *Back to the Future*,' Maddy said. 'It's bloody bonkers.'

'More like *Groundhog Day*,' Talantire said. 'And I can't make any sense of it.'

Chapter 7

'Someone's having a giraffe at our expense,' Nuttall said, once Talantire and Maddy had returned to Barnstaple CID. 'How can it be the same bloke?'

Primrose's face crinkled up in bafflement. 'A giraffe?'

'It means having a laugh,' Talantire said.

Maddy was already typing away furiously, searching the offender database. 'Entwistle is registered as being at Ashworth Hospital in Merseyside.'

'That's the place that Ian Brady was in,' Nuttall said.

'Brady died there in 2017,' Maddy said. 'Gone to hell, along with her.' Moors Murderer Ian Brady and his partner in crime Myra Hindley were the most notorious killers in British history. They had tortured and murdered five children in the early 1960s. There was hardly an adult in the country who could not bring to mind the haunting newspaper images of them.

'But is Entwistle still there?' Talantire asked.

'There is a release date. October last year, but the file is redacted,' Maddy said.

'Why would it be redacted?' Nuttall asked, walking over to take a look at her screen.

'I've got a two-line summary,' Maddy said, pointing at it. 'When you click on the PDF it won't open, and the attachment, a photocopy of the original release paperwork, has black lines drawn over bits.'

'That can only mean one thing,' Talantire said. 'It's a Special Branch job. He was released on the quiet, and has been given a new identity.'

'I never read anything about that,' Nuttall complained.

'I think that's the idea,' Maddy said, with a glance at Talantire.

'That's disgusting,' Nuttall said. 'Blokes like that deserve to die.'

'You just proved why they don't let us ordinary plods know,' Maddy said. 'We're the ones who they reckon would slip his new address to the vigilantes.'

'And what's wrong with that?' Nuttall asked.

'What if he didn't do it?' Talantire asked.

'What do you mean,' Nuttall said. 'Of course he did it. His DNA is on the bloody murder weapon. I mean, it's still there, for fuck's sake.' He rolled his eyes.

'Dave, you exhibit tabloid policing at its best,' Maddy said.

'What—' Dave spluttered.

'Hang on a minute,' Talantire said. 'That's exactly right. Like you said, Dave, there might still be DNA from the original crime still on the original murder weapon.'

'Right,' he said.

'But what baffles me is how someone could get access to that piece of evidence, that murder weapon, to use it again,' Talantire said.

'You mean one of our lot?' Nuttall asked.

'Whoa, a murderer in our ranks, eh Dave,' Maddy said. 'Who'd have thought that in this day and age?'

'Save us the sarcasm,' he muttered. 'This isn't the Met.'

'Well, Devon is full of orchards,' Maddy said. 'The perfect place to find a few bad apples.'

Talantire fixed her with a glare. 'It doesn't mean anyone in the police was the killer, Maddy, but it might be indicative of complicity.'

'Right, while you've been gallivanting off to Exeter, I've been getting some serious info,' Nuttall said, cracking his knuckles. He showed them a whiteboard, which was covered in illegible marker pen scrawl with red arrows pointing backwards and forwards.

'What have you got, then Dave?' Talantire asked.

'I'm trying to piece together the life of the victim's husband James Quince,' he said, gesturing at the board. 'Which is a bit difficult because he was killed in a road accident in India in 1999.' He handed Talantire a faded newspaper clipping in a plastic sleeve. It was a newspaper article from the *Daily Mail*, headlined *Holiday Brit Dies in Indian Road Tanker Horror*. The piece was dated 25 February 1999.

'That dovetails with the cremation in March of the same year,' Talantire said. 'We've got the order of service somewhere in the evidence file,' she added, gesturing to the pile of documents stacked up on the spare desk.

'Here it is,' Nuttall said, brandishing another clear plastic sleeve. 'I can't find any evidence of a marriage to Mrs Lyle; however, the pension firm has provided some information on our Mr Quince, and, thanks to the National Insurance office at Long Benton, I've got most of his contribution and employment records. He was pretty well paid, for the time.'

'What exactly was his job?'

'A consulting mud engineer, whatever that is. In 1978 Ruth Lyle was put on his occupational pension, as his spouse and beneficiary, and the address given was the same one in Aberdeen. Land Register of Scotland records show she was a joint owner on the freehold, which was bought in 1979 and sold in 2002. They were both there on the voters' register at that address for all that time.

'But she kept her own name.'

'Yes, which makes it likely they were just living together.'

'You reckon he was an oil worker?' Maddy asked.

'Yes, the original employer was Lamprey Offshore Equipment Ltd. It was taken over in 1983, by a Norwegian company, AKQ Norge A/S, and then in 1991 part of it was sold to a British company called Enterprise Oil, which itself was bought by Royal Dutch Shell in 2002. Aviva's records are the only ones we have. It took over pension administration from the

Norwegian firm in 2006. Unfortunately, AKQ Norge's original records "aren't available" according to the Shell admin people, which I presume means lost.'

Talantire tapped her pen on the desk in front of her. 'What about Mrs Lyle's working life? That's our focus. There's a small occupational pension in her own name, isn't there?'

'Yes, she worked in maritime insurance for a firm in Liverpool for a number of years in the 1990s, and was on income support there for a while later on. There are big gaps in her early contribution record. In fact her National Insurance record shows that she later bought back some of her contribution years.'

'Financially savvy, then,' Maddy said. 'I helped my mum buy back gaps in her contribution record so she could get a full pension. Of course, by marrying Quince she was automatically entitled to sixty per cent of a full state pension, whatever the state of her own contribution record. Not many people know about that.'

'Have you got any later addresses for Mrs Lyle?' Talantire asked.

'Yes, in Liverpool. That's where the insurance office was, though it closed in 1997.'

'What else do we know from her National Insurance number?' Maddy asked.

'The earliest P60 for Ruth Lyle is 1988, but that is ten years after she appeared on Quince's pension. But if she lived in the UK, she should have had a National Insurance record from sixteen.'

'Dave, this is good work.'

Talantire leafed through the various reports and documents in front of her, and the latest emails. Exeter University had just reported back that no one called Ruth Lyle had studied there in the 1970s or 1980s.

'We haven't got very much, have we? No early photos, no friends, no colleagues, no college record. Who on earth was

Mrs Ruth Lyle?' Talantire felt that the woman was slipping through her fingers, like some kind of ghost.

–

They spent the next hour examining all of the DNA results that had come back. Most of them were not a surprise. The murder victim's DNA was all over Bluebird Cottage, and there were a few traces of Mrs Lee's, the landlady, too, along with that of PC Dowling. A couple of door handles and the toilet cistern handle produced matching traces to a third, unknown person, whose traces were also found on the murder weapon along with those of the victim and Entwistle. There were fingerprints too, overwhelmingly from the victim, but a thumbprint and a fingerprint on the kitchen sink and taps whose associated DNA showed they were from a different person than the four traces on the crucifix. None around the home matched those of Gawain Entwistle. His DNA was only on the murder weapon.

Talantire went to a whiteboard and noted down the four traces on the murder weapon. 'One is the victim. Two is Entwistle, the original murderer. If so, it stands to reason the third must be the original victim. If his traces survived, so must hers.'

'Sounds reasonable,' Nuttall said. 'Which still leaves one more trace on the murder weapon, which must be the killer.'

'Not necessarily. Mrs Lee and one other person left dabs elsewhere but not on the cross. Imagine you're the killer, and just stabbed Mrs Lyle. You might have a lot of blood on you that you wanted to wash off. After you've done that, you strip off your rubber gloves, or whatever it was you used to stop getting your dabs on the crucifix, because you don't want to step outside and be seen wearing them. And even though you cleaned up, you still feel dirty. So you wash your hands again, and then turn off the taps.'

'We could get more analysis done,' Maddy said. 'Find out if there's a lot of bleach splashed about.'

'I'm going over to Middlemoor now,' Nuttall said. 'To see what records they've still got from the original crime.'

'I'll come with you,' Talantire said. 'Primrose, can you try to get some older electronic records from the phone? Go back beyond the six months you have so far.'

'Yes, ma'am,' she said.

'I'm going to go through the rest of Mrs Lyle's paperwork,' Maddy said. 'One other thing, the local newspaper has just put this up on its website.'

Talantire looked at the screen. The piece in the *North Devon News* was headlined: *Detectives baffled by holiday home killing*, and went on, *Police are yet to name the woman found dead in a holiday cottage in the centre of Ilfracombe on Saturday. All they will confirm is that a woman in her sixties was discovered with stab wounds, and may have been dead for a day or two. A spokesman for Devon and Cornwall Police said they remained open-minded about the motive for the killing, and called on members of the public to help identify both her and anyone who may have been seen with her in recent weeks.*

'That's all right, as far as it goes,' Talantire said. 'I told the press office not to mention the name or the crucifix.'

'That Tim Harvey from *North Devon News* has rung the station a few times,' Maddy said. 'Everyone's been warned not to say anything. Luckily, he doesn't yet seem to realise that Bluebird Cottage is the same place that young Ruth Lyle was killed.'

'Not surprising,' Talantire said. 'He's only in his twenties. He's probably never heard of it. And as long as we keep the victim's supposed name to ourselves, they might never know.'

–

Nuttall drove, as always, like he was on the track at Brands Hatch. He had the seat reclined, and his arms fully extended as if he was in a racing car. Even though it was an overcast day he was wearing wraparound shades, and chewing gum energetically. Talantire tried to use the time to read up on the latest emails on her phone, but soon started to feel bilious from the bumps and swinging of the car. She gave up and turned to Nuttall.

'Go easy, Dave, you might not want to see what I had for breakfast.'

'What?'

'Kippers with scrambled eggs.' It was a lie, but a useful one.

'Kippers *and* scrambled eggs? That is so wrong,' he said, but slowed down anyway.

'So what have you learned so far, about the case records?' Talantire asked.

'Well, Princess Avenue police station in Ilfracombe was already built when the 1973 murder took place. All records then were kept on site. But by 1986, due to lack of space, all evidence associated with closed cases was moved to a warehouse on site at Middlemoor. As you know, all cases after 1991 were entered onto the police database and the huge job begun to scan in case files prior to that.'

'From what I recall, they never finished,' Talantire said.

'Yeah. Budget cuts, and it got worse during austerity, that's what the archivist told me. Around 2010 the whole process ground to a halt. It was around that time that a whole lot of physical evidence was chucked out. They needed the space for new cases. But obviously, anything that had been in the fridges would have deteriorated by then anyway. To complicate matters, in 2013 they weeded out all remaining items in cases more than twenty years old where there was no active appeal. What was left of the pre-2000 evidence and the paperwork still to be scanned was shifted to a commercial storage facility on the Moorland Road industrial estate. And that's where we're heading first.'

'So is there anything from the original Ruth Lyle murder case on the database?'

'Only the stub reference, awaiting attachments of scanned files.'

'…which, as you said, has never happened,' Talantire said.

'Correct.'

They arrived at the industrial estate, and Nuttall turned right into the driveway of StoreULike Ltd, a low-rise 1960s industrial building with peeling paint, and missing plastic letters in the display sign. 'Doesn't inspire confidence, does it?' he said.

They parked and the two detectives made their way inside. The receptionist was a young woman with pink and green hair and an infected-looking facial piercing. Nuttall reminded her who he was, and she led them along a corridor to a lock-up unit with a roller door. She crouched down to undo the padlock, revealing a tattoo of a lion on the small of her back. She pulled up the door.

The unit was about the height and width of a lock-up garage, but twice as deep, and packed to within a foot of the roof with sagging cardboard boxes, some at the point of collapse, spilling loose files, sheafs of paper secured by treasury tags, and crumpled brown paper bags. Somewhere within that lot was the evidence they were looking for.

Talantire shook her head. 'What a mess! It'd take months to go through this lot.'

'Years, I'd say,' Nuttall replied.

Talantire picked up some loose papers at random. A case number dated 1981, an allegation of rape in Plymouth. There were witness statements, all written in looping handwriting, and various stamps that showed the evidence had been formally entered. The complainant claimed to have been raped by her former boyfriend in a car, and it was her word against his. The sheaf of papers in her hands was far from complete and did not detail what eventually happened with the case, and she wondered where the victim was now, and whether this event had tainted her entire life. She hazarded a guess that the case would have come to nothing, just as most such cases still did today.

Nuttall reached into the mess and pulled out an evidence bag. The handwritten number was clear enough, but the ink describing the contents had faded. There was a damp stain on the brown paper, but the date was still discernible: October 1978. He opened it and pulled out a bloodstained dental plate, lifting it towards his boss.

'Alas poor Yorick,' he said in Shakespearean tones. 'I knew him.'

'All right,' Talantire said. She had realised long ago that Nuttall was a fellow of infinite jest, but her gorge, like Hamlet's, had risen. 'Put it back. This is a dead end.'

—

On their return to Ilfracombe they had a quick incident room meeting to summarise the limited progress they had made. Maddy and Nuttall sat on stools at the bar, their laptops open, while Primrose had arranged her work on the pool table. The whiteboards were now populated with photographs, dates and arrows linking several boxes around the name Mrs Ruth Lyle. 'All right everybody,' Talantire said, 'here's what we know. On or around the evening of April first someone came to visit Mrs Ruth Lyle at Bluebird Cottage. There is no sign of a forced entry, so we must presume he or she was let in by the occupant. An argument ensued, heard by a witness, and Mrs Lyle was gagged with a pair of tights before being stabbed, on her kitchen table, with an iron crucifix.' She pointed to a photo, pinned to a board by a magnet, showing the entrance to Mercer Lane. 'There are no obvious candidates on the CCTV, but of course we don't know who we are looking for. And this is the point. The major line of enquiry, unsurprisingly, is that the killer was either obsessed with the original crime or connected with it. The answer to today's killing, I am convinced, lies in the past. For someone to restage this could not have been a coincidence.'

'Especially if he got hold of the original murder weapon,' Nuttall said.

'Yes, especially then,' Talantire said. She moved to a different whiteboard, on which were fixed cuttings from the 1973 killing.

71

'This is what we've gleaned from the original murder case. There are no physical records surviving, that we are aware of, but if we have to go through that entire lock-up of old records we will.'

'What normally happened to those old records?' Primrose asked.

'The records should all have been scanned onto a database, particularly with notorious cases like this,' Talantire said. 'But I think it's down to budgets. Why resource looking after old records when there are stacks of new ones with live evidence piling up? Unfortunately the SIO at the time, DCS George Hogley, died in 1992, so we can't ask him.' Talantire looked across to her detective sergeant. 'Maddy, have you found out who else was on the team?'

'Yes, Detective Sergeant Keith Howell, who retired in 1983, is still alive and lives in Marbella, Spain.'

'Retired for forty years?' Talantire said. 'How old is he?'

'He's only in his eighties. He took very early retirement.'

'Nice for some,' said Nuttall. 'Bagsy I'm on the team to visit him.'

Maddy laughed. 'Nah, we won't be allowed. Haven't you read the latest regs, Dave? You can get a Zoom set up for witnesses like him. No foreign trips without the sign-off of the chief constable.'

'Okay, well, we do need to talk to him,' Talantire said. 'Anyone else on the team still alive?'

'We don't have a complete list of who was on it,' said Maddy. 'A DC named Ian Collins, who definitely was, died in a road accident just a couple of years ago.'

'Shame.'

'There's one part of this that bothers me,' Nuttall said. 'The crucifix had Entwistle's DNA on it, right?'

'Unless it's cross-contamination,' Maddy said, with a mischievous grin.

Nuttall looked up. 'Very funny. Okay, so that means either it was the same murder weapon, and therefore retrieved by someone with the authority or nous to find it, or Entwistle himself, newly released, actually used a new murder weapon, a replica of the original, to kill a second time.'

'Neither of these possibilities make us look good,' Talantire said.

'Tell me a time when the police ever looked good?' Maddy asked. 'I mean, just once, ever.'

Chapter 8

Alan Lyle was the manager of an estate agency in Bideford, a historic town straddling the River Torridge, ten miles south of Ilfracombe. Talantire and Maddy had arranged to visit him shortly after the shop closed on Monday. The Fountain, Swire office was a double-fronted Georgian riverside building overlooking the Long Bridge. Lyle showed them in. He was an attractive and well-dressed sandy-haired man with the same blue eyes that his late sister had possessed. He seemed very happy to see them and ushered them into a back office, closing the door behind them. There seemed to be nobody else there.

'How is your mother?' Talantire asked.

He blew a sigh. 'Well, she is conscious, but a little confused. Look, I must thank you both for the prompt action you took. The doctors tell me it almost certainly saved her life.'

'Well, we were happy to help,' Talantire said.

'Detective Inspector, I will always be indebted to you,' he said, with a slight nod of his head.

'Is she able to speak?' Talantire said.

'After a fashion,' he said. 'She's regained the movement of her left arm, too. They're arranging for a language therapist to come next week.'

'Ah, bless. That's very good news,' Maddy said, glancing obliquely at Talantire. The sooner they could talk to her, the sooner they could start to unravel the conundrum of who Mrs Ruth Lyle really was.

'Now, Mr Lyle,' Talantire asked, offering him an iPad. 'Do you recognise this person?' The image was of Mrs Ruth Lyle, a selfie at the seaside, taken on her phone.

'No, I can't say I do.'

'We believe your mother recognised her. She showed a reaction when we presented her with a passport photograph of this lady, immediately before she had her stroke.'

'I see.' He looked more intently at the image. 'Is this the woman who was killed at Bluebird Cottage?'

'Yes.' Talantire swiped through several more pictures. 'Did this lady ever come to your estate agency in the last year? She might have been looking for rental properties.'

'No, I don't think she did. What name was she using?'

'Mrs Ruth Lyle, or possibly Susan Lyle.'

'You're joking,' he said. 'Well, that certainly proves she didn't come here. Someone would have notified me of the name.' His expression then changed. 'Of course, we did have an impostor, about five years ago. Claiming to be my sister.'

'What?' Talantire said.

'Some woman knocked on my mother's door, spouting some nonsense about her being Ruth and having come back from the dead.'

'Did you report it?'

'I certainly did, but the police didn't seem to take it very seriously. They just thought it was somebody trying to extort money and told my mother she should take no notice. But she was profoundly upset. She cried for days.'

'I can well imagine,' Talantire said. 'Did this woman leave any contact details?'

'No, but she did say she would return. I told my mother to make sure she rang me if that happened so I could have a stern word with the woman. But she never came back.'

'Was this while your mother was in the care home?'

'No. She lived at Blyth Road at the time, number seventy-nine. Of course, after this she did deteriorate quite rapidly. I think it was a major contributing factor to her loss of independent living, and having to go into residential care. You know, it was such a terribly cruel and heartless act, quite unforgiveable to cause such pain to a woman already as deeply wounded as my mother.'

Talantire could see that it wasn't just his mother who was wounded. Alan Lyle had lost his older sister and seen his family shrivel before his eyes. The pain seemed etched into the lines around his pale blue eyes, and the creases in his forehead.

'It would certainly be useful if you could recall the exact date the complaint was made to the police,' she said.

'Won't you be able to trace it anyway?'

'If the officer in question filed a report, yes. Sometimes they don't.'

Alan Lyle raised his eyebrows. 'Mum may have written it in her diary.'

'One final thing,' Maddy said. 'Can I just take a cheek swab for DNA elimination?'

He looked baffled. 'Why? I wasn't at the crime scene.'

'No. But the woman claiming to be your dead sister was. With samples from you and your mother, we will be able to check if you were indeed related,' Maddy said.

His face widened in alarm. 'So you *do* think she might be my sister!'

'Stranger things have happened,' Maddy said.

'This gets more ridiculous by the minute,' Lyle muttered.

'Look, it's only an outside possibility,' Talantire said. 'Building the evidence base ensures we are on the right track.'

'My poor sister has been lying dead in the grave for fifty years,' he said. 'And now you come here, casting doubt on whether she is really dead at all!'

Maddy put on blue nitrile gloves, and reached into her pocket for the DNA testing kit. 'Calm down, Mr Lyle. Much better to get your DNA now than have to dig Ruth up, isn't it?'

76

He looked even more astonished. His mouth hung open.

'Bit wider,' said Maddy, reaching forward with a cotton bud. 'There, that's it.' She swirled the bud around the inside of his cheek. 'All done.'

'One final thing, Alan,' Talantire said. 'Your mother told us that she gave you most of Ruth's childhood possessions when she moved into the home.'

'Yes, they're in the loft.'

'All right if we come and take a look? We'd like to get a sample of her DNA.'

'Would it survive after all that time?'

'Yes. The tests we have now pick up even the tiniest scraps, even from decades ago.'

'Yes, of course.'

After they had left and were sitting in the car, Talantire turned to Maddy and said: 'You shouldn't have mentioned exhumation, Maddy. We're a long way from having to do that. Especially if we can get a match from a childhood toy or something.'

'Sorry, me and my big gob again.'

They looked back through the window of the estate agency. Alan Lyle was closing the blinds, but he stopped, and his hand rested on the glass. His head slumped, shoulders shaking.

'Oh God, he's crying,' Maddy said. 'I am such an idiot.'

'I understand his upset, it's natural. Mrs Lyle sullied the memory of his sister,' Talantire said, as they sped away. 'But we shouldn't overlook the fact that it might have given him a motive to have killed her.'

–

Alan Lyle watched the detectives depart, then closed the blinds, reached for a tissue and blew his nose. A young couple arrived, hand in hand, and began looking at one of the listings in the window. They looked at each other with excited eyes, and then at him. He sensed that, despite the sign showing the agency

77

was closed for the day, they wanted to come in, brimming with the joy and enthusiasm of love, and thirsting to buy a home together. Right now, he wanted no part of it. He didn't want them spilling their bliss on him.

He was in another place, bleak, dark and cold as a sepulchre. He was in no state to see anybody, and turned away. He retreated to the rear office, closing the door behind him. He shifted a stack of *Country Life* magazines on a bookshelf, revealing the office safe. Tapped in the digits of his dead sister's date of birth. The door released with a click, and he pulled it open, revealing a space just big enough for the two box files of client documents inside it. He slid them out and placed them on a desk. He then picked at the corner of the carpet tile that formed the floor, and peeled the adhesive back. There was a slight depression built into the floor of the safe, and an aged manilla envelope lay in it. He carefully lifted the brittle item and brought it into the light. On it was written, in neat handwriting from an unknown hand, *Ruth, for you*.

He gently lifted the flap, and slid out the Polaroid photograph within. He knew every millimetre of this illicit image, the possession of which had haunted him for half a century. So many times he had thought of owning up to possessing it, aching to deploy its power to shatter the many lies told about the death of his beloved sister, and to give clues to the identity of her killer. But there would be costs. He would have to confess to how he had acquired it, something that had been uppermost in his mind in his teenage years. But that fear had been eclipsed in recent years. Now he was terrified of the effect it would have on his mother. This picture, even the description of what it showed, would simply kill her. He had no doubt about that. So it remained his secret, his cross to bear, until such time as his mother died. Then, he had decided, he would send it anonymously to the police.

–

Talantire returned to Ilfracombe, and spent the early part of Monday evening on her own in the incident room in the Stag and Hounds, reading the entirety of the press coverage of the original case, which had been photocopied by a trainee detective constable at Ilfracombe Library that morning. It ran from April to July 1973, after which it began to die down. At its height there was front-page coverage in the nationals, which resumed a year later when Gawain Entwistle stood trial. The newspapers made clear that a 'young man' had been arrested two days after the case broke, along with his father, presumably the verger, and then both were released on police bail. Then a few days later, two other young men were arrested, and again released after a day or so. The papers did not identify them. It was two weeks later when Entwistle was re-arrested, charged and remanded in custody.

It was nearly eight p.m. when she looked up. Outside the pub she heard youngsters, laughing and joking, making their way past along the High Street. She packed up her notes and the remaining unread photocopies, planning to read them at home. She glanced over at Nuttall's desk, and saw that he had hand-written an itinerary of the victim's movements, cross-referenced to paper receipts found in her purse, plus credit card entries and cash withdrawals on her bank account. In the week before her death, Mrs Lyle had spent a lot of time in Ilfracombe, but had taken a bus to Exeter on the Saturday, where she had bought clothing in a variety of shops. On the Tuesday she returned she had, according to one paper receipt, bought two slices of cake at the Flamingo Cafe at 3:54 p.m. Nuttall had ringed where both tea and coffee were shown on the bill and written beneath: *possible companion? CCTV?*

This was diligent work. If there was CCTV near the cafe, they might be able to get a peek at whoever Ruth Lyle had been with. She knew that Primrose had been looking at triangulating the victim's phone, which would put more detail on the map of her last movements. The GPS on the Android phone would have produced a more accurate record, but it had been turned off, and the location history deleted. Getting the underlying data from Google would take longer. Mrs Ruth Lyle was certainly a mystery, but she would inevitably give up her secrets.

Now it was time for a run. She had missed three days and was feeling the pull of exercise. She returned to her car and drove back to Barnstaple, leaving unsolved mysteries for another day.

–

Running in the dark through Watchett Woods, with only a head torch for guidance, would not be many people's idea of a fun way to spend a mizzly Monday evening, but for Jan Talantire the loneliness of the path, the uncompromising stony track as it rose over to Oxcombe, and that long haul up Modge Hill were hard to beat. It also cleared her head. She often had her best investigatory ideas while she was exercising. The full loop was a little over four miles, started close to her own home, and was little used. The path ran along between the side of a petrol station, long closed, and an industrial unit. The county council hadn't repaired the wooden stile, and the old metal footpath signpost was now algae-stained, shrouded in hawthorn, and difficult to spot. It was often muddy, especially at the start, and that put off many of the fair-weather walkers. Pounding her way up the hill, her feet chewing noisily into the chocolatey mud, she crested the ridge and stopped to get her breath back. There was a wooden bench here, set up for the view and dedicated to some old gent who'd died years ago. She rested an ankle on the back of the bench, careful not to drop goops of mud on the seat, and leaned over to grasp her calf. She stretched both hamstrings until they burned, then stood back, hands on hips, watching her breath plume in the light of the head torch. She gazed over the lights of Barnstaple, and the distant sheen of the River Taw, winding out westwards to the sea.

She knew she had to have a press conference soon, probably tomorrow at six p.m. after the post-mortem. The weight of media queries had been building up, and the press office at Middlemoor had been pleading for some more information to throw to the salivating hounds of Fleet Street. So far they had released nothing but the bare minimum: the suspicious death of a woman in her mid-sixties. She was experienced enough to know that going public too early was often a mistake. Asking the public for information and sightings of the victim was all very well, but it also indicated lines of enquiry, and once they were out there it was hard to then change them. Asking the right questions often took a little time.

She gritted her teeth, and ran home.

–

Alan Lyle got home at seven o'clock that evening, gave his wife a peck on the cheek as usual, and ruffled the hair of his two children as they sat doing their homework on the dining table. Then he went to the garage and pocketed a powerful torch. He brought out a pair of stepladders and carried them carefully up the stairs to the landing underneath the loft hatch. He set up the steps, climbed up to the hatch and gently lifted the wooden block and slid it onto the joists. The torch showed a dark forbidding space. The hanging cobwebs showed how rarely it was visited. This was the realm of the past, a place visited only in his nightmares. He found the wooden shipping chest, old and heavy, freighted with emotion. He slid it to the edge of the hatch, and pulled it after him. He retreated down the steps with the weighty object and placed it on the floor.

'Ugh, what have you got all that lot out for?' asked his daughter, as she slid past him on her way to her bedroom.

'Don't be disrespectful, Tamsin. These are all Auntie Ruth's childhood things.' He lifted up the chest and carried it through to his home office, and placed it on his desk. He lifted the lid, and was immediately awash with memories. A stack of framed photographs of Ruth's school years, her photo albums, school reports and much other paperwork. At the bottom was a pink plastic vanity case, its casing now cracked and yellowed. He lifted it out and undid the zip that ran round the edge. Inside was a colourful crayon with a rubber gonk on the end, a stack of vinyl singles, and a threadbare teddy bear Ruth had had as a baby.

He leafed through the singles in their paper sleeves: 'I Think I Love You' by the Partridge Family, several by the Osmonds, Roberta Flack, Gladys Knight. He picked up a particularly heavily loved version of 'Without You' by Nilsson. On the sleeve was a stuck-on heart, and a faded word in biro, written out again and again: *Envy*. Envy of what, or of whom? He had no idea, but presumed it was connected to the man in the Polaroid.

Chapter 9

Tuesday

Talantire woke up at six after a night of disturbing dreams in which she was naked and exploring the Dimpsy Chapel, and had chanced across the crucifix, still on the wall. As she slipped out of bed and put on her bathrobe she could still imagine the chill of the time-worn flagstones of the crime scene beneath her bare feet. It took a long hot shower before she felt right again. As she washed her hair and massaged her scalp, she tried to imagine why a woman would come back to Ilfracombe and to Bluebird Cottage, to pass herself off as someone who everyone old enough to remember knew was dead. Who was she hoping to persuade? There didn't seem to be any money in this. Gwen Lyle's records showed that the local authority paid for her care at The Chestnuts, and she had sold her house at seventy-nine Blyth Road to repay them. Though her son Alan seemed comfortably off, it was hard to see an impostor getting hold of any of his money. So where was the angle?

She made her way downstairs, and saw her own rented home through fresh eyes, as if she'd been on a long journey and just returned. After she and Jon had broken up nine months ago, she had moved in here halfway along a winding road on a treeless estate on a hill in northern Barnstaple. A dull three-bed semi, a turgid symphony in beige woodchip wallpaper and yellowing paintwork. Devoid of character or life. The landlord had said she could repaint it if she wanted, but at her own expense. She demurred. She'd already lain on her back outside the back door to replace the dishwasher outlet pipe, had climbed the roof to fix a rattly tile, cleaned out the gutters that had overflowed in heavy rain, and rodded the drains. The landlord, having ignored the required work himself, took offence when she asked to deduct money from the rent to cover her time and expenses. She had often thought about moving out, but having fixed everything wanted to stay to get the benefits. Besides, the emotionless tundra of Cornwallis Avenue suited her mood, as she reflected on Jon's departing text message. *We never had much in common, Jan, did we?* She had thrown herself into work to such an extent that she barely recognised her neighbours, nor they her. The only one she registered was Derek, the thickset man opposite, whose noisy moped often woke her at two a.m. as he got back from his shift at the hospital. Then there was some elderly woman two doors down whose name she didn't know, but who habitually dragged her wheelie bins out into the street before six in the morning, the sound waking Talantire like a prolonged rumble of thunder.

Breakfast was stale cornflakes and milk. It tasted like soggy wallpaper. She had to get herself a life, she thought. *I can't subsist on work alone.* The dating apps she had been on had produced only disappointments. The pool of available men within an hour's drive was just too shallow. She was being offered sixty-year-olds, callow young surfers, and a procession of balding beer-gutted divorcés. A gust of loneliness swept through her, just as the real wind rattled the lids on the wheelie bins. Her phone, on charge on the kitchen worktop, showed a message on the dating app.

Adam.

She seized the phone like a drowning woman. They had already agreed to meet this week, but there had been no follow-up. He was now proposing Wednesday at the Bank of Swans in Bideford, a well-known gastropub. *Really pleased they found that little girl safe and well,* he added. *Hope we can manage a whole evening this time.* He had finished off with a wink.

That was a bad choice of emoticon, no doubt about it. Too suggestive. But the sheer fact he wanted to meet, after she had baled out of their first date, outweighed everything. She felt a little wave of happiness, then a backwash of stupidity for being so girlishly enthusiastic. *Come on, Jan, we've only had half a date. Get a grip.*

In the car on the way to work, she had music on loud, and very nearly broke the speed limit past the Gatso camera near the junior school. That would never do. Still, the smile persisted for the rest of the journey and was only wiped from her face when she logged on to her computer at work. Her ray of sunshine completely erased.

—

It had taken thirty-six hours for Jan Talantire's request to see the files of Gawain Entwistle to be answered by Special Branch. And it had come back as a 'no'.

'Can you believe this?' Talantire asked Maddy, who was sitting opposite her looking equally glum. 'How are we ever going to get to the bottom of this if we can't see the documents?' She fired off an email asking for a rethink, and reminded them she was investigating a live murder case.

'I don't know. Sounds crazy to me.' Maddy was hammering at her keyboard, the angry percussion of keys telegraphing her mood.

'What's up?' Talantire asked.

'Neville has let the house insurance run out,' she said. 'And now I'm trying to get a reasonable quote from somebody else before he burns the bloody place down.'

Maddy's husband was an artist. Even for that financially cursed occupation, he was horribly, desperately, disastrously unsuccessful. For six years, he had been making sculptures from old ship's ropes, coiled, twisted and spliced, sometimes painted brown or grey, but sometimes covered in tar. He had a shed full of them, like inedible jumbo spaghetti, and had only ever sold two. One was to his mother, the other to his sister, and that latter one had soon found its way into a skip at her husband's insistence. Maddy had supported Neville and their three young children solely from her own earnings for the entire decade of their married life. In exchange he was supposed to run the household, but a stay-at-home dad is supposed to do more than rough-and-tumble with the kids. She finished her email with a flourish, just as her phone rang.

She picked it up, wearily. 'Hello darling,' she said, and mouthed the name Briony to Talantire. 'Why aren't you at school?'

Maddy's hand fell over her eyes as she listened to her eight-year-old. 'Spilled it where, darling?' There was a long explanation. 'Our double bed. How?' The explanation lasted thirty seconds. 'And where is he now?' Maddy waited while the child explained. 'Well, he shouldn't go to B&Q and leave you on your own to look after Bethany and Hughie. Ah, you did tell him. Yes, it's illegal, and I'm a policewoman. Yes, I suppose I could arrest Daddy.'

'If you need to go I can give you an hour,' Talantire whispered.

Maddy smiled at her, but held up a hand. 'Briony, is Carol next door? Can you ask her to look after you all until Daddy gets back?' After a few seconds, she asked, 'Briony, darling, was it oil paint or tar?' She waited and then muted the phone as she looked up at the ceiling. 'Linseed oil, oh for the *love of God*!' she yelled. 'Thank you for taking off the bedspread,' she said, after she'd unmuted. 'Did you look it up in Stickipedia, darling?' Another wait. 'Bicarbonate of soda. That sounds right, and then vinegar after twenty-four hours. But, darling, B&Q doesn't sell baking powder, so why did he...?' She sank even lower in her chair. 'We've actually got some in the larder, but it's on the top shelf. Don't try to reach it. Go and get Carol.'

Maddy's domestic firefights were a familiar feature of Barnstaple police station's CID department. This one was no more than par for the course.

Talantire's phone rang before Maddy had finished. It was a DS Gerald Ferris from Special Branch in Exeter, the officer who had poured cold water on her requests for oversight of the Entwistle case notes. 'I'm afraid you've trod in a very sensitive area,' he said. 'Mr Entwistle has been released, having been judged by a panel of clinicians to no longer be a danger to the community. Because of the notoriety of his crime and fears of retribution, he has been given a new identity.'

'I understand that, but there was no announcement or release about this development,' she said. Ferris had a reputation as a stickler, and she wasn't optimistic about her chances of changing his mind.

'No, there never is. If contacted and asked specifically, the Ministry of Justice would have confirmed it. However, the offender was allowed to change his name by deed poll while in Ashworth, and once released it was changed again.'

'You mean someone helped him,' Talantire said. 'He had learning difficulties.'

'Yes, he was helped,' Ferris said.

'You must be aware that the mother of the murder victim is still alive, and would want to know.'

'I am fully aware of that, and she had been discreetly informed of the decision to release. Normally that is only done for those in the Victim Contact Scheme. However, this whole matter went to the highest level within the Home Office before a decision was made. The advice to the Home Secretary was that there was a real and immediate risk to his safety if his identity and location were revealed. You also have to be aware that he was a child when he is alleged to have committed the crime.'

'Alleged? He was convicted. Are you saying there are doubts?'

'Well, not specifically. But the panel of judges who reviewed the clinicians' decision suggested there remained considerable doubt over the burden of proof, and with modern forensic techniques it might well have been the case that no conviction would have been made. The provision of a new identity seemed to be the least that the state could do to recompense him. Obviously a pardon would only have drawn attention to his release.'

'Okay, I understand all that,' Talantire said. 'But I do still need to interview him about a current murder.'

'You mean that copycat crime in Ilfracombe?'

'Well, you can't conclude it's a copycat. It would be dereliction of duty on my part if I didn't investigate this line of enquiry.'

'I'm sure we'll be able to let you email some questions, which we can put to him.'

'That's no good,' Talantire said. 'Come on, Gerald, I'm sure you've been an investigative officer. I need to see his face, and look into his eyes.'

'I do understand. Well, I'll see what I can do,' Ferris said, with a sigh. 'It may take a while. And no promises.'

'Look, I don't have the luxury of time,' Talantire said. 'I'm sure you don't want to stand in the way of a murder investigation.'

'Take it from me, he had nothing to do with the crime you are investigating. He's easily confused, and needs help even with the basics of everyday life. He's never learned how to drive and lives a long, long way away from Devon. I'm told he's struggling to use even a basic mobile phone.'

'So does this mean he's getting an official alibi?'

'Not exactly.'

'You seem pretty sure, but here's the thing: I have in my possession the murder weapon found stuck in the body. Lab tests show it has Gawain Entwistle's DNA on it.'

There was a long, shocked silence. 'That can't be right,' he said.

'No, it can't can it? But what I want to know is, Gerald, whether you are going to be part of the problem, or part of the solution.'

88

Another sigh. 'I'll see what I can do, Jan. I see where you're coming from, but honestly, something like this is like turning a supertanker round.'

'Well, perhaps it's time to at least start to turn the wheel. In the meantime, can you tell me the name Entwistle was released under, before the second name change.'

There was a pause, then he replied. 'I suppose so, seeing as it's a matter of public record. The name's Gary Endle, and I'll send you the release docket.'

He ended the call, and a few minutes later the promised document arrived. Dated 24 December 2022, it was a list of prisoners slated for release, and sure enough, Gary Endle was amongst them. Somewhere out there was a convicted murderer, found guilty of a terrible crime in 1973, and now implicated in an equally terrible one. With a new name and identity, courtesy of the Home Office, he could be anywhere. She needed to find him, but how?

—

The Zoom call to Marbella was set for two p.m. Talantire and Maddy sat in the incident room with the curtains drawn, side by side, on their respective laptops. An image of sunny Mediterranean climes appeared on the screen and gradually the swimming pool and bougainvillea pivoted from view until a tanned face, a pair of sunglasses and a thick head of white hair appeared, shaded by a large, gaily coloured beach umbrella. Keith Howell radiated smugness, having apparently secured for himself an idyllic life.

'Hello, Keith, are you enjoying your retirement?' Talantire asked.

'I am indeed,' he said. 'I wasn't surprised to get your call. I was reading about the copycat killing just this morning.'

'I know it was many years ago, Keith, but we would be very grateful for your recollections about the original crime.'

'I'll help you all I can. It's nice to feel useful at this stage in my life.'

'We are convinced that the perpetrator isn't simply somebody who read about what happened back in 1973, but much more intimately involved.'

'Oh, why is that?'

'We're not confirming anything officially, as yet, but you may have heard the rumour about a crucifix being used, as before. As far as we can tell, it's not simply a replica but the actual one.'

'I can't see how that's possible,' Howell said. 'We're talking about someone with access to evidence.'

'I just want to stress that this particular fact is completely confidential between us, Keith. We know that retired cops have a tendency to gossip, and, seeing as you are the only person we have told, if this emerges we would know who it was from.'

'Your secret is safe with me,' he said. 'But it's shocking!'

'We've been trying to gain access to the original evidence, Keith,' said Maddy. 'You may not be surprised to hear that the evidence bags can't be found, but more worryingly the paper files, which should have been scanned back in the 1990s, are not on the database either.'

'Well, all that was after my time. I retired in 1983.'

'We know that, Keith,' Talantire said. 'We're not blaming you. However, we also know why you retired so early.'

'Listen, that was all bollocks. It was someone I had put away just trying to frame me. I couldn't prove I hadn't taken the money. So I just thought, well…'

'We are not here to judge you on that, Keith,' Talantire said. 'I know a lot of officers retired rather than face disciplinaries. But if you took with you any of the Ruth Lyle murder files, we want to know.'

Howell shook his head. 'I haven't got anything.'

'Come on, Keith,' Maddy said. 'We know that was easily the biggest case you ever worked on. A lot of officers take trophies, don't they?'

'I've got newspaper cuttings, sure. But not evidence. I'd never do anything like that.'

'You never retained the murder weapon?' Maddy said. 'It wouldn't have been hard, would it? The case had been closed for ten years when you retired, there was no likelihood of an appeal. It would have been a nice little thing for you to boast about with your mates down there on the sunny coast of Spain.'

'I didn't do it, all right?' The image of Howell jumped as he slapped his hand down on the metal table that was holding his laptop. 'I wasn't the only one working the case, was I? There were more than a dozen others on the team. Anyone could have had access, long after I left. Besides, at some point when they changed evidence storage it might have just been chucked out. Tossed in a skip, for someone to find.'

A grey-haired woman in a short-sleeved white blouse appeared on camera, and placed a drink in front of Howell. 'Gin o'clock, dear,' she said. The sound of clinking ice cubes and the fizz of poured tonic was mesmerising to the watching detectives.

'All right, Keith,' Talantire said. 'It's not an accusation. Were you aware of any others on the team who liked to take trophies?'

He shook his head, and gazed away. Talantire wished he'd take off his shades so they could see his eyes. The better to see whether he was lying.

'The whole case was horrifying,' Howell eventually said. 'They didn't use the term PTSD in those days, but the first constable who found the body was never the same again. PC John Cook. He was only twenty-two, got divorced and years later took his own life. He wasn't even fifty when he died. And then PC Collins, I heard he'd died too.'

'We haven't got a full list of the team,' Maddy said. 'If you can email the names, that would be a real help.'

'I will, so far as I remember.' He took off his sunglasses now and ran a thick hairy hand over his face. 'I do recall the evidence officer. Lorraine Parkes. You should talk to her. She was only young, so she should still be around.'

'All right, that's a decent start.'

Howell put his sunglasses down. There was a stripe of sunlight across his face, and he squinted against the light. 'You do know there was an additional set of suspects, don't you?'

'We read about two arrests in the cuttings, but there was no detail,' Talantire said.

'Yeah, it was two likely lads, on the pull for easy lays. Seen buying the victim drinks in the Stag the week before she died.'

'The Stag and Hounds Hotel?' Maddy said, and looked at Talantire. The very same place where they were sitting.

'That's the one.'

'Do you know their names?' Talantire asked.

Howell put his glasses back on, and quirked his lips. 'Gimme a break, it was fifty years ago. But they gave statements, and they should be there, somewhere.'

Somewhere. Talantire thought of the lock-up, and its tons of unsorted papers. Somewhere in there, possibly.

'If you think of the names, Keith, do let me know, all right?' she asked.

'Yes, I will,' he said.

After they'd ended the call, the two women looked at each other. Maddy shook her head. 'Just think, two blokes, here, sitting in this pub with young Ruth all those years ago.'

'Chances are they are still alive,' Talantire said, getting up and picking up her shoulder bag. 'Let's double down on finding them. Once I get back from seeing Dr Holcombe cut up Mrs Ruth Lyle.'

–

The Royal Devon Hospital in Barnstaple was the usual combination of brown brick and stained concrete and, with marvellous *Soylent Green* planning, the mortuary was opposite the refectory in the basement. Dr Holcombe was already busy on the body of Mrs Ruth Lyle when the technician escorted Talantire inside. Holcombe was dictating into a suspended microphone, but acknowledged Talantire's presence with raised eyebrows. The body on the stainless-steel slab was a waxy white, the only colour being the russet red of her hair, her scarlet varnished fingernails and matching toes, and the blackened gore around the wound. Small pearl earrings remained in the lobes of her ears. Her eyes were closed and she looked peaceful, considering the horrifying injury she bore.

'The deceased is a white female appearing to be in her mid-sixties, weight 58.2 kg, height 1.74 metres, blue eyes, apparently healthy dentition, appendix scar—' Holcombe stopped.

'Hello, Jan, how are you?'

'Fine, thank you.'

'You might be interested that there is some evidence of fightback,' he said.

'Fingernail scrapings?'

'Yeeess,' he said tentatively. 'But certainly abrasion on the knuckles of the right hand, with extravasation.' He lifted her hands to show Talantire where the knuckles were scraped and had bled.

'She punched her attacker?'

'It's one possible explanation. There is no associated contusion, so my guess is that the injuries were sustained a few minutes at most ante-mortem. I oversaw the removal of the body myself, so there is no possibility of damage to the corpse in transit, which would be the only other likely explanation. There is some residue beneath the nails as well, which I have bagged for analysis, along with a swab from each of the knuckles.'

'I hope we get the assailant's blood and DNA on those knuckles,' Talantire said.

'If we are lucky,' Holcombe said. 'Are you going to stay for the evisceration?'

It was a year since she'd attended an autopsy, and that hadn't been with Holcombe. Talantire wasn't squeamish, but seeing a body cut open and the brain and the entrails removed was a challenge for all but the most hardened observers. However much you know the theory, seeing that the interior of a human being is little more than a series of bags of liquids, fleshy pipes and connective tissue was always philosophically profound. On top of everything was the smell, which even the powerful overhead extractor rarely masked. This woman had been six days dead, three of them in unrefrigerated surroundings. The stench would soon be appalling.

'Yes, I'll stay,' she said.

Holcombe moved around the body, describing every abrasion, mark and blemish, while the technician arranged a tray of instruments including a scalpel and a small electric bonesaw. Talantire took from her pocket a pad of tissues doused in perfume that she had prepared earlier. She held it beneath her nose as she watched the pathologist make an incision across the scalp from ear to ear, and then fold forward the skin of the forehead, sliding off the top part of the face. At the appearance of the saw, Talantire stepped back a couple of paces. The whine of its motor was distressing enough, but on contact with the skull it changed to a screech. A couple of minutes later, the forensic pathologist lifted out the brain of Mrs Lyle and put it into a metal dish held by the technician for weighing. Returning to his scalpel, Holcombe made a Y-shaped incision in the chest, and then used a pair of what appeared to be bolt croppers to crack the ribs so that the viscera could be removed. She watched the whole process with the same morbid fascination as she had experienced as a child watching the Daleks on *Doctor Who* from behind the settee. Fascinating, repellent and quite scary. Not quite looking between her fingers, but safely back from the scene of such horror. Dr Holcombe was standing with his back to her, and the technician a little to his left. Then he said: 'Ah, now that *was* unexpected.' He turned to Talantire. 'You might want to come and see this.'

She walked up to his side and peered round him. His gloved hands were glistening with human goop, poised above the open slit of the woman's body, which ran from sternum to pubic bone.

'What is it?' Talantire asked.

'She doesn't have a uterus. Nor Fallopian tubes, nor ovaries.'

'You mean a full hysterectomy?'

'No, a bit more fundamental than that. Your murder victim was born a man.'

Chapter 10

'So there was a sex change operation?' Talantire asked.

'Gender-affirming surgery, we say these days. But yes, some decades ago, I would say. A very neat job.' He moved the body's legs apart. 'As you can see, externally, a woman. I have already noted that the external genitalia, labia major and especially the clitoris, seemed a little underdeveloped, but still within the normal range. There was no external scarring whatsoever, though internally one can see scars from what looks to be a penile inversion. I'm going to have to do a little bit of research on this.'

Talantire nodded. 'This opens up whole new lines of enquiry. I'm glad I hadn't already had a press conference. Rowing back on the cause of death would be one thing but having to do a U-turn on the sex of the victim is a bit more embarrassing.'

'Of course the autopsy report will still identify her as female, as that was her clear preference.'

'I don't think we will be revealing this publicly,' Talantire said. 'If she's lived as a woman for decades then there's no reason to believe it should have any bearing on the case. Except, of course, if it somehow tied up with the original murder.'

'That indeed is your conundrum,' said Dr Holcombe, washing his hands at the sink. 'In any case you'll have my full report in a couple of days. I'll try to find out a little bit more about the style of the gender-affirmation operation to see where and when it may have taken place.'

'Thank you,' Talantire said, and made her way out.

Two minutes later, standing in the car park, she took several deep inhalations to clear the smell of decomposing intestines from mind and body. Mrs Ruth Lyle had been born a man, but possessed a birth certificate corresponding to the girl who was murdered back in 1973. She had used it to create a fully female identity that matched not only her chosen gender, but a particular person. It was a sophisticated and all-consuming act to recreate a woman, as if to somehow expunge the act of murder. To bring back from the dead a child, and create a new life for her as if she had continued to live. There was one obvious motive for such an action, perhaps a misleading one, but powerful nonetheless.

Guilt.

–

'Trevor Goswell and Andrew Hinks,' Maddy said as Talantire walked in. 'Keith Howell has just emailed the names of the two blokes he interviewed about the 1973 murder.'

'Good,' said Talantire, sitting down and blowing a sigh.

'You look a bit white. Did you chuck up?'

'No, I was fine. At least until the moment when the pathologist held up a glistening mass of entrails, minus uterus, and pointed out that our murder victim had been born a man.'

'What?'

'Yes, a pretty perfect operation, so he said. It helps that the bloke had originally been quite slim with androgynous features, small hands and feet. He did make a very good woman. Holcombe showed me that they had even done a tracheal shave, which trims the size of the Adam's apple.'

'Bloody hell! But when had he had it done?'

'Decades ago. That type of surgery's been going on for a lot longer than you might imagine.'

'So what is his real name?' Maddy asked.

'We are no closer to that now than when we thought he had been a woman all his life.'

'Well, I've been trying to find Goswell and Hinks, and there aren't any of that name locally,' Maddy said.

'It's not surprising,' Talantire said. 'If you'd been questioned in connection with a notorious murder like this, you'd want to go and live almost anywhere else, wouldn't you?'

'I expect so,' Maddy said. 'But it's my job to bring them back for a few questions.' She picked up the phone. 'I'm going to start with National Insurance and NHS numbers. Uncommon surnames, and both male, so I reckon I've got a good chance of making quick progress.'

'That's a good start,' said Talantire. 'I spoke to Wells on the way back from the hospital, and we'll have a press conference this evening, seven o'clock.'

'At Middlemoor?' Maddy said, staring at the clock. It was five thirty. 'We'll have to set off now.'

'No, we'll do it here, at the Stag, in the conference room upstairs. The bigwigs will have to travel here.'

'They won't like that,' Maddy said. 'Forty-four miles into the sticks on slow roads, with hostile natives round every bend.'

'It is short notice, but Wells has been pressing me. We've agreed to keep the gender discovery out of it, but we do need Nuttall's reconstruction of the victim's last known movements.'

At that moment DC Nuttall walked into the incident room, looking at his phone.

'Dave,' Talantire said. 'Can you run us through your reconstruction. We've got a press conference here at seven p.m.'

'Whoa! You never mentioned that.'

'It's only just been decided,' Talantire said. 'The press office at Middlemoor is going ape trying to fend off the media enquiries, so we've got to throw them something.'

He looked shocked. 'Not me? I'm not presenting it to the press, am I?'

'No, no, Dave. That would be cruel.'

'…to them,' Maddy muttered. Nuttall's presentational skills, written and verbal, were not great.

'Wells will be running the conference, and he'll hand over to me as SIO. I'll present the reconstruction, and we'll ask the public to give us their sightings of the victim and any visitors.'

Nuttall looked relieved.

'All right, off you go,' Talantire said, pointing to the heavily populated whiteboard.

'Okay, so this is what we know of the movements of Mrs Ruth Lyle for the week prior to her death,' Nuttall said. 'On Thursday, a week before her body was discovered, she left Mercer Lane at 9:17 a.m., visited the Co-op and come back via the High Street with two carrier bags of shopping, as shown by CCTV. She also visited the library, and her online library card shows she borrowed two audiobooks, of the thriller genre. That day she also rang Keane Wale Harbyttle at 3:15 p.m. She was spotted on CCTV near the harbour later that evening.'

'But presumably we don't know how she got there?' Talantire asked.

'Well, we still have this problem that only the top end of Mercer Lane has CCTV coverage, when you come out on the High Street. If she leaves via Wilder Road, we won't see her. On this occasion though she was seen entering a convenience store on Fore Street, and, once Primrose examined the footage from inside the store, we discovered that she had visited regularly.'

'She bought a half bottle of Stolichnaya vodka a couple of times a week,' Primrose said. 'We looked back over the previous month, which was as much footage as was stored.'

'Was anyone seen walking with her?' Talantire asked.

'Not exactly,' Nuttall said. 'There was a homeless man, apparently quite well known locally, who she was seen to give money to outside Aziz Flame Grill, which is a kebab-type takeaway. The CCTV on that street on the Saturday captured her walking with him for a short distance, and then going together into the Flamingo Cafe.'

'Ah, was that the receipt for both tea and coffee?' Talantire asked.

'Yes,' Nuttall said. 'And a couple of slices of chocolate cake.'

'So she had a charitable nature,' Talantire mused.

'Well, if you've already died once at sixteen, you probably have a philosophical take on life,' Maddy said.

Nuttall gave her a quizzical look, then turned back to his whiteboard. 'Certainly her bank accounts show regular direct debits to national charities, including the NSPCC.'

'So we don't have images capturing her with anyone else?' Talantire asked.

'Transactional interactions only,' Nuttall said. 'The swimming pool, the Co-op, and various other shops. There was one GP appointment at the local surgery, but they're a bit slow on letting us have medical records.'

'Right,' Talantire said. 'So we're going to show them a map of known sightings, ask if anyone saw her or spoke to her.'

–

The Stag and Hounds Hotel conference room was packed with journalists long before the press team arrived from Middlemoor, looking suitably grumpy at having had to make the slow and tedious journey. Half a dozen hacks from national papers as well as the Press Association and numerous local reporters had already trooped out to the crime scene, less than a hundred yards away. There was no room for satellite vans, which had to park some distance away, but there were plenty of well-known TV faces already doing pieces to camera before the conference began.

Detective Superintendent Michael Wells arrived only ten minutes before the start, but came into the incident room to greet Talantire and the rest of the team. Moira Hallett, from the press office, who Talantire had spoken to before but never seen in person, accompanied him.

'We've got to throw them a bit of fresh meat,' Moira said. 'They need something new to say, they keep trying to get me to comment on various hare-brained theories.'

'Well, the one thing we can give them now is the victim's name,' Talantire said. 'We refrained at the start because we thought it was an alias, but it is now clear that this woman has been living under this name for decades.'

'That will certainly put the cat amongst the pigeons,' Wells said. 'Once they get the link to the historic crime.'

'I'm really surprised you managed to keep it secret this long,' Moira said. 'All they had to do was to ring the landlord and ask the tenant's name.'

'Ah, but she's gone to Bristol to stay with her son,' Maddy said. 'We did suggest to her it might be sensible to move away for a while.'

They made their way upstairs and shoehorned their way into the crowd. Talantire sat next to Wells, with the PR chief on her other side. A press pack had been prepared, containing three pictures of the victim from her own phone.

Wells began by saying: 'We are investigating the horrific stabbing of a sixty-six-year-old woman in her home. We have her name, Mrs Ruth Lyle, but know very little about her. So we are asking the public if they knew her, had talked to her and, most importantly, if they had seen anyone coming to her home, Bluebird Cottage, on or around Thursday last week.'

'Did you say Ruth Lyle?' asked one reporter. 'The same name as the girl who was killed in this town fifty-odd years ago?'

'Yes, that's right,' Wells said, then turned to his right. 'At this point, I'd like to introduce Detective Inspector Jan Talantire, who is the senior investigating officer.'

'Now, we've tried to recreate the movements of Mrs Lyle during the last week of her life,' Talantire began, as a slide popped up on the screen behind her.

'Just a second,' called out another reporter. Moira whispered his name in Talantire's ear. 'John Tullow, *Guardian*.'

'We've got the same name for a murder victim, killed in roughly the same place—'

'No, exactly the same place,' shouted out someone else from the back. 'Exactly fifty years on.'

'Is this a copycat killing?' shouted a female TV reporter.

Talantire held up her hand. 'That is certainly a line of enquiry we are pursuing.'

'The original killer is out, isn't he?' asked a reporter in the front row.

'Gawain Entwistle,' called someone else from the back.

The press conference descended into a series of shouted questions that Talantire wasn't prepared to answer. Wells brought proceedings to a close, but there was immediate uproar, and the detectives were soon pressed into a throng by the reporters.

The final question she heard yelled as she made her escape was: 'What was Mrs Lyle stabbed with? Was it a similar weapon?'

Talantire, DS Wells, Maddy and Moira took cover in the incident room as the reporters filed out.

'Well, that went well,' Maddy said, as she listened to the loud complaints from journalists who were gathering in the street outside.

'It was inevitable,' Wells said. 'It's perfect tabloid fodder, isn't it? The same woman killed twice, fifty years apart.' He looked at his phone. 'Seems the public reporting line is already going crazy. Maybe four officers aren't enough to handle all the calls.'

Already, the first trickle of leads were being forwarded to Talantire's email. Someone who had seen the murder victim in the centre of Ilfracombe. Someone who had seen her in Exeter. Someone who had apparently seen her in Skelmersdale in Lancashire, nearly three hundred miles away. Inevitably it brought forth more tenuous ideas: someone who thought they had seen Gawain Entwistle in Lincoln, another who'd seen him on a bus in Somerset. But who these days would know what he even looked like?

What she was hoping for was a member of the dead woman's family; a cousin, a brother, even a boyfriend, who could shed some light on her.

That got her thinking about Ruth Lyle's husband, James Quince. The first record of them being together was in 1978, just five years after the murder, when she was first listed as a beneficiary on his pension. The gender reassignment operation had presumably happened some years previously. So where had they met? Could have it been at university? Nuttall had been checking, but had made little progress so far.

-

'Are you going for a pint, boss?' Maddy asked as she saw Talantire putting her coat on. Tuesday was their normal evening for a quick drink at the Coach and Horses.

Talantire looked at her watch. It was gone eight and the Prince of Darkness had just arrived to take over the nightshift. She and DI Lockhart bumped fists as he headed off to the gents, and she slung her bag over her shoulder. 'Yes, all right. I could really do with one.'

Maddy was closing down her PC and tidying up her desk. She turned to the young digital evidence officer, who looked deeply engrossed in something on her screen. Her shift should have finished an hour ago. 'Primrose, fancy a drink?'

'In a pub? I don't drink alcohol, but I'd love to come.'

'What are you working on?' Talantire asked.

'Recovering deleted files from Ruth Lyle's handset. It's not done yet.'

Ten minutes later they were in the quiet back bar of the Coach. Talantire had bought a half of Titanic plum porter, Maddy had a double gin and tonic, while Primrose had a Coke with a slice of lemon and plenty of ice.

'I can just imagine what the papers are going to say tomorrow,' Talantire said.

'It'll be a total shit storm, as we say in the trade,' Maddy said.

Primrose stared around the pub. Talantire followed her gaze, and felt slightly embarrassed at the dive they frequented. Dark, low beams, slightly dingy, with the ever-present smell of stale beer. Seats repaired with gaffer tape, the wooden tables defaced with the initials of customers past and present. There was a gambling machine behind them and an electronic jukebox to the right, underneath the screen which normally showed the football.

'We only come here because it's the closest,' Talantire said.

'And because they always have a good dark beer on,' Maddy reminded her.

'I tried English beer once and it was so bitter,' Primrose said.

'That's kind of the idea,' Talantire said, taking a sip of her porter. She'd have to savour every drop, knowing that she could be called back to work if DI Lockhart needed help.

'I like things sweet,' Primrose said with a smile. Her teeth were perfect.

'We only come here on Tuesdays,' Maddy said, folding her arms. 'The firearms unit's darts team plays here on Wednesdays, and on Fridays it's karaoke, and you might run into your mate Venables.'

'You mean the racist sergeant?' Primrose said.

'Yeah, fancies himself a proper Roy Orbison,' Maddy said.

Primrose made a face as if she'd bitten a lemon. 'Orbison? He's, like, ancient.'

'Extinct, but I think he represents the time and place Venables would like to go back to,' Maddy said. 'With the other dinosaurs.'

Primrose laughed, then walked over to the jukebox and perused the selection before finally plumping for 'Everything I Wanted' by Billie Eilish. Without self-consciousness, Primrose swayed gently to the soft voice, one arm floating up, then down as she looked through the other offerings, her back to them. Talantire looked at Maddy and smiled, but didn't need to say anything. *We've got to look after her.*

Above Primrose, the TV was now showing the local news. The sound was down, but the image of Mrs Ruth Lyle flashed onto the screen, followed by some footage from the press conference. Talantire saw herself talking through the murder victim's last moments. Primrose turned to them with a big smile, and pointed at the screen above her.

'I should have worn the blue jacket, this one makes my face look pale,' Talantire said.

'A man wouldn't care about that,' Primrose called across. 'And nor should you, ma'am.'

'There, that's told you,' Maddy said, with a laugh.

Talantire looked down at her phone. She'd had a message from Adam. She looked at it and said, 'Shit! My cover's blown.'

'What's that?' Maddy asked.

'Adam said he saw me. He just wrote: "Wow! So *that's* what you do."'

'Is that your boyfriend?' Primrose asked, coming over to join them and peering towards the phone.

'No, just a date.'

'Go on, show her!' Maddy said. She, of course, had already had chapter and verse.

Talantire shrugged, and turned the phone to show Adam's picture, with the message beneath.

'Hmm, nice eyes,' Primrose said, grinning. 'Are you seeing him tonight?'

'No. Tomorrow, fingers crossed. And not here!'

They both laughed.

'The Bank of Swans in Bideford,' Talantire said.

'Ooh! That's a bit posh,' Maddy said, raising her eyebrows. 'They have linen napkins there, so I've heard tell. Not bog roll, like you get here.'

Primrose laughed. 'So do you have a boyfriend, Maddy?'

'I've got a Neville, which is a bit like a husband, but without the income or any smart clothes.'

'Do you have a picture?'

Maddy blew her cheeks out. 'Now you're asking.' She ferreted through her phone, swiping past a dozen clearly unsuitable images, until she displayed one. 'That's on our wedding day.' The photo showed a gangly bearded man with a lot of hair, combed only at the front, and gappy teeth. He was clearly delighted, his arms round his bride.

'How did you meet?' Primrose asked.

'At college. He was my official stalker, all three years.'

Primrose laughed. 'Why did you marry a stalker?'

'Well, it just seemed easier, you know. I'd had some bad relationships before, but knew this one'd be devoted.'

'Is he?' Primrose asked, clearly amazed.

'Yeah, to these.' She cupped her hands under her hefty bosom. 'I'm not sure he'd recognise my face.'

Talantire laughed, but Primrose seemed shocked.

'So what about you?' Maddy asked her. 'You don't wear a ring. Is there anyone in your life?'

'My mom,' Primrose said, rolling her large brown eyes. She showed them a picture on her phone of a tiny lady with grey hair and a sweet smile. 'I live with her in Plymouth now. My dad's still back in Virginia. They split up, so she needs me.'

Chapter 11

Wednesday

Talantire hauled herself out of bed at six the next morning, pulled on her running gear and headed out into the cold blowy morning. She didn't have time to go up to Modge Hill, but instead ran two miles along the edge of the B road that passed the estate out towards the village of Goodleigh and then back through the riverside pastures. She deliberately didn't look at her phone until she got to the furthest point. As she stopped to catch her breath, she scrolled with a rising sense of dread through the day's headlines. *Ilfracombe killing linked to fifty-year-old crime,* was the *Daily Telegraph's* take on it. *Back from the dead?* was the headline in the *Daily Star,* juxtaposing the photograph of Mrs Ruth Lyle with the girl who died in 1973.

Talantire hated to have to get her head into work mode this early; it was intruding into her already limited time for exercise and reflection. But she also knew she would have to be prepared for a very challenging day. She had experienced this before. Once a crime was seized upon by the media, it became difficult to retain control of the investigation. Pressure would begin to trickle down from the police hierarchy to follow up various lurid claims made in parts of the press, all of which only distracted from the job in hand. She knew that her boss DS Wells understood this, and his experience in social services and child protection made him well-qualified to help protect her from the pressures.

She got back home before the rain began in earnest, and had almost finished drying herself after her shower when she got the first call, from Moira at the press office. It was not quite seven a.m.

'Good morning, Jan, sorry to disturb you so early. I've had a call from the police and crime commissioner, who wants to know why we don't have the records of the original 1973 crime.'

Talantire snorted. 'Well, it's because people like him kept cutting the budgets.' She towelled her hair with one hand, then put the phone on speaker so she could make a turban with the towel. The Honourable Lionel Hall-Hartington, a millionaire dairy farmer who owned thousands of acres of the Devon countryside and was the proprietor of the nationally known Sleepy Monk Creamery cheese brand, had been elected commissioner a year earlier. He was proving himself a complete pain.

'Why is he so interested anyway?'

'You know what it's like, Jan,' Moira said. 'Crimes as lurid as this turn everyone into an amateur detective. And unfortunately he has power to push his own theory.'

'Which is?'

She sighed. 'That the real killer is quote, a religious psychotic, unquote, was never found and has lain undiscovered in the community for fifty years, awaiting his chance.'

'I see.' Talantire knew that LHH, as he was referred to, had been poking his nose into almost every ongoing investigation, to the irritation of the entire force.

'Of course that theory has just been lifted in its entirety from today's *Daily Mail*,' Moira said. 'But he wants to know that you've been told it.'

'Consider it done,' Talantire said.

'Knowing him, he might try to FaceTime you too.'

'Christ, I'm only wearing a towel, and that's on my head.'

'Just warning you. Bye!' She hung up.

–

Talantire managed to dodge three calls from the Hon. LHH, and arrived at the office at 7:20 a.m. to find Primrose already there, hard at work. The moment she logged on she saw hundreds of messages: most from the crime helpline officers, twenty-five from the overnight duty press officer, and a similar number from various other officers.

'God, I need coffee,' she gasped, then glanced towards Dr Crippen, humming away quietly to himself in the corridor. No, she didn't need it that badly.

She sat down and started to sift through the leads that had come from the public. These supposedly were the ones that had passed the test of plausibility from the officers taking the calls. She would hate to have seen the ones that they rejected. Mostly they were vague sightings of someone who may or may not have been Mrs Ruth Lyle, from all over the country.

Someone had left a copy of the *Sun* on her desk. On the front was a huge picture of Mrs Ruth Lyle, and the headline *You Only Die Twice*. A subheading said: *Murder victim had same name as 1973 victim*. The article went on:

Police in Devon are clearly baffled by last week's copycat killing in Ilfracombe. It has been revealed that the dead woman, sixty-six-year-old Ruth Lyle, is of exactly the same name as a sixteen-year-old girl murdered in the same spot exactly fifty years previously. Locals in the pretty seaside town reacted in horror to the news that the killer who struck half a century ago may once again be stalking their streets. While police have not named sixty-four-year-old Gawain Entwistle as a murder suspect, sources close to the investigation reveal that the savage killer, caged supposedly for life at the Old Bailey in 1974, was last year released from Liverpool's high-security Ashworth Hospital, and given a new identity at public expense.

She looked up to see the Prince of Darkness looming over her. 'I guessed you could do with a coffee,' Lockhart said, passing her a lidded cup. 'I've just been to the Italian Place, I remember that you liked their macchiato. No sugar, that's correct isn't it?'

'Richard, how sweet of you,' she said.

'And Primrose, here's your cappuccino.'

'Thank you, sir,' Primrose replied.

'Busy night?' Talantire asked. He looked pale, even for him, but still delicious in a brown-eyed-vampire type of way.

'Non-stop. Mostly your case. There was a serious domestic incident in Redruth, but I got the local DC to handle that.' He stifled a yawn and apologised. 'Right, I'm off to take Laura and Henry to school. Oh, I took a call last night from a woman who claims to have had a conversation with Ruth Lyle at a bus stop in Exeter near the university. The date and time tallies with the electronic record of her journeys, so I think it must be true. The caller said that the victim had mentioned studying at Exeter University, though when I checked the file contradicted that.'

'That's right. No Ruth Lyle there. Still, I think we're beginning to narrow down where this woman came into being.'

'Sorry?' Lockhart said.

'Well, she was born a man, with a different name that we don't yet know. I can imagine that as a male he went to Exeter University sometime in the Seventies, because this story was also told to the landlady of Bluebird Cottage. I can't see a reason to make it up. And this man, whoever he is, decided to become Mrs Ruth Lyle for what purpose we still do not know. However, presumably after gender reassignment surgery, we do know that she was in a relationship under that name, with a man called James Quince, by 1978. That was the year she was registered as next of kin on his pension, and shortly after she appeared on the deeds of a house in Aberdeen with him. They lived together there until 1999, when he died while on holiday in India.'

'Could they be the same person?' Lockhart asked.

'Not easily. We have evidence of them living in different places in the 1990s, and Nuttall says they arrived separately in India before his death in 1999.'

Lockhart stroked his chin. 'The whole thing is weird. Why would someone go to such trouble to assume such a notorious identity?'

Talantire sipped her coffee. 'The classic reason for changed identity is simply to escape your own. Like in the Frederick

Forsyth book, *The Day of the Jackal*. Our murder victim possessed the original 1973 Ruth Lyle birth certificate, when it should have been with the family of the dead girl. We have no idea how she came to have it, and of course it is a foundational ID that can be used to apply for bank accounts and passports. But such a notorious dead child isn't really one you'd choose, if you just wanted to disappear. Especially given that she came back to the scene of the crime. So we think the motive must have been something else. She really wanted to be this person, but why?'

'Was there any money in the Lyle family?'

'Not that we can discover. Gwen Lyle lived in a basic cottage most of her life, and the local authority funded her move into care until the house was sold. She has a son, Alan, who's an estate agent, so he's probably doing okay. But that's much more recent. No, there would be far better targets to choose if you wanted to extort money.'

Lockhart said, 'Well, good luck with it. I'll be late if I don't go now.'

'Thank you for the coffee, Richard.'

'You're welcome.' He winked.

Maddy, who had just arrived to witness this, asked him, 'Do you have a coffee for me, Richard?' She batted her eyelids in faux winsomeness.

'Next time, Maddy, next time,' he said, laughing and resting a hand on her shoulder before departing. Maddy shrugged off her coat, held the part Lockhart had touched to her cheek, sighed briefly, then dumped it over the back of her chair. 'I don't know what you two are looking so smug about.'

Talantire and Primrose smiled at each other. 'Coffee from the dark side,' Talantire said.

—

Tony Healey, the man who had been seen with Mrs Lyle in a cafe, lived in a small flat in Oxford Grove, just two minutes' walk from the crime scene. Talantire parked next to the flat, outside which a stained and sagging three-piece suite had been dumped. As she was getting out she saw PC Rod Jenkins, one of the community team, striding down towards her. Jenkins apparently knew Healey well, so she waved to him and waited in the car for him to join her.

'Healey's not a bad sort. He used to live down there, in the doorway of the Liberal Club,' Jenkins said, pointing to the High Street behind him. 'They were less minded to move him on than others. He spent a few nights in the cells over the years, but is basically harmless, despite his intimidating appearance. He moved in here last week, and has been seeing a counsellor for alcohol addiction.'

'Right, let's go and see him.' They levered themselves out of the car and made their way to the entrance to consider the bewildering array of bells on the rotting door frame. Jenkins rapped on the glass and after a couple of minutes a figure appeared and opened the door. Healey was tall and rough-looking with a lined and tattooed face and neck, wearing a moth-eaten pullover and ripped jeans, no shoes or socks. He could have been any age between fifty and eighty. He invited them in, and they had to make their way around carrier bags full of empty beer cans and bottles in the hall. The place stank like an abandoned brewery. 'Been having a bit of a clear-out,' he said. He showed them into a back room, which boasted magnificent original wide floorboards and a lovely high corniced ceiling, stained by decades of nicotine.

'This has the makings of a lovely place,' Talantire said, looking at the ceiling.

'Yeah, not bad,' Healey said. 'Needs a bit of work.'

'We'd like to ask you about Mrs Lyle, the lady who took you to the Flamingo Cafe.'

'Ah, yes. Very sad, what happened to her.' He looked at them both, his hands clenching and unclenching in anxiety.

'Did you know her?'

'She gave me some money a few times when I was on the street. Her name was Ruth.'

'Did you ever go into her home?'

'No, I didn't know where she lived until I heard about the killing.'

'What can you tell me about the day she took you to the cafe?'

'She asked me if I'd eaten anything that day and I told her no, which wasn't strictly true. She invited me to come with her to the cafe and bought me a cuppa and a bit of cake.'

'Was that the only time she did that?'

'Yes.'

Fifteen minutes later, they were both relieved to escape back into the street. Everything he said accorded with the details recorded on the receipt they had, and the CCTV recording. His DNA was already on file, and didn't match anything at the crime scene; neither did his fingerprints. It looked like he was in the clear.

–

'This is interesting,' Nuttall said, looking up from his screen. 'Ruth Lyle may not have studied at Exeter, but James Quince did. A BSc in geology from 1972 to 1974 and then did a master's degree at St Andrews, 1975 to 1977. I suppose that fits well with the job at the offshore company.'

'We seem to be finding out a lot more about him than we did about her,' Talantire said.

'It's all as clear as mud, or mud engineering,' Maddy said.

'I've got a call in to the Exeter alumni office to see if we can find who his contemporaries were,' Nuttall said. 'I've also got a picture of him, in the annual report of his Norwegian employer in 1981.' He brought over the document, which showed an oil rig under sunny skies. A caption on page four identified Quince as being on the extreme left of a picture of five people in hard hats, sunglasses and pristine protective overalls standing on an unusually clean rig. He wasn't tall, and had a sandy-coloured beard, but with shades it was hard to really see what he looked like.

'Where did you get the annual report?' Talantire asked.

'An obscure website run by aged oil anoraks,' he replied.

'Sounds very niche, as hobbies go,' she replied.

'But thank God for them, eh?' Nuttall said. 'If we can get a better picture, then we can try to find colleagues. I've already discovered a Petroleum Wives Club based in Norway, with records back to the 1970s, and a networking group called The Oil Club, based in Surrey. Got emails out to them, each of the companies where Quince used to work, to see if they have an archivist.'

'Anything else?'

'Yes. I have a copy of his CV, from 1986, which was in the personnel records at Enterprise Oil. He claimed "good downhole understanding, and experience with kick-tolerance software", though I'm none the wiser.'

'That's good work, Dave,' Talantire said. 'Let's just see if we can fill in the blanks on both of them.'

She and Nuttall used a flipchart to draw two parallel columns, labelled for Ruth Lyle and her husband, starting at the top with the most recent dates and going back to 1970 at the bottom, filling in all the information that they had. Most data was from 1972 up to the death of James Quince in 1999. Ruth Lyle's column ran from 1978, shortly after Quince began working for the offshore firm Lamprey, and they had all the documentary evidence to show that they had both lived in Aberdeen for a number of years.

Talantire pointed to the start of Ruth Lyle's job in Liverpool in 1992. 'Quince is still based in Aberdeen at this point, so it looks like they broke up.'

'Except they were both in India when he died, seven years later,' Maddy pointed out. 'The article makes that clear. She came back with his body.'

Nuttall nodded. 'Yes, and that's proven. For those of us who suspected he and she may be the same person, this is quite a blow. The Indian immigration authorities keep paper records right back into the 1990s, and have been very cooperative. Quince and Lyle arrived separately in India, but were definitely both there, and the local police records confirm the death of Quince, Mrs Lyle's witness statement, and the documentation for repatriating the body.'

'Okay, but how are you doing on Mrs Lyle's early years?' Talantire asked.

'Not as well,' Nuttall said. 'I've been through every bit of the stuff she left behind at Bluebird Cottage. There is no diary, no family photographs, no receipts for anything deposited in storage. There's plenty of clothing, some of the stuff that she brought from India, fabrics and so on. So, basically, there are no clues.'

'And social media?'

'I've now contacted more than half the Ruth Lyles I previously listed, and they're not connected with ours. Either of them.' He paused for a wry grin. 'Some are abroad, obviously. I've had several contacts through the information line, but nothing pertaining to her earlier years. And there's another couple of sightings of Gawain Entwistle, one of them supposedly in Ilfracombe itself.'

Primrose said: 'Mrs Lyle had a Twitter account, but only tweeted three times in seven years. Her Facebook account was deleted two years ago, and even Facebook no longer has the records on any of its servers. After 180 days most of it is gone.'

'We need to know who she was sending messages to and still has an active Facebook account,' Maddy said.

'How about Roger Keane, the solicitor?' Nuttall said.

Maddy laughed. 'You'd find nothing from him. It's just a new way for a solicitor not to return your calls.'

'Is this based on your experience using one?' Talantire asked.

'Got it in one,' Maddy replied. 'Tell you what, I'll ring him, right now.'

Talantire watched. Amazingly, Maddy seemed to get straight through, and with little preamble went straight for it. 'Mr Keane, we find it hard to believe the number of contacts between you and Mrs Lyle if she had nothing specific in mind. Would you care to think again?' There was a pause, and Maddy could be seen making notes. 'Right, so why didn't you tell us before?... I see.'

After she hung up, she turned to Talantire. 'Well, now it makes sense. Mrs Ruth Lyle had wanted to buy seventy-nine Blyth Road, which just happened to be Ruth Lyle's childhood home.'

'Why?'

'No reason was given. Keane told her it wasn't on the market, but said he contacted the occupants anyway. A premium over the market price was offered, but refused.'

'And why didn't he tell us before?'

'He said it's the solicitor's reflex: client confidentiality. Mrs Lyle had asked him never to tell anyone.'

'She really wanted to take over young Ruth's life in every detail, didn't she?' Talantire mused. 'But I can't really see the point.'

–

Maddy was peering between the venetian blinds into the car park at Barnstaple police station. 'Oh shit, it's the commissioner!'

Primrose looked out of the window alongside her.

'It seems everyone wants a piece of the action,' Talantire said. 'I don't know how we're going to get any work done.'

'He's here with Wigwam's sister,' Maddy added. Victoria Carnegie was the local MP.

'Being a Wednesday, it's probably the usual Rural Crime Committee meeting at the George Hotel,' Talantire said. 'They'll have been on the sauce for a couple of hours.'

'They drink during meetings?' Primrose asked incredulously.

'Before, during and after, probably,' Maddy said. 'It's not actually referred to as booze, it's called Devon networking juice. Yeah, look. He's a bit wobbly.

'The Met rules are very strict for alcohol on duty,' Primrose said. 'They told us just a small glass of wine can put you over.'

'Ah, but the Honourable Lionel isn't a member of the police, he's elected. He's probably polished off a bottle on his own, which is why Victoria's driving, not him.'

The officers fled back to their desks, and looked busy. Two minutes later Sergeant Ken Venables opened the door into the CID department and showed in the commissioner, followed by the MP for Devon North West. Victoria, never Vicky, was the older sister of Inspector T. P. Carnegie. She was a tall and stylish woman in her sixties; her cropped blond hair gave her a little of the Annie Lennox look. She had married astutely, to a rising local businessman, and had survived many years in the Commons giving as good as she got from the farmers, property developers and ambitious social climbers who populated her side of the house. While Hall-Hartington stuck with tweedy jackets and jeans for the country squire look, she sported leather trousers, high-heeled boots and a pale blue designer jacket. There had been rumours of an affair between the two some time in the past. Those with the lowest opinion of him suggested that, now the commissioner's wife was recently diagnosed with multiple sclerosis and using a wheelchair, he might be eyeing pastures old.

'Ah, Jan,' rumbled Lionel Hall-Hartington. 'Too busy to return my calls, I see.'

Talantire stood up. 'It's been pretty manic, sir, actually, as you can imagine.'

'Well, never mind, it's good to see one of our best girls doing such a fine job.' He leaned forward, as if to kiss her on the cheek, but she inclined her head away from the gammon, jowly face and its mist of alcohol.

Turning away, defeated, he spotted Primrose, who was resolutely staring at her screen. 'Ah, a nice touch of diversity, eh. Brings a bit of colour to the drabness, that's what I always say.'

Talantire eyed Victoria, whose horrified brown eyes were locked on to the side of the commissioner's face, broadcasting something along the lines of: *shut up, you drunken fool.*

'Sorry, to interrupt, ma'am,' Maddy called to Talantire, holding a telephone receiver in her hand. 'It's the Home Office forensic pathologist. Says it's urgent. Line two.'

Talantire smiled at her and picked up the call. It was actually the Devon weather service recording, but she greeted it anyway, before muting and turning to the guests.

'I'm sorry, these are confidential forensic details that we're not allowed to discuss in front of anyone. So, if you'll excuse me.' She gestured towards the door behind them.

'Look, I'll take you both for a coffee,' Maddy said, leading the guests away towards Dr Crippen. 'I can thoroughly recommend the cappuccino.'

Talantire struggled to keep a straight face as she watched Maddy guide the bigwigs through the reconditioned machine's settings. She heard the buzz, the clack of the plastic cup and the final hiss of the machine, before a long pause, and then the boom of the commissioner's voice.

'Gah, Jesus wept. That's bloody AWFUL.'

The receding sound of VIPs descending the stairs announced the coast was clear. Once Maddy returned, all three women burst out laughing.

'He spilled most of it down his jacket,' Maddy said.

'Serves him right for inflicting the damn thing on us,' Talantire said. Her phone rang. 'Ah, now it really is the pathologist!' She paused to drain the laughter from her voice. 'Yes, Piers.'

'Jan, I've been doing a little research on gender-affirming operations. I think Mrs Lyle may have visited George Burou's Casablanca clinic. There are some indicative surgery marks internally, from the penile inversion vaginoplasty that he pioneered.'

'Are they sufficiently definitive to allow us to date the procedure?'

'Well, no. Burou died in 1989, but the technique lived on and has been improved still further. However, I have to confess that is one of the most convincing gender affirmations I've ever seen. In fact the only surviving indication externally of Ruth Lyle's sex at birth is one of the most obscure: in men the zygomatic arches of the skull tend to end behind the auditory meatus, in women they are in front.'

'Well, thank you for that,' Talantire said, none the wiser.

'The DNA under her fingernails matches that of an unknown individual from the crime scene and on the murder weapon, but none was lifted from the grazed knuckles apart from her own.'

'So whoever she scratched could well be the killer,' Talantire said. 'And that means Entwistle is in the clear.'

'Unless there were two or more killers,' Holcombe said.

'True,' Talantire conceded.

'The final tox tests have come back. There was nothing indicated besides alcohol, and my report will also mention some slight liver scarring, indicating a sustained and excessive intake for many years. And then something really interesting. I asked a forensic odontologist consultant colleague of mine for help, and he has managed to find the original dentition records for young Ruth Lyle from 1972, made when the school dentist came to visit. Quite impressive that those records still exist, isn't it? And your victim has fillings in exactly the same place as hers.'

'You're saying the dental records are identical?'

'Well, no. There are some extra fillings in the older victim, which are a mixture of porcelain and modern glass and resin isomers, and a couple of porcelain crowns, which is what you would expect over the course of a lifetime. The crucial point is that the three amalgam fillings described in the 1972 dental report are still there, in exactly the same places, as is the one extraction.'

'Could that be coincidence?'

'Well.' He sighed. 'Statistically, it's highly unlikely. With twenty-eight teeth usually present at age sixteen, and several positions where a filling can be made for each tooth, and at least two types of filling used in the 1970s, the variables are considerable. Less than one in a million chance of this being random, was my colleague's calculation.'

'So are you saying that our murder victim is the real, genuine Ruth Lyle?'

'Ah, no, that's still a leap. But it is nonetheless fascinating, wouldn't you say?'

Talantire sighed. 'I can't get my head round this, Piers. Obviously, somebody was murdered back in 1973, and the family identified the body as hers. We're still waiting for the lab result for the elimination sample from Alan Lyle. I'd requested a familial comparison, so we'll soon know if he is the brother of our victim.'

'Yes. You wouldn't want to exhume the original victim, would you?'

'No. Anything but that.'

Talantire thanked him and hung up, then stared at Maddy.

'What's up?' she asked.

'Mrs Ruth Lyle, though originally born a man, has the same dental records as the original murder victim from 1973.'

Maddy's jaw hung open. Talantire could see her fillings.

Chapter 12

The incident room at the Stag was dismantled by early on Wednesday afternoon, and the premises, so well known for the antics of riotous youth, were returned to the pub company management to allow the refurbishment to continue. The inquiry team was now back full-time on the first floor of the Barnstaple police station building. Jan Talantire decided she just needed one last check of the crime scene, so that the rota of long-suffering PCs on the door day and night no longer had to endure the indignities of the daft questions, drunken antics and endless selfies of the great British rubbernecking public. At the same time the family who lived in the cottage opposite, and had been asked to vacate their home while the crime scene was investigated, were now allowed to return from the bed-and-breakfast hotel that they had been put up in at public expense. All of this had been arranged by Inspector Carnegie.

One final flourish was required. While Talantire was happy enough for a hefty police padlock to now secure Bluebird Cottage, she had asked Carnegie to install a discreet CCTV camera under the window ledge of the first-floor window of the opposite home, and a doorbell camera on Bluebird Cottage. The great cliché of the perpetrator returning to the scene of the crime looked a racing certainty in this particular case. Two Ruth Lyles, both dead at the same address fifty years apart.

While the contractors were busy on their stepladders opposite, Talantire let herself into Bluebird Cottage, unlocking the police padlock. Mrs Lee had installed a five-lever mortice above the original church lock, but it wasn't locked. She took the padlock in with her, then bolted the door behind herself. The place still stank: of vomit, stale blood and decomposing human innards. This was what she imagined an abattoir would smell like. Closing the outside door behind her, she undid her shoulder bag, and from it took blue plastic booties and gloves. Something was nagging in her, suspicions, something that she had overlooked. Bluebird Cottage, formerly St James Without, a.k.a. the Dimpsy Chapel, might still harbour secrets, if not from the most recent killing then perhaps from the original one. She remained convinced that the answer to who killed Mrs Ruth Lyle was hidden in some overlooked detail of the original crime in 1973.

According to Mrs Lee, the chapel was partly refurbished in the 1980s, long before her own work to turn it into Bluebird Cottage four years ago. It had been used to store church equipment for a while. Talantire started in the modern kitchen, in which last week's killing had taken place. The modern units, all tastefully painted in Farrow and Ball: Clunch and Cromarty. Everything was handmade to fit the unusual non-rectangular shape of the cottage. She made her way into the lounge, and once again admired the spacious way it had been remodelled, drylined but still incorporating the vaulted ceilings, ten-foot-high narrow lancet windows and even higher clerestories, all of which lit the galleried bedroom. Right at the back of the lounge was an original wooden door, about four feet high, possibly to a cupboard. It had been varnished and rehung, and was now locked. She wondered what it contained. She put her hand over the mortice keyhole and could feel a slight draught. She then made her way to the boxed-in pillar in the centre of the lounge, from which the vaulted ceiling was supported. From the accounts she had read it was roughly here that the first murder had taken place, with Ruth's body spreadeagled on a stone altar. The photograph sent by the historical society showed that this pillar was where the crucifix had hung. The altar space was now occupied by a wood-burner. Where was that altar now? She wondered what they would find if they removed the dry-lining and pulled up the carpets.

She climbed the spiral staircase to the large bedroom under the clerestory windows, which occupied half of what would have been the vaulted roof of the chapel. The top halves of the lancet windows looked down onto the street at the rear. The double bed was neatly made and had a colourful Indian-style counterpane, with tiny mirrors sewn into it. There were no wardrobes, just a rail fixed to the wall with a few plastic clothes hangers. Above the wooden bed was a tapestry with some curlicue writing in another language. Yellow plastic evidence markers left by CSI were dotted about, and she cross-referenced them to the records on her iPad. One on the pillow, for hairs to match the victim. One inside the middle of the bed sheets, for body fluids. She lifted up the bedspread to check. The sheets looked fresh. There was a reference to samples taken from the linen basket, which she found in the second bedroom. All good forensic thinking. The results, however, had been unequivocal. No DNA apart from the victim's was found in either bedroom. The drawers had already been checked, and there were no apparent signs of blood or any disturbance at all. The book-case in the room was heavy with religious texts, particularly of Eastern religions, and there were Asian and vegan cookbooks. By the bed was a framed photograph of the victim with a South Asian woman of similar age, in some tropical setting. They were both wearing saris. They knew from her passport that Mrs Lyle had visited India on several occasions.

After photographing everything, Talantire stared down over the railing and tried to imagine what the Dimpsy Chapel had looked like before conversion. The nave would have been narrow, and taller than it was long. Of course the addition of the cottage next door, which now housed the kitchen, bathroom and second bedroom, had made possible the conversion to a home. For all the carpets and soft furnishings, the place still felt cold. The kind of place to chill you to the marrow. But maybe that was because she knew what had taken place here. Twice.

She took a final look round, and then descended the stairs and retreated back towards the entrance. She was still ten feet away when she heard footsteps outside and a rattling noise at the door. As there was no longer a PC outside, it was probably some joker trying to enter a place of murder to show off to his girlfriend. Ignoring the racket, and safely bolted in, she stripped off her booties and gloves and pressed them into the disposal bag.

The small shaft of light through the original medieval keyhole was suddenly cut off. She crouched down, just as something was slid smoothly into the lock. Her body turned to ice as she realised this key was actually turning the mechanism. She slid back the bolt and turned the heavy iron latch, ready to confront the would-be intruder.

Locked.

The door wouldn't open. She was shut in. She tried to force it, pulling on the large iron handle, but only succeeded in rattling the door. Who on earth could have a key that worked for that ancient lock? She couldn't think. She banged on the door and yelled. The key was quickly withdrawn, and she rushed to the kitchen and scrambled onto the draining board to peer outside from the high window. The angle was all wrong to see the front door, but the contractor she'd seen on the ladder opposite was still there, working on the camera installation. She could hear his radio. There was a window lock on the frame and she didn't have the key to open it. She banged on the window, but couldn't attract his attention.

Talantire texted Maddy, who rang back quickly and told her a locksmith would be there in half an hour to let her out. 'I need a DNA swab off the lock first, Maddy,' Talantire said.

'Righto, I'll be round directly,' she said. 'About fifteen minutes.' Before she hung up she gave Talantire the mobile number of the contractor opposite and Talantire rang him. He answered and looked over his shoulder towards the window from which she was peering.

'Someone just locked me in. Did you see anybody at the door?' she asked.

'No, I was busy here,' he replied.

She cursed inwardly. 'Is the camera working yet?'

'Five more minutes.'

'That's no good to me,' she said.

'I'll come and see if I can get you out.' He started clambering down his ladder.

'No, don't. You mustn't touch it. DNA and all that.' She hung up, then cursed again as she slid off the draining board and started working her phone. She began with the landlady of Bluebird Cottage. Mrs Lee said she hadn't ever had a key for the old lock, and had assumed it didn't work any more. Talantire rang the Diocese of Exeter, and was put through to the team rector of Ilfracombe. This turned out to be the Reverend Neal Vaizey. She explained what had happened, and asked if the church still possessed a key or a copy of one.

'I really don't think I can help you on this issue,' Vaizey said. 'I was only ordained in 1993, and didn't come here until 2002. So it's really before my time. I'm sure that we don't keep keys to church buildings once they're sold. I'll ask the churchwarden, but that's my understanding.'

'I get that, Reverend,' Talantire said. 'The point is, that the number of people who could possess such a key now is very small. I think whoever had access to it might well have got it decades ago.'

He didn't say anything for a moment. 'So you think this may connect to the original killing?'

'It's certainly possible.'

'Well, I'm a little dubious myself. But good luck getting yourself out. I take it you don't believe in ghosts?'

'No, I have enough trouble with the real world to keep me busy without worrying about the spirit world.'

He laughed. 'I'm sure you do. Well, not many people would relish being locked in that building, given what happened there.

I would certainly be most reluctant to return. By the way, have you had a chance to think about letting us look at the crucifix?'

'No, I'm sorry.' Hearing the clatter of tools outside, she quickly ended the call. The moment she did so, Maddy rang her to tell her that she was outside with the locksmith and had just swabbed the lock.

—

Once Talantire was released and they were standing outside, Maddy asked: 'Did you hear a voice when the lock was turned?'

'No. The impression I got was that whoever it was assumed they were unlocking it, because they'd tried to open it earlier but it was held by the bolt. They were scared off when I yelled through the door.'

'What did you yell?'

'Something like "Hey, what are you doing?" I've already checked the landlady and the church and no one seems to have a key, I mean a big old key for that original lock.'

'So you think this is another lead going back to the original crime?'

'Well, maybe not that far...' Talantire stopped when she saw a familiar woman approaching.

'Hello, Jan,' said Victoria Carnegie. 'Returning to the scene of the crime?' The MP was elegantly turned out in white jacket, leather trousers and ankle boots. She appeared to have been shopping, and was carrying two bulging carrier bags.

Talantire smiled. 'It's part of my job description.'

'Look, I'm sorry about Lionel. He means no harm. I hope your colleague wasn't offended.'

'She survived the Met, so I imagine she'll be all right here,' Talantire said.

'Except maybe with Sergeant Venables,' Maddy muttered.

'Oh, do you have a particularly misogynistic colleague?' Victoria said, her eyes narrowing. 'I'm on lots of committees, and carry a fair amount of clout. I'm sure a transfer could be arranged. I hear dog handling is a useful receptacle for these individuals.'

'I'll bear it in mind,' Talantire said.

'I realise that making a report on someone you work with can make life difficult. Just say the word.' She winked. 'We women have to stick together, right?'

'Certainly.' It occurred to Talantire that Victoria might have no idea of the reputation of her own younger brother, a uniformed inspector, for putting his hands where they weren't wanted.

Victoria glanced at Bluebird Cottage. 'It's all right if I go inside, isn't it? You're all done and dusted on the forensics?'

'We are, yes,' Maddy said.

Talantire glared at her. 'Well, actually...' she began.

'I've always been intrigued by the place,' Victoria said, moving up the steps. 'Ever since my father got involved as the coroner on the original case. It almost did for him, you know. The stress.'

'Yes, Wigwam told us,' Maddy said, following her in.

'Wigwam?' she said, laughing. 'So you call my brother that too? It was how they teased him at school.' She stared around at the hallway, then advanced into the lounge. 'They have done a really good job on this conversion,' she said, running a hand down the lacquered woodwork. 'Shame about the terrible pong.'

'Actually, Mrs Carnegie,' Talantire said. 'We do have some additional tests to do, so we would appreciate you not going any further or touching anything.'

'Oh, of course, sorry,' she said, retreating.

Once she had gone, Talantire turned to Maddy. 'We can't let all and sundry turn this into a tourist attraction, Maddy. She will no doubt mention it to the commissioner and he'll want to be round, and then will get councillors and goodness knows who else.'

'But we are done, aren't we?'

'No, I don't think so. I want to get that dry-lining off the walls in the chapel itself. We need to Bluestar the place and re-examine the original crime from scratch, treat it like a cold case. Old blood is still blood, and it's full of DNA.'

—

In Talantire's absence, Keith Howell had sent them a surprisingly large amount of information from Spain about the 1973 investigation, including names and original addresses of witnesses. One of the original suspects, Andrew Hinks, had by his recollection admitted sleeping with the victim, who was underage at the time. He was never charged. Maddy and Nuttall worked the phones for a couple of hours, following up with neighbours, friends and former associates, until they had a breakthrough.

'Hinks is a property developer, based in Essex,' Maddy said. 'I'd seen the name before, but ruled it out until a former neighbour sent me this link.' She showed Talantire a website for ALH (Homes) Ltd, based in Braintree. There were plenty of photographs of new homes, but none of the chief executive. 'I've used Companies House to prove it was him. The date of birth on the director registration matches the one I got from his school records.'

'Good work, Maddy,' Talantire said. She picked up the phone and tapped out the company number. After explaining who she was to a receptionist, she was put through to the man himself. Even before he spoke, it was clear from the background noise that he was in a vehicle.

'My name is Detective Inspector Jan Talantire. Before we proceed, Mr Hinks, can I ask if you are a passenger or driving the vehicle?'

'I'm driving, but don't worry, it's on a hands-free. How can I help?'

'It's about Ruth Lyle.'

She heard the sound of braking, with some background clattering.

'I'm just pulling over into a lay-by,' he said. His voice was deep and patrician, without any trace of a Devon accent. That was all the clearer once the background traffic noise had dimmed. 'Well, Ms Talantire, I really thought that had all been left behind in the dim and distant past.'

'So did we. However, a serious crime has taken place in exactly the same location in Ilfracombe, exactly half a century later.'

'What, at the Dimpsy Chapel?'

'It's part of an Airbnb cottage now, but yes.'

'How extraordinary. I hadn't heard about it. What happened?'

'A woman of sixty-six was found murdered. You can read that much in the press.'

'How does it relate to the previous crime?'

'We can't share too much of that but, as I know you were interviewed as a suspect back in the original case, there may be information that will help us.'

'I'd be happy to be of assistance, but I'm not sure how much I can tell you. As you know, I was cleared, and the real killer was identified as—'

'There's nothing to worry about, Mr Hinks,' Talantire said. 'We can do it by Zoom, although I'm going to ask one of my colleagues at Essex Police to be present in person to take a cheek swab, just to eliminate you from enquiries.'

'There isn't any point, is there? I've not lived in Devon since 1974, and DNA testing didn't exist at the time of Ruth's killing.'

'Like I say, it's just a formality.'

He sighed. 'Okay, I'll get my PA to set up a call,' he said.

After they had arranged a time she asked: 'One final thing, do you have an address for Trevor Goswell?'

'Trevor? Good God, no. I've not seen him for decades.'

'Not friends any more?'

'Just drifted apart, I suppose. Hardly surprising is it? The case made our lives a living hell.'

'I'm sure,' Talantire said. 'Still, you can be thankful that it was before the days of social media. The trolls now would follow you everywhere, not just to the county border. Adults sleeping with fifteen-year-old girls was always illegal.'

'A girl, singular,' Hinks corrected her. 'And I didn't sleep with her. It was just heavy petting. In any case, she had told me she was eighteen. She was very willing. And I was only twenty-one at the time.'

The caveats and excuses tumbled out. Talantire had lots she could have said at this point, but she'd save it for the interview. She didn't really expect that Andrew Hinks was anything to do with the latest murder, but he had spent time with Ruth Lyle, and could perhaps cast some light on who might want to bring her back from the dead.

–

The public information line hadn't yielded many clues, but one that came straight through to Talantire was from a retired oil worker from Aberdeen. 'I've seen posters in the library that you're looking for a Jamie Quince who used to work on the rigs.'

'That's right.'

'I lived opposite him on East Main Avenue, Aberdeen.'

'What year was that?'

'Well, I lived there from 1977 to 1989. I don't recall if he lived there all that time, but I saw him and his wife from time to time. I think he was still there when I left.'

'What was her name?' Talantire asked, pen poised over her notepad.

'From your press release, I see her name was Ruth Lyle.'

Talantire rolled her eyes. 'Yes, I know what we have written, but were you ever introduced to her?'

'I think so, but I didn't recall the name. She didn't live there much. It's quite common in the oil industry because everybody is a few weeks on then a few weeks off. My late wife might have had a better grasp of the comings and goings, but...'

'Did you ever socialise?'

'No. He and I shovelled snow side by side one winter, I do remember that. They kept themselves to themselves. No kids, from what I remember.'

This was progress. If someone had seen James Quince and his wife side by side, it proved they weren't the same person.

'Can you remember what she looked like?'

'Well, I've seen the picture on the poster. Obviously she was younger then.'

'Yes, but is there a resemblance to the poster?'

'Um, can't really recall, to be honest.'

'Do you know anyone who worked with him at Lamprey?'

'Not offhand. If you try the company...'

Talantire ground her teeth. 'It doesn't exist any more.'

'Ah, well I'll ask around.'

'Thank you.'

After she'd finished the call, she shouted out in frustration, 'God! It's like pulling teeth. It can't be that hard, surely, to find someone who worked with him.'

Maddy, who was on the phone, muted the receiver and turned to her. 'Well, I've just got someone who worked with Mrs Lyle.'

'Ah, a miracle!' Talantire declared, putting her hands together. The woman had lived the life of a ghost; perhaps now she would assume some more solid form. 'Put her through.'

The woman's name was Lizzie Snell, and she told Talantire she'd worked with Mrs Ruth Lyle for eighteen months in Liverpool from 1992 to 1993.

'What do you remember about her?'

'Well, she was in telephone sales, and pretty good at it. Most of the time she had permission to work from home, which was quite unusual at the time, but she'd come in one week in three, to catch up on paperwork. She was very good at the job, I have to say, and obviously extremely bright. But...' She hesitated. 'I also have to say, she was slightly peculiar.'

'Peculiar in what way?'

'She seemed quite, well, masculine. These days you would probably say she was transitioning. A couple of girls in the office just thought she was a man in drag, and I had to have a word with them.'

'But she used the ladies' toilet?' Talantire wasn't going to mention that Mrs Ruth Lyle was born a man, but clearly at this point the transformation had been far from complete.

'Yes.'

'Did you ever meet her husband? A man called James Quince.'

'We heard about him. She used to go off to see him most weekends in Aberdeen. I remember being shocked when I heard about him dying in India.'

'Was she still in contact with you then?'

'I did get a letter, from India, about his death. I may still have it. It was quite moving.'

Talantire put the phone down. 'Maddy, I'm not sure where this is getting us. We've got a vague witness statement to someone seeing Quince and Ruth side by side, but then it could be someone else. And now evidence of these independent lives in Liverpool and Aberdeen. But none of it is conclusive, really.'

'If she's not Quince, who the hell is she, this invisible woman?' Maddy asked.

'I don't know,' Talantire said. 'She seemingly sprang into life in middle age in 1978, and then departed on April Fool's Day 2023.' She picked up her coat. 'Right, it's a mystery for another day. I have a date tonight.'

'Good luck!' Nuttall and Maddy chorused.

Chapter 13

Talantire sped off to meet Adam at the Bank of Swans in Bideford. The radio was on, and she was singing along. They had agreed to go for a quick early bird special, a fixed-price menu for two courses in the bar, rather than the full restaurant experience, which would take at least a couple of hours. She had got permission from her boss to take the work unmarked car, its boot loaded with a kitbag of all the equipment she might need if she was called away. She could be back in HQ in fifteen minutes, if she needed to be. She wouldn't have a drop to drink, but prayed she wouldn't suffer another broken date.

That would be down to Adam. She was relieved that thus far the news conference that had blown her cover hadn't changed anything. Knowing she was a cop had not diminished his enthusiasm at all. If anything she detected a little bit of excitement in his messages. She had always recognised that her job carried a little bit of unwarranted glamour. The TV idea that plucky detectives spent all their time wrestling drug dealers to the ground, kicking open doors, and racing at high speed from one crime scene to another was nonsense. The grinding hours spent on paperwork, in case conferences with tedious and nitpicking Crown Prosecution Service lawyers, the hideous bureaucracy of filling out warrant applications. TV drama never showed much of this. And for good reason. It would make for very boring viewing. She spent as much time at the computer terminal and on the phone as any BT call centre operator. Her pay was probably comparable, too.

Still, if a hint of police procedural mystique gave her an unfair advantage she would use it. She hadn't had a decent date with an attractive man for months. Last time she'd had decent sex? Indecent sex even? She didn't dare think about that. She turned on the radio, and found some good driving rock. She'd chosen this life because of what had happened to her years ago, or maybe the circumstances of life had chosen her. Buried pain from her teenage years, the great secret, which now only surfaced in her nightmares but provided jet fuel for her energy when running or training at the gym. A little bit of rage, well channelled, but used only when needed. She wouldn't need it tonight. She had to take her pleasures in the brief gaps between work, and tonight was hopefully going to be one of those moments to enjoy.

She was ten minutes early, turning in to the car park. Adam's car was already there. She parked next to it and couldn't help noticing the barely legal tread on the front offside tyre, the still-broken indicator glass at the rear. She made her way up the steps into the pub, which was already busy. A young woman at a lectern greeted her and asked her if she had a reservation. She gave the details, and the woman said, 'Adam, is that Mr Tuppen? For the early bird?'

Ah, so that was his surname. 'I'll wait until he's here,' Talantire said. She retraced her steps to the entrance just in time to see Adam, on foot, coming back in from the main road with a puppy on a lead. The dog was clearly very young, and raced backwards and forwards until the leash restrained it. Adam looked up at her, and grinned as he shouted a hello. Talantire went over to meet him, and Adam scooped up the dog.

'Meet Scamp,' he said, restraining the wriggling puppy, which tried to scrabble out of his arms. 'The destroyer of furniture, the chewer of carpets and stainer of clothing.'

'Aren't you lovely?' Talantire said, tickling the dog behind its fluffy ears, one white, one black, then under its chin. The puppy's wet pink tongue caught her fingers as it panted excitedly. 'You never told me you had a dog,' she said. However, she did recall, from their first date, seeing Adam bend over and talk to something in the estate car. The dog must have been asleep that time.

'Well, it's been a bit complicated. My ex doesn't get on with him, in fact it's half the reason she is my ex. I didn't want to mention her on our first date.'

'Understandable,' Talantire said. Her detective brain kicked in immediately. This ex must be quite recent, given the age of the dog. Very recent, in fact.

'I can't leave him alone at home,' Adam said, lifting the dog to his face. 'Because you whine all the time, don't you? And the neighbours think you are an unhappy bunny.' The dog licked his face.

'He's absolutely gorgeous,' Talantire said, stroking Scamp again.

'He'll be all right in the car. When he's in there he thinks he'll soon be off on another walk, so he's happy enough, at least for an hour.'

Adam settled the dog down in a big pile of blankets in the rear of the BMW, and gently closed the tailgate. Once they were back inside and at their table, they ordered a seafood sharing platter and some soft drinks. Meeting the dog had cast a warm glow over the date. Talking about him was easy and enjoyable, and led them through the first half-hour of their time together. But inevitably a new subject emerged.

'So you're actually a big-shot detective?' he asked, biting into a seafood samosa.

'Well, not always, but this is a high-profile case. And I have to say now, and I'm sure you understand, that I can tell you absolutely nothing about it.' She glanced at her work phone, which was sitting unobtrusively behind her glass of fruit juice where he couldn't see the screen.

He leaned forward, all boyish enthusiasm. 'Can I ask you about being in the police, in general?'

'Of course you can.'

There then followed a series of questions about shifts, pay, what she enjoyed and what she didn't. She answered in the most generic terms, aware that this was only half an hour into the second date. The last thing she wanted was, if they didn't meet again, him sharing her innermost thoughts with all his mates.

'Have you ever used a gun?'

'No. I was never in an armed response unit.'

'A Taser?'

'I've been on the training course, and as part of that had one used on me.'

'How does it feel?'

She smiled and looked around the restaurant. 'Absolute agony. Brief but unendurable. We were warned to empty our bladders beforehand.'

'Have you been taught self-defence?'

'For years, yes. I used to fence at school and university, though these days I'm rather rusty. But since joining the police I've been on a couple of mixed martial arts courses. Of course the really valuable part is de-escalation training for stressful situations. But yes, I can look after myself.'

He looked at her with new respect. 'A dangerous woman, eh? So you can bring down a man my size, say?'

This was *so* schoolboy. 'You are, what, five-ten, thirteen stone?'

'Six foot,' he protested.

'If you are untrained, I'd generally reckon to have you immobilised face down, within five to ten seconds. I know limb restraints, finger- and arm-holds that no one can endure. We are also issued with PAVA, an incapacitant spray. It's like rubbing a vindaloo into your eyes.'

'Wow.' He stared at her with undisguised admiration.

'Now, of course, that's in the gym and when I'm prepared. Real life is messier. Seven years ago, I was in the drug squad on the first-floor walkway of a council estate in Plymouth, facing a huge guy who'd just knocked a male sergeant unconscious. He ran for me, and I had nowhere to go, my back was to the balcony. So I flipped him over the edge, using his own momentum, plus a hand in his beard. He made an awfully big dent in the roof of the riot van parked underneath.'

'Bloody hell!'

'I got into a lot of trouble with the chief inspector for that.'

'Why?'

'I didn't know the van was there. It had arrived literally five seconds before, full of uniformed plods.'

—

The journey home was pleasant and unhurried. She and Adam had got on really well and, amazingly, the date hadn't been interrupted by work. Maddy had worked late and held the fort. DI Lockhart had come in earlier for his evening shift, and Maddy never minded being in the office with the handsome Prince of Darkness. The nearest to a snag was him being appalled by her crunching the entirety of a prawn, including shell, legs and even antennae. They had then had a discussion in which Adam confessed to not eating the skins of jacket potatoes, nor apple cores. He wasn't much fond of leftovers, either.

'You've never been hard up, then,' Talantire said. He frowned at that. It was the nearest thing to a hitch in the entire evening. She felt good about him, though she was a little alarmed about the ex, whose name was Pepsy, short for Philippa. They had only broken up six weeks ago. That was still well within the 'reconciliation possible' phase.

She allowed him a chaste peck on the cheek, and a brief hug before they parted.

While she was on the way home, she heard the ping of a text on her personal phone, and pulled over to take a look. Adam. Yes, he wanted to meet again. She smiled to herself, and turned the music on. It wasn't yet eight thirty when she got in. She needed to find time to do a bit of long-overdue housework and some laundry, but not now. She felt too hyped up. Too full of food for exercise, she rang her best friend Amy to update her. Disappointed when there was no answer, she left a long message, finishing with: 'I've got a good feeling about this one, Amy. Speak to you soon.'

Thursday morning brought new leads. The most important was the DNA tests on the blood recovered from underneath Mrs Ruth Lyle's fingernails, forwarded by the pathologist. It matched the remaining unknown trace from the crucifix. Talantire went to the whiteboard with its list of confirmed forensic samples. Firstly, from the apartment alone, Mrs Lee the landlady, Stephen Dowling the vomiting PC, and the mystery trace on the taps. Then those from the cross:

1) Mrs Ruth Lyle

2) Gawain Entwistle

3) Young Ruth Lyle

4) Unknown – Murderer?

At number four she removed the question mark, and added 'matches trace under Mrs Lyle's fingernails'. Could that logic be faulted? Whoever Mrs Lyle had fought had left a trace on the murder weapon too. Could there be any other explanation except that this was the killer?

She couldn't think of one.

There had been several new calls and emails from former contacts of James Quince. One had worked with him at Lamprey and another was Susan McDonald, wife of a former colleague of Quince's who had died ten years ago. Mrs McDonald recalled her husband inviting James and his partner over for drinks in Aberdeen on one occasion in the early

1980s. Talantire had arranged for Mrs McDonald to be interviewed locally by Police Scotland and sent them a selfie of Mrs Ruth Lyle from her own phone. The answer came back pretty quickly: even allowing for the passage of years, this did not look like Jamie's woman, who had been a dark-haired local lass and was introduced as Cally. She'd had a strong Scottish accent, and had seemed quite a few years younger than James. Mrs McDonald didn't think that James and Cally were married either, at least when she met them.

It couldn't be Mrs Ruth Lyle.

Talantire was baffled. She had experienced trouble enough getting information about James Quince, but Mrs Ruth Lyle was another order of difficulty altogether, and the discovery of another woman in Quince's past didn't help. Mrs Lyle had seemed to spring from nowhere, from the moment she appeared as his next of kin and beneficiary on his pension, using information essentially stolen from the 1973 murder victim. The National Insurance and NHS numbers popped up a decade and a half later, along with her name on utility bills, and, a few years later, a passport. The place of birth, in line with the birth certificate, was given as Ilfracombe. There was no driving licence. No photographs of her from her marriage or life with Quince, nothing else.

It was time to go back to somebody who had seen Mrs Ruth Lyle and had spoken to her. Gwen Lyle, mother of the original victim.

The moment Talantire got off the phone, she was aware that Maddy was waiting to speak to her. Even in her peripheral vision she could pick up a sense of excitement from whatever was on her colleague's screen.

'What is it, Maddy?'

'I found out who locked you in at Bluebird Cottage!' she hissed. 'The DNA tests on the door handle and lock have come back. There were twelve traces detected—'

'Clearly all and sundry trying to get into the crime scene.'

'—including both of us, but one of them was Gawain Entwistle.'

Talantire's jaw dropped. 'So he must be here, there's no other way. Maybe we should have taken that sighting in Ilfracombe more seriously. Why would he come down from wherever it was that they resettled him?'

'To commit a murder, perhaps?'

'Bloody hell, I've got words to say to Detective Sergeant Ferris, that's for sure.'

It took two hours to get hold of Gerald Ferris of Special Branch. 'Jan, I'm afraid I don't yet have an answer for you on your request,' he said when he picked up on the fifth call.

'I'm not calling about that, Gerald. Entwistle is back in Ilfracombe. He locked me in at the crime scene yesterday.' She explained about the medieval key being used.

'Did you see him?'

'No. But we swabbed the lock, and his DNA came up on it, just as it did on the murder weapon.'

'Good grief. Look, I'll have to make some calls but I will get back to you as soon as possible.'

'I need a picture of him, for a start,' Talantire said. 'As he is now.'

'Now, I really think that's unlikely. It would be in violation of the lifelong anonymity order.'

'I don't give a monkey's,' Talantire retorted. 'He is the major suspect for a second killing. Just look at the papers! Surely reoffending should trump whatever protections were put in place for him. Once word gets out that he's around, there will be a lynching party. It would be for his own protection.'

Ferris said he'd look into it, then got back to her within twenty minutes.

'I think we can all calm down a bit,' he said. 'Mr Entwistle attended a meeting with his psychiatrist on Thursday afternoon last week. She confirmed he didn't leave until a quarter to five. Now I understand the time of death for the murder victim was roughly the same. We can assure you that he couldn't have travelled from his new location to the scene of the crime in Devon in less than twelve or so hours on public transport. He cannot drive, and he hasn't the kind of money for a taxi journey of that length. So it couldn't possibly be him.'

'I'm sorry, you're still not playing ball with me,' Talantire said. 'His DNA is on the murder weapon—'

'But I understand it is the same murder weapon used previously, so it must just be an old trace—'

'We're not convinced it *is* the same weapon. It's remarkably uncorroded for an object originally found during the Crusades. And what about the lock?'

'I suppose you have to get the crucifix analysed, then,' Ferris said. 'You prove to me it's a new weapon, then I agree it will be hard to come to any other explanation.'

'What about the lock?' Talantire repeated.

'Okay, I suppose he could be in Ilfracombe *now*. Just not at the time of the killing. We'll certainly have an idea if he doesn't turn up to this week's psychiatric appointment. It starts in half an hour.'

—

Talantire and Maddy found Mrs Gwen Lyle sitting up happily in her bed in Alexandra Ward, North Devon District Hospital.

'How are you feeling now Mrs Lyle?' Talantire asked, while a nurse rearranged the pillows behind the patient's back.

'Much better, thank you. They came and washed my hair yesterday.' There was a slight sibilance to her speech that not been there before, and her left eye wasn't fully open. 'I'm a bit wobbly on my feet.'

'She is doing much better,' the nurse said.

'This is the one who saved my life,' she said, pointing to Talantire.

'I heard you were very quick,' the nurse said. 'And knew exactly what to do.'

'My mother is a retired GP,' Talantire replied. 'She showed me in case she ever had a stroke.'

'So what was it you'd come to see me about? I forgot all about it,' Mrs Lyle said.

'It was about your daughter, Ruth.'

Her face darkened. 'She died, you know. Fifty years ago.'

Maddy and Talantire exchanged a glance. While the woman looked to have largely recovered from her stroke, it was clear that her memory was impaired.

'We know, dear,' Maddy said. 'You told us about it last time.'

'Did I? Oh.'

Maddy took out her iPad and showed her a selfie from the dead woman's phone. It had been taken by a beach. 'Do you know this woman?'

The woman squinted at the picture. 'No, who is it?'

Talantire glanced again at Maddy. She had recognised her previously, before the stroke.

'Are you sure?' Maddy asked.

'Oh, well.' She looked closer, adjusting her glasses.

Talantire watched a dawn of understanding illuminate the old woman's face, widening it. Even the lazy left eye flickered up.

'Is this the woman that came to see you?' Maddy asked. 'Your son said that you had a visitor, a few years back.'

'Is that her?' Talantire asked.

Mrs Lyle reached into her handbag, her arm a bird-like claw, scrabbling about until she found what she wanted. A cotton handkerchief, which she raised and, removing her glasses, dabbed at her eyes. The bottom half of her face seemed to dissolve. Not a stroke this time, but something profound. Her mouth moved, unable to restrain horrors of some kind.

'Alan said someone came to you, pretending to be Ruth,' Talantire said.

She nodded, her mouth still moving. 'It was years ago, at Blyth Road. Before I lived here.' She seemed to forget she wasn't at the residential home. 'When I was at my house.'

'Do you remember when, exactly?' Maddy asked.

'No, but it's written down. My son was furious when he heard. He tried to get me to arrange for the woman to come again, so he could be there to confront her. But she never did.'

'And was it this woman?' Talantire said. She swiped to a different selfie, taken by Ilfracombe Harbour, a big smile, partially masked by windblown red hair.

'Yes, yes it's her. Bit older in that picture.' She began to cry, and dabbed her eyes. Her tiny bony shoulders shook underneath her cardigan.

'We don't want to upset you, Mrs Lyle,' Maddy said. 'But can you recall what she said?'

The woman sobbed, trying to coax out the words through a thickened throat. 'She knocked on my door. She was all neatly dressed with ginger hair and nice shoes and those same dimples and everything. I'll never to the day I die forget what she said.' She paused and closed her eyes. 'She said, softly, "Hello, Mum, it's me."' Mrs Lyle's body began to quiver, her mouth distorted and her face folded inwards. She sobbed uncontrollably.

Maddy reached for her hand, and looked at Talantire.

When she was able to speak, Mrs Lyle said, 'She said, "Mum, it's been a long time. I've come back to see you. Don't you recognise me?" Anyway, the room started spinning and I had to sit down. I brought her in for a cup of tea while I got my head straight. Then she said, "I know this must be a shock to you, but I am Ruth, and I have come to tell you that everything is fine."'

'Did she ask for any money?' Maddy asked.

'No. She didn't ask for anything. Besides I didn't have any money, never did have. You know, I could've sold my story to the papers. They asked me many times, but I wouldn't.'

'It's generally a good decision, I would say,' Maddy said.

'My son reported it to the police at the time, and a constable came round. He just said, "Pay no attention Mrs Lyle, it's probably someone trying to get money off you. Just a crank probably."'

Maddy rolled her eyes. 'They should have done more.'

'Do you have this woman's phone number?' Talantire asked.

'No, she didn't give it me. The constable asked that too. The woman said she would come round again, because she cared about me and all the suffering I'd had. Before she left, she said, "Mum, I have missed you so much." She kissed me on the forehead and hugged me.'

'What did you do?' Talantire asked.

'I held her in my arms as tight as I could, and I didn't want to let go. And I howled my heart out.' Mrs Lyle had begun to sob again, huge breathless sobs. An agony, borne for a lifetime, momentarily lifted and then dropped back on her.

Talantire could see that Maddy, as tough a woman as she'd ever known, had tears in her eyes. Her own eyes were moist too.

'That was very cruel of her,' Talantire said, softly.

Mrs Lyle's voice had sunk to a hoarse whisper. 'She offered me the one thing I have wanted, every minute of every day, for fifty years. So of course I wanted to believe. My Ruth, my own dear daughter, come back to me.'

Chapter 14

Talantire was reeling as they returned to the car. Why would anyone want to do this? To put an old lady through such agony, by pretending to be her dead daughter. There were elements of Eastern mysticism in Mrs Lyle's book collection; perhaps reincarnation had something to do with it. But why try so hard to inhabit this particular lost soul? A long-dead Devon schoolgirl?

Maddy put her foot down as they drove back to Barnstaple, while Talantire worked the phone. She rang DS Ferris at Special Branch, and got straight through.

'Jan, I was just going to call you. First things first, Gawain Entwistle missed his psychiatrist appointment this afternoon, and when a social worker went to his home there was nobody there. So you may be right—'

'We know he's here,' Talantire said. 'But I need a picture from you, urgently.'

'I'm sorry, there was a meeting earlier this afternoon, involving senior Home Office and Ministry of Justice officials, and, despite representations by your assistant chief constable, they are not ready to break the lifelong anonymity order.'

'Why on earth not?' Talantire demanded.

'Quite simply because Entwistle was not in Ilfracombe on the day the murder was committed. We can be quite certain about that. CCTV footage from a mental health day centre shows he was there at the time. I've seen and can verify it.'

'Can you send it to me?'

'No, I'm afraid not, because it shows his appearance and may give away where he lives. I'm afraid you're just going to have to take my word for it.'

'Do you know where Entwistle is now?'

'No.'

'Well, we're going to track him down. I promise you that.'

The next call she made was to Dave Nuttall, who had been researching Entwistle's family. He told her that although Entwistle's parents were dead, there was mention of an aunt, his mother's younger sister Sheila Woodley, who lived in Woolacombe, just a few miles down the road from Ilfracombe. The woman was in her eighties. 'I got a warrant for Entwistle's visiting records at Ashworth Hospital, and it shows that she visited him several times in the last five years before his release,' Nuttall said.

'All right, let's get some uniformed resources over there straight away. As he has learning difficulties and was travelling a long distance, he is most likely to seek out the one friendly face he can rely on. Maybe we'll even find him there.'

-

Once they'd arrived back at Barnstaple and clambered up the stairs to CID, Talantire peered through the glass-panelled door of the CSI room. Pavel Kaminski was sitting, bent over, at a desk, with his back to her, confronting a pile of paper evidence bags. In his nitrile-gloved hands, she saw, he had the murder weapon. The crucifix was close to his face, as if he was about to kiss it. She opened the door, and he gave a start, almost dropping it.

'My God, you almost gave me a heart attack!' he said.

'Didn't mean to make you jump,' she said. 'I know you're a good Catholic, but I'm not sure this is an object worthy of worship.'

He turned to face her, and she could see he was wearing a jeweller's eye-loupe, one that clipped onto his spectacles. 'It is a fascinating object,' he said. 'I've been doing a bit of research. Medieval roofing nails aren't like modern nails, they often have a flange just on one side rather than a circular cap. But these have a pyramidal cap, which is a Roman influence, and an unusual notch—'

'Is this relevant to the case, Pavel?' She could see that on his screen there was a document open describing the characteristics of medieval ironwork.

He blinked owlishly at her, one eye magnified enormously by the loupe. 'Well, the more we can find out about it…'

'We're hard-pressed to get results, and I'd rather you concentrated on the other evidence. As the evidence officer I would have thought you had enough on your plate. We have got bags of Mrs Lyle's clothing still to examine, have you finished all that? If so, I haven't seen the documentation.'

'Is this a bollocking, ma'am?'

'No, but I'd honestly prefer if the murder weapon was only handled when absolutely necessary, even in gloves. I'm not sure that knowing the historical provenance is relevant.'

'Well, I'm trying to establish if it's the original,' he said.

'I only need to know if it's the same one that was used in 1973. Not whether it's typical of the period. I want it back in the safe.' She pointed at the secure cabinet. As Pavel packed away the item, she leaned over his desk and picked up the evidence log clipboard. She scanned the initials to see who else had looked at it.

'What's this?' she asked, pointing to a ten-minute-long sign-out from the day before.

'Ah, the commissioner wanted to see it. I wouldn't let him touch it – it stayed in the box. He just wanted a photograph.'

'For God's sake, Pavel!'

'What could I do, ma'am?' Kaminski complained. 'Detective Superintendent Wells was with him, along with the MP. I could hardly refuse, could I?'

'Victoria Carnegie too? This is not a kids' excursion to the bloody V&A!' Talantire shouted. 'This is secret evidence, withheld, not in the public domain. Fat bloody chance of it staying that way when all and sundry come in here taking pictures!' She turned on her heel and walked out, slamming the door behind her so hard that she heard the glass crack. Looking across into CID, she saw Maddy, Primrose and Dave Nuttall staring at her, open-mouthed.

'Haven't you lot got some work to do?' she shouted, then turned sharp right and thundered down the stairs. She stormed out into the car park, breathing hard, past the gaggle of civilian staff smokers who congregated between the riot vans. Her breath pluming the air, she peered beyond the half-dozen parked police vehicles, and out across to the builders' yard opposite where a forklift truck was busy lifting timber. A BBC local radio van was parked nearby, amid a knot of photographers. She turned away, took half a dozen deep breaths, exhaling hard. From the press crowd, someone bellowed at her, using her Christian name, asking if there had been any progress.

She ignored it, to examine the anger that had built in her like a thunderstorm from a clear sky. As usual it was the ghost, sliding through the keyhole of memory: held helpless, the prying hands, the soft voice, the odd smell of embrocation. Our little secret, he had said, back when she was eight. And it was. 'Why are you such an angry child?' her mother asked, when Jan quarrelled with other children, broke their toys, bit her older brother. 'Such a temper!' But when she had tried to tell her, she was called a liar. She never attempted to again, but sealed the horror back into its mental tomb.

Along with Bella.

Jan's identical twin sister, who suffered brain injuries from birth, had been institutionalised since the age of three, and every time Jan had been naughty, her mother had said: 'Bella wouldn't behave like you do. Sometimes I wish I could go back to 1985 and make it the other way round.' It being the injury. The rarely-mentioned curse that had maimed her family.

Maybe she should visit Bella. She was only in Bristol. She'd not been for years. But she couldn't bear to stare at her own features on a now-bloated body. Bella, with a face somehow full of reproach; the might-have-been, the guilt. Unbearable.

Other things to think about.

Okay, it was annoying that the prime exhibit was being treated like a tourist attraction, but she knew she shouldn't have taken it out on Pavel. He was powerless to stop someone of Wells' seniority interfering. The chance of contamination was minimal, seeing as they had already conducted all the forensic tests that they needed, but the risk of disclosure was real. It was really getting to her. Pavel was right in one respect: there was something strange about that crucifix, something powerful. Everyone wanted to see it, to touch it. She had even dreamed about the damn thing herself. Above all, she was terrified that it would disappear once again. Maddy was right; this was a cursed object, slipping through history, from one death to another, for a thousand years. To resurface in yet another murder.

–

She headed back inside twenty minutes later, apologised to her team for the outburst, and then went in to see Pavel. The cracked glass, right across the panel diagonally, had already been fixed with clear tape. It still rattled as she opened the door. He glanced up at her, then looked back at his screen.

'Look, I'm sorry about that, just then.'

He shrugged, but wouldn't look at her. Pavel was a sensitive soul, prone to moods, but a first-class CSI technician.

'I've put it away,' he muttered, gesturing at the security cabinet.

'Thank you. Look, we're all under pressure. No suspect, a week after the killing.'

'And we don't even know who the victim is,' Pavel said.

'Right. So hands up, I was out of order.'

He extruded a smile of acknowledgement. She left quietly. It wasn't the greatest apology, but would never have been made by a man, she was sure of that.

She returned to CID. 'So what was that you were telling me, Maddy?'

'It's about the uniforms who visited Entwistle's aunt. Sheila Woodley apparently denied that her nephew had come to visit her, but refused the officers' permission to look around the house. Shall I get a warrant?'

'Yes,' said Talantire. 'That's a good idea. There is a good chance he may have gone to ground in the area. Primrose, can I get you to track down any CCTV from the Woolacombe to Ilfracombe bus?'

'Yes, ma'am.'

'We have to remember that Gawain Entwistle was plucked from the modern world at the age of fifteen, and incarcerated in an institution. He can't drive, doesn't know how to use a mobile phone, and is probably travelling around by public transport.'

'That limits his options,' Primrose said.

'Yes. In practical terms the outside world for him is frozen at 1973. He has of course some severe learning difficulties. But it doesn't mean that he will be easy to find,' Talantire said. 'He knows things about Ilfracombe that most people have forgotten. I discovered that when I came up against him in the Dimpsy. And he could be dangerous.'

'Right,' said Maddy, picking up the phone. 'One other thing. I've tracked down Trevor Goswell, and I'm going to call him.'

'Well done. How did you find him?' Goswell, the other man who had briefly been a suspect in the original crime.

'Through his National Insurance number. He's a retired mental health nurse living down in Falmouth. Do you want to listen in?'

Talantire listened in on her extension as Maddy rang Goswell's landline. After she'd introduced herself, Goswell interrupted: 'It's about this murder in Ilfracombe isn't it?'

'What makes you think that, Mr Goswell?'

'You're raking over the coals, aren't you? Considering I was arrested back in 1973. Well, I don't know anything about it, see?'

'I haven't asked you anything yet,' she said. 'But I would very much like to come and speak to you.'

'Well, I don't want to speak to you.'

'Come on now, Mr Goswell, we can do this the easy way, just two of us, in plain clothes and an ordinary car, or we can do it the hard way, with uniforms and flashing lights. Time to make your choice.'

There was a heavy sigh on the other end of the phone. 'All right. You can come here.'

After they had arranged a time that evening, she asked: 'One final thing, do you have any contact with Andrew Hinks?'

'I've not seen him for decades.'

'Not friends any more?'

'Hardly surprising is it?'

—

Trevor Goswell lived in a tidy-looking bungalow at the end of a cul-de-sac of social housing. Maddy parked the unmarked white Nissan hatchback immediately outside, and she and Dave Nuttall made their way up the short concrete path to the front door. The presence of a ramp and a railing indicated that the home had been converted for the disabled.

The doorbell rang with soft chimes, and set off the distant barking of a dog. The door was opened by a shortish bald man in his seventies, in a stained grey cardigan and slippers. He waved them in quickly after they'd introduced themselves, showed them into the main lounge and turned off the TV. A woman with frizzy white hair and spectacles peered out at them from the doorway of the kitchen, with a quivering yorkshire terrier yapping at her feet. After dispensing a cup of milky tea to each of them, she disappeared into another room, taking the dog with her.

Goswell lowered himself into the settee, and indicated to the two detectives to sit opposite him.

'So what is it you want from me after all these years?' he asked.

Maddy began. 'As you probably know, there's been another killing in Ilfracombe, with some similarities to the previous one that took place at St James Without back in 1973.'

'And you think I had something to do with it?'

'No, we don't think that. However, we would like to tap into your recollections of what happened when you were interviewed in connection with the original crime.'

Goswell laughed. 'You've lost the original paperwork, haven't you?'

'It's not normally stored for fifty years,' Nuttall said. 'I also need to get a DNA sample to eliminate you from our enquiries.'

'I've not been to Ilfracombe for years, so you'll not find any traces.' Goswell nevertheless opened his mouth to allow the inside of his cheek to be swabbed.

'I just wish DNA tests had been available then,' he said, after the swab had been withdrawn. 'Would have put me in the clear and stopped my life falling to bits.'

'I agree with you,' Maddy said. 'It would have helped all round. But I still need to know what was said when you were interviewed.'

Goswell looked out of the window. 'All I can remember is being asked by Hogley what I got up to with Ruth Lyle. The answer was nothing. They knew my prints weren't on the murder weapon, nor were Andy's.'

'Why would he have assumed that you did know her?' Maddy asked.

'You'll have to ask him, won't you?' he asked, with a sly grin. It seemed obvious that Goswell knew that Hogley was dead.

'So, what was the connection with Ruth?' Nuttall asked.

'She used to frequent the Stag, along with a load of other underage drinkers. She asked me and others to get her drinks from the bar. And she didn't always give us the money afterwards. She liked a glass of cider. These days of course you would classify her as vulnerable. She was a flirt, liked attention, especially from older men. And was a bit forward.'

'Forward, how?' Nuttall asked.

'That was covered in the original trial. I mean, it's a bit innocent by today's standards. Instead of paying for her drink, she'd often just snog you.'

Nuttall looked down at the information he been given by Howell, which didn't detail this at all. 'You were twenty-two when you met Ruth Lyle, and Hinks was twenty-one. How old was she?'

'She said she was eighteen, but I knew she was younger.'

'Did you ever have sex with her?' Nuttall asked.

'No.'

'Did Andrew Hinks?'

'No idea.'

'Press reports at the time said one of the arrested men had been seen with the victim in an alleyway, and an act of intimacy was alleged to have occurred.'

Goswell snorted his derision. 'Bloody tabloid tittle-tattle.'

'Someone must have seen it happen, to be the source,' Nuttall said. 'You or Hinks had been seen going off with Ruth.'

'Who says?' Goswell replied.

Maddy knew that this snippet had come from Howell's recollection and nothing more. A thin thread of memory in a retired officer, and utterly inadmissible. How they needed those original case files.

'Listen, as I said at the time, I've done nothing to be ashamed of. I was friendly with her because she was fun, that's all.'

Maddy knew that Goswell had no criminal record, but she was far from convinced he was telling her the whole truth. He seemed to have an inkling that there were no surviving records that would contradict a sanitised version of his behaviour at the time.

'Do you remember when you first met her?'

'Yes. Andy Hinks and I had gone to see a band at the Stag, and she was there.'

'Do you remember the date?'

'No.'

'The name of the band?'

'I don't recall. But I do remember their lead singer. She's now that MP.'

'Which one?'

'Victoria bloody Carnegie.'

'I see.' Maddy tried to hide her surprise. This was the same woman who'd tried to talk her way into the crime scene. Maybe she actually knew Ruth?

Goswell was in his element now. 'Yeah. She believed in violent revolution, as I did at the time. She was also gorgeous. Couldn't believe that she's sold out, and now she's right up there in the land-owning establishment.'

'It happens to a lot of people,' Nuttall said.

'That's right,' said Maddy. 'Dave here used to be into punk.'

'Was I hell,' Nuttall muttered, scowling at her.

'So, Mr Goswell. What was the name of the band?'

'I don't recall.'

'Did they play at the Stag a lot?'

He scratched his head. 'No, I only ever saw them the once, and they were a support act.'

'To whom?' Nuttall asked. 'Then we might be able to trace them.'

Goswell blew a sigh. 'Maybe Andy knows more, he was more into the music. I was into the politics.'

'Just like Victoria is now,' Maddy said.

'No, no.' He held up his hands. 'Not those politics. But how she was *then*. I wouldn't give her the time of day now.'

154

Chapter 15

By seven, Talantire was exhausted. With Maddy off in Falmouth with Nuttall, and DI Lockhart not yet in, everything fell to her. She'd just finished a long phone call with her boss, trying to persuade him not to let anyone else in to see evidence. Detective Superintendent Wells heard her out, but couldn't see why it was a problem letting the police and crime commissioner into the CSI room. He clearly had a higher opinion of the Hon. LHH than she did. Likewise with the MP, whom Talantire thought had been far too interested in the crime scene. All Wells would agree was that he'd give Talantire the opportunity to veto any future requests to see the crucifix.

'You can just say it's off for tests,' he had told her.

After all that, she needed to get out of the office. Tomorrow they were going to start pulling apart Bluebird Cottage, or at least the parts of the Dimpsy Chapel that had covered over the original crime scene. Mrs Lee the landlady had been notified, and, though furious at the damage that would be done, was partially mollified once she'd heard that the beautiful fitted kitchen, located in the new part, was likely to escape the constabulary crowbars.

Talantire picked up her handbag, and quickly checked the CSI office to make sure it was locked. Part of her wanted to check the safe, to be sure the crucifix was still there. She dismissed the idea that it might not be as ridiculous. But she did need to get some fresh insight, a new perspective.

Thursday was her normal night to go running with the Black Bull Harriers, and according to the schedule they'd all be up on the cliffs west of Ilfracombe this evening. It would be a perfect opportunity to go back to the crime scene en route. Was there something she was missing?

It was already quite dark when she parked the unmarked Ford Focus just round the corner from Bluebird Cottage. From the boot she took her toolkit and a holdall containing a fresh Tyvek suit, gloves and booties. If she had expected Mercer Lane to be empty, she was wrong. An enterprising tourist guide, a middle-aged man in a pirate hat and a jacket covered in badges, was standing on the step outside, describing the 1973 murder to a group of a dozen cagouled visitors: 'And just a week ago today, another woman was murdered here. Rumour has it that she was also stabbed with a crucifix, though the police are saying nothing.'

'Excuse me,' Talantire said, showing him her warrant card. 'Perhaps you'd care to move away.'

The man urged his group back, and as they shuffled away he said to them. 'Well, as you can see, Tyrell Tours always gets you to where the action is.'

Numerous camera flashes illuminated Talantire as she brought out the keys. She opened the hefty police padlock that now secured the door, and slipped inside, bolting it behind her. She set the padlock on a table by the door, along with her holdall. The smell of stale vomit lingered, along with a vague butcher's dustbin pong. She changed into the Tyvek suit and booties, and then noticed that a light was on inside, towards the back of the building. She didn't recall leaving one on. The entry log had shown she was the last to sign in.

'Anybody there?' she called out.

No reply. She unzipped the holdall and withdrew a meaty screwdriver. Best be prepared, just in case.

'Hello?'

She advanced slowly into the lounge, the screwdriver poised ahead of her. The silence stretched out, such that she imagined she could hear the echo of her own heartbeat from the vaulted ceiling. She peered round the central pillar, and turned on the main light, a chandelier with eight bulbs on a dimmer switch. She turned the brightness to maximum. It was clear no one was in the room. She checked the kitchen, which seemed to be as she had left it, and then climbed the spiral stairs to the galleried bedroom. The Tyvek crackled as she raised each leg, and her footsteps thrummed on the metal.

Someone had disturbed the double bed, as if they had sat on it, and there was an empty crisp packet on the floor next to it. How on earth had anyone got in? She backed away, then crouched down and peered under the bed. There was no one there, and this was the one place that someone could hide on this level. But on the other side, just beyond the frame, was a plastic carrier bag. She didn't recall that having been logged on the evidence file. She stood up and made her way round to have a look.

Then a click. Everything was plunged into darkness.

She gasped. How could that happen? There was no one by the pillar where the switch was. As her eyes adjusted, she realised it wasn't quite pitch black. A faint orange glow from the streetlamps filtered through the rear lancet windows, and she could make out the walls and ceiling. She couldn't hear the hum of the fridge, nor see any light on the wi-fi unit on the wall above her. That must mean the power had been cut. Only someone who knew the place well could do that. She fumbled inside the Tyvek and took out her work phone from an inside jacket pocket. With trembling fingers and in the blue nitrile gloves, it took her three attempts to unlock it. The light from the phone temporarily dazzled her, and she made her way slowly beyond the foot of the bed towards the gallery's wooden balustrade. As she leaned over and pivoted left, a shadow appeared on the wall next to the bed.

Of a huge man-sized cross.

A crucifix.

She gasped, and fumbled the phone. It dropped over the edge to the floor beneath. There was a crack, and darkness returned. *Shit!*

Then, below her, she felt as much as saw a shadow move, slowly, crawling like a reptile across the far end of the floor beneath the lancet windows where the darkness was deepest. A sizeable movement, stealthy and almost silent, making its way towards the cupboard to her left. A cold shudder slid through her entrails, and she had to stifle a sob. This was nightmare territory. She was alone, without a phone. But she still had resources, and she steeled herself.

'Stay exactly where you are,' she yelled, in her most authoritative tones. 'I'm armed with a taser. Stand up, where I can see you.' She hoped the lie would be convincing, but to her own ears it rang weak and hollow. The shadow froze and made a low threatening exhalation. An animal noise. Then, after a few seconds, it resumed its crawl. She leaned over the banister, hearing the squeaking of footwear and the movements of outstretched hands. She reckoned the figure to be at least six foot long.

'I said stop, this is your final warning.'

The slow creak of a hinge to the left indicated an opening door, which must be the cupboard, previously locked, that she'd seen before. That's where this individual must have come from, and where they were now returning. With a final quick movement, the shadow disappeared inside the cupboard. The door squeaked closed. The click of a key turning was followed by the sound of descending footsteps. Only when she was sure that the coast was clear did she make her way carefully downstairs, feeling the banisters, moving right until she arrived at the spiral staircase. She made her way down, perspiring heavily in the suit, her breath coming in sharp gasps. She tried the light on the column. Dead. She then crawled over to where she'd dropped her phone. It took a couple of minutes to locate it. It wouldn't switch on, and she could feel the screen was cracked. In the deeper darkness away from the glow of streetlamps, it took her another two minutes to find her way back to the front door. She slid back the bolt and stared out through the crack in the door. Light and air! She found the foot traffic passing back and forth quite reassuring. She took a deep breath, then slid the bolt again. Then she turned to the holdall and found a torch, along with her personal phone.

She rang the control room, and called in what had happened. 'I think he's trapped in a cupboard, or has got some secret way out. No, I don't have a description.'

A patrol car screamed in within five minutes, containing four burly male officers. She left two of them in the doorway of Bluebird Cottage and went with the other two out into Mercer Lane. They turned left up the steps into the alleyway, which ascended to the High Street, turned left again at the top and arrived at the front of the building that backed onto Bluebird Cottage.

It was a nightclub, called Secrets, and there was a throng of youngsters outside, dressed for a night out, chatting, laughing and smoking. A subwoofer thump rattled the windows. Talantire could feel it in her ribs. She and the two uniforms jumped the queue and were allowed in by the security staff. It was still quite early by nightclub standards, and there were only a few dozen people in the place. The music was deafening. Alerted by the doormen, the manager, a stocky and bearded individual of about forty, came out to greet them.

'Turn it off, please,' she bellowed, pointing at a freezer-sized speaker. The manager turned and signalled to some headphoned DJ, and the sound was turned right down.

'That's better. I'd like to check any cellar or store areas that you have at the back,' Talantire said. 'Have you seen any suspicious individuals this evening?'

The manager gestured to the punters. 'We get quite a few, as you might imagine, but it depends what you mean by suspicious.'

Giving up on this line of reasoning, Talantire got him to lead them to the gents and ladies toilets and cloakroom and then down into a storeroom, which looked like it had genuinely been carved out of the rock beneath hundreds of years ago. 'Are you aware of any back way into St James'?' she asked.

'You mean the Dimpsy? No, I mean it does back onto us and there is a tiny garden between the two, which is full of beer kegs right now. One of the doormen used to work at this place years ago, when it was called the Malthouse. He reckons there were several underground rooms but they've been sealed off for health and safety.'

'Under your management?'

'No, long before mine. Here, look.' He led them behind a series of pallets of bottled cider to a waist-high door. The door was clearly old, but had been roughly whitewashed numerous times.

'So you don't have the keys for this?' she asked.

'No, sorry.'

She turned to the uniformed sergeant next to her, a tall guy called Whittaker. 'We need this place closed down for the evening, can you see to it? We'll probably need another four or five bodies, if you can spare them. Crowbars, a locksmith and some powerful lights.'

'Yes, ma'am,' he said.

'What? You can't do that,' said the manager, who had been joined by an intimidating-looking doorman, all tattoos and shaven head. 'We're just getting busy, aren't we, Carl? We only just survived lockdown and now you do this to us. For God's sake.'

'We are investigating a serious crime,' Talantire said.

'Can't it wait until the morning?' the doorman asked.

'No. It can't. The intruder I'm looking for may still be on the premises somewhere.'

'You got a description, then?' he persisted.

'No.'

The doorman laughed. 'So how you do know when you find him?'

'Yeah, that's a bloody good question ain't it?' the manager said.

It was. A very good question.

Talantire left the sergeant with instructions to post a PC on the door to the storerooms and cellars and get all the nightclub's CCTV for the last week. She was just making her way up along the curving alleyway back towards the Dimpsy when she saw the looming figure of Inspector Carnegie coming the other way, along with three other uniforms.

'Been getting yourself into trouble again, have you, Jan?'

'Someone's been getting in, despite the police padlock, and I intend to find out who.'

'What, into the crime scene?'

'Yes, through a cupboard door in the back, which I think comes out in the storage room of the nightclub behind.'

'How did CSI miss that?'

'That's a question for another day,' she said, and squeezed past him to return to the chapel. She signed in at the door with a uniformed PC, stepped inside, and found another two, staring hands on hips into the gloom, playing their torches along the walls and vaulted ceiling. She then saw the shadow of the crucifix again, on the wall next to the bed.

How stupid she'd been.

It was simply moonlight from the clerestory windows, the cross being the panes in the frame and the Christ figure the shadow of a long central catch that allowed it to open with a pole. It was the shock of seeing it that had made her drop and break her work phone.

Sighing, she thought about putting her Tyvek back on, but there didn't seem to be any point seeing as all and sundry were now walking in and out in their constabulary boots. She knelt at her holdall, opened the toolbox and pulled out hammer and chisel.

'Have you found the fuse box?' she asked the PCs.

'No, it doesn't appear to be in the kitchen,' one of them replied.

Talantire made her way past them using her phone light, and homed in on the corner where the shadow had seemed to emerge. In it was an unvarnished tallboy wooden cabinet, quite in keeping with the history of the place, one door slightly ajar. She donned a fresh pair of blue gloves and gingerly eased open the door. As she suspected, the back of the cabinet had been crudely cut out to fit out over the protrusion of the Bakelite fuse box mounted on the wall behind. Shining her phone on it revealed it had no cover, and the master switch was off. Talantire flicked it on, and suddenly she could see.

She scrambled out of the cabinet, just in time to hear one of the PCs say: 'And God said, Let there be light: and there was light. And he saw that it was good.'

'So long as you pay the bloody bill,' said the other, and chuckled.

'Now you can see, would you be kind enough to fetch my holdall, by the door? I need some evidence markers, the gel lift kit and some DNA swabs. And you' – she pointed to the other PC – 'come over here with me.'

The young PC followed her over to the locked cupboard door that she had seen the previous day. She knelt down and pressed her fingers against the bottom of the door. It was locked. She waited until the other officer had returned with the goodies from her bag. She started with a DNA swab on the brass lock, and then followed it up with a gel lift for the entire section of the wood around it, hoping to pick up some fingerprints. After she had completed and bagged the evidence, she weighed up the hammer and chisel against the door, and then had second thoughts.

'I really don't want to smash this,' she said.

'We could wait for the locksmith, ma'am,' the PC said.

'No, the firm we use have got to come from Barnstaple and won't be here for ages.' She took a meaty flathead screwdriver,

162

and used it to scrape off the paint over the hinges. The screw heads were old and rusted. 'Let's give it a go,' she said, pressing the screwdriver in and attempting to turn it. Unable to make any progress, she passed the tool to the PC, who had no better luck.

'Right,' she said delving into the toolbox again. She came out with a set of Allen keys, designed for use with hexagonal headed bolts. 'These are all roughly key-shaped, right? Let's see if we can tickle the lock. It's pretty old and basic for a mortice lock.' She tried various sizes, starting from the smallest and eventually working up to the largest that would fit through the hole. Using a pair of pliers on the shaft of the Allen key, she was able to get enough torque to turn the lock. It opened with a resounding clunk.

She grinned at the PC. 'There. My dad showed me how to do that when I was thirteen and had lost the keys to the shed.'

'That's pretty clever,' he conceded.

'Right, let's see what we have here.' Using the Allen key, she gently pulled open the cupboard door, which squeaked alarmingly. It revealed a steeply descending set of stone steps set in a rough whitewashed stone corridor. There was a stub of candle in a niche, along with a set of electrical cables strung along the ceiling. There wasn't much headroom.

'Right, I'm going down,' she said.

'It should be me, ma'am.'

'It's all right, I'm not expecting to find anybody down there. He'll be long gone. Besides, you're too wide to fit down there.'

Borrowing the PC's more powerful torch, she went down the steps, holding onto the roof. After five feet of descent, the corridor turned sharp right to a T-junction. To the right was an alcove over a grating that seemed to drop a long way. Cold damp air drifted up. To the left was three feet of corridor and a solid-looking metal door, unbolted, with a latch. Through it she could distinctly hear the babble of voices. The nightclub.

She lifted the latch and eased the door open. It moved easily, and opened into a storeroom stacked with aluminium beer kegs almost to the ceiling. She made her way through, squeezed past the kegs, up a wooden staircase, and surprised the PC who was on guard in the nightclub.

Talantire wanted to see the nightclub's CCTV footage before leaving. She sat with the manager in his cramped and untidy office to have a look at what had been recorded in the previous hour. It was a modern system and the images were clear. They quickly found what they were looking for in a camera positioned to oversee the drink storage area. At 8:05 p.m., a tall man wearing a hooded jacket and gloves was captured by this camera, seemingly on his way to the gents' toilet, but then passed under the device and right, out of sight. The manager explained this would take him to the metal door, which he had assumed was sealed from the other side. But she knew this was the same passageway that she had exited from, and which led to the Dimpsy. They fast-forwarded through the next hour, ignoring the typical nightclub customers in their evening finery as they came and went to the toilets, and then the same camera caught the man hurriedly returning at 8:47 p.m. It coincided with the time that Talantire had had her encounter in the chapel.

'You recognise this man?' she asked. His face could not be seen, but he moved a little stiffly.

'Yes. He asked for a cup of tea, shortly after we opened. We don't do tea but I served him a soft drink and he complained bitterly about the price. He seemed to know a bit about the history of the place. He told me his cousin used to work here when it was a printworks.'

Talantire nodded. 'That's great. Can you copy last week's records onto a data stick, and I'll have an officer come round to collect them.'

She looked at her watch. It was after ten. The Black Bull Harriers would be back in the pub by now, with the warm glow of a 10k run behind then. All she could do now was go home, and hope for an undisturbed sleep. But it wasn't to be. She dreamed of crucifixes, and awoke from a nightmare about darkened chapels seething with monsters.

Chapter 16

First thing on Friday morning, Talantire arrived to find the Prince of Darkness sitting at her desk. He swivelled round in her wheeled chair.

'Morning, Jan. I heard you tangled with some shadowy intruder last night.' DI Lockhart grinned at her, and as usual she couldn't help smiling back into that handsome face.

'Yes, it was a bit scary for a while.'

'Well, you're in luck. The nightclub manager forwarded all the relevant CCTV by two a.m. and we can actually get a look at who it was.'

She looked over his shoulder, breathing in his musky scent, as he pulled up the video programme and clicked on the red memory tab on the time bar. The CCTV footage showed a tall and intimidating-looking man, sipping from a glass. He had dark and very deep-set eyes, thick dark eyebrows and a mane of iron-grey hair.

'Do you recognise him?'

'No, but I'd lay you a pound to a penny that he is Gawain Entwistle. He's about the size of the figure that I saw in the Dimpsy. If that's the best image, let's get a screenshot and I can send it to Ferris at Special Branch. Maybe that will persuade them to cooperate with us.'

'What about publicising it?' he asked.

'No, not for now at least. Could you imagine the headlines? "Notorious crucifix killer on the loose." There are enough people who remember the original killing to be absolutely terrified. It'd be a witch-hunt, with vigilante gangs trying to hunt him down and kill him. However, I am going to make sure every single officer knows what Entwistle looks like. We've got an incident room meeting set for nine a.m.' She looked at her watch. Just over an hour to go.

'Do you think that the original murderer is also the killer we are looking for?'

'Well, his DNA is on the murder weapon, and on the Dimpsy's door handle. They certainly can't deny that he is here,' Talantire responded.

'That's a slippery lawyer's answer, if you don't mind me saying,' Lockhart said.

'Yes it is, isn't it?' She laughed. 'But in my gut, I have to say that I don't think he's our killer. It would be too neat. Besides, though his DNA was on the crucifix, it wasn't anywhere else at the crime scene, and someone else's was.'

'So why is he down here?' Lockhart asked.

'I don't know. Curiosity, maybe, once he heard of the new murder. Or perhaps the Dimpsy has a magnetic attraction for him. It certainly seems to exercise a hold on plenty of others.'

'Including you, so it seems. Going in there, on your own, at night seems a bit risky.' He rotated her chair backwards and forwards. 'And you've done it twice.'

'Richard, there are questions to be answered.'

'You sound just like Pavel, about the crucifix,' Lockhart said.

'What's he been up to?' Talantire asked. Her eyes strayed to the CSI office.

'He came in last night at around ten, and locked himself in there with the blinds down.'

Talantire narrowed her eyes. 'But Pavel wasn't rostered on nights! The Exeter crew had the CSI duty last night.'

Lockhart shrugged. 'Well, he was still here at midnight when I went out to attend a shout at Bude, but had gone by the time by I got back at two thirty.'

Talantire got up and tried the CSI room door. Locked.

'You could always smash the window again,' Lockhart called out to her, and began to laugh.

Talantire didn't see the funny side and went to fetch the keys from the desk sergeant downstairs. By the time she had come back up and opened the door, she had convinced herself that Pavel himself might be lying dead on the floor with the crucifix stuck in him. But in fact the room looked tidy. She checked the log, which showed no fresh examinations of the cross. She crouched at the security cabinet and tapped in the code. Opened the door.

It was still there, in its knife container.

The incident room was packed for the nine thirty meeting. With Talantire were Maddy, Primrose and Dave, along with Pavel from CSI. Talantire's boss, Detective Superintendent Michael Wells, was there too, along with Inspector T. P. Carnegie and a dozen uniforms. She had put up a series of whiteboards in the main conference room, dotted with pictures and notes, many of them connected by arrows.

'All right everybody, in summary we have some pretty solid forensic evidence. Just over a week ago, an intruder was let into Bluebird Cottage, or at least got in without forcing an entry, and then stabbed to death the woman he found there. That at least is incontrovertible,' she said, pointing to a series of photographs taken at the crime scene and a couple of images of the murder weapon. 'Everything gets more complicated after that.'

Nuttall chuckled and whispered to Primrose, 'You're telling me.'

'The dead woman was carrying identity documents in the name of Mrs Ruth Lyle, including the original birth certificate that would originally have been given to the family of our first murder victim. She also seems to have dentition that matches young Ruth Lyle, as evidenced by records of the school dental examination in 1972. However, post-mortem records show incontrovertibly that our victim was born a man.' She pointed to photographs that had been taken by the pathologist, of the internal scarring. 'Efforts to find out who she really was are ongoing—'

Wells interrupted. 'Jan, are we absolutely certain that the grave of the 1973 victim actually contains her remains?'

'It is our assumption,' Talantire said. 'The victim's mother is still alive and an exhumation, for understandable reasons, would be our last resort. Of course that crime pre-dated DNA testing, but we have no reason to believe that the actions of the police surgeon and the coroner of the time were anything other than professional. To switch a body is a substantial conspiracy, and even if it were to have occurred it would still leave us with the fact that our new murder victim was born a male.' She pointed to a picture of the young Ruth Lyle. 'This young girl was definitely born female. They cannot have been the same person.'

She pointed to a Gawain Entwistle's name on the whiteboard. 'We have to assume at this point that the forensic evidence is leading us towards a second crime by the original perpetrator. Since his release four months ago, we know he has a new name and a new life apparently a long way away, and is protected by a lifetime anonymity order. While it is conceivable that his DNA on the murder weapon is solely that remaining after the original crime, the fact that traces have also been recovered from the door handle of Bluebird Cottage shows that he must be in the area now. In fact, I'm pretty sure I ran into him last night. We've got some more DNA to test, including an empty crisp bag left by the bed, but I'm pretty confident.'

Talantire pointed to a still from the CCTV, printed out and attached to the whiteboard. 'This, we think, is him.'

'Looks like a murderer to me,' Nuttall said, folding his arms. 'Like the butler from the Addams Family.'

'Lurch,' said Maddy.

'Is there not an official mugshot?' Carnegie asked.

'I've asked, believe me,' Talantire said. 'Setting up a lifetime anonymity order is so unusual that they are very loath to destroy it, which is what releasing a photograph would do. Ferris from Special Branch says the decision has to go a long way up the Home Office.'

'The further up the better,' Nuttall muttered, then grinned, looking for anyone who got the joke.

'How are we supposed to catch him if we don't know what his name is now?' Carnegie asked.

'We have some reasonable lines of enquiry, don't we Maddy?'

'Yes, his aunt, Sheila Woodley, lives in Woolacombe,' Maddy said. 'We've interviewed her already, and because she didn't cooperate we've now got a search warrant for the house. If Entwistle visited anyone in the area, it's likely to be her.'

'What about your interview with Goswell?' Talantire asked Maddy.

'Now, that was interesting,' She described Goswell's recollection of seeing a band fronted by the young Victoria Carnegie. 'As far as we can tell, it was a month or so before the first murder in 1973.' There was some laughter at the back, presumably at imagining a local sixty-something MP as a 1970s amateur rock singer. 'I've put in a call to the MP's office, but they tell me she's away, so I'm awaiting a call back from her.'

'Keep on to her,' Talantire said. 'She may know something.'

'I'm fascinated by this murder weapon,' Wells said. 'I see that it is supposed to be some medieval artefact.'

Pavel Kaminski shook his head. 'It's an enticing idea, but I doubt it. I spent last night comparing it to the photographs from the historical society. I'm increasingly convinced the one we have is a replica. First, for an iron object of that age we would expect signs of corrosion, and second because the crossbar of the crucifix seems to be a little shorter than that in the original.'

Talantire hadn't heard this second point and asked him to explain.

'Well, in the original the crossbar is clearly a nail with a sharpened point. The version we have seems to have lost its point.'

'Perfectly describes the entire investigation,' Nuttall muttered, earning a glare from Talantire.

'So if this *is* a replica, then Entwistle must be our murderer, right?' she said. 'Because the only innocent explanation for his DNA being on it was if it was the original, and the trace survived from 1973.'

'It looks that way,' Kaminski said.

'That would be huge progress,' Talantire said. 'If he didn't already have an alibi. Courtesy of Special Branch.' She looked around, and got nothing but shrugs from her team.

'I invited Ferris,' Wells said. 'But he's got a meeting in London.'

'Right, Dave, tell us what you have to share,' Talantire said. 'Where are we with identifying our victim?'

Nuttall stood up and made his way to a flipchart. 'As you asked,' he said, flipping over the top page. On it was written: *Who is Mrs Ruth Lyle?* On the second page he flipped to was written: *Not the 1973 victim.*

'Two reasons for that,' Nuttall said. 'One, as we know, because he was male at birth. And, perhaps the most obvious, she was still alive up until a week ago. Which the 1973 victim was not.'

This produced some laughter in the room.

'C'mon Dave,' said Maddy. 'Tell us something we don't know!'

Talantire had been told what Nuttall was about to say and kept her counsel. The detective constable smirked and flipped another page. On it was written a giant question mark. 'I am now about to tell you who Mrs Ruth Lyle really is.' He took a red marker pen and with his back to the audience wrote on the flipchart underneath the question mark. He stepped aside to show what he had written:

Ruth Lyle = James Quince.

'That's nuts,' Maddy said. 'We've discounted that idea. For three years she lived in Liverpool while he lived in Aberdeen.'

'They were the same person,' Nuttall insisted.

'But you said yourself we've got witnesses to him living and working on the oilfields,' Maddy said. 'And we've got witnesses to her work in insurance in Liverpool.'

'True,' Nuttall said. 'But remember this. Quince worked three weeks on, two weeks off. Mrs Ruth Lyle's job was only part-time too. Logistically, it's quite possible that Quince was testing his female persona by living a separate parallel life, travelling back and forth between the two locations.'

'He had a beard!' Maddy said. 'Are you telling me he shaved and regrew it each time?'

'We've only got that one photograph of him with a beard,' Nuttall said. 'Asked to describe him, most of those on the same rigs that I've been able to talk to do not mention a beard.'

'I only heard this a few minutes before we were due to start,' Talantire said. 'But it does make sense. Mrs Ruth Lyle was invented by James Quince. She does not exist in any way that we are able to tell prior to the moment she appeared as his next of kin on his company pension.'

'He created her,' Nuttall said. 'It was a first in history: a woman who was of man born.'

'That's bonkers,' Maddy said.

'There's more,' Nuttall continued. 'Quince erases himself from history, when he conveniently disappears in a road accident in India in 1999 that is almost impossible for anyone to check.'

'Have you tried?' Maddy asked.

'Yes. There is a police report at the time about an oil tanker that crashed and killed at least twenty people in the state of Uttar Pradesh, and I have a translated copy of it. It was an inferno, with many of the victims completely unidentifiable. Likewise, there is a witness statement from Mrs Lyle that describes seeing him just before the accident walking into a restaurant that was destroyed in the blaze. There is also an insurance claim for repatriation of remains.'

'What about flight records?' Primrose asked. 'I thought you said there were separate flight records for the arrivals of Quince and Mrs Lyle in India? If there were, isn't that evidence that she existed?'

'You would think so,' Nuttall said. 'Certainly both individuals were noted as being on holiday from their employers in India at the same time. Mrs Lyle arrived on a BA flight from Manchester to Delhi on 9 January 1999. Quince arrived four days later on an Air India flight from Kathmandu to Delhi. The Indian embassy confirmed that they both had visas. And I agree, that this looks like evidence they both exist. But I realised it was quite possible for Mrs Lyle to have arrived on her passport in Delhi, to have then taken a train or bus from Delhi to Nepal, and then, using Quince's passport, to have flown back to Delhi again. Thus one person becomes two.'

'All the while changing clothes from male to female and back again,' Maddy said sceptically.

'Why would anyone do that?' Wells said. 'The gender reassignment operation, dental work, all this to-ing and fro-ing to make a convincing audit trail. Why would anyone so much want to become a person who is dead?'

Nuttall shrugged and looked at his boss. Talantire replied for him: 'That's the question none of us have an answer to. In the meantime, we've got a man with no name to find. Right, over to you, Inspector.'

Carnegie stood up. 'Right, everybody, as you've been told, this is the man we're looking for,' he said, pointing at the enlarged CCTV picture on a whiteboard. 'Born Gawain Entwistle, aged sixty-four, but now with a new name thanks to the Home Office. With luck, we'll find him at the aunt's house. He'll probably answer to his birth name, and when you arrest him you'll probably find his new ID.'

'Is he likely to be violent?' asked a smallish female officer.

'We should assume so,' Carnegie said, rubbing his hands together with what seemed like enthusiasm.

'Not so fast,' Talantire interrupted. 'As he has learning difficulties it would be worth going softly–softly to start with. Remember, he's had a lifetime in institutions, he's probably feeling lonely and lost. So I'd use brains not brawn.'

Carnegie looked at the wall clock. It was 10:38 a.m. 'Right. I want one team to Woolacombe, to his aunt's house, one team at Bluebird Cottage while CSI and contractors remove the dry-lining, and the rest on foot patrols around Ilfracombe. Is that clear?' He looked across to Talantire. 'Anything to add, Jan?'

'No. We'll catch up with you later. Good hunting!'

The assembled uniforms trooped out. It was a while later, when Talantire was looking through the latest forensic test results, that she became vaguely aware of Dave Nuttall, sitting the other side of Primrose, having a frustrating phone call. 'That's amazing, I'm really having trouble believing it,' he said. 'Okay, thank you anyway.'

'What's up Dave?' Talantire asked.

'I've been trying to track down Lorraine Parkes, the evidence officer for the 1973 case. Keith Howell said she should be around because she was only young, but she left the police in 1984 and, I've now discovered, drowned in 1988 in a canoeing accident at Llangollen in Wales.'

'And another one bites the dust,' muttered Maddy without looking up.

'This is crazy!' Talantire said. 'Do we know how Hogley died?'

'I don't know. But we could ask Howell,' Maddy said.

'There is bound to be up an obituary online,' Talantire said. 'He was the man who cracked the case, after all.'

'I've got it,' Primrose said, staring at her screen. '*The Times*, September 1992. It says here that he died after a short illness. No other details.'

173

'That's often the code for a heart attack,' Talantire said. 'Wigwam was in the force back then, he might know a bit more, I'll give him a call.'

Talantire got straight through to Carnegie, who was in a car on the way to Woolacombe. The answer wasn't what she expected at all. 'He fell off a ladder at home, and cracked his head on his patio. He died in hospital a few days later,' Carnegie said.

'Not really a short illness, then,' Talantire said.

'Well, it's a bit embarrassing for a top policeman to fall off a ladder, isn't it? He'd had a bit of a run of bad luck. His son had become a drug addict around that time – oh, and he was burgled. I think that's why he was on the ladder, putting up an alarm.'

'Did you know Lorraine Parkes?' she asked.

'The name is familiar but no. Why do you ask?'

She explained about the young officer's untimely death.

'I'm not sure what you're driving at, Jan.'

'Well, I'm not superstitious but three out of the four CID officers who I can trace that worked on the 1973 case are now dead. We've only got Keith Howell.'

'Best look after him, then,' Carnegie said.

'I know you were a young officer in Exeter in the 1980s. We're struggling to find any of the original evidence or case files for the 1973 case. Did you ever see them?'

'I do recall looking at them during training. Seeing the full gory details was like porn for a young police cadet.'

'The trouble is none of it is around any more. Unless it's in that lock-up on the industrial estate. We've got three PCSOs wading through it, but I just thought for the sake of the budget I'd have one final go to see where the paperwork has got to.'

'Can't help you, I'm sorry,' Carnegie said.

Talantire thanked him and hung up. She had an idea. Maybe the burglary was the key. This was clearly a job for Nuttall.

At Talantire's request DC Dave Nuttall spent a precious hour of Friday morning looking through the local police database of recorded crimes from the 1990s. It was only sorted by date or conviction of a known offender, and hadn't been indexed by type of crime as more modern records had. But he eventually found what she was looking for. When Talantire saw it, she rang Howell in Spain and passed across the information that Carnegie had given them.

'I hope you're looking after yourself, Keith, you're the one survivor from the case. Make sure you look both ways before crossing the road.'

He laughed. 'I've never felt better, Jan. The move to Spain has done me a power of good. I never want to come back.'

Talantire had to agree that when she'd seen him on the Zoom call he'd looked a picture of good health. 'Okay, Keith, I've got a bit of a hunch here. Do you recall that George Hogley was burgled at home?'

Howell blew a sigh. 'Yes, I do recall something about it, it was in the 1990s I think. There were quite a lot of jokes about it in the force.'

'He lived in Croyde, on a quiet country lane,' Talantire said. 'And according to the records we've found, he and his family came back from a holiday abroad on 18 July 1992, and found his house and garage had been ransacked.'

'He was pretty upset about it, I do remember that,' Howell said.

'The statement here is pretty thin,' Talantire said. 'Some money was stolen, and a handful of apparently low-value jewellery that belonged to his wife. Plus some unspecified items of great sentimental value. Any idea what they were?'

'No. Hogley was old school. Very little emotional sharing in those days.'

'Well, here's my theory. It's possible that George Hogley kept some of the evidence from the 1973 case, and took it home as a souvenir. When he was burgled, he might have lost it. And whoever burgled him had possession of it.'

'Are you talking about the crucifix?' Howell asked.

'It's good to see your detective skills haven't deserted you,' Talantire said. 'That's exactly what I'm talking about. It's a plausible route for the evidence to have found its way back into circulation to be used in the second crime.'

'It's a bit of a long shot, isn't it?'

'Look at it this way. The only other plausible explanation is that someone here in the force is a murderer or at least an accomplice to one. Which theory would you prefer?'

'I see your point,' Howell said.

Chapter 17

Talantire ended the call with an impending sense of dread. The original investigation seemed to be coming to pieces in her hands: lost or stolen evidence, no original police reports, and most officers involved now dead. Yet the original suspect, the murder weapon, even the victim, were seemingly back in circulation.

An email popped up on her phone, and she seized on it. The latest sheaf of DNA tests had come back. Entwistle's DNA had turned up on the crisp packet and the plastic bag in Bluebird Cottage, as expected. Samples taken from Ruth Lyle's childhood teddy bear matched an unidentified sample on the murder weapon, alongside those identified as Mrs Ruth Lyle. That proved, as if there could have been any doubt, that the two Ruth Lyles were not the same person. You cannot, despite all rumours to the contrary, be murdered twice. However, the tests dashed one line of enquiry. Alan Lyle, the original victim's brother and the only person with a clear motive to kill Mrs Ruth Lyle, was in the clear. His was not the mystery DNA found at the crime scene.

She rested her head on her hands, hoping that all this would just go away. She closed her eyes for ten seconds, and then heard someone coughing gently nearby. She looked up and saw Primrose.

'Sorry to disturb, ma'am.'

'No need to call me ma'am. Jan is fine.'

'Okay. I've now restored all of the deleted files on Mrs Ruth Lyle's phone, and have finally been given access to the GPS data on the phone app, so that we can see everywhere she went for the last six months, if you'd like to come and see the maps.'

Talantire eased herself up and made her way over to Primrose's terminal. The young technician had created 180 maps, each covering in GPS a day in the life of their murder victim. Talantire clicked through them, moving back from the day of the murder, one day at a time. 'This is brilliant work. Of course it only tells us where the phone went. I know youngsters take their phones with them everywhere but it's not always true of older generations.'

Most of the maps showed movements in and around Ilfracombe, but Talantire looked more closely at the days when Mrs Lyle had left the area. There were some longer journeys, involving train trips to London, and right at the beginning of the six-month period a trip to Amsterdam for a week.

'We can cross-reference that to her passport, but I'm not sure it would get us anywhere. What about the deleted files?'

'Here they are,' Primrose said, switching the screen to a folder packed with hundreds of subfolders. 'They're mostly photographs, maybe 10,000 in total. There are lots of pictures of James Quince, and some images that appear to be old, and cover the gender-transition process. It does seem to prove that they were right about Mrs Lyle and James Quince being the same person. There is not a single picture of them together. There are also loads and loads of photos of old paperwork, which I haven't really had chance to look through. But there is this.' She clicked on a folder, which opened to show a series of pictures of young Ruth Lyle. Most were the best-known images in black and white used by the press, but there were colour versions too, including several that Talantire hadn't seen before.

'The datestamp on the images is in the last five years, but that is just when they were scanned in,' Primrose said.

'How did Mrs Lyle get more pictures than the press?' Talantire asked. 'Only the family should have these.'

'Maybe Ruth's mother gave them to her when they met, when she was impersonating the murdered girl,' Primrose said.

178

'Or maybe they were unreleased images from police records.' That, she knew, would be worse, but tied in to the loss of evidence that was already becoming apparent. 'Right, let's look at the transition process images,' she said.

Primrose clicked through a series of subfolders, and set a slide show for the images within. The pictures were seemingly taken in the same bedroom, but at different times, because of the altered light conditions. They showed a gradual change in James Quince's appearance over days and months. The earliest pictures had him with a full sandy-coloured beard and glasses, then clean-shaven and with different glasses. Then with make-up, including red lipstick and red nail varnish, then wearing a dress and necklace with eye make-up.

'He still looks like a man to me,' Primrose said.

'Yes,' Talantire said. 'Maybe just experimenting at this stage.'

The glasses disappeared in the next series, and the colour of the bedspread in the background was different. Then there were a shocking series of Quince with a bandaged face and huge bruises.

'I think he was beaten up,' Primrose said.

'Perhaps,' Talantire said. 'Or it could have been cosmetic surgery.' Sure enough, in the following images Quince's brow seemed softer, his eyebrows shorter and higher; but the most obvious change was to his cheeks.

'He never had those dimples before,' Talantire said. 'Show me the pics of young Ruth again.'

Once Primrose had flicked back to the file, it was clear that Mrs Lyle had similar cheek dimples to that of the child.

'It's amazing, isn't it, she's really trying to replicate Ruth in her entirety,' Primrose said.

Finally, there was a folder of images taken much later, which showed Mrs Ruth Lyle with flowing red hair to her shoulders, in her underwear, with a woman's body, broadened hips and a modest bust.

'Wow, that is amazing,' Primrose said. 'So much effort, and so much surgery.'

Talantire nodded. 'Hormones too, by the look of it. But what we don't know is why. The only thing that makes any sense is that it was she who killed young Ruth and is now trying out of a sense of guilt to somehow bring her back, as if the crime never took place.'

'That's crazy,' Primrose said.

'You have any other explanation?' Talantire asked.

'No. But then who killed Mrs Lyle?'

'Well, it appears not to be Alan Lyle, the one person with a motive,' Talantire said. 'Okay, take a look through the rest of the pics and document them. This is clearly a bit of a treasure trove.'

—

Talantire took a short walk outside the police station to clear her head. Smokers were as usual gathered around the back of the riot vans, enjoying a bit of springtime sunshine over a Friday lunchtime. Her phone buzzed. It was Maddy. She said: 'I'm patching through someone on a withheld number who claims to be Entwistle's shrink. Her name is Dr Sophie Weiss.'

'Hello, Dr Weiss,' Talantire said. 'I've been looking forward to this conversation for a long time. I'd been waiting in vain for Special Branch to forward me your name and details.'

'I'm speaking off the record, actually, Detective Sergeant Ferris knows nothing about this, nor does the Home Office.'

'That's fine, I can guarantee this won't go any further.'

'Thank you. As you know, conversations that I have with the client are protected under patient confidentiality. However, the one priority above that is a duty of care. So I think it might be useful for you to know that the client telephoned me this morning, from Ilfracombe. After having talked to him I rather fear for his safety, and have urged him to hand himself in.'

'Why is that?'

'Well, you won't be surprised to hear he is labouring under a lifetime of guilt for what happened in 1973. When he came to me a few days ago with news of another murder in his home town he was quite distraught. I have to say his mental state has regressed substantially and much of the work I have tried to do with him over the last three years, and that done by colleagues over previous decades, seem to have unravelled. We had been gradually working towards an appeal against the original conviction. His original defence was that he was guided in his actions by what he called the "dark angel of the Lord", who had appeared to him and guided his hand.'

Talantire vaguely remembering reading about this in one of the press cuttings. 'What did he mean by that?' she asked.

'He thought it was real. A manifestation, a physical presence. Of course you have to bear in mind that he is a highly religious individual. He remains utterly devoted to God and prays many times a day. Almost every time he comes for an appointment, my secretary tells me that he sits in the waiting room gabbling through the Lord's Prayer under his breath.'

'He sounds very vulnerable.'

'Oh, there's no doubt that he is. He professes to be a deeply moral man, and is always seeking guidance, but he finds himself utterly tainted by his past. I had encouraged him to try to relive what actually happened on the day of the crime, and, though I never completely succeeded, it is my professional opinion that someone else was there with him in 1973 when the crime was committed.'

'This so-called dark angel?'

'Yes. I think this was an actual person, not a fantasy.'

'Not a part of his imagination?'

'No, because he describes his hands being squeezed onto the weapon, which was forced down into the body of the victim, until the palms of his hands bled.'

'Stigmata.'

'Yes, indeed.' Weiss sounded impressed that Talantire knew about the bodily marks on hands and feet manifested by Christian mystics. 'That's exactly how he interprets it, as corresponding to the wounds of Christ. He believes it was the will of

God. I think he was very suggestible particularly to comments of a religious nature.'

'Does he have a name for this person?'

'No. I don't think he even remembers. It is simply the way that his memory has been transformed by devotion. He describes an abusive childhood. His father Arthur, the verger of the church of St James Without, was a cruel, cold man who detested his "backward" son. With his mother's encouragement the boy instead threw his hopes upon a holy relic, a crucifix made out of nails that was kept in the church.'

'And which turned out to be the murder weapon.'

'Yes, the client remembers his mother telling him she put this cross into his pram as a baby, to calm his crying. She told him she made him kiss it, because it would bring the power of the Lord into him. He had what he terms "fits" as a child, I suppose they may have been seizures, in which he saw visons. In the last decade he has started having seizures again, quite serious ones that have been diagnosed as epilepsy.'

'Why is he back in Ilfracombe?'

'I think he wants to find the crucifix. It's never out of his conversation for long.'

Talantire closed her eyes, and blew out a huge sigh. 'He won't get his hands on it. It's in safe keeping with us.'

'That's what I told him, but his reply was interesting: "It always finds the seeker, as it has done for 1,000 years."'

'Not if I can help it,' Talantire muttered.

'But is it not true that the item was under lock and key before?'

'Yes, and it was lost, but long after the case was finished. That isn't going to happen again.'

'Well, let's hope not,' Dr Weiss said.

'We know that Gawain was released under the name Gary Endle, but it was changed again. I'm afraid I have to ask: what is Gawain's name now?'

She hesitated. 'I'm sorry, I cannot tell you.'

'Look, if we are to find him before he gets hurt, we need all the help we can get.'

'I get that, but I'd lose my Home Office accreditation and be frozen out of the profession.'

'We won't say where we got the information. You can trust me.'

'Very few people know who he is, and the information could easily be traced back. So, I'm sorry, but I can't take the risk.' Her voice broke, and Talantire heard what sounded like a tearful sob. 'I'm so worried that something terrible is going to happen to him.'

'What specifically did he think would happen?' Talantire was conscious that she was turning the tables on the psychiatrist, drawing out her fears.

'He described his last seizure to me. He was reading the Bible, something he does every day, and he suddenly lost all track of time. He didn't know the year, yet alone the day or time. He felt remote, as if there were a transparent membrane between him and reality, with a strong sense of déjà vu. This is the classic description of an aura associated with an epileptic seizure. In his case it had one quite specific manifestation. With him in this little timeless bubble he still sees the dark angel, holding out the crucifix to him.'

'Does he describe what this angel looks like?'

'Yes, a big imposing man, wearing a white clerical vestment over black clothing. He has long dark hair, a moustache and dark eyes, but is made up like a woman, with black fingernails.'

'Black with dirt or varnished?'

'I don't know.'

'You're sure this is not simply a fantasy? It sounds like a dark version of Christ.'

'Yes. I wondered whether he'd seen or visited the black madonnas in Spain, but I doubt it. But the Virgen del Pilar from Zaragoza and the Virgen de Guadalupe from Extremadura seem to be based on similar religious fantasies. Seizures are strongly associated with visions, and that has been true throughout history. In fact I took my doctoral thesis on the association between religious ecstasy, epilepsy and the visions of saints.'

'So we shouldn't take this at face value,' Talantire said.

'No, but I would still take it very seriously. Remember this, Detective Inspector. Something doesn't have to be real for the fervent belief in it, if widely enough shared, to have world-shaping consequences. Every one of the world's great religions are built upon stories that in the modern scientific world we have trouble taking seriously. Nevertheless, they not only create their own reality for their own believers but shape the world in which the rest of us have to live, whether we believe or not. We have thousands of years of human history to attest to this.'

'I take your point, but I still haven't a clue whether this dark angel is flesh and blood or not.'

'Neither have I,' Dr Weiss said. 'But if my client is completely convinced it is real, then we can best predict his actions by going along with it.'

As soon as they got off the phone Talantire went back to her desk and googled Dr Weiss. She turned out to be based in Berwick-upon-Tweed, by the Scottish border. Assuming this was where Entwistle had been resettled, it would certainly mean a long journey by bus to Devon. She forwarded the call details to Primrose and asked her to dig up the psychiatrist's withheld number, then get a list of all the numbers that had rung it from the Devon area in the last couple of days. There weren't many phone boxes left, and Talantire was pretty sure she could find which one Entwistle had been using.

She was interrupted by a phone call from Graham Dodds, one of the CSI technicians who were overseeing the dismantling of the interior walls of Bluebird Cottage. Dodds, normally a sober individual, was excited, and the tale he had to tell was compelling.

Five minutes later Talantire was on her way to Ilfracombe. It was 2:30 p.m.

She parked halfway up Mercer Lane, as near as she could get, and almost ran the last hundred yards. She signed in with the PC by the crime scene tape and entered Bluebird Cottage through a CSI tent. Waiting for her there in his hooded Tyvek suit was Graham Dodds, the technician who had rung her.

'You've really got to take a look at this,' he said.

'I can't wait,' she said, wriggling into full protective gear. He then led her into the building, where Tyvek-suited technicians were clearing up under dazzling lighting. The carpets had been rolled up to reveal the original flagstone floor, and most of the dry-lining covering the walls had been removed and ferried to a couple of builders' bags, which sat by the entrance to the kitchen. A lightweight folding table sat on a plastic sheet in the centre of the room. On it was every piece of evidence they had found: a partially shattered Bic ballpoint pen, a few ancient cigarette ends, the dried and cracked remains of a used condom, a collection of hairs and a fragment of a Polaroid photograph.

Talantire looked at the image and drew a sharp intake of breath. 'Amazing. Where did you find this?' she asked.

'Just here,' he said leading to the central column, which supported the vaulted roof, and was now shorn of its dry-lining. He crouched down. The mortar at the base of the pillar had a crack, credit-card thin, around part of the base.

'On its edge, deep in this gap. There was all sorts of crud around there, paint chips, dust. The stuff we couldn't reach with tweezers we vacuumed out. And that's when this came up.'

She looked around and could in this intense light now more clearly see scratches and discolorations on the flagstones. 'These four areas presumably are where the legs for the original stone altar were.'

'I think so,' Dodds said, standing up. 'And up here on the column above is where the crucifix was originally mounted. It matches the position on photographs that we have.'

Talantire looked where he was pointing. There was a rudi-mentary iron mounting cemented into the column, which had previously been masked by the dry-lining. 'Have you Blues-tarred this area too?' she asked.

'Yes, just before I rang you.' Dodds turned to his crew and told them he was dimming the lights. The moment he did so, the original gloom of the Dimpsy Chapel reasserted itself. Gradually, a constellation of tiny blue points of light appeared. They were thickest right in front of her, on the column, and spattered on the flagstone floor. There were just a very few smaller dabs further away, thin crescents that added slivers of moon to the galaxy of light.

'Bloody footprints,' Talantire said, pointing at the arcs. 'These are all from the original crime, because that entire area was under carpet at the time of the second killing.'

'Yes, it's incredible isn't it?' Dodds said. 'What we can pluck out from the past with modern forensic techniques. Those furthest dots, by the way, right up into the vaulting, are likely to have been blood carried on the feet of flies. That's how sensitive this stuff is.'

'Can we get any DNA from it, do you think?'

'It's possible. Certainly, I have high hopes that the hairs retrieved from the same gap could give us some ID.'

Talantire wondered if it was really possible to reinvestigate the 1973 killing with what had emerged in the last twenty-four hours: new bloodstains uncovered, potential sources of DNA and a scrap of a photograph. Would these now confirm that Gawain Entwistle was guilty all along or that he was innocent?

She looked at the Polaroid again. It was the torn-off bottom right-hand corner, and showed a woman's partially naked torso, with a curve of breast visible under a mauve blouse on the right-hand side, and just at the tear on the left-hand side a fuzz of what could have been pubic hair. But the picture was dominated by a masculine-looking hand, gripping the crucifix that had now become so familiar to her. Most of the murder weapon was lost above the tear, but she recognised the serpentine blobs of lead that marked the feet of the Christ figure. The point at the bottom of the cross was dimpling the woman's stomach. But that wasn't the thing that most gripped her. It was the fact that, on the three visible male fingers, there appeared to be nail varnish.

And it was black.

Chapter 18

Talantire needed to step outside after this revelation. She made her way out of the building, through the CSI tent, then emerged into the street. As usual there were a dozen or so spectators, chatting and taking selfies by the crime tape. Still wearing her Tyvek suit, hooded up and masked, she was a perfect photographic subject. She leaned against the wall catching a little bit of the watery April sunshine. According to Dr Weiss, Entwistle had described a vision, a dark angel with black nail varnish. It had sounded like nothing more than the product of his fevered imagination. But now there was photographic evidence to back it up.

The female body in the Polaroid was presumably Ruth Lyle, but the male-looking hand was a mystery. Black nail varnish on a man wasn't so uncommon now, but fifty years ago it was rare, surely. It reinforced the idea that Quince, toying with gender reassignment, was the man connected with this crime most likely to wear nail varnish.

But if Quince was the original murderer there were going to be forensic problems. As Mrs Ruth Lyle, his DNA was already all around the current crime scene – as victim. To prove Quince was there at the original crime, his DNA would also have to be found in places only now revealed by the removal of interior cladding.

Talantire moved back inside to speak to Dodds. She found him kneeling over a section of flagstone flooring.

'Graham, just want to double check that you have been DNA-sampling all these recovered objects?' she asked.

He clambered to his feet and turned to her, looking over his mask, clearly needled that she doubted his professionalism. 'Yes of course, it's standard practice. We took a sample from each of the objects you saw before we picked them up, including the cigarette butts and the Biro. Naturally, we did the condom too. Of course some of them, such as the fag ends and the scrap of Polaroid, have been whirling around together in the vacuum cleaner, so there is a chance of cross-contamination between them.'

Talantire thanked him and made her way over to the evidence log on the table. Each sample was clearly marked with a location and a photographic reference number. Dodds followed her, and she could hear his suit rustling behind her.

'This is great,' she said. 'You see my major line of enquiry is that the victim of the second crime is the perpetrator of the first, and the only way to disentangle the many samples of Mrs Ruth Lyle's DNA in this building is to make sure we do not mix up those two types. I've got to persuade the Crown Prosecution Service that our evidence logging is top notch – and, thanks to you, it is.'

Dodds pointed to the ceiling. 'That's the only place where we won't be sure,' he said. 'What was carried up there by last week's flies can't be distinguished from what flies may have left there fifty years ago.'

At that point she got a call. Someone had been camping in Holy Trinity churchyard. A sleeping bag, a Thermos flask and a change of clothing had been found. Along with a Bible. She was pretty certain whose it was.

–

Talantire de-suited, ran to her car and drove the short distance from Mercer Lane to Church Hill. The brooding stone silhouette of Holy Trinity dominated the skyline. She was met at the entrance to the churchyard by a uniformed PC and three young volunteers wearing hi-vis and strimming gear. They told her the story of having started work clearing the overgrown north side of the graveyard when they came across what was clearly a sleeping place.

Talantire unloaded her go-bag of forensic kit and followed them as they led her up a steep incline through a graveyard crowded with mossy stones, very few of them recent. Many of the graves were overgrown with nettles, bindweed, ragwort and goosegrass. One of them pointed out the grave that belonged to a man who had fought with the Kaiser on Ilfracombe beach when they were both young men. It was right at the back, in the shade of a sycamore tree and close by railings that led to a sharp embankment down to Church Road. Beyond that grave was what, Talantire saw, had been a very cosy encampment. The sleeping bag was basic but seemingly quite new. A T-shirt and boxer shorts looked to have been discarded, along with a pair of very large socks. The Thermos flask lay on its side, and Talantire knelt down to do a gel lift from the plastic cup and metal cylinder.

'That's going to be pretty much perfect for fingerprints,' she said.

The Bible, a compact edition little bigger than a cigarette packet but with the thinnest of pages, she tested for DNA.

'So am I right in saying that nobody saw anyone?'

The volunteers shook their heads. 'We started strimming over there,' the woman said. 'And obviously we were making a racket as we worked our way up, so he had plenty of chance to make an escape.'

'I take it there's no CCTV at the church?'

They shook their heads. She thanked them and headed off. Their fugitive was proving adept at escaping, but they would catch him. She just hoped it wouldn't take too long. It was 3:30 p.m. and she wanted to have him in custody today, before the weekend, when uniformed resources were always harder to muster. Where was Entwistle?

Reverend Neal Vaizey was thinking the same thing. He was sitting in his Nissan Micra in the car park by Ilfracombe Harbour, staring at *Verity*, the huge statue of a pregnant woman with upraised sword and scales of justice sculpted by Damien Hirst. The sixty-foot-high figure, based on a Degas sculpture of a young girl, wasn't to his taste, particularly the cut-away anatomical sections. Nevertheless, every time he looked at it he couldn't help thinking how it symbolised Ruth Lyle, that helpless innocent who had trusted too much. He blinked away the memories, and his own guilt. If only he'd been able to do more. That was why now, half a century later, he wanted to help rebalance those scales of justice, to put right what was still wrong.

After twenty minutes, he saw in the rear-view mirror the looming figure he had been waiting for. In his hooded jacket and woolly hat, and with a rucksack, Gawain Entwistle looked from a distance like a typical walker, one of tens of thousands who visited the resort every year. Perhaps a little taller than many, and with a distinctive stiff gait. He had spotted the car, and made his way over.

Vaizey opened the passenger-side door for him, and Entwistle clambered in. The seat had already been set back to its maximum for the required legroom.

'Right, we should get out of here,' Vaizey said, peering around him. 'I've seen quite a few police patrols.'

'It's good of you to give me a lift. Thank you,' Entwistle said. His voice was deep, slow and almost mechanical. 'Thank you again.'

'Well, I want to help you. No need to keep thanking me, I'm happy to do it.' Vaizey had already given Entwistle a lift to see his aunt. 'But I think you should lie low now.'

'What about the cross?'

'Frankly, Gawain, I think we should ease back on that. I've tried my best to get a look, but I can't keep asking. It looks suspicious.'

'Thank you. Thank you again.'

'Have you removed all your camping gear?'

'No. I had to run.'

'They would have found you, you know. You can't keep camping out.'

'I can't stay with Auntie Sheila.'

'I know. And I've been thinking. I've got space at the rectory.'

'Thank you,' Entwistle said, staring out of the window. 'I'm grateful.'

Vaizey glanced across at him. 'So what about an appeal? Going to the police.'

'I'm scared.'

'Yes, you said. But there really isn't any other way, is there?'

'What about the second murder? Was she really called Ruth Lyle?'

'Yes,' he said cagily.

'Risen from the dead, and slain by the enemies of God.'

Vaizey creased his face in doubt. 'Well, I shouldn't go hunting for too many biblical parallels, Gawain.'

'They might think I did it.'

'They might well. But you weren't here, were you Gawain? You didn't arrive until Saturday, did you?'

Entwistle ferreted in his pocket and produced an already tatty bus ticket, which he waved towards Vaizey.

'That's it? It's not much of an alibi is it?'

'Dr Weiss knew I was still in Berwick-upon-Tweed. Can I ring her from your house?'

'Yes, of course.' Vaizey put the car into gear and pulled away. Well, the die was well and truly cast now.

–

Victoria Carnegie was in her constituency office in Lynton, holding her mobile phone in her hand. After a frustrating series of calls the Home Office had finally officially confirmed what was in the papers: that the convicted murderer Gawain Entwistle had indeed been released four months ago and was living under a new identity. She had been informally tipped off weeks before, but only now was someone willing to go on the record. She leaned through the door to her receptionist and said: 'Right, Sharon. Hold my calls please.'

'The police rang again. I said you were out.'

'If they ring any more, just remind them I'm up in London for the weekend,' she said in a conspiratorial whisper. Sharon looked uncomfortable, so she added: 'Don't worry, I will return all messages on Monday.'

She closed the door that separated her office from that of the receptionist. She then tapped out her brother's mobile number. He answered and she said: 'Wigwam, is this a good time? Well, never mind, I'll be brief. I'm hearing rumours that Entwistle is not only released, but is now back in the area. Was this something you were aware of?' The long silence told her almost everything she needed to know. His response, when it came, was couched in that detestable officialese of the reflex bureaucrat. 'Can't you just answer the question, Wigwam? No, I'm not going public with it. But I'm concerned about the safety of my constituents.' Another long-winded response came, laden with caveats. 'Yes, but the man could be anywhere,' she said. 'This is an outrage. People need to sleep safe in their beds at night.' She paused as he replied. 'No, I'm not practising making a speech, I just want to know.'

She hung up and looked out of the window. What she hadn't told him was that she had been sounded out by the prime minister to become a junior minister at the Home Office at the next reshuffle. With the responsibility for crime, of all things. There was a huge danger here, and it was out of her hands. A convicted killer as notorious as Entwistle once again on the loose in her own constituency could be a catastrophe, politically. He had to be caught, and quickly. But there was no sign of that happening. A policing disaster could never be ruled out. It would rub off principally on Lionel as commissioner, but might taint her too. She couldn't afford that. That obdurate detective Talantire seemed to be determined to follow some murkier lines of enquiry. Perhaps it was time to call in some favours. She made a call and left a message.

Now she had prepared the ground, she needed to destroy some evidence, just in case. From her personal filing cabinet she took a slim manilla file and, from it, an aged brown paper envelope. In it was a letter sent to her thirty-odd years ago, accompanied by a series of aged yellow newspaper cuttings, along with a photocopy of a fifty-year-old photograph. That picture, reputationally deadly, was a reminder of who had the power. She had hung on to it for years, but now knew what had to be done, what should have been done weeks ago. She stuffed the letter, picture and cuttings back into the envelope, walked out into reception, and fed them both into the shredder. She was aware that Sharon was eyeing her quizzically, especially when she detached the almost empty plastic bin from the shredder.

'It's all right, I'll do that, Victoria,' Sharon said.

'I'm on my way out anyway,' she replied. 'Oh, could I borrow your lighter for a moment?'

The receptionist handed it across. Victoria walked out of the office, down the steps and into the enclosure at the side of the office where the wheelie bins were kept. She tipped out the shredder bin onto the ground, took out the lighter, and set the fist-sized mass of shredded paper ablaze. It quickly flared and then died down. She stamped out the embers, hoping the smoke wouldn't damage her court shoes. When she returned, and passed back the lighter, Sharon asked, 'More hate mail from the trolls?'

Victoria thought for a moment. 'Actually, yes, in a manner of speaking.'

'Finally I am getting somewhere,' Nuttall said. He lifted up a sheet of paper. 'The Exeter University alumnus office came good with a list of everyone who studied with James Quince, and I've been working through it over the last few days. I didn't get much from the fellow students in geology, but I found two female friends from his first year, Jenny Clarke and Angela Howard. And they both say the same thing. Something happened to him in his second year, during the spring term.'

'Would that coincide with the date of the murder?'

'Yes it would, but neither of them drew that connection. They say he missed a lot of classes, was absent a lot and became quite withdrawn. One of them believes that Quince had been having a relationship with someone outside the college, which ended badly.'

'Any more detail?'

'Only one, but it's pretty significant. One of these women remembers that he was a regular visitor to Ilfracombe. And in ten minutes, if you've got a moment, you can join me in a Zoom call with her.'

—

Angela Howard was a silver-haired sixty-eight-year-old grandmother, a retired academic with the Open University. Over a Zoom link from Nottingham, she described to Talantire and Nuttall what she recalled about her former boyfriend James Quince during their brief time together in Exeter. They had met at the freshers' party, then dated on and off for a few weeks in their first term.

'So what kind of person was he?' Talantire asked.

'Oh, he was a very sweet young man: sensitive, intelligent, emotionally open, but lacking in self-confidence. Not at all macho, and quite unlike most of the male geology students. Quite good-looking in a Pre-Raphaelite kind of way, too.'

Nuttall's face furrowed as he tried to imagine this. Talantire continued: 'Did he talk about his childhood at all?'

'Well, you could hardly stop him! He had a very troubled upbringing. After my conversation with DC Nuttall here I looked in my diaries, just to be sure. He had told me he was fostered at the age of six, and had seven wonderful years with this loving couple in Hampshire. He had only just taken their name when they died in a road accident. It obviously traumatised him – he was just thirteen. He was transferred to a children's home, where he was bullied and miserable, but eventually managed to get the grades to go to university.'

'Do you know his birth family's name?'

'No. But he did tell me that just a few months before coming to Exeter, when he turned eighteen, he tried to make contact with his birth mother. She rejected him. He was wounded by it, and I imagine that he was always damaged. He once told me, "I'd like to be somebody else." I told him that he was lovely just as he was.' She paused and looked away for a moment. 'I may have contributed to his hurt. I wouldn't sleep with him. He was a virgin, and I just thought that if I did, with all his other baggage, I would just become a huge emotional liferaft for him and I didn't want the responsibility when I'd just started college. Jamie was so desperately needy. He radiated it, which, at that age particularly, is such a turn-off.'

'Did you meet many of his friends at uni?' Nuttall asked.

'Well, he didn't have many at the start. I think he found it all a bit overwhelming. But he gravitated to women, who were kinder to him. Did you speak to Jenny Clarke?'

'Yes,' Nuttall said. 'She pretty much backed up what you've said.'

'Was he religious?' Talantire asked.

'Not as such. He was quite interested in the idea of religions, particularly Eastern ones. But not a believer, at least when I knew him. And music. He was a good classical pianist.'

'How did your relationship end?' Talantire asked.

'Well, after I'd made it clear I couldn't sleep with him, he sulked and I think he sought solace elsewhere. I started seeing someone else, and by the second year he'd drifted away, got a flat outside hall. So I just didn't see him.'

'So how did you know about the visits to Ilfracombe?' Nuttall asked.

'Oh, it wasn't from him directly. A female friend, I forget who, said she'd seen him with a girl in Ilfracombe. I just hoped that she, whoever she was, would have made him happy.' She looked away, a hand to her mouth as if to prevent an outpouring of guilt. 'Then of course, many years later, I read that he'd died in India. It was very sad.' She looked at the two detectives. 'Unless of course, he didn't die in India. I suppose you wouldn't be asking me all these questions unless he was still alive.'

'We really can't say anything at this stage—' Nuttall began.

'—Look, if it's about this murder, he couldn't kill anybody – you do understand that don't you?' she said. 'Jamie was the gentlest soul. He just wanted to start all over again, in life. To shrug off his past like a worn-out overcoat, and escape.'

'Thank you, Mrs Howard, this has been very useful,' Talantire said, then ended the call. She asked Nuttall to get on to Hampshire Social Services, to see if the foster parents who died could be traced, and in turn the birth mother's name. Given that this was the 1960s, it was a long shot. They'd probably have the same problem that they had encountered with the 1973 killing. Then she remembered something else.

'Dave, the books and wall-hangings in Bluebird Cottage seem to show Quince's interest in religion was sustained,' Talantire said. 'Has anyone been through all those books?'

Nuttall shrugged. 'I flicked through, looking for any annotations, correspondence or papers, but I didn't read the books themselves. I'll take a closer look at them when I get a chance.'

Talantire looked through the list of uncompleted tasks, which, like the examination of Mrs Lyle's book collection, seemed to stretch out to the horizon. She walked across to her sergeant's desk. 'Maddy? I see here that we didn't formally request any documents that Keane Wale Harbyttle might have held on Mrs Lyle's behalf,' she said.

'Keane didn't mention any,' Maddy replied.

'Well, he wouldn't, would he? It only invites us to ask to look at them.'

'I'll ring him,' Maddy said, with a shrug. 'But seeing as it's Friday afternoon they will probably be closed.' She rang the number and the receptionist told her that none of the partners were at the office on a Friday. Maddy turned back to Talantire. 'I have put in a request for any documents held for Mrs Ruth Lyle.'

'Good.'

'But don't hold your breath. Keane is going on holiday today apparently, she would have to refer it to him.'

Twenty minutes later an email dropped into the CID mailbox from the solicitors. 'Listen to this,' Maddy said "'To whom it may concern. Thank you for your enquiry. However, we are bound by legal professional privilege from revealing any documents that may or may not be held on behalf of a client. We refer you to the relevant paragraph of statute, which reminds you that this privilege overrides the power of a warrant." It's PP'd on behalf of Roger Keane.' She looked up at her boss. 'Is that true?'

'Yes, it is,' Talantire said. 'However, from what I remember from the legal course, the privilege is that of the client. If the client is dead, and we're trying to find who killed her, I recall that it would change things.'

'Sounds like we have to go to court to make the case,' Maddy said. 'And presumably with the backing from those higher up.'

'True. And likewise, we can get them if we suspect fraud, but that will never fly.'

'Awkward sods,' Maddy said. 'They won't even tell us if there even are any documents.'

'Nope. We'll have to add them to the list of awkward Arthurs.' And what a list it was: The Home Office, which clung on to the idea that Gawain Entwistle was going to be able to stay anonymous, the MP who wouldn't return their calls, the commissioner who was more interested in pushing his pet theories than trying to back her to solve the case, and the crime scene technician who thought the crucifix was a historical research project. Then, of course, Entwistle himself, who was somewhere in the area and lying low.

By seven, the CID office had emptied out of clerical staff, leaving just the three detectives and digital evidence officer Primrose Chen working quietly at their desks. Nuttall then left to re-examine Mrs Ruth Lyle's possessions, leaving Maddy examining key sections of the CCTV footage from the new camera opposite the door to Bluebird Cottage. She had marked up sections that showed that someone resembling Entwistle had come past on numerous occasions in the last few days, staying several minutes, even since a PC had once again been posted on the door.

'We captured him on the bus CCTV two days ago as well, presumably travelling in from his aunt, who's on that route,' Maddy said. 'The local plods searched her place this morning and found plenty of evidence he had been there, but he's clearly not any more.'

'Maddy, we really should be able to catch him,' Talantire said with a sigh.

'I'm sure if we could go public, we'd get sightings.'

'Yes, but we can't go public can we? Not without unleashing the fury of the Home Office. Wells told me he got a bollocking from the ACC this morning, for not reining me in.'

'He shouldn't even be so senior,' Maddy said. For such a forgettable individual, Assistant Chief Constable Jeremy Noone stirred up strong emotions. Parachuted in from fraud, he was reputed not to have left his desk in ten years. His nickname in the force was Jeremy No-one.

'Wells says he still backs me, but so long as Special Branch continue to give Entwistle an alibi the Home Office is holding firm. I'm not to go public.'

'So what next?' Maddy asked.

'We have to get inside his head. If we can't get to him we have to bring him in to us.'

'You mean lure him in?'

'Yes, set a trap. We just need the right bait.'

'What are you thinking?'

'Well, based on conversations with his shrink, Entwistle is fixated on this crucifix.'

'Like Pavel, then.'

'But not out of historical interest, more from a kind of religious ecstasy. It's personal. His mother used to put it in his pram when he was crying.'

'You're joking,' Maddy said. 'You shouldn't do that, with a baby.'

'It's certainly a sharp object.'

'I don't mean that. I mean there's lead on it, isn't there?' They retrieved the CSI office key from the desk sergeant, let themselves in and opened the safe. Part of Talantire was convinced that the crucifix wouldn't be there. But it was. Slipping on nitrile gloves, they lifted out the knife container and placed it on the desk.

'Yes,' Maddy said, looking at it. 'That's bound to be lead, given how old it is. It's poisonous, particularly for young kids, and you know how kids are for sucking things. No end of times at home I had to tell Neville not to leave his reels of lead solder about in front of the toddlers.'

'That could certainly explain Entwistle's developmental difficulties,' Talantire said.

'Or at least have added to them. Anyway, it's yet another victim for the bloody thing,' Maddy said, shuddering. 'Let's put it away.'

'Actually, I was thinking that this could be the bait.'

'What?'

'Look at it this way. Entwistle has come all the way down here, and has made several attempts to get back in to the Dimpsy Chapel. He's obviously looking for something – isn't it likely to be this? That's certainly what Dr Weiss believes, and she's the only person we know of who has spoken to him recently, and who has a chance of getting into his head.'

'So are you going to put it back in the building?'

'I don't know, I've got to think about it.'

'Apart from anything else, how are you going to let him know without announcing it to all and sundry?' Maddy asked.

'It was something Dr Weiss said. Entwistle believes that the crucifix finds its way to the seeker.'

Maddy rolled her eyes. 'If you believe that, Jan, you are as bewitched as the rest of them.'

Talantire steepled her hands over her nose as she stared down at the two simple nails and the leaden Christ figure. 'Maybe I am, Maddy. But I keep coming back to the facts: this thing was in police custody for years and, presumably after Hogley was burgled, it's found its way into the hands of a killer again.'

'Pavel thinks it might be a replica, though.'

'He does, but forensically we now know that's impossible,' Talantire said. 'We've got DNA traces on the murder weapon from the original 1973 victim. How did traces of young Ruth Lyle get there, if it isn't original?'

'And even Gawain's,' Maddy added. 'Given that he wasn't here in Ilfracombe at the time she died, it must have been from the original killing.'

'Exactly.'

Pavel hadn't been in today, and would not be on shift until Monday. But this afternoon he'd sent her an email from home. Now, at nine p.m., she finally opened it. The contents were amazing. He'd completely changed his mind, again.

Chapter 19

Pavel's email said that he had been working in his own time on the origins of the crucifix. He was now convinced that it *was* the original one, found in the Crusades. But more than that, he believed the nails it was made from were already a thousand years old when they came tumbling from the burning roof of the Accursed Tower at the siege of Acre.

There is a good possibility, both from the style of the nails and from what we know was stored in the treasury in that tower roof, that these weren't medieval roofing nails at all, but Roman. And if they were from the reliquary bestowed there by the church on behalf of St Helena, they could be from the cross on which Christ was crucified. The One True Cross.

Pavel had appended dozens of documents, including a *National Geographic* piece and numerous links to various historical websites. One was entitled the Iron Crown of Lombardy, and described how the Emperor Constantine had been given four nails from the crucifixion of Christ by his mother, St Helena. This artefact was still in place in the Monza Cathedral in Italy. Other nails, supposedly from the One True Cross, were kept in reliquaries in Germany's oldest church, the High Cathedral of St Peter, Trier. One link went to the website describing the properties of an ancient iron column in India, the Qutb Minar, which despite being nearly 2,000 years old looked like it had been made recently, so free was it from corrosion. In India's monsoon climate, that was not easy to explain.

At the bottom of the email, Pavel had copied across some text from a piece of scientific research at the Polytechnic

University of Milan, which had taken a sample from the iron pillar in India and found it to contain little or no sulphur or magnesium, as most cast iron does, but an unusually high proportion of phosphorus. Below that was a reference in a historical journal, claiming that the nails from the crucifixion likewise did not rust.

Pavel wrote, *They have the same pyramidal Roman cap, with a notch, as the ones used in the de Lisle Crucifix. I know it's not strictly relevant to the crime, but I think we may be in possession of a unique historic relic.*

Talantire looked up from her email and caught Maddy's eye. 'Pavel's completely lost the plot,' she said. 'He's now banging on about the murder weapon being part of the One True Cross.'

'Good grief. The trouble with that kind of thing is that, if enough people believe it, it has a way of becoming true. Like those images of the Virgin Mary that people see in their dinner.'

Talantire rubbed her face. 'We need him to keep his eye on the ball. I have enough aggro with this case as it is. God forbid that any of this should get out into the public domain.'

'Well, I'm going home, if that's all right,' Maddy said. 'I've got three kids who need attention, and I'm so tired that I'm going cross-eyed.' She eyed her boss, and then added, 'And Jan, you should go home too. I can see this case is getting to you.'

Talantire had to agree. She closed down her workstation and locked up the evidence cupboards, returning the key to the desk sergeant. DI Lockhart was around, somewhere, and there was an overnight DC on the public information line in Exeter. The case could tick over for a few hours without her presence. But tomorrow would be a big day.

–

It took most of Saturday to arrange, but the trap was almost ready to spring. Talantire and Maddy had spent hours on the phone to Entwistle's psychiatrist Sophie Weiss, and liaising with Northumbria Police to get a phone trace. Four p.m. seemed the right time. Talantire went into the CSI office, worked the safe combination and retrieved the crucifix in its knife container. She slid the box into a plastic carrier bag and came out to join Maddy. The two officers descended the stairs, greeted the desk sergeant as they departed, and entered the internal garage where the unmarked cars were kept, away from prying criminal eyes. They picked a bottle-green electric Renault that was rarely used, and, with the crucifix stored safely in the boot, Maddy hit the button to release the roller shutter. With Talantire driving, they headed for Ilfracombe on the B3230. It was one of the first genuinely warm and sunny days of spring, leaves in the hedgerows unfurling, and through the open window they could hear the trilling of skylarks.

Maddy looked at her phone. 'Still no luck getting hold of Roger Keane, at home or the office, only the receptionist. She now says he's on a family holiday in the Canaries for two weeks, and can't do anything until he gets back. Just what I always said about solicitors.' She folded her arms as if nothing more needed to be said on the matter.

'And we're still awaiting the DNA results from the various items found at the Dimpsy,' Talantire said. 'I'm told we should have fingerprint results, if any, later this afternoon.'

'I hope they manage to get something from that condom,' Maddy said, rubbing her hands in anticipation.

'I hope Wigwam has managed to get enough uniforms to stake the phone boxes out,' Talantire said. 'Even though there's only three.'

'Unmarked vans?'

'That what I asked for, so with luck Entwistle won't spot them. The previous time he rang was from his aunt's place,' Talantire said. 'But I don't think he would dare go there now.' She checked her watch. Not yet three. Dr Weiss had told her that Entwistle was a creature of habit, usually ringing her at four o'clock, in line with his twice-weekly appointments, though these had never been on a Saturday.

'Just ring her again,' Talantire said. Maddy rang Dr Weiss's number, and put the phone on speaker. She answered immediately.

'Everything all right your end?' Talantire asked.

'Yes. I'm not sure he will call, seeing as it's Saturday. But it's been four days now, and he does get agitated.'

'Just to remind you that we will be able to hear the call, and trace the number it came from. You won't be able to hear us, but we will ring straight afterwards.'

'Yes, I know. As I mentioned, because client–patient calls are privileged I'm going to keep the conversation to administrative matters, if I can.'

'Whatever you need to do,' Talantire said. 'Just so long as you mention the crucifix now being back in the Dimpsy Chapel.'

'I will, he's bound to ask.'

Talantire thanked her and cut the call. They were now coming down New Barnstaple Road. They headed left towards the High Street, then swung round the sharp bend right, next to Body Aware Pilates, down Fore Street, towards the harbour. There were a few tourists about, enjoying the sunshine, but nothing like the high-season crowds. Talantire was hopeful that something would emerge from this entrapment. They would either get Entwistle in person, or, if he rang from somewhere new, they would quickly be able to trace the call through the software that Northumbria Police had loaded onto Dr Weiss's phone.

Talantire parked in the harbour car park, within sight of the *Verity* statue and twenty yards from the phone box that Entwistle had used before. Lights flashed her from an unmarked grey Renault van nearby. She returned the greeting, and then saw the officer at the wheel slurping an ice cream. Not the brightest thing to do fifteen minutes before an interception.

All they had to do now was wait.

–

At four o'clock exactly, her earpiece clicked on to the sound of Dr Weiss's phone ringing. It was answered immediately, and the other voice on the line was very deep, and halting.

Hello, Dr Weiss.
Hello, Gary. How have you been?

Talantire and Maddy exchanged a glance at hearing Entwistle's secret assigned name.

Not very happy, but thank you for asking.

There was no background noise, no traffic, none of the echo that is common within a telephone kiosk. Maddy showed Talantire her iPad, on which the software was crunching the location. A mobile phone, unlisted, calling from within Ilfracombe.

'I thought he couldn't use a mobile,' Maddy said.
'Someone's taught him,' Talantire replied.
When are you coming back? Dr Weiss asked him.

I don't know, but thank you for asking. I need to find it. It's here somewhere.
The crucifix is back in St James now, did you know?

Maddy grinned and gave a thumbs-up to Talantire.
There was a long pause before he answered.
Is it?

Yes, I read it online.

Talantire nodded. That was intelligent. Entwistle apparently couldn't use the Internet. There was just one thing that she hadn't asked, that Talantire really hoped that she would.

So Gary, where are you staying? Have you got
somewhere comfortable?

Yes, thank you for asking. I've got my own
room with a comfortable bed, but there's no
window. I don't like it when there's no window,
because it's like before, like the special room in the
hospital.

Cell site triangulation had come through now, and was indicating Castle Hill less than three hundred yards from where they
were. Talantire flashed her lights at the grey van. She got an
answering response, put the car into gear and drove off out of
the harbour. The van followed. Maddy kept her eye on the cell
site map, but it was clear this was not going to be the kind of
precise location that you might get in the centre of a big city.
Ilfracombe was hilly, with lots of signal shadows, and there were
only four cell sites. The call between Weiss and Entwistle had
finished, but the signal arrow held steady. Five minutes later the
two vehicles were parked on Castle Hill. It was a steep residential street with lots of short side roads. At the signal bullseye
they stopped. On one side was a large zinc-roofed garage, and
on the other side an imposing Victorian house with extensive
gardens and a large bay window overlooking the harbour. The
plate on the brick gatepost said *Castle Hill Rectory*.

Talantire and Maddy stepped out of the vehicle and
approached the grey van, which had pulled up behind. Two
uniformed officers emerged and headed towards the zinc-
roofed building, whose entrance was in a lower side street, while
Talantire and Maddy opened the gate and climbed up towards
the door to the rectory. As they were doing so they saw a tall
gangly figure run from the back of the house across the garden
and vault down over a high garden wall into a side street.

'That's him!' Talantire shouted. The two detectives raced
back to the car, to see that Entwistle was now running down the
steep street, about fifty yards ahead of them. Talantire, the better

runner, headed after him, thankful that she had chosen to wear trainers. A chase had always been on the cards. Maddy headed for the car, started it and, heading downhill, soon overtook Talantire. Entwistle was eating up the ground with his long strides, and had pulled off his green hooded jacket. As Maddy slowed the Renault next to him, he tossed the jacket onto the car's windscreen, blocking her view. As the car slowed, Talantire overtook, and was soon only twenty yards behind her quarry. At Portland Street Entwistle raced across the road, oblivious to the traffic. He was only just missed by a lorry, which forced Talantire to come to a halt. The fugitive earned himself a long honk of air horns as he headed away down an alleyway between houses on the opposite side. Talantire set off in pursuit. She was realising that Entwistle knew this town like the back of his hand.

Running downhill is much less tiring than running up, but the trick is not to lose your balance. The alleyway soon gave way to steep descending stone steps set into the hillside, with a tremendous view over the harbour beneath. Entwistle took these four at a time, then used a handrail to pivot right at the bottom, where the path flattened out. Talantire arrived to find the narrow alley continued with a high laurel hedge on the left and a breezeblock wall on the right. She could hear Entwistle's footfalls in the next steep zigzag below. For a man of sixty-four, he was certainly fit. She sprinted to the corner, jumped down the next flight of steps in two quick leaps, and turned the corner left to see that the alleyway was now wider, but hemmed in by shoulder-high stone walls and shrubs beyond.

There was no sign of the fugitive.

Nor indeed of any of the uniformed officers, who should have been keeping up with her. She unclasped her PAVA spray, and on tiptoe peered over the walls, to the left, where there was nothing to be seen, and to the right. There she could hear heavy breathing, not just her own. Then she saw him, on high ground behind the upslope wall, lying on his side, behind a compost heap.

'Come on out, Gawain,' she said, softly.

He didn't move and his deep-set dark eyes bored into her.

'Come on, it's all over now.'

'I didn't do it,' he said.

'I know you didn't do it, Gawain. I know.' She smiled at him. 'We are here to help you.'

'Thank you, thank you very much. I didn't do it.'

By now, the two uniformed cops had caught up with her, one of them sporting a bloody gash in his cheek. 'Fell over,' he said by way of explanation. 'Ah, there's the bastard,' he went on, starting to climb the wall.

Talantire grabbed his arm. 'Wait,' she hissed.

'Don't send me back to the hospital,' Entwistle whispered.

'Come with us, we can get you a nice cup of tea,' said the other uniform, having picked up on Talantire's softly-softly approach.

Entwistle didn't move. Trying to climb the wall and shift him by force would be tricky, so Talantire tried one final gambit.

'We can let you look at the crucifix, Gawain. Then you can tell us all about it.'

His eyes widened. He began to crawl towards her, in the same stealthy fashion that she had seen, or sensed, inside the chapel.

–

Gawain Entwistle sat, handcuffed and cautioned, in the back of the Renault next to Maddy. Talantire realised that he was only two feet away from the object he most craved, which was in the boot. The nearest place to take him was Ilfracombe police station, less than half a mile away. The aged 1970s building was staffed for less than twenty hours a week but it did have one interview room, though it had probably not been modernised since the day Entwistle was sentenced. Perhaps he would feel at home there.

They arrived and brought him in. The place smelled musty, with a hint of stale coffee. There was a working tape recorder, which Maddy set up, while Talantire brought in the carrier bag and stowed it in a cupboard in the main office. The two uniforms who had followed in the van stood with Entwistle in the corridor until everything was ready. He could be heard thanking them, though what for was unclear. A search of him had revealed two keys: the big medieval key to the front door of St James Without, and the smaller key for the passageway that led through to the nightclub.

'Should we offer him a solicitor?' Maddy asked. 'Seeing as we arrested him.'

'No. I don't anticipate charging him with anything and the fewer people who know about this the better. If he admits either crime, then we'll call a brief.'

They brought the tall figure in, and his eyes searched the room. They knew what he was looking for. Talantire nodded to the uniforms and the handcuffs were unlocked.

Once Entwistle was seated, his back to the door, he immediately started rocking backwards and forwards, throstling his thighs up and down so his feet tapped out a beat on the floor. 'Can I see it, please,' he said. 'Please.'

'In a while. First I need you to answer me some questions,' Talantire said.

'Okay.'

He looked down, his long, broad fingers gripping the edge of the table. The backs of his hands were criss-crossed with wounds, mostly old scars, but some scabbed and recent.

'What is your new name?'

'Gary Moss. I don't like it. Moss was my grandma's maiden name.'

'Would you prefer Gawain?'

He nodded.

'Gawain, I want to take you back to 1 April 1973.' This was the approach that Dr Weiss had suggested.

Entwistle shook his head. 'No, no.'

'I need to know what happened.'

'I'm sorry, I'm so sorry. I didn't mean it.'

'I know, Gawain, I know. You were there with Ruth, weren't you?'

He nodded.

'Gawain, speak up for the tape,' Maddy said, not unkindly.

'Yes,' he said. 'She was there.'

'How did she get in?' Talantire asked.

'I had given her a spare key, for the back door. Weeks before.'

'Why?'

'Because she asked.' He looked almost shy now.

'Why did she need access?' Maddy asked.

He bowed his head, but put his hands together and started to gabble under his breath. 'Have mercy on us according to your love. Wash away our wrongdoing and cleanse us from our sin. And restore us to the joy of your salvation, through Jesus Christ our Lord.' When he'd finished, he bowed his head.

'She had a boyfriend, didn't she?' Talantire said, softly.

Gawain nodded, then recited the prayer again.

'Gawain, was anyone else there with you?'

At this, he squeezed his eyes shut and emitted a prolonged whimper. His throstling intensified, and he rocked as if he was riding a horse. Talantire knew this was a symptom of mental stress, very common amongst those who had been institutionalised. Only now did she wonder if Gawain was taking his medication. Presumably he was supposed to be on something. She asked him, but he didn't reply.

'Were you alone with Ruth?' Maddy asked.

He shook his head and whimpered again. Talantire had never seen anything like this. The man was petrified of something.

'Who was it? Male or female?' Talantire asked.

Entwistle's knuckles were white. He whispered: 'The Dark Angel of the Lord.'

'A real person?'

He started sobbing then. 'Can you show me, please?' he pleaded.

Maddy indicated to the uniforms to fetch the knife container. Entwistle almost dislocated his neck trying to turn to look as it was brought in and handed it to her.

'This is it, isn't it, Gawain?' Maddy was holding it about three feet away from him.

'I want to hold it,' he implored them, starting to stand up.

'No, stay seated, Gawain,' Talantire warned. Maddy stepped back, and the two uniforms stood either side of her. Maybe this was a bad idea, Talantire thought. He mustn't get his hands on it.

'Was this a real person, Gawain, or something in your imagination?' she asked.

'Look,' he said, showing the palms of his hands. In the centre of both hands there were livid wounds, one of them clearly infected, the other scabbed. 'He pressed my hand onto the cross!'

'Those are recent,' Maddy said, looking at the scars. 'They weren't done in 1973.'

'I do not heal,' he said. 'Without the cross.'

Talantire and Maddy exchanged a glance. 'Gawain, you don't let them heal,' Talantire said. 'You have been self-harming for years. Dr Weiss told me all about it.'

He began to pray again, this time the Lord's Prayer, so fast that the words slurred together.

Talantire exchanged a glance with Maddy. They weren't getting anywhere. The man's ramblings would be inadmissible, even if he told them anything. She could just imagine the case conference with sceptical CPS lawyers. No, they had to find another route to the truth. They ended the interview and retrieved the tape. Maddy made a couple of calls, and Entwistle was passed to the care of adult social services, whose mental health support team came over to pick him up.

One thing that Entwistle had let slip was that he was staying in the basement at the rectory, courtesy of the Reverend Neal Vaizey. Talantire and Maddy interviewed the rector in his rather grand front room, sitting on high-backed chairs under a crystal chandelier. He looked urbane and relaxed, wearing jeans, deck shoes and a rugby shirt, his silver hair neatly arranged. He offered them coffee from china cups and opened a packet of Sainsbury's petit fours, which he placed upon the high table between them.

'What is your connection to Gawain Entwistle?' Talantire asked. 'How come he was staying here at the rectory?'

'I've long had an interest in the case, which I have regarded as a miscarriage of justice. I did visit him once at Ashworth Hospital, about a decade ago. As you know, my concern with the victim's family is ongoing and I see Gwen Lyle quite regularly.'

'What makes you think there was a miscarriage of justice? You presumably would have been quite young when he was sentenced,' Talantire asked.

He steepled his fingertips and looked up at the fine ceiling, with its ornate ridged cornices, as if seeking help from a higher authority. 'Oh no, I would have been in my twenties, and I didn't grow up here, but in Sussex. But when I took the cloth in 1991, and was posted here, it didn't take me long to realise that there was a deep wound in the community hidden beneath the conspiracy of silence over this historic crime. And I thought I should help to mend it.'

'Very commendable,' Maddy said, eyeing Talantire. 'But there's a difference between an academic interest in the case and letting a convicted killer stay in your home.'

'Christ teaches us that forgiveness and understanding are practical concepts not theoretical. I suppose I was hoping that a reappraisal of the case in the light of modern understanding of mental illness would clear him. Whether he is guilty or not, Gawain is clearly a devout man.'

'So did he contact you or did you invite him here?' Talantire asked.

'His aunt, Sheila Woodley, rang me in a bit of a panic after news of the recent murder, and asked if I could help. Gawain was coming to stay at her home. So I said I would do what I could.'

'Were you aware the police were seeking him?' Maddy asked.

'I had no idea. Of course I'd heard rumours, but in this job it pays to discount idle gossip.'

'Yet, several days ago you approached Devon and Cornwall Police on behalf of the historical society asking to see a piece of evidence connected to the murder of Mrs Ruth Lyle. Was this simply because Entwistle wanted to see it?'

Vaizey recoiled. 'Of course not. Your "piece of evidence" is in fact a crucifix, not only a powerful religious item but a historical one of great importance. I'm happy to give you a list of members of the historical society – and if you doubt me you can ask them. Indeed, my request was made several days before I was made aware that Mr Entwistle had in fact returned to North Devon.'

He was clearly a smooth operator. Everything that he had said made perfect sense, but somehow Talantire felt there was something he wasn't telling them.

Maddy asked if she could use the toilet, and Vaizey said, 'Of course. The downstairs loo is on the right, under the stairs.'

While she was gone, Talantire asked, 'Did you ever meet Mrs Lyle, the victim of the recent murder?'

'No, not knowingly. I've seen the photographs and under-stand that she came to Marlborough Road Cemetery. But I think I would have remembered her.'

'And have you ever visited St James Without?'

'No, I think it had ceased to be a chapel by the time I arrived in Ilfracombe.'

'So you've never seen the crucifix?'

'Only in photographs, unfortunately.'

'Nevertheless, I hope you don't mind if I ask for an elimin-ation sample.' She reached down to her go-bag and pulled out a plastic test tube.

'What on earth for?'

'Well, we have no reason to doubt anything you say, but there is nothing like forensic proof to put you in the clear.' She unscrewed the lid of the vial and pulled out a sealed swab.

There was a flash of something in his eyes and the set of his jaw, little more than a twitch, before the affable expression returned. 'Of course, you have your job to do.'

She took the sample from him and screwed it back into the vial, then bagged it for analysis.

'Thank you for your cooperation.'

'It was my pleasure,' he said. 'I'm just sorry I couldn't be more help.'

Maddy arrived back, telegraphing something to Talantire with widened eyes. She waited until they had left and were making their way down the garden path before she turned to her and said, 'There were some of the Reverend Vaizey's certificates framed in the bathroom. And one caught my eye. BA in history from Exeter, 1974.'

'Ah, he would have known James Quince.'

'That's what I was thinking,' Maddy said. 'Shall we ring the doorbell again?'

'No, let's do some research first. Nuttall may have more information.'

Chapter 20

Talantire rang Nuttall from the car, put the phone on speaker and asked him to check Vaizey against his list of Exeter graduates. 'Yes, he's on there,' Nuttall replied. 'Same year as Quince, but different departments.'

'Is there any way to check whether they knew each other?'

'I can ask the two women we found who knew Quince while at college. Unfortunately, the university already told us there are no hard and fast student accommodation records going back that long, so we can't find out if they shared a room or anything. We are just relying on people's memory.'

'Okay.'

'Ah, but we've just had some DNA results back from the lab. Let's have a look.' They could hear him logging on to the system. 'Yes, there's half a dozen DNA signatures at the Dimpsy, including some matches to the database. One of the cigarette ends is a partial match to what was found on the taps in Bluebird Cottage.'

'How partial?'

'Hmm. It's a bit technical. But there's a 42 per cent chance that it's the same person. However, on another piece of evidence there is another match; this one is much stronger. Let's see the cross-reference number... Yes, it's from the condom found in a crack in the floor.'

'Brilliant,' Talantire said.

'There are two DNA traces on it. One matches the murder weapon, tiny specks of blood found on the ceiling and walls, as well as the teddy bear we got from the Lyle family.'

'That would be young Ruth Lyle,' Talantire said. 'That's a fundamental confirmation that the crucifix was used on her.'

'And so the condom was used on the original 1973 victim, whose blood we found under the dry-lining. The second trace on the condom— Whoa, it's dynamite! You're not gonna believe it.'

'Try me.'

'It's Mrs Ruth Lyle.'

'What?' Maddy yelled.

Nuttall blew a huge sigh. 'Yes, Mrs Ruth Lyle screwed young Ruth Lyle. When Mrs Lyle was still a man. So today's murder victim had sex with yesterday's.'

Maddy sat with her jaw hanging open. 'This case gets weirder and weirder.'

'Hang on, these are just two traces,' Talantire said. 'You can't deduce an act, Dave.'

Nuttall snorted in disagreement. 'Come on, Jan. It's a condom for Christ's sake. What else is it used for?'

'Look, James Quince could have opened a condom packet to show young Ruth, who may never have seen one, who then chucked it away. Never jump to conclusions. Is there any evidence of semen?'

'Those tests aren't back yet. CSI has sent them off to some specialist lab. But sperm doesn't last long, does it?'

'It's the DNA, not the sperm, Dave,' Talantire said. 'In rape cases, DNA in semen recovered internally is hard to detect after three days, mainly because it's swamped by female cells. However, there is a published case from Italy where a hundred-year-old semen stain on a piece of cloth *did* yield a DNA sample.'

'So mind you wash your undies, Dave,' Maddy called out, laughing.

After they'd hung up, Talantire said: 'This is so exciting, Maddy. We're actually recreating the forensic record for a fifty-year-old crime from original source material.'

'It does sound to me like James Quince raped and murdered young Ruth,' Maddy added. 'That ties in with the nail varnish seen in the photo and everything.'

'It's not the only interpretation,' Talantire said. 'But yes, you could be right. But then who in turn killed the killer?'

–

Now desperate for a coffee, Talantire and Maddy drove down towards the harbour, parked the car and assessed the choices available. There was a new pub, the Ship and Pilot, but late on a Saturday afternoon it already looked full. They passed by and on to the quay. 'Look,' said Maddy. 'There's Victoria Carnegie.'

The MP, smartly dressed as ever, was thirty yards ahead of them, heading into the Ilfracombe Yacht Club with a briefcase.

'Right, that's got her,' Talantire said. 'She's been avoiding us for days.'

The two detectives made their way upstairs to the bar, discovering that the Yacht Club was not really a club; it was just a pub, though an attractive one. An upstairs balcony at the back had a beautiful view of the shoreline, and seemed sheltered from the wind, which was whipping white caps up on the sea. The MP was sitting alone at a table, with a laptop, phone and cup of coffee in front of her. She didn't look up until they were almost upon her.

'Good afternoon, Victoria,' Talantire said.

'Oh, hello.'

'I didn't expect to find you here. Your receptionist told me that you were in London for a long weekend.'

'That was the plan, but things change. Look, I'm sorry, but I've got a meeting here in a few minutes. I promise I'll make time for you on Monday.'

'Things change, as you said. We're making time for you now.'

The MP pointed a finger at Talantire. 'Now look, this is a public place—'

'I'll make it a private place,' Maddy said, getting up.

'Get us some coffees while you're at it, Maddy,' Talantire called. Maddy went back to the bar, closing the terrace door behind her.

'This is preposterous,' Victoria said.

'Would it be less preposterous if we took you to the station for an interview?' Talantire said, sitting down across the table.

Victoria stared harshly at her, then relaxed a little. 'All right, what is it you want to know?'

'You grew up here in Ilfracombe, didn't you?'

'You've delayed my meeting here to ask me that? It's on my website, a matter of public record!'

'Well, here's something that isn't a matter of public record. Where were you on 1 April 1973?'

'What do you mean? It was fifty years ago. I don't remember.'

'Did you ever go to the Dimpsy Chapel?'

'God no, I was an atheist at the time.' Maddy had just arrived with the coffees, which she set down next to Victoria's half-finished one before returning to guard the door.

'And a revolutionary, so I hear.'

She rolled her eyes. 'A brief rebellious streak, before I grew up.'

'And a wannabe rock star. Your band played at the Stag and Hounds in February 1973.'

'The Winnowers? Well, we hardly played any gigs before we broke up, but we may have played there.'

'And in the audience, we have been told, was a young Ruth Lyle.'

Her reply was very cagey. 'It's possible, but I never met her.'

'Do you recall the exact date of the concert?'

She laughed. 'No. Life was a bit chaotic then.' She looked away towards the sea, as if scanning far-distant memories.

Talantire turned to her notes. 'You probably think this is a bit obscure, but we are trying to recreate the last few weeks of Ruth Lyle's life. That gig was two months before her death, and it's quite possible that she was there with somebody else, someone who might have been her killer, or at least known the killer.'

'Well, there were two other men arrested at the time—'

'We know. We have been in contact them. They have been eliminated from our enquiries, just as they were from the original investigation.'

'Well, well, so you have tracked down Trevor Goswell.' She smiled at the memory.

'You know him?'

'I did. He was two years above me at school. And I recall he asked me out after the gig.' She rolled her eyes. Victoria clearly considered herself to have been well out of Goswell's league even then.

'What about members of the audience? Did you see a young girl with red hair?'

'You clearly don't know what it's like onstage. There are bright lights in your face, the audience are nothing more than silhouettes, except perhaps at the very front. The only things I recall about that night were the cheering and whoops of delight. We played three encores. We were a little bit self-obsessed, I think it's fair to say. And it was fifty years ago.'

'What about other members of the band?'

'The Winnowers was just a bunch of students and me, who had dropped out.'

'Students from which university?'

'Exeter.'

Talantire felt she was getting close to something. 'Give me their names.' She looked up at Maddy, still guarding the glass door onto the terrace. With her was Tim Harvey, the *North Devon News* journalist. Talantire made a note of the names that Victoria gave her, and thanked her for her time. 'I think the press is here for you,' she said as Maddy let Harvey through. 'I'll leave you to it.'

As the MP and the reporter greeted each other, Talantire collected up the empty cups. At the bar, she returned two of them, retaining the one that Victoria had drunk from. Standing face-to-face with Maddy to hide what she was doing, she slipped a swab from her pocket, stripped it of its protective wrapper, then surreptitiously took a sample along the rim where Victoria's dark red lipstick had stained the cup. She slipped the swab into a plastic tube and put it into her pocket. Then she left the cup on the bar. Then she emailed the names of the band members to Dave Nuttall. Researching a fifty-year-old band? Right up his street.

–

Five minutes later, as they walked back to the car, Talantire's phone rang. Nuttall had some results. He had already discovered just how obscure the Winnowers were. 'Nothing on YouTube, no discography,' he said. 'The two band members mentioned – Colin Young was the bass player, and Ian Jones was lead guitar. Young, an Exeter University student, went on to become an accountant in Leeds, but left a couple of reminiscences on Facebook, which linked to Ian Jones's LinkedIn account. Want me to pursue it?'

'You think it's a dead end?' Talantire asked.

'Well, it's not generating any fresh leads. Okay, maybe young Ruth Lyle was in the audience, but it doesn't prove anything.'

'Okay, thanks,' Talantire said. 'Perhaps you might get more luck if you try to see what his mate Hinks remembers. He didn't show up on the DNA list, but his memory might be useful.'

'All right,' Nuttall said.

–

It turned out to be good advice. The property developer, erstwhile friend of Trevor Goswell back in the 1970s, seemed to have a much better recollection of the concert at the Stag and Hounds. He remembered it taking place on Saturday

10 February 1973, but he didn't recognise a band called the Winnowers.

'The main band was, as you probably know, the Car Crash Three,' Hinks said. 'Of course that was before David Archer arrived as lead guitarist…'

Nuttall recognised that he had stumbled upon someone with an even deeper knowledge of obscure British rock bands than he himself. 'What was the support act?'

'I don't recall, but it wasn't the Winnowers. I don't know that name. Whoever it was, they weren't bad, though. I do remember Trevor lusting over the lead singer. She was a tasty piece in a short leather skirt, preaching revolution, which was right up Trevor's street.'

'Do you remember her name?'

'No.'

'Trevor said she was Victoria Carnegie,' Nuttall prompted.

'No idea,' Hinks said.

'She's one of our local MPs now.'

'Really? Anyway, the lead guitarist was very good, with riffs a bit like Ritchie Blackmore. The girls seemed to love him. I do recall they seemed quite inexperienced as a band, not together, out of key. The drummer looked the part, but was off the beat half the time. I also recall Trevor moaning that the singer he fancied was going out with the guitarist.'

'You have a good memory,' Nuttall said.

'For obscure and irrelevant stuff maybe. I can never find my reading glasses, and I can't remember my daughter's birthday for the life of me. So why is it you want to find out who was playing there that night?'

'We are trying to put together the movements of Ruth Lyle.'

Hinks snorted. 'Well, if they didn't crack it fifty years ago you are going to have trouble doing so now, I would imagine.'

Nuttall thanked him and ended the call. He wrote up what he'd learned and emailed it to Talantire. Hinks was right, of course. Although they didn't have the original paperwork, the original inquiry had, after arresting Goswell and Hinks, returned to the obvious conclusion that Gawain Entwistle was the killer. He had access to the crime scene, knew the victim, and last but not least his fingerprints were on the murder weapon. The current investigation of Mrs Ruth Lyle's killing was struggling to do better and, even with modern forensic techniques, had no credible suspects. Only that morning, Nuttall had seen the *Daily Mirror*, which had published a scathing piece about the police investigation under the headline *What are they up to?* Below the headline was a photograph of a gaggle of Tyvek-suited CSI investigators taking a break outside the Dimpsy, one smoking, another looking up at the sky, one bending over, looking for all the world like a Teletubby convention.

He did a bit more searching online, until he was interrupted by Hinks returning his call. The property developer had now remembered the name of the support band from the 1973 gig. It was Silken Subway, not the Winnowers, and when Nuttall googled that a whole lot of interesting information came tumbling out, including a very scratchy YouTube video, in black and white, below which were comments identifying Victoria Carnegie as the singer and 'a promising keyboard player: Jamie Quince'.

James Quince! So here was a historic connection between the recent victim and the MP. Nuttall recognised that Talantire's gut instinct had been good. Moreover, they had discovered that Victoria had played in two bands, but had directed them to the wrong one. If deliberate, that *was* incriminating. He picked up the phone and rang Talantire.

Chapter 21

Meanwhile Talantire and Maddy sat in the car watching the procession of tourists coming to and from the quay. Amongst them they saw Tim Harvey, who seemed to have had a very quick meeting with Victoria Carnegie. The *North Devon News* reporter spotted them and made his way over to the car.

'Time to leave,' hissed Maddy.

'No, hold on, we might find out what he wanted to ask her,' Talantire said.

'Could I ask you a quick question please, Detective Inspector?' Harvey asked, leaning towards the open window. 'What was it you wanted to speak to Victoria Carnegie about?'

'I can't discuss operational matters with you, I think you know that,' Talantire said.

'Were you talking to her about the property deal?' Harvey asked.

'What property deal?' Talantire asked.

'The purchase of Bluebird Cottage.'

'Sorry, I'm not aware of this.'

'Oh, I thought you would know. That a company owned by the police and crime commissioner, and in which our MP is a director, is buying the building from Mrs Lee.'

Maddy let out an audible gasp. Buying the crime scene!

'How did you discover this?' Talantire asked. She was horrified. Not so much about the MP's involvement, but that of Lionel Hall-Hartington. The man was insufferable anyway, but this just looked so very bad.

'There's a planning application,' Harvey said. 'I always look at them, part of the job.'

'Well it's not part of mine,' Talantire said. 'Whoever owns the building, I'm afraid the police will retain control of the property until such time as the investigation is completed.'

Harvey smiled at her. 'Just surprised you don't know, seeing as there is a yellow public notice posted on the lamp post just outside Bluebird Cottage. The same one the crime scene tape was attached to.'

'Since when?'

'A couple of days. They are planning to extend the building, and have applied for a change of use.'

'So is that what you wanted to talk to our MP about?' Maddy asked him.

He laughed. 'Yes, but you seem to have left her in a bad mood. She wouldn't say anything.'

'And neither will we,' Talantire said. 'However, it's nice to get more information out of a journalist than we have given.'

'Glad to be of use,' he said, then smiled. 'Maybe in return, you can—'

Before he had finished, Maddy had buzzed up the window, ending the conversation. She waved at him as Talantire started the car and began to drive off. They watched him in the rear-view mirror. He was still managing to smile.

'What the hell is the commissioner up to?' Maddy asked.

'Making money, one way or another,' Talantire said. 'I'm going to let Wells know. It's above my pay grade.'

'Yeah, but it's above his too, and Noone's.'

They both knew the assistant chief constable was too limp to say anything, and, with the top post vacant, that was as high as it could go.

'Victoria Carnegie and James Quince could well have met before they played together,' Maddy said. 'He studied at Exeter University, she dropped out after a term. Most of the band of Silken Subway were students. And according to Hinks, she was going out with the guitarist.'

'It doesn't get us very far,' Talantire conceded, as she took the sharp bend back onto Portland Street, heading east. 'But I tell you what is interesting. We've been wondering all along how evidence such as the crucifix got back into circulation, but also how James Quince managed to get hold of the birth certificate for young Ruth Lyle, on which he was able to build a new identity as Mrs Ruth Lyle. But of course, as coroner, Victoria's father would have had access to all that documentation.'

'True,' Maddy said.

'What if Victoria had stolen it from his files, and passed it to Quince?'

'That presupposes Quince was already planning to steal Ruth's identity all the way back into the 1970s.'

'Not necessarily,' Talantire said. 'She might have done it for a bit of a laugh, undermining her father as a pillar of the community. She was by own admission a revolutionary in her youth. Winding up your dad is often a part of that.'

'It might explain why Carnegie senior had a bit of a break-down,' Maddy said. 'That's what Wigwam said. The case nearly destroyed his parents' marriage.'

'Trouble is Wigwam was too young to have seen it first-hand. He only remembers it because his mother told him.'

'Still, it's worth asking him,' Maddy said. 'He only lives up the road.'

'I know. That's where we're headed.'

Inspector Carnegie lived in Chambercombe, just off the main A399 to Combe Martin. When the two detectives arrived they saw him in the garden of his large Victorian home, undertaking a typical Saturday activity: mowing the lawn. They saw him swing the motor mower effortlessly, imprinting another neat green strip into the carefully tended grass. As they entered through the gate, he stopped the mower, and stood waiting for them with his hands on his hips.

'What's happened?' he asked.

'Operationally, not too much,' Talantire said cagily. 'You probably heard that we found and interviewed Gawain Entwistle.'

'Yes, I did. Where is he now?'

'Deposited with adult social services,' Maddy said.

'Would you like to come in for a cuppa?' Carnegie asked. 'I could murder one myself.'

'No, we're a bit pushed for time,' Talantire said. 'We're here because we wanted to ask you about your father's role as coroner.'

He scratched his head. 'Well, as I mentioned I was only young, so I don't know too much. Have you tried the Exeter office at the county council? That's where all the records are kept. Of course in theory they are sealed for seventy years.'

'We've seen the original inquest summary, by special request,' Talantire said. 'But there are no supporting documents. He wouldn't have kept anything here at the house, would he?' She was aware that Wigwam had inherited the parental home.

'It would be better to ask my sister, she'd know.'

Talantire and Maddy glanced at each other.

'Most coroners' inquests take place close to the location of an unexplained death,' Talantire said. 'So it is possible he would have kept files here rather than lugging them backwards and forwards to Exeter?'

'Again, you'd have to ask Victoria. She and my late mother dealt with all his paperwork after his death. I was only twelve when he died, but Victoria had been working for him as a clerical assistant after she dropped out of college.'

To Talantire, the pieces were falling into place. There was definitely a possibility that Victoria Carnegie was the conduit through which confidential documents had found their way to James Quince. But what of the crucifix? Surely that couldn't have been retained by the coroner, who was after all a lawyer and not a forensic expert.

'One last thing,' Maddy asked. 'Hope you don't mind me asking. But why didn't your sister inherit the house, as the eldest?'

He grinned and shook his head. 'They fell out, years ago. It was a big family feud. At the time she said she didn't want it, as she was going to live, quote, an alternative life of hedonistic freedom without the trappings of materialism, unquote. Now, between you and me, she's seething about it.'

It was only a short drive from Chambercombe back to the rectory. The Reverend Neal Vaizey, a history graduate from Exeter University, certainly had more questions to answer. The two detectives again mounted the steps, and rang the doorbell. There was no reply, but the faint sound of rock music could be heard. They rang again, and rapped sharply on the glass. No reply.

Talantire beckoned Maddy to follow her. They moved around the edge of the house negotiating flowerbeds and lawns, passing through a gate in a wooden fence to the extensive rear garden from which Gawain Entwistle had bolted a few hours earlier. The rear of the house boasted a rather lovely Victorian sun lounge, and they made their way round it towards the back door on the far side. As they approached, they saw a semi-basement window. It was from here that the music was coming. They descended a couple of steps towards the back door from where they could see into the basement room. There, in what looked like a music studio, Vaizey was playing an electric guitar, wearing headphones. He was giving it the full treatment, his face screwed up, waggling his hips. *Dad Dancing*, the musical.

'"Highway Star", by Deep Purple,' Maddy said. 'He's good.'

'Maybe a member of the band with Victoria?' Talantire rapped on the window loudly and repeatedly, before getting the reverend's attention. He took off his headphones, stowed the guitar on a stand and indicated that he would come to the back door.

There was a rattling of keys and the door opened. 'I'm afraid you rather caught me unawares, ladies. I'm not used to performing in front of an audience.'

'Oh, I think you are,' Talantire said. 'Didn't you have a gig at the Stag and Hounds Hotel on 10 February 1973?'

–

Vaizey invited them inside, but there were no cups of coffee or petit fours this time. He rounded on them in the hall. 'I would have thought that with an unsolved murder on your hands you wouldn't be that interested in obscure gigs in forgotten pubs in the 1970s.'

'There's no need to take that attitude,' Talantire said. 'We're pretty certain that whoever killed Mrs Ruth Lyle last week was connected with the original crime in 1973. Mrs Lyle, who was once Mr James Quince, seemed to be determined to take over the identity of the original victim. The truth of why he did that I think lies in what happened in the Dimpsy Chapel in the weeks leading up to 1 April 1973.'

'I told you I've never been there.'

'However, you were part of a student band that included Mr Quince.'

'Yes, but that was decades ago.'

Talantire looked at her phone, on which Nuttall's email was displayed. 'You were the lead guitarist for Silken Subway, weren't you? With Mr Quince on keyboards, and Victoria Carnegie as lead singer?'

'We played two gigs before we broke up,' Vaizey said. 'It cannot possibly be relevant, surely?'

'You never mentioned to us that you knew Mr Quince,' Maddy said.

'Why would I? I thought the name of the murder victim was Mrs Ruth Lyle. I wasn't aware that Mr Quince was even relevant to your enquiry. It's not been publicised, has it?'

Recalling how little information had been put in the public domain, Talantire had to concede that he was right.

'Well, now you *do* know, we need to get you to come in for a formal interview. We need to know exactly what you knew about Mr Quince.'

'Are you arresting me?'

'No, but you are an important witness,' Talantire said. 'Can you come now?'

'I'm sorry, I really can't. I have an urgent Zoom call with the diocesan council in half an hour, and tomorrow morning being Sunday, of course I have a service to lead at Pip and Jim's. However, I'm more than happy to come in tomorrow afternoon, for as long as you'd like.'

Talantire and Maddy exchanged glances. 'We'd prefer this evening. The station is only just up the road,' Talantire said.

Vaizey looked at his watch and blew a sigh. 'All right, but I need an hour or two to rearrange my meetings.'

'All right, we'll send a car for you at seven o'clock,' Talantire said.

Outside, sitting in the car, Talantire looked again at the scratchy video on her phone that Nuttall had sent her. It was impossible to see much detail in the tiny phone screen, so she sent it to her iPad for a better look. The video, from a fan website for the Car Crash Three, the headlining band, began near the end of Silken Subway's set. The lead singer was announcing their final song. Her dark hair was damp with sweat, her dark eye make-up typical of the glam rock era, but she certainly had something, something beyond the long legs, short skirt and skimpy leather waistcoat. She had presence, and, when the final song began, she belted out the vocals as if she really meant it.

'Young Victoria Carnegie, eh?' Maddy said. 'Did she really just yell, "kill the fucking rich"?'

'Sounded like it to me,' Talantire said. She watched as Victoria ground her hips against the guitarist – Vaizey – and then pretended to lick the head of the guitar while he held it towards her.

'Bloody hell!' Maddy said, eyes wide. Both detectives were transfixed. The audience too, seemed to be going wild, a forest of clapping arms obscuring the view to the stage. There was no view of the other band members, except a final brief pan across the stage.

'Hold it there,' Maddy said. Talantire hit the pause button. 'So that must be Quince,' Maddy said. 'He's modelled himself on Rick Wakeman. Long sandy hair, and wizard sleeves.'

'The drummer looks more heavy metal,' Talantire said. The frozen image showed a beefy-looking man wearing a vest, Frank Zappa droopy moustache and sunglasses, with his arms in the air, both drumsticks in one hand.

Talantire gasped, and stared more closely. 'Look! He's wearing black nail varnish!'

Chapter 22

After he had closed the door on the two detectives, the Reverend Neal Vaizey steepled his hands over his face and blew a huge sigh. For a minute or two, he paced about in the hallway, muttering to himself. He made his way upstairs to his office, and picked up the landline handset. He began to punch out a number, then stopped. He had just stopped himself doing something very stupid, something that would immediately bring the temple crashing down around his ears. Instead he replaced the handset, pulled open the bottom drawer of his work desk and pulled out a blister pack in which was a new dumbphone. He'd bought it when he'd heard about the murder, less than two weeks ago, but had hoped he would never need it. He powered the device up, saw there was no charge on it, and plugged it in. He needed enough juice to at least make a few calls. In the bedroom next door, he pulled down a suitcase and began to pack, then stopped. Where on earth could he go, to escape what was coming?

Nowhere.

After ten minutes he went to the phone, saw there was some charge, and punched out a number for another mobile, one that he had called only once before, just two weeks ago. There was no reply, and no facility to leave a message. He was caught between a rock and a hard place. He was tempted to tell all, to spill the beans to the police and seek forgiveness, but that would bring disaster. There could be no absolution for what he had done, even though his entire life since that time had been a symbol of atonement for errors of judgement made over a few short weeks in 1973. He had feigned shock at hearing that the murder victim had been Jamie Quince, and was pretty sure that they had been taken in. Yet there was something very dogged and tenacious about that Detective Inspector Talantire. Yes, of course Ruth Lyle had been at that concert, he had noticed her in the front row, dancing and staring at him as he played. And then of course there was a visit to him backstage, afterwards, when he had agreed to autograph her arm. If it had stopped there, then it would have been harmless. But no, it had its own momentum, which had ended up with him and Victoria making a Faustian pact. That was when the evil really began.

Now, what Entwistle had called the Dark Angel of the Lord was coming to collect the souls that he was owed. There was no way out.

Vaizey fell to his knees and prayed.

—

Victoria Carnegie stood by the entrance to St Nicholas Chapel at the top of Lantern Hill, and pulled her pale blue leather jacket closely around her shoulders against the freezing wind. The chapel, built in 1321 was now a museum, but incorporated the country's oldest working lighthouse. It had closed at six p.m. and she had the place to herself. There was a fabulous view to the right over Ilfracombe Harbour and the Damien Hirst statue, and to the left over Capstone Hill and Wildersmouth Beach.

This was one of those times when she wished she hadn't given up smoking all those years ago. She had to admit she was scared. The police had been diligent, far too diligent. Detective Inspector Jan Talantire was turning out to be far tougher to deal with now, even from her own position as a powerful MP, than that idiot DCS George Hogley had been back in 1973. Yes, she was a failed student back then, a long-haired dropout, but she was also the daughter of the eminent local coroner. She had charmed Hogley and she had flirted and her view had prevailed. He had never seen through any of her lies. And that, she had thought, was done and dusted. Jamie had retreated into his shell, then gone off to work in the oil industry; Neal had dumped her and broken her heart. And then there was Groz, the man everyone had underestimated. The wolf she had invited into the sheep pen. Well, that bastard had dramatically overreacted to the re-emergence in Ilfracombe of a woman who they had thought was dead.

She scrabbled in her handbag, and pocketed her iPhone. She then pulled out a cheap unregistered Samsung smartphone she had bought for cash a few weeks ago. She took a deep breath and punched out a number. Then she stared out to the horizon, and the brooding dark green sea under heavy grey clouds. The storm was about to break, and she had just one last desperate chance to stop it.

–

The two detectives sat in the car and stared at the video. Jan screenshotted the frame that showed the drummer's black nail varnish and emailed it back to Nuttall to see if it could be enhanced.

'Victoria has been lying to us through her teeth,' Talantire told Maddy. 'She may have been in a band called the Winnowers, but it's this one, Silken Subway, that ties James Quince to Neal Vaizey and her.'

'Is this drummer the same one who was in the Winnowers or is it somebody else?' Maddy said.

'No idea.'

Talantire rang Nuttall, and told him about the nail varnish she had spotted.

'It's a bit thin, isn't it?' Nuttall said. 'Just a vague reference from fifty years ago from a man whose spent his entire adult life in a mental institution.'

'If you'd spoken to Entwistle, Dave, you'd know it's not just a vague reference,' Talantire said. 'He's terrified of this Dark Angel. So, do you have a name for the drummer?'

'No. There are a load of comments beneath the video but, as you can see, the drummer is only referenced by the prefix crap, as in "what a crap drummer". None of the comments that I can see are from anyone who sounds like they know him. Of course you have to bear in mind that most of the audience were there to see the Car Crash Three, who were quite big. at the time, and the only information about Silken Subway I found on this website is from fans of the headline band. I get the impression that Silken Subway existed for only two or three gigs, and none of the musicians ended up pursuing it as a career choice.'

'What about Hinks? Would he know the drummer? He sounds like he's got a good memory.'

'He has, but he too was there to see the Car Crash Three. Why don't you ask Victoria Carnegie?'

'I will, but she'll lie,' Talantire said. 'She's covering something up, is clearly involved, but I can't work out how. By the way, I've got a DNA sample from her and one from Vaizey that we need tested, pronto. I think it's even more urgent now, so could you get a courier to meet me at Ilfracombe police station on Princess Avenue?'

'Yes, I'll get it booked in online on the overnight service.'

'Thanks, Dave. We'll be up there to formally interview Reverend Neal Vaizey too,' Talantire said, and cut the call.

'I have a feeling he isn't gonna turn up,' Maddy said.

Chapter 23

PCSO Sandra Willis was feeling fed up. It was gone six on a
Saturday night and she and her two fellow trainees Jon Dawkins
and Hilary Edwards were up to their ankles in stinking old
paperwork in an industrial unit in Exeter attempting to find
the ultimate needle in a haystack: CID investigation documents
from a fifty-year-old crime, which apparently had been dumped
here along with decades of other paperwork, surplus to police
requirements. All three of them agreed that it was not what they
had joined up to do.

This afternoon they had found other 1970s case files,
from burglaries, assaults and rape investigations. She had been
shocked at how cursory some of the documentation had been.
Handwritten, sometimes almost illegible witness statements,
clearly written by the police themselves and handed over to
be signed. Even the language was evidence of a police origin. 'I
was proceeding in a northerly direction by foot' was the type of
phrase she had come across several times. It was not something
a normal person would say.

When she had first agreed to take overtime for this task
four days ago, she had assumed that the files would be in some
kind of date order, grouped by case, alphabetically or by some
index number. There were indeed some like that, and others
where they had the godsend of a treasury tag – a metal-ended
string used to keep related documents together. They didn't
seem to be used in modern offices. But there were also heaps of
completely random papers, as if a hundred filing cabinets had
been emptied into a skip ready for disposal before somebody

had decided that they should be shovelled somewhere else. Well, now there really was a skip outside, to which they were ferrying all the demonstrably irrelevant information prior to incineration. Otherwise there was nowhere to separate the stuff they had looked at from that they had yet to see.

As well as paperwork they had found a metal cabinet, in which was lying a heap of knives big enough to make a cutlery drawer. The results of some kind of amnesty. They had also found folders of thousands of photographs, of crime scenes, of victims and of witnesses. It was a horrific litany of crime and criminality.

Jon, who was in charge, had called time. They were supposed to work until seven, but they weren't being supervised, so leaving half an hour early wouldn't be much of a problem. As it was a Saturday, everyone had places to be. Sandra decided to do one last lot, a group of three files, held together with a loop of faded sticky tape. They were the old bottle-green type of suspension files with skinny metal edges that scrape on the drawer runners, fat with faded documents, and she lugged them on to the examination table. After cutting the tape, they flopped open, as if inviting examination.

And there they were.

–

The Princess Avenue interview room had been prepared, and the aged tape machine checked. Talantire and Maddy were now wargaming the various questions they would ask the Reverend Neal Vaizey about exactly where he was on the day that young Ruth Lyle was murdered, and the location of other members of the Silken Subway band. What they really needed was a rapid result from the DNA test.

At precisely seven p.m. they got a call from a patrol car waiting outside the rectory, just a few hundred yards down the road from the police station. 'We rang the doorbell and there was no reply,' an officer told Talantire. 'Steve has just gone round the back to see if there's any sign of him.'

'Keep me posted,' Talantire said, and cut the call. 'Maddy, I think he's done a runner.'

'I've had this bad feeling in my stomach,' Maddy said. 'Like the time I was invited to a cannibal wedding and saw the finger buffet.'

Fifteen minutes later it was confirmed that there was no sign of the Reverend Vaizey. Talantire stared out of the window, looking numbly over the cars parked in the secure enclosure beneath.

'We should have arrested him,' Maddy said.

'How could we? We've got nothing on him,' Talantire said. 'He's a prominent clergyman and a pillar of the community.'

'Or maybe just a pillock. And fifty years ago he was a spotty student, thrusting his guitar at young girls in the Stag and Hounds. An audience that included Ruth Lyle.'

'If you believe Hinks and Goswell.'

'Okay, but nothing yells guilt to me like him doing a runner.'

'In hindsight, yes,' Talantire conceded.

Her phone rang. It was the control room, with a message from the PCSOs wading their way through the evidence. She listened with mounting excitement, and asked that one of them drive over with everything they had on the case. After she'd cut the call, she turned to Maddy.

'They found a stash of the Ruth Lyle murder case documents. Witness statements, case summaries, evidence dockets. We're getting it blue-lighted over to Barnstaple, and we'll meet them there.'

'Here comes an all-nighter,' said Maddy, with a sigh.

'I'm going to get a search warrant for the rectory,' Talantire said, reaching for the phone.

'What about Victoria Carnegie?'

Talantire shook her head. 'I'll have enough trouble convincing the duty magistrate that we should burst into Vaizey's home. There'd be no chance for the MP, not until we've got some serious forensic evidence. But tomorrow morning, hopefully.'

She tapped out the number.

–

Having got her warrant, Talantire dropped Maddy off at the rectory to lead a team of four uniforms in the search, and then blue-lighted her way back to Barnstaple in the gathering darkness. Fortunately traffic was light and, even though she had spent twenty minutes trying to cajole the magistrate into accepting the warrant request, she still arrived back at CID headquarters a few minutes before the car from Exeter.

In her absence, Nuttall had drafted in three support staff and instructed them to start scanning in the documents the moment they arrived, and then pass them to Talantire to peruse. DI Lockhart was there too, planning to single-handedly cover almost everything else that might happen in Devon and Cornwall on a Saturday night. They all hoped for a quiet night with no punch-ups or stabbings. They couldn't afford any distractions.

The thunder of footsteps on the staircase heralded the arrival of two hefty PCs lugging up the paperwork in four large plastic stacker boxes. Talantire lifted up the first folder and flicked it open. Despite years of being buried in a lock-up storage facility, it still reeked of tobacco smoke, an unwelcome reminder of office conditions in another time. She'd love to be able to read the minds of Hogley's investigatory team, but all she was getting was the contents of their lungs.

She passed it into the scrum of support staff, who were busy at three scanners, and waited for the first pages to emerge. The first were typed pages of legal argument, which she put to one side. Then came the first witness statement, from a neighbour who had heard a scream. The language was laborious, but comprehensive. Next was the alibi given by Gawain Entwistle's mother, in which she maintained the boy had been watching television with her at the time of the killing. Next came a copy of the judge's summing-up, whose tone was familiar from the newspaper coverage, and a statement by a passer-by who'd seen no sign of anyone leaving the building at the time of the screaming. Finally they were really into it, and found what had been missing all along: statements from the first two constables, who had arrived about fifteen minutes after the alarm had been raised, found the door of St James Without open, and went inside, to be faced with a young girl lying dead on the altar, impaled with a crucifix.

As she speed-read the documents, Talantire felt the horrible familiarity of the crime, of which the modern investigation was such an echo.

–

Detective Sergeant Maddy Moran was relieved they had gained entry to the rectory. The locksmith had been ten minutes late but had opened the UPVC rear doors into the sun lounge in less than five seconds with a big pair of pliers, by twisting the exterior locking mechanism. He made it look so simple, it reminded her to review the safety of her own home, which relied on identical locks. The warrant had partly been granted on the basis that there were concerns for the safety of Reverend Vaizey because of his failure to turn up for a police interview. However, a quick reconnaissance showed that there were no bloodstains, no signs of a body, no sections of rope thrown over a suspended beam. Having discounted the worst possibility, she now had to recalibrate the search. What exactly was she supposed to be looking for?

The uniforms did what they had been trained to do, and went straight for the computers. There was one aged desktop, along with a router that held the unique MAC address of any device using the wi-fi, even those no longer connected. There were no mobile phones, only a rather aged answer machine, clear of messages. Maddy stood in the centre of the rather grand lounge, turning slowly to take in the period architectural features of this fine house, while officers bustled in and out carrying plastic bags for the electronics. Talantire, in her rush to return to Barnstaple, had given her only the vaguest outlines of what to look for, so Maddy fell back on common sense; she looked for used cups and glasses in the kitchen, and bagged them for DNA testing. She thought back to how they had caught the priest playing his electric guitar in the basement. Of course – that would be where to look for something to link Vaizey to the past.

Music.

She descended the stone steps into the music room and found one of the uniforms already busy, leafing through a large collection of CDs and vinyl LPs. There was a fair quantity of electronics here too. To her untrained eye it looked like a recording studio.

'There's some valuable stuff here, I would think,' the PC said, showing her a pile of heavy metal LPs.

'We're looking for any tapes, gig demos, anything that would prove who was in the band with him,' Maddy said.

They delved into boxes and cupboards for the next ten minutes, until the PC gave a chuckle of amazement. 'Until now I thought he had good musical taste,' he said, brandishing a paper-sleeved vinyl single, which he held in one corner with his gloved hand as if it was poisonous.

'What is it?' Maddy asked.

'"Puppy Love", by Donny Osmond.' He grimaced.

'Where did you find that?'

'There's a shoebox full of this kind of stuff. It was in the bottom drawer of the cabinet.'

'Let's have a look.' Maddy took the box from him. There were a dozen singles of the era, including 'Tie a Yellow Ribbon', Simon and Garfunkel's 'Bridge Over Troubled Water', 'Without You' by Nilsson and the haunting love song

'Killing Me Softly' by Roberta Flack. On the sleeve of that single was a verse penned in florid handwriting.

> *I hear the sound of Envy, feel it pulsing in my soul.*
> *I want the taste of Envy, moistening my hole*

The last word had been scratched out in the same hand. The verse may not have been intended to be read by anyone else. But who or what was Envy? Of course! NV – Neal Vaizey. With a rising sense of excitement, Maddy delved further into the box. Underneath the singles was an aged envelope, worn with use, and addressed to Neal Vaizey at an address in Exeter. Inside was a love letter, date 26 February, in the same handwriting.

> *My darling Neal,*
> *I'm really hurt that you've been avoiding me, and my heart is wild with desire. That trip to the seafront was special to me, our hot kisses in the salt breeze. And I did say I would let you, if we could find somewhere. Now I know there is a place, to which I can get the keys, if as you say we can no longer go to your flat in Exeter. I'm really longing to be with you and feel your arms around me, and I did love hearing you play the guitar so brilliantly. Please meet me at seven p.m. by the Scarlet Pimpernel. If you don't come it will break my heart.*
> *Love and kisses*
> *Ruth*

'Bingo,' shouted Maddy, showing the letter to the constable. 'We've got a clear 1970s connection between Neal Vaizey and Ruth Lyle. Now what we have to do is find him.'

She rang Talantire and told her.

Chapter 24

Talantire was excited to hear Maddy's news, which she shouted out to the rest of the team. There was a round of applause, although it was equally obvious that the clerical staff who were helping with the evidence, and who seemed most enthusiastic about this latest development, probably didn't have the faintest idea of its significance. Still, if it created a little bit of camaraderie for weekend working, it was worth it.

'Did Hogley know?' Maddy asked. 'Is this a genuinely new connection?'

'Yes! Nobody's seen anything in the 1973 paperwork that shows that DCS Hogley and his crew were aware of the connection between Ruth Lyle and Neal Vaizey. No statements, nothing.'

'Right, got to get back,' Maddy said. 'Vaizey's car is missing, so I'm off now to Princess Avenue to get the ANPR search under way.'

Talantire thanked her and cut the call. It was good news that the affair between Ruth and Vaizey had not hitherto been uncovered. New evidence was a powerful tool, capable of reopening cases and launching appeals. If conversely Hogley had been aware of, but discounted, Vaizey's involvement, then it would be a much more difficult conversation with the Crown Prosecution Service to resurrect the case. Either way, firm evidence would be needed. Vaizey was a pillar of the community, as far as Dave Nuttall could establish; he had never had any suspicions levelled at him since he joined the clergy in 1991.

He had been in Ilfracombe almost all of that time, and in his current role at Pip and Jim's for a decade.

At half past ten they took a break. They ordered in pizza, boxes of it, for the whole team. Talantire made them move into a conference room to eat, mainly to get away from the stale tobacco stench, which now permeated the whole office, but also to avoid contaminating any of the precious paperwork with greasy fingers.

'Thank you all for giving up your Saturday evening,' Talantire said to the assembled crew. 'It may feel like basic routine office work, but I can't tell you how important it is. Whoever killed Mrs Lyle had something to hide back in 1973.'

'So the murderer must be an old person,' said one of the male uniforms, who was lifting a slice of ham and pineapple pizza to his mouth. He looked about twenty-two. His idea of old might be anyone over the age of thirty.

'We can narrow it down more than that, I would say,' Talantire said. 'The suspect is likely to be in his or her late sixties or early seventies, quite possibly a graduate or at least an attendee of Exeter University, and associated in some way with the band Silken Subway. However, to get any closer we really need a couple more forensic results. That will save a great deal more work.'

'What about that cross of nails?' asked a female assistant. 'Pavel said it might go all the way back to the time of Christ, which would be amazing.'

'I wouldn't go back that far—' Talantire said and then stopped. Where was the crucifix? She had last seen it in the interview room at Princess Avenue, but had forgotten to put it back in the car before she rushed back to Barnstaple. She cursed under her breath. She could have sworn the damn thing was trying to escape.

She rang Maddy, but the line was busy, so she left a message, then rushed down to the ground-floor garage where the unmarked cars were parked and confirmed that the boot of the electric Renault was empty of evidence bags. While she was down there Maddy returned her call.

'It's not here, Jan. In fact I don't recall seeing it after it was shown to Entwistle.'

'Good grief. I think I'm going crazy here.' She hung up, and leaned against the rough breeze blocks of the shadowy parking garage, panic rising in her. Where was the crucifix? She certainly did remember Entwistle being escorted out of Princess Avenue into a van from adult social care. The cross, in its knife container, was at that point still in the interview room. A fluttering nervousness was eating into her ability to recall, gnawing away at her concentration. They simply could not lose this piece of evidence, again. It was even easier now to imagine that whatever dark forces had conspired to retrieve the 1973 murder weapon from police custody were still out there. When paranoia is in control, the most lurid possibility congeals into fact.

She closed her eyes. *Think, Jan, think!*

A nearby noise startled her. A large male silhouette was framed in the doorway to the corridor, with light behind. 'What you doing down here, Jan?' It was DS Wells. 'I've been looking for you.'

I could ask you the same question, she thought. Late on a Saturday night. What on earth was her boss doing creeping about in the dark? But all she said was, 'I'm thinking, sir.'

'Good, we need some fresh insight on this. I'm getting a lot of pressure from upstairs. It's ten days, Jan, since the killing. Are you going to charge Entwistle or not?'

'No, because he didn't do it.' She stared at Wells. Hadn't she told him this already, several times? 'Sir, he wasn't here at the time of the murder. According to Ferris there is CCTV footage showing that Entwistle was at the other end of the country when the killing took place. I think I mentioned that.'

'Yes, but you haven't seen that CCTV. I've been talking to a friend at the CPS.' Seeing the expression on Talantire's face, he quickly added, 'No, not treading on your toes, but vague generalities. A bit of wargaming, you might say. And it does seem that the easiest way to get a conclusion on this case is to go with the flow.' He edged into the garage and let the door wheeze close behind him. He loomed over her, a dark grey shadow.

'What are you saying?' Talantire was too angry to add the honorific, sir, to the end of the question.

'Look, Jan, she is very senior and very experienced, and she just told me: "If you need a result that badly, and it seems that you do, then you already have all the forensic evidence you need to put Entwistle away a second time."'

He lifted a cigarette to his mouth and clicked a lighter. Talantire had had no idea that he smoked. Seeing his face lit from below by the flame gave him a devilish countenance, those bushy eyebrows now arched. She was alert now, and dipped her hands in her jacket pockets. Phone, keys, evidence bags, but no PAVA spray. Why was she suddenly scared?

'No way, absolutely no way,' she said, taking a step backwards. 'We now have a clear romantic connection between the Reverend Neal Vaizey, and a sixteen-year-old Ruth Lyle. Vaizey, aged twenty, was the lead guitarist in a student band called Silken Subway, in which James Quince, a.k.a. Mrs Ruth Lyle, was the keyboard player, and none other than Victoria Carnegie was the singer.'

'So what?' Smoke billowed from his nostrils, dragon-like.

'We have witnesses who say that Ruth was in the crowd in the Stag and Hounds when Silken Subway were playing, just a few weeks before her death. She had a connection to these people.'

Wells blew smoke over her head. 'Jan, it's a house of cards.'

'No, not at all. We now have a condom, on which we have found the DNA of both James Quince and young Ruth Lyle. None of this was uncovered by the original investigation.'

'And you are seriously trying to implicate Victoria Carnegie? She would be a very powerful adversary.'

'She's been leaning on you, hasn't she?'

Wells laughed. 'Why are you trying to make this so difficult?' He edged a little closer to her.

'Because I believe in justice.'

'So do I, believe me. Look, Victoria has the ear of the commissioner, as I think you know.'

'And his balls, apparently.'

'Justice requires resources, Jan. I have to think about budgets, the big picture. We're only just recovering from austerity. We really don't want to jeopardise boots on the ground, do we? For one hopeless case? Victoria is widely tipped to be the next policing minister, in the Home Office. The reshuffle is expected at any time.'

'And she doesn't want anyone frightening the horses?'

'You've got it. You're a very bright woman, Jan. But it's been clear for a long time that you've been struggling to get traction on this case. So I want Entwistle to be formally charged on Monday morning, and I think you'll find it easier than you expect. Don't make life hard for yourself. Go with the flow.'

Talantire said nothing, but was seething with anger. Wells took a final drag on his cigarette and extinguished it against the breezeblock wall. He turned to go, heaving the heavy metal door open, and slipped out into the light of the corridor. Once the door had sighed closed, Talantire began to kneel to retrieve the cigarette end. The door opened again.

'By the way, just a little down payment on gratitude. The annoying Sergeant Venables is being transferred to dog handling next month. We can't have racists in our force,' he said.

The garage door gasped closed behind him. Talantire retrieved the cigarette end with a plastic evidence bag as if clearing up after a dog, then inverted it and pulled off the sealing strip. Then she checked her phone. Yes, it had worked.

–

Talantire raced up the stairs and into CID and peered around to see if Wells was there. 'The boss was looking for you,' Nuttall said, looking out of the window. 'Bloody weekend ambush, to see if you're skiving, I s'pose. But he's just driven off.'

'He showed a lot of interest in the latest revelations,' Maddy said. 'Congratulated us on our diligence.'

'Maddy, just a quick word,' Talantire said. She led the detective sergeant to the ladies' loo, and closed the main door behind her. 'We're being stitched up. Listen to this.' She replayed the voice note from her phone. She had only managed to capture the second half of the conversation with Wells but it was clear enough what was going on.

'It's incredible,' Maddy said.

'Yes. I mean I'm not surprised Victoria tried to throw her weight around, but to have succeeded like this. And with Wells, of all people. I always thought he was straight as a die.'

'So what are you going to do?'

'I'm going to solve the case, by Monday morning, Maddy. Before the deadline Wells set me.'

'Wow, you *are* angry, aren't you?'

'I'm incandescent. I didn't join the police to just find the most politically convenient conviction, I joined to nail the person who actually committed the crime. No ifs no buts.'

'They could destroy us, Jan.'

'Bring it on. And Maddy, I'm so thrilled that you used the word "us" just then.'

'Of course, we are in this together. I believe in the work we've done, and I've always believed in you. So what's next?'

'We're taking the offensive, Maddy. I've decided I need to know a bit more about our detective superintendent boss.' She held up the cigarette end in its evidence bag. 'I'm sending this off for analysis, just in case he is minded to interfere with evidence. He'll be person W. If he's been anywhere in the crime scene, I'll have him, especially in combination with that recording.'

'There's night-vision CCTV inside the garage too, though there's no sound,' Maddy added. 'I'll download a copy.'

'Yes, he won't be able to deny that he was there.'

'We also need somewhere to act as a confidential incident room, somewhere just for us two, where we can be sure that Wells won't stumble across us.'

'There's the storeroom downstairs next to the rape suite, which has got a spare workstation and plenty of whiteboards,' Maddy said. 'But are you going to tell Nuttall?'

'I don't know, Maddy. The fewer people who know, the better.'

'He's not stupid, he'll soon figure out that we are up to something.'

They exited the ladies and returned to their desks.

Nuttall immediately glanced up. 'What have you two been up to? You look like you're plotting something.'

Maddy looked at Talantire and rolled her eyes. Were they really that transparent?

'Dave, have you seen the crucifix at all?' Talantire asked.

He stared at her. 'I thought you took it with you to Ilfracombe?'

'I did. But it's gone.'

He shook his head, and sucked his teeth in mock anxiety. You're in trouble now, he seemed to be saying. But Talantire knew his sense of humour.

'You've bloody got it, haven't you, Dave?' she yelled.

Nuttall slid open his desk drawer, and brought out the knife container. 'The courier picked it up at Princess Avenue by mistake along with the DNA samples, and dropped it off here when he realised there was no accompanying paperwork.'

Talantire blew a huge sigh. She didn't know whether to slap him or kiss him. In the end she playfully pinched his cheeks. 'Don't wind me up, Detective Constable, I'm on a short fuse as it is.'

'Don't we all know it,' he replied, rubbing his cheek.

Talantire headed off to Dr Crippen, not for coffee of course but to steal a quiet moment to check her personal phone. She had texted Adam earlier to ask if he wanted to come to a world music gig with her in Barnstaple the following Saturday. He'd not replied, so she sent him a reminder. Tickets were going fast, so she needed a decision. This time the reply was quick.

> Sorry. Can't make it. Let's put everything on ice for now. Things just got complex here.

On ice? They'd had only two dates. Correction: one and a half; they'd shared a brief peck on the cheek and a bit of food. This thing had hardly got going and it was already over. What was this about complex 'here'? To her that meant only one thing: Adam was back with his ex. As she had suspected, they had still clearly been within rapprochement time.

She looked up. Maddy was staring at her, and asked, 'What are you muttering about?'

'Bloody Adam. Wants to put everything "on ice".' She rabbit-eared the words with her fingers.

'And you never even got a chance to shag him, eh?'

'Maddy, that wasn't the objective of the exercise. I wanted something more.'

'Pardon me,' Maddy said and pulled a face to no one in particular. 'I hadn't realised that you were on a crusade to explore the universal ecstasy of human existence.'

Talantire stared hard at her. Maddy held up her hands in apology. 'I always go too far, sorry. I'm just jealous of your opportunity.'

'What bloody opportunity? I work, eat and sleep CID. I'm forty next year, and sure there's no end of officers, usually senior to me, trying it on for a quickie, so they can go home to the wife with a smug grin on their face. But on the rare occasions I get home at a reasonable time, there's no one there to hand me a glass of wine, no one there to give me a cuddle. Just faded woodchip wallpaper, and a pile of bills on the mat.'

She hadn't meant to say that much, anywhere near that much. She just hoped that Dave Nuttall further down the office hadn't caught any of the details. But it was true. Since she and Jon had split up, she'd become lonely. Horribly lonely.

—

Talantire returned to the fray with renewed ferocity, going through each of the scanned-in documents from the original case along with some of the legal papers from the court case. Her initial suspicion that Hogley had done a poor job in 1973 was proving ill-founded. There were witness statements from many dozens of people who had spoken to or seen young Ruth Lyle in the weeks leading up to her death, including school friends and relations. It was only in the grey area of her unusually active social life that the inquiry seemed to lose focus. Yes, they had a statement from Hinks, in which he had admitted to 'heavy petting' with the girl, in an alleyway near the pub on the night of the gig, but he had an alibi for the date of her murder. By homing in on those like Andrew Hinks and Trevor Goswell, who had been seen flirting with her publicly, they had completely overlooked or at least failed to find the evidence of her other affections. There was no mention whatever of Neal Vaizey. Indeed, there seemed to be an element of class preju- dice, because one of the victim's female friends had mentioned an association with students from Exeter University but it wasn't followed up. Nothing was written, but it was clear there was an assumption that those well-brought up youngsters couldn't possibly be involved with a crime like this.

When she looked up, she saw it was nearly one a.m. The clerical assistants had gone home an hour ago, leaving just her, Maddy and Nuttall. They were all dog tired. Maddy had just emailed Talantire the results of a web trawl on Detective Superintendent Wells. Links she had appended showed a great deal of coverage of his work in social services in Southampton, and in that most fraught of public service roles he really did seem to have achieved great things. He wasn't a student at Exeter University but at Essex, where he had studied sociology. He was born in Bridgwater in Somerset. In Talantire's conspiracy-tainted mindset, she had become convinced that Wells was a member of Victoria Carnegie's 1970s band. But Maddy could find absolutely no evidence of that.

She steepled her hands and thought about going to Jeremy Noone with the recording. Of course it could well have been the spineless assistant chief constable who had been putting pressure on Wells, having in turn been leaned on by the commissioner or Victoria Carnegie, maybe both. The Honourable Lionel Hall–Hartington in turn appeared to be in a business venture with the MP. It was so bloody incestuous. Who needs murky Masonic meetings when you have this kind of influence-peddling? How high would she need to go to find an incorruptible ally?

As she considered her options, an email marked urgent dropped into her box.

The results of the two emergency DNA tests. One sample from Vaizey's cheek and the other from the MP's coffee cup. If they matched anything at the crime scene it could make the case. She clicked on the link, and held her breath.

Chapter 25

The first news was a disappointment. Vaizey was in the clear. The rector's elimination sample didn't match anything that had turned up at the crime scene. But for Victoria Carnegie, it was very different. The mystery sample on the tap in Bluebird Cottage was hers, which put her in the frame for the recent murder, but it also matched one of the cigarette ends turned up from the recently uncovered cracks in the stone floor of the Dimpsy Chapel. Potentially, it was a link to the original crime.

'Maddy, this is dynamite,' Talantire said.

'Have we got enough to arrest her?' Maddy asked.

'I'm not sure. The remaining unknown trace on the crucifix, and under Mrs Ruth Lyle's nails, is now the only one we haven't identified. It doesn't match Victoria's. If it did, we could charge her. However, we have enough to justify a warrant to search her home and office in Lynton, and get her phone records. Magistrates are cautious when it comes to implicating those with political connections but, yes, I think we have enough.'

'Primrose didn't find any calls or emails between Mrs Ruth Lyle and Victoria,' Maddy said. 'She checked the entire call log for the previous six weeks.'

'I know, but we must be able to turn up something. Get Primrose in ASAP.'

'She's not on the rota till Monday.'

'We don't have time to waste. I want her at her desk first thing tomorrow morning,' Talantire said. 'Ready for when we bring in a huge stash of Victoria Carnegie's computers.'

'Good job that Wigwam isn't on duty this weekend. You couldn't expect him to organise a raid on his sister's home and office.'

'Not without tipping her off. No, we've got DI Blundell, who's also from Lynton. Would you ring him and set up the raid for six a.m. while I get on to the magistrate?'

'Righto,' Maddy said, resignedly. 'And I'll dig up some benefit application forms too, for when we get sacked for taking on the high and mighty.'

Talantire picked up the phone and dialled the duty magistrate hub. It was two a.m., a perfect time to get an awkward one, annoyed to have their sleep disturbed. She realised that, without the support of her boss, this was a high-risk operation.

The number rang out and was answered by a woman with clear Home Counties vowels. Talantire crossed her fingers and then said: 'I'd like to request a warrant to search the home and office of the sitting MP for North West Devon, Mrs Victoria Carnegie, in connection with the murder of Mrs Ruth Lyle in Ilfracombe on the first of April.'

There was a sharp intake of breath at the other end. The die was cast.

–

Primrose Chen certainly knew how to impress her team. She arrived before five a.m. with a welcome tray of coffees from the all-night place on the industrial estate. While Maddy and Nuttall sipped their drinks, Talantire briefed the digital evidence officer.

'So you got the warrant?' Primrose said, her eyes wide.

'Yes, after a long conversation with a sceptical magistrate. Two teams of three uniforms are going in at six o'clock sharp, to the MP's home and her office. In an hour.'

'Welcome to Operation Kamikaze,' Maddy said.

'Yeah, we're all toast,' Nuttall added.

'So are we all going to get fired?' Primrose asked, looking from one to the other, her voice already beginning to quaver.

'No,' Talantire said. 'We are going to catch the killer of Mrs Ruth Lyle, wherever that trail takes us. And if, for whatever reason this all blows up in our faces, I give you my personal guarantee that I will protect you, as well as the other members of the team, from the consequences. Everything you are doing today is because I ordered it, as your superior officer and the senior investigative officer in this case. If there is blame, I will take it personally.'

'Then ma'am, that is good enough for me,' Primrose said, sitting down and logging on to the system. 'I'll trace the relevant service providers as we already have the numbers, so I'll be able to get results by the time the raid takes place.'

—

It was 6:15 a.m. on Sunday, and Victoria Carnegie was smouldering like a volcano in the rape suite at Barnstaple police station. She had kept up a continuous harangue against the custody sergeant, the uniformed officers who had arrested her, and, when they came downstairs to begin the interrogation, against Talantire and Maddy. Finally, when the duty solicitor had arrived, she bitterly complained about the interview not being deferred long enough for her own solicitor to arrive.

'I mean, how is this pimply youth supposed to defend me against this noxious conspiracy?' she said, gesturing to the pale and tired-looking young man paid at public expense to represent her. Talantire knew the brief had already spent most of the previous evening at the station dealing with the usual quota of Saturday-night drunkards who occupied six of the eleven cells.

'I am fully qualified, and you can be sure that I will do a professional job,' the solicitor said, watching as the two detectives set up the tape machine. 'However, if I may advise you, it might be sensible to calm down.'

Victoria snarled at him, and turned round to face Talantire, pointing an accusatory and perfectly manicured finger at her. 'I'll have your pension off you, as well as your job, madam. And you, Detective Sergeant, you're going to spend your old age eating dog food, that's how poor you're going to be.'

'Going... to... spend... your... old... age... eating... dog... food...' Maddy repeated as she jotted down the threat in her notebook. She smiled at the MP as Talantire started the tape, recorded those who were present and cautioned the interviewee: 'Victoria Carnegie, you do not have to say anything. But it may harm your defence if you do not mention when questioned something which you later rely on in court. Anything you do say may be given in evidence.'

The MP glowered at the detectives. 'I would like it placed on record that I object to the manner in which uniformed police, without prior notice, descended upon my house and constituency office first thing on a Sunday morning, waking up my family, upsetting my pets, taking away computers, ransacking confidential files. I've always made myself available to officers in the pursuit of their duties, and my record will show that I am a firm supporter of the forces of law and order, yet I think I can say, without fear of contradiction—'

'— we don't have time for a speech, Mrs Carnegie,' Talantire said. 'You're not at the House of Commons now. You are suspected of involvement in the murder of Mrs Ruth Lyle on the first of April this year, and of perversion of the course of justice in relation to the 1973 killing of Ruth Lyle. Other charges may follow.'

'That is utterly preposterous,' Victoria responded.

'Did you know Mrs Ruth Lyle?' Maddy asked.

'Not really. I was briefly acquainted with Jamie Quince at university, and after the murder I was told that he – or I suppose I should now say *she*, or perhaps even *they* – was, or in the latter case possibly *were*, the victim.' She rolled her eyes at the solicitor.

Talantire didn't need to guess where the MP stood on gender rights. 'How did you get this information?'

'I suppose I read it in the papers.'

'There was nothing about Mr Quince released to the press,' Maddy said.

'Well. My brother is an inspector in Ilfracombe police force, as you well know.' She smiled coldly.

It was clear to see she had no compunction about dropping Wigwam in it. 'So are you saying that you had no contact whatsoever with Mrs Lyle after her return to Ilfracombe?'

'No, I didn't say that. I was leafleting for the council elections in the town towards the end of March, and I did get invited inside by a lady who lived at the top of Mercer Lane, and it wasn't until I was inside I recognised her, him or them. When I passed by the building after the murder, I realised it was the same place.'

'You never mentioned this before,' Talantire said.

'Simple reason: you never asked me.' Victoria rolled her eyes at her brief again.

'Exactly what date was that?' Maddy asked.

'The Monday of the week she died, I think.'

Talantire knew she hadn't appeared on the CCTV, but she might have come in from the Wilder Road end. 'Was somebody with you?'

'No, I was alone, I do remember that.'

'Canvassing is normally done in groups, isn't it?'

'Canvassing is, but I was just leafleting. I always make sure I have a stash of leaflets in my handbag anywhere in the constituency so no journey is ever wasted.'

'And when you were invited inside, where exactly did she take you?'

'Into the kitchen, as I recall. She, he or they made me a coffee.'

The two detectives exchanged a glance. The MP had just completely neutered the only forensic evidence against her for the recent crime. Whether this constituency visit was fiction or not it, would provide a plausible explanation for how her DNA had turned up on the tap in the kitchen where Mrs Ruth Lyle was later murdered. All she had to say was that she had washed her hands. Without something else, the case against the MP was going to crumble to pieces.

'No election leaflet was found,' Talantire said, weakly.

'Sadly, people *do* throw them away,' Victoria answered with a sarcastic smile. 'I try not to take it personally.'

'Was that the first time you had ever been into Bluebird Cottage?'

'Oh, I'm not sure. I had probably been there when I was working as an assistant to my father, who was the coroner.'

'You mean in relation to the 1973 killing?' Talantire asked.

'Yes, obviously.'

The two detectives excused themselves and paused the recording. They headed out into the anteroom, from which they could see through the one-way glass.

'She's a clever one,' Maddy said. 'There's nothing incriminating left. Not even the 1973 fag end with her DNA on it. We can't disprove anything she said.'

Talantire steepled her hands across her nose. She was looking at the end of her career. She had ignored her boss, gone out on a limb to make a high-profile arrest, and now it was all rebounding horribly upon her. There would be no one higher up who would back her. As Nuttall had so succinctly said, they were all toast now.

She sat down with a coffee to think, and idly checked her work phone, something she hadn't had a moment to do yet. There was the usual digest of overnight crimes from the control room. Assaults, drunk and disorderly, an allegation of rape, and an apparent suicide. There was also one forwarded message from the Prince of Darkness, simply saying: *Jan, I think you should see this.*

The original email was from the Reverend Neal Vaizey late the previous evening, and had been sent to many people in the church community, several of whom had forwarded it to the police. It had taken seven hours to reach DI Lockhart mainly because non-urgent police email addresses are not constantly monitored over the weekend.

Dear Friends,

You may have noticed my absence in recent days, and apologies to everyone for my failure to return calls. This is my last chance to apologise. I have tried to live my life in a moral and principled fashion in the sight of God, but it seems that my attempt to rehabilitate Gawain Entwistle has been a grave error. He stayed with me and confessed, as God is my witness, to both the 1973 killing and that of Mrs Ruth Lyle. I did not confirm this to the police as I should have done. There is nothing to do now but say goodbye. God will judge me for my mistakes, and I commend my soul to him.

Neal

Talantire almost screamed with horror: 'Maddy, Vaizey's sent a suicide note.'

'Shit! I don't believe it.'

They told the custody sergeant to make sure Victoria got something to eat, then both trooped upstairs to the CID office. Talantire logged onto her terminal, looked back over the crime log from the control room, and rang up to get a better report. It didn't take long for her to be sure.

'Yes, it's the suicide report from the log. A fishing vessel has reported a body at the base of cliffs near Hele Bay. There is no ID as yet, but it's described as a middle-aged male.'

'It must be him,' Maddy said. 'It's got to be.'

'Damn it! Why couldn't we find him?'

'Because he didn't want to be found, Jan.'

'Aargh! Everything is going wrong,' Talantire yelled, grabbing her own hair in frustration. 'He was our best hope.

He had a relationship with Ruth, and he might have told us everything.'

'No good crying over spilt milk,' Nuttall said, unhelpfully.

The full implications of the news were continuing to crystallise in Talantire's brain. 'Two members of Silken Subway are dead, one is telling us nothing, and we still don't know who the mystery drummer was. How are we going to get an insight into what happened back in 1973?'

Maddy leaned across her desk towards Talantire and said, 'In light of this, with Vaizey implicating Entwistle too, maybe...'

'Maybe what?'

'Maybe we should just go with the flow and charge Entwistle,' Maddy said quietly. 'Events are conspiring against us.'

Talantire stared at Maddy like she had just been stabbed in the back.

The detective sergeant candidly returned her gaze. 'Look, I'm sorry Jan, it's all well and good for you to go on a crusade for truth and justice. You've only got yourself to look after. But I've got three young kids to support, a useless husband, and a mortgage the size of Exmoor.'

Nuttall looked across from his desk, and said, 'Maddy's right, Jan. You've got to pick your battles. But if you insist on going on a righteous crusade you'll be needing this,' he added, lifting up the knife container that held the crucifix.

'Thank you, Dave. You're a great help,' Talantire said.

Primrose, who had been working at the data kiosk, looked up. 'I'm still on your side, ma'am. I think we've got to find the real killer. Otherwise, what are we here for?'

'Thank you, Primrose,' Talantire said. 'I'm glad somebody is offering some moral support.'

'Well, it's not just moral actually,' Primrose added. 'I just stumbled across something odd in Victoria Carnegie's burner phone. Take a look.'

Chapter 26

10 p.m. the previous night

The Reverend Neal Vaizey parked on Hele Beach Road, and made his way through the woods up onto the cliffs, heading towards Forthglade on the South West Coast Path. There was just enough light to see where he was going, but in truth he knew exactly what to expect. A final meeting to end this damnable conflict. After ten minutes he ascended the final, steep, worn-out section of path, which promised a wooden bench at the viewpoint. There was no one around, and little sound bar the wind. The cliffs were just ten yards away, and the last of the evening's gulls slid above, scything the buffeting air. They watched him speculatively: gliding grey, ruthless, opportunistic. Not the only such creatures up here; breathing heavily, he rounded the final turn and saw that, as expected, the bench was occupied.

'Hello, Neal,' the man said.

'You've got to stop this, now,' Vaizey said. 'Or it will end in disaster.'

'No, no, Neal. You worry too much. Entwistle is going to go down for it, I have it on good authority.'

'So are you going to give up the photographs?'

There was no reply.

'You said you would, Groz,' Vaizey said.

He laughed. 'No one calls me that now.'

'You've worked hard to reinvent yourself, that's why. But I want the pictures. That's why I'm here.'

'My Polaroids are my guarantee, Neal, you know that.'

'For God's sake man, it's been fifty years!'

'Ah, but they've never been needed more than now. That lovely picture with your arm round young Ruth, and the one with her giving you that adoring look. And some of the others, of course. Really incriminating ones. Maybe I will give them to you, I'm not sure.'

The faint urgency of sirens drifted up to them. They both looked behind them, down into the town, all twinkling lights, where a police patrol car, tiny as a toy, raced from the direction of Combe Martin towards the centre of town, blue lights flashing. 'You better not have been followed,' Groz said softly.

'No, I kept a lookout.' Vaizey turned and peered at the car. It had already passed the turn-off for Hele Beach, and now it disappeared from view, the siren dwindling into the distance.

'Then that's all right,' he said.

'The police are unravelling everything,' Vaizey said. 'The photos won't save you, Groz. They are better destroyed.'

'I'm not so sure.'

'The police want to know who the drummer was, and they will find you out.'

'But it doesn't prove anything does it? Just being in the band.'

'Have they got your DNA?' Vaizey asked. 'They've certainly made sure they got mine.'

'I don't think so. It wouldn't prove anything anyway. The only thing that would be dangerous, is if someone talks.' He stood up, hands deep in the pockets of his heavy trenchcoat, and looked out to sea.

'I won't talk.'

'I'm not sure, Neal. You've always had a bit of a conscience. Unlike her. She's hard as nails, focused on greater things, I hear. I've no need to worry there. But you – I have a horrible feeling you might want to sacrifice yourself to the greater glory.'

'No need to worry. I won't.'

His hands were still deep in his pockets, eyes searching the horizon for answers. 'Ah, but look at all the motives you might have, Neal. Self-sacrifice for truth, for justice, in self-conscious Christian piety, in pursuit of blessed martyrdom.'

'You can mock my conscience, but you've never had one, Groz. Not a hint of one. I saw that all the time we were sharing a house.' Vaizey thought back to 78d Cranmer Road, Exeter, the nightmare of 1972–73. Cramped, cold and dingy. He was lucky enough as a student on a grant to have the large airy ground-floor room. Jamie was upstairs. And then Groz, two years older, a hospital porter, already resident in the basement, the filthiest room in the place. The noises he used to hear from below, in the night. Women, and girls, halfway between pleasure and pain. Always gone by morning. And here was Groz, after all these years, reinvented in a new life, but still with such a hold on all of them.

'Neal: it's a good name for a priest, isn't it? A man who spends his time on his knees.'

'Only to God, I bend for no other.'

'You've bent to me, Neal. For half a century.' Groz laughed, and turned to look at him. 'And for good reason. It was six years after you when I finally went to university. But I always understood the tools of the world as it is: power, opportunity, leverage, control. Anticipation of the actions of others.'

'Those are the tools of war, and I never believed in them.'

'But they are the tools of society, economics and politics too. And they work whether you believe in them or not. Unlike your God.'

'It is the power of Christ within us that works.'

'Not within me, Neal. Nor her. She's a lot like me. She knows what works and what doesn't.'

'Is she coming to join us? You said she might.'

'She did say she'd message you.' He smiled. 'Have you got a signal?'

'I think so.' Vaizey checked his phone. 'No message though.' He looked up. 'I'd have been surprised. We never talked, you know. Not afterwards.'

'I know. She never forgave you. Her jealousy is as pure and undimmed as an emerald, isn't it?' He looked around. 'Look, I'm a reasonable man. Here's what you want.'

Vaizey looked down at the envelope Groz offered to him in a gloved hand. Why was he wearing gloves? It wasn't that cold.

He didn't see the other hand. Didn't see the hammer until it was too late, until the pain had exploded and snatched away his consciousness. After collapsing, he didn't feel Groz take his phone, didn't feel being dragged towards the cliff edge over the rough path. He didn't feel being rolled off the precipice. The Reverend Neal Vaizey came to, briefly, once he had begun to fall, in the final millisecond of his life, barely enough time for a prayer. He glimpsed a bright welcoming light. But all he heard was the shriek of gulls, alerted to a feast on the sea-thrashed rocks below.

Chapter 27

Talantire, Maddy and Nuttall gathered round the data kiosk, a desktop unit about the size of a photocopier. Primrose had it linked into her workstation. 'This phone was found in her handbag, but it's not the one registered to her. I suspected it might be a burner phone and thought I would look at it first. I'm glad I did, because she forwarded an email to an unregistered mobile at around 7:46 p.m. last night. Look at this.' She brought the email up on the screen, and the three detectives looked over her shoulder.

'It's a copy of the rector's suicide note. He probably sent it to her,' Nuttall said.

'But Vaizey didn't send out his note until nearly eleven p.m.,' Maddy said. 'The MP sent this copy at a quarter to eight.'

'Ah! It was forwarded,' Talantire said, 'and look at the extra line in the forwarding email. "I tweaked it a bit, I think it will do the trick." And it's signed V, presumably for Victoria.'

'Victoria wrote it for him?' Maddy said, puzzled. 'Why on earth didn't he write his own…?'

'She didn't write it for *him*,' Talantire said. 'She wrote it for whoever killed him, who immediately after throwing him off a cliff emailed everyone in Vaizey's contact list with a bogus suicide note, which just happens to incorporate a confession that no one can ever verify.'

'So not a suicide. It's a third murder,' Nuttall said, leaning back in his chair and yawning, his arms behind his head. 'Just as well – we were running out of work, weren't we?'

'Maddy, can you make sure there's a CSI team sent to the site of the body recovery?' Talantire said. 'And to the clifftops above. We've got almost no time.' She turned to Primrose, and tapped the screen she'd been working on. 'This, young lady, is a fantastic piece of work.'

The young digital evidence officer beamed, and flushed slightly. 'Thank you ma'am. I would also direct your attention to a later text that came in to her burner phone from the same sender.' She moved the mouse and clicked. 'It just says, "It's done". That was at 10:18 p.m.'

'That would be the killer,' Talantire said. 'But you say it's from an unregistered phone?'

'Yes, but I have some triangulation data. It's slightly awkward because we have to rely on masts in South Wales because of the signal shadows in Ilfracombe itself. But this is a map trace of the location of the phone from yesterday evening.' Her fingers danced across the keyboard and switched to a map that showed a red trace that crossed and recrossed a Google Map of Ilfracombe.

'Can you cross-reference the times, Primrose?' Talantire asked.

Primrose hit a couple of keys, and the trace was marked by time stamps.

'Right, here we are,' Talantire said. 'At ten o'clock it was moving up towards the cliff from Hele Bay, the furthest point at the cliff edge is reached at... ten... twelve p.m. So that's it, the killer threw Vaizey's body off the cliff at say 10:12, texted Victoria to say it was done at 10:18. She had already sent him a revised suicide note, which he then copied from her message into the rector's phone, and sent to everybody on his contact list at around eleven.'

'How did he lure Vaizey up there?' Maddy asked.

'I don't know,' Talantire said. 'But he may have had some-thing on him, perhaps about the 1973 relationship.'

'I feel a bit sorry for Vaizey,' Maddy said. 'The fact he befriended Gawain Entwistle indicates that he felt guilty. It wasn't just Christian charity for those fallen on hard times.'

'Right,' Nuttall said. 'We have a murdering MP downstairs, and proof that it was she who wrote Vaizey's suicide note.'

'Let's get a little more ammunition,' Talantire said. 'Primrose, do you have a triangulation on the phone found in Victoria Carnegie's bedroom?'

'Yes. The trace was right there in her house at the time she forwarded the suicide note.'

'Good. Print out a screenshot. Did we get fingerprints on the phone itself?'

'No, I don't think so,' Maddy said. 'Blundell didn't mention it, and the raid officers were just a bunch of plods. But if it was in her own bedside cabinet she can hardly deny it's hers, can she?'

'If it's possible, she will,' Talantire said. She knew they could hold the MP for twenty-four hours. In theory they could double that at least with a sign-off from a senior officer. But, given the attitude of DS Wells, they would need really solid evidence. The discussion was interrupted by a phone call from the control room that said that Vaizey's car had been found in Hele Beach Road.

Maddy logged into the ANPR system to check if it came up anywhere else. It hadn't, but something else was flagged up. 'Shit, why didn't I notice that?' she said. 'One of our previous vehicles of interest in the last twenty-four hours triggered cameras between Bideford and Barnstaple, and then back again.'

'Which one?' Talantire asked.

'A Toyota Prius belonging to our favourite solicitor, Roger Keane.'

'He's supposed to be in the Canaries until next week.'

'That's what I was told, but it could be a member of his family.'

'The receptionist at the firm said it was a family holiday, so somebody is lying,' Talantire said, turning round to look at Nuttall. 'Dave, can you chase this down for me while we have another go at our MP downstairs? I need to know if Keane is in that car.'

'Righto.' He picked up the phone.

'And Dave, when you find it, get that vehicle swabbed for DNA and prints.'

–

Just after eight a.m., down in the interview room, Talantire set a printout of the emails in front of the interviewee. 'How do you explain this, Victoria?' she asked.

'I don't know anything about it,' the MP said. 'Where did you get it?'

'From the phone we found in your handbag.'

'Oh, that's not my phone.'

'You identified it as being yours to the officer who seized it at your home,' Maddy interjected.

'No, I was mistaken. I think it belongs to a constituent who left it behind after a meeting.'

'Which constituent?' Talantire asked.

'I'm sure my secretary can tell you, she was looking into it.'

'So you haven't used this phone.'

'No.'

'Were any constituents in your home at ten o'clock yesterday?'

The MP didn't answer. Her eyes darted around as if she were searching for the least incriminating response.

'Mrs Carnegie, please answer—'

'No, but—'

'Explain this: we can prove this phone was used in your home at around ten o'clock yesterday evening, in contact with another burner phone that was located on top of the cliff above Hele Bay, just above where the Reverend Neal Vaizey was this morning found dead.'

'Dead? Oh God, poor Neal.'

The look of faux shock on the MP's face wasn't convincing. 'We believe that the so-called suicide note sent from the Reverend Vaizey's phone last night was actually written by you, and emailed from this burner phone of yours to the killer, who then typed it in on Vaizey's phone.'

She said nothing, but held Talantire's gaze without blinking.

'You used to go out with Neal Vaizey, didn't you? During the days of Silken Subway?'

Victoria raised one eyebrow but said nothing.

'But we know that you had a rival. A very pretty, vivacious schoolgirl, who looked eighteen but was in fact two years younger. Ruth Lyle poured out her affection to Neal, and some of those letters survive and are in our possession. We believe they met on several occasions.'

'This is nonsense.'

'You knew about this relationship, didn't you?'

'Detective Inspector. Have you found my fingerprints or DNA on the murder weapon?' she asked, arching her eyebrow again. 'If you had, I think you would have told me.'

'We have plenty of evidence linking you to the killing.'

'You are, if I may say so, avoiding the question, Ms Talantire.'

'We are asking the questions,' Maddy intervened. 'And here's three: did you conspire to murder Ruth Lyle in 1973? Did you conspire to kill Mrs Ruth Lyle last week? And did you arrange for the killing of the Reverend Neal Vaizey last night?'

'No, no and no.'

While Maddy continued questioning the MP, Talantire looked at her phone. After reading a message, she suspended the interview and again beckoned Maddy outside. 'Uniforms have followed the car back to Keane's home in Bideford. His wife answered the door, but said he wasn't there. She expressed bewilderment at the idea that they were on holiday.'

'We're not going to crack Victoria, are we?' Maddy said.

'I doubt it. She's brazen, that's for sure. Let's leave her stewing for a while and go after Keane.'

–

Talantire and Maddy ran downstairs and jumped into the first available unmarked car. Unusually, it was the two-year-old blue race-tuned BMW, the Prince of Darkness's preferred vehicle, almost never available to anyone else. As they were heading out, they recognised the black four-wheel drive of the police and crime commissioner, turning in to the police station car park. 'Whoops, that's Victoria's cavalry by the looks of it,' Maddy said. 'And he's got somebody with him.'

'Did he recognise us?' Talantire asked as she hit the accelerator and flicked on the blue lights.

'I don't think so, but he must have a big bee in his bonnet to be out of bed before nine o'clock on a Sunday morning. I think it's you he's come to sting.'

'Maybe. Who was the other person?'

'A white-haired geezer, maybe Victoria's personal lawyer?'

'Venables is this morning's custody sergeant. He'll take over at nine.'

They roared around the roundabout outside the industrial estate, and sped off to the A39 heading west.

'I wonder if he's heard that Victoria is getting him moved to dog handling?' Maddy said, with a chuckle.

'Either way, he knows it's more than his job's worth to release her.'

Talantire turned on the police radio to find out the latest on Keane. The control room told them that four uniformed officers were now at Keane's home. His wife had now admitted that her husband had returned home in the Prius, then slipped out of the side entrance on his mountain bike.

'Right, I think we can catch him,' Talantire said. She asked the hands-free to connect her to Primrose Chen.

'Hi, Primrose,' she said when the digital evidence officer picked up. 'Do you still have a trace on the phone used at the clifftop to contact Victoria Carnegie?'

'Yes, ma'am.'

'Good. I want a live trace, or as up-to-date as you can manage on triangulation. First, I want you to coordinate it with an ANPR hit on a Toyota Prius on the southbound A361 from Ilfracombe to Braunton. I want to know if that phone was in the vehicle. Second, I want to know if that phone is turned on and where it is now.'

'Okay. As it's a burner phone, he probably won't guess that we are tracking it.'

'That's what I'm hoping. We're heading off now to Westward Ho! Keane's home backs onto Abbotsham Cliffs and it wouldn't surprise me if he's heading down the coastal path. We should be there in three minutes.'

She cut the call, hit the sirens and overtook a couple of trucks at over eighty. Maddy held on to the dashboard as Talantire swung the car round the Devon bends. By the time she arrived outside Keane's house, confirmation had come through from Primrose. It was the same phone, and had been in the Toyota Prius.

She saw that a CSI unit was there, with officers crawling all over the Toyota. She buzzed down the BMW's window and was approached by the senior uniform, an Inspector Patel based in Woolacombe. He told her that two officers had set off along the cliff path, heading west, and, thanks to the tracking screen forwarded to them by Primrose Chen, a separate patrol car with two officers was heading to Fairy Cross to try to head Keane off.

'So is he our murderer?' Patel asked.

'Yes, I certainly think he threw the Reverend Vaizey off a cliff,' Talantire said. 'It's a bit murkier for the other two killings, but I'm sure he was involved. Right, we're heading off now to Fairy Cross too.' Gunning the engine, she executed a screeching turn and headed off with sirens blaring, back onto the A39 heading south-west.

'I'm just googling Roger Keane,' Maddy said, looking down at her iPad. 'I've read the profile on the partnership website before, and there's nothing about where he went to university. He wasn't on the list of Exeter graduates either.'

'Well, that's probably what threw us off the trail.'

Once they arrived at Fairy Cross, they headed down a narrow country lane ending in a National Trust car park. A patrol car was already there, blue lights flashing.

'He's turned the phone off,' Maddy said, looking at her iPad, where the live trace had been showing. 'But he should be passing here soon.'

The hands-free came through with a call from Primrose. 'Ma'am, as you've probably seen, the trace has gone dead. But two minutes before that a call popped up onto the log for the target phone.'

'So somebody else knows of the burner.'

'Yes. In fact I've just traced the number, and it's from here, a landline.'

'What!'

'Yes, here, the police station.'

'Let's get this clear, Primrose. You're saying one of our colleagues tipped him off? A police officer?'

It all made sense. A bent cop, perhaps even Wells, someone involved in recycling the murder weapon, passing across the documentation. But it would have to be someone who'd been in the force a long time. Or maybe several people.

'Primrose? Can you find out which phone, on whose desk?'

'Yes. I'll need a few minutes.'

The paranoid possibilities spiralled in her head until she saw suspects everywhere. Finally, she thought of the commissioner, who had arrived moments before they left. Of course! He was in on it, with the property deal, and in cahoots with Victoria. Talantire now realised she was standing, almost alone, against the biggest guns in Devon and Cornwall Police.

Chapter 28

She hung up and turned to Maddy, who had got the gist of it. 'If someone at the station is working with Keane, and Victoria, and they have DS Wells on their side, we don't stand a chance, do we?' Maddy asked.

'Probably not,' Talantire conceded.

'Right, I'll get down to Asda and load up on pet food.'

'What?'

'To see if I like the taste, seeing as I'll be eating it for the rest of my life. According to Victoria Carnegie.' She folded her arms and stared out of the window.

'Right,' Talantire said. 'Let's get out and find Keane at least.'

As she opened the door, the phone rang. It was Primrose. Talantire put it on speaker. 'It wasn't a desk phone, Ma'am. I was confused, so I went down to check, and the outbound number is actually the payphone next to the custody suite.'

'That makes sense,' Talantire said. 'They wouldn't want to be overheard tipping Keane off.'

'Actually, I asked Sergeant Venables who had used it, and he told me the MP had. She had insisted on her right to make a call, and he had agreed.'

'Bloody hell, she's warned him off.' Talantire turned to Maddy. 'It wasn't a cop!'

'Well, so Venables says, if you believe him,' Maddy replied.

Talantire shrugged and turned back to the phone. 'Is the commissioner still there, Primrose?'

'He's gone. He marched up into CID, made a huge fuss, said we'd all gone mad, and spent the next fifteen minutes on the phone to the assistant chief constable. He was shouting at him, and we could hear it even though he was in one of the meeting rooms.'

'But Venables didn't let her go?'

'No.'

'Good.' Talantire hid her surprise. Venables appeared to have some backbone, one virtue despite all his other vices.

'She's got some top London lawyer with her now,' Primrose said.

'Okay, thank you for that.' Talantire cut the call. She and Maddy left the car and approached the patrol car. One female PC emerged to greet them.

'The suspect's out there somewhere,' she said. 'The phone's gone dead, and there are loads of gullies and gorse. PCs Davies and Compton are out there, but we need loads more bodies to track him down.' She looked up at the heavily clouded sky. 'It looks like we're in for a soaking too.'

They could feel the first drops of rain. Talantire rummaged in her go-bag on the back seat and pulled out a showerproof jacket and a pair of trainers. Maddy had nothing, but found in the boot one of Lockhart's police fleeces. She wasted no time in putting it on and hugging herself. 'I feel his warming presence already,' she said, with a smile.

The two detectives squelched off down a narrow muddy path, into the face of a rising wind. Several hundred yards ahead of them, Talantire could see the hi-vis jacket of either Davies or Compton, close to the cliff edge. She ran ahead towards the PC, leaving Maddy floundering to catch up. The path dipped into a huge brake of yellow-flowered gorse. 'I've got him, he's over here,' came a breathless voice from nearby.

'I'm coming,' Talantire said. She rounded the corner into a marshy area surrounded by gorse, and glimpsed a chequered constabulary cap and flash of hi-vis. The officer was standing over a body. She ran to his left side, and crouched down by the prone figure, a young bloodstained man, half in a large gorse

bush. Not the man they were looking for, but clearly unconscious. A police radio crackled in the bush nearby, a broken
bodycam lay near it. Something strange, something familiar.
Something wrong.

'Hang on a minute,' she said, glancing up at the officer.

Not a cop, but wearing a police hi-vis jacket and cap.

Roger Keane.

His big hand reached out and grabbed her by the throat.
She tried to scream, but no sound emerged. He rose to his full
height, lifting her, and from his other hand swung an already
bloodstained hammer. Instinct kicked in, and she raised her left
arm to block it, and felt the hammer smash into her forearm. In
her agony, she reached out to his hammer arm with her right,
but was forced onto her back. She couldn't connect properly,
but at least got a grip on his wrist, stopping the hammer. But
he was strong, and his grip on her throat relentless, his knee
now on her stomach. She was starting to see stars. That poor
policeman, on the ground nearby, who might be dead. And she
was fighting for her life. Could they be seen? They were in a
dip, in the shadow of a drystone wall.

Keane was breathing heavily, and she was emitting a low
whine, but over this she could hear Maddy calling out her name,
not far away. He was distracted by the sound for a moment,
which gave her the chance to bend back the thumb that was
over her windpipe. It released for a moment, and she yelled at
the top of her voice. Maddy was nearly there, panting heavily,
and suddenly Keane let go. He tried to kick Talantire in the
side of the head, but her bruised left arm again got in the way.
Then he was off.

Talantire levered herself up as Maddy came into view. 'Look
after him,' she said, pointing to the prone officer, who had a
bloody wound on the side of his head. 'I'm going after that
bastard.'

Looking up, she could see the other male officer approaching
from the right, while Keane mounted his trail bike, which had

been hidden behind a bush. She was heavily out of breath but she had to go for him. Keane headed left, bumping up over the path through narrow gaps in the gorse. She sprinted after him, and saw him rise up on the pedals. She had to get him in the next ten seconds or he would get away. She filled her lungs and raced, extending her legs and pumping her arms. She was in so much pain, but focused it like a laser on her objective. The bumpy path was impeding him, and she closed to within a few feet as he put a foot down to negotiate the bike across some rocks.

She threw herself at him, hitting him from the side. He tumbled from the bike and they rolled into the gorse together. This time he was underneath, without his hammer, and Talantire punched him twice in the face. He tried to grab her throat again, but this time she caught his thumb, twisted it backwards, forcing him to rotate. He roared in pain as he rolled over, and she finished subduing him with PAVA spray.

By the time the other officer had arrived, he was helpless, with blood, tears and snot pouring down his face.

'Okay,' he gasped. 'Enough, I give up.'

When PC Davies arrived, Keane was handcuffed, then marched back to the patrol car while paramedics were called for PC Compton. The young officer was unconscious, but breathing. Once the ambulance had arrived, and departed again carrying the injured officer, Talantire returned to the patrol car, where the bloodied Keane was sitting handcuffed in the back.

'You've got nothing on me,' he said. True enough. Talantire searched him and couldn't find any sign of the phone. That would be something to track down in the hours ahead. However, she did take a DNA swab from him, with the intention of getting it couriered for the fastest possible service.

'Roger Keane, I am charging you with the murder of the Reverend Neal Vaizey, and with the attempted murder of PC Ian Compton.' She then cautioned him, and told him he would be held in custody until a magistrate's hearing could be arranged. 'I will now be getting a warrant to search your home as well as your offices.'

Maddy, who had been with the injured officer, approached, grim-faced.

'How is he doing?' Talantire asked.

'I'm not sure but it looks bad. The paramedic said he's unresponsive, but thank God there's no sign of spinal injury, so they could move him. They'll get him an MRI.'

Talantire turned to the suspect. 'Three dead, one seriously injured, one innocent boy unjustly jailed for a lifetime, lives and reputations ruined. How on earth did all of this start?'

Chapter 29

They got Keane back to Barnstaple in half an hour, during which time he complained that Talantire had broken his nose. He remained truculent and uncooperative during the first half an hour of interrogation, after which he was cleaned up and given an hour to stew in the cells. They then hauled him up, still red-eyed from the PAVA spray, and now with a dressing over his nose. He merely folded his arms, and demanded breakfast 'As is my right', and refused to answer any questions. He was left again for another hour, but at 9:45 a.m., as Talantire watched through the one-way glass, the duty sergeant arrived with a cold Greggs sausage roll and a plastic cup of Dr Crippen's best tomato soup for the prisoner, and pronounced it brunch. Keane's hitherto smug solicitor face dissolved into sneering contempt.

'Green tomato soup? Right. I want to speak to her,' he said. 'And I will give a statement.'

Talantire let him stew another few minutes, in time for the arrival of a new duty solicitor, a middle-aged woman, then with the sergeant led her into the interview room. The moment the door opened, Keane pointed at the uneaten food: 'Police and Criminal Evidence Act 1984, I'm entitled to at least two meals a day,' he declaimed. 'A sausage roll is *not* a meal.'

The sergeant, a cold-eyed fellow called Hipkiss, retorted: 'There's nothing in PACE that says it ain't. We have operational difficulties in the kitchen, so I sent a PC out to get this specially. There's M&S chicken balti if you are still with us this evening, so think yourself lucky. I haven't had any breakfast myself.' Talantire, whose own hammer-bruised arm was bandaged, found herself wishing she had managed to hit Keane a few more times. After prepping the tape, and repeating the charges and the caution, she brought in DC Nuttall and began the interview.

'Right, Mr Keane. We've heard from the hospital that PC Compton has a bleed on the brain. You're going down for a long time, for that alone, let alone the other charges. So it's in your interests to cooperate. Will you?'

He shrugged.

'So let's start right at the beginning, when you first met James Quince, Neal Vaizey and Victoria Carnegie.'

He emitted a huge sigh and began: 'It was at seventy-eight Cranmer Road, in Newtown. I lived there for three years in Flat D, the basement, and the students were upstairs, because they could afford to pay more rent. It was a pretty wild house, to be sure, with lots of parties and a fair amount of drugs, and it was through selling some of my supplies that I paid my own rent.'

'So were you employed?' Talantire asked. 'Or were you dealing full-time?'

'No. I worked part-time as a hospital porter, and that's how I was able to get a plentiful supply of uppers and downers, through a friend at the dispensary.'

She looked at him, the successful conveyancing solicitor, and tried to imagine what he would have been like back then. Long hair, black nail varnish, a sideline in drugs and an affinity for heavy metal. And a darker side that no one had yet discovered.

'So the students all lived upstairs?'

'Yes, it was always a student house.' He cupped his arms behind his head, the same smug pose he'd adopted when she first interviewed him at home. But this time there were dark sweat patches in his armpits.

'Tell me about Neal Vaizey.'

'I met Neal in the autumn of 1972. He was the cool, good-looking, self-assured type. He lived immediately upstairs

279

from me, and I used to hear him playing his guitar. He was damned good, and it was that first Christmas, his second year at college, that he set up Silken Subway. He recruited his girl-friend Victoria Carnegie, who had previously been in another band, I don't recall—'

'The Winnowers?' Talantire interrupted.

'Yes, that's right.' Keane looked impressed that she knew this detail.

'They had a Christmas gig at the student union. That went okay, but the drummer dropped out of university in January, having been caught with a pack of Mandrax.' Keane couldn't restrain a sly smile.

'Drugs supplied by you?'

He nodded. 'Contained methaqualone and diphenhyd-ramine. Anyway, they were desperate for a replacement for their main gig, the Stag and Hounds in February 1973, where they were supporting a genuine professional band.'

'The Car Crash Three,' Nuttall supplied. 'Before Dave Archer was on lead guitar, before they hit the big time.'

'You've done your research,' Keane said. 'So I told them I'd do it, but in truth I'd never really played the drums. I didn't know exactly what I was doing, and unfortunately it showed. I was as high as a kite for most of the set, so no surprise there was no third gig. I think Neal was angry for me having misled them, but—'

'Tell us how you met Ruth Lyle,' Talantire said.

He said nothing.

'Come on, we know you must have met her,' she said.

He sighed. 'I had noticed this lively girl dancing at the front, really gyrating and into it. I don't recall what happened after the gig, as I'd mixed cider and amphetamines and God knows what, so I was wrecked, but next afternoon Victoria banged on my door, and said they were going out for some fresh air. It was cold at the seafront, and when we got there Jamie Quince came along, with this girl in tow.'

'Ruth Lyle,' Talantire said.

'Yeah. He looked pretty pleased with himself, so we drew the appropriate conclusion.'

'That he'd slept with her?'

'Yeah, Jamie later told me that Ruth had the keys to a disused chapel and had sex with him on the altar, which was an impressive story. But even in my state I could see she was spending more time staring at Neal than Jamie, and from Victoria's face I knew that was going to be trouble. She'd only been going out with Neal a few months, and she was always the jealous type.'

'You mentioned photos?' Nuttall said, looking back at the early partial statement.

'Yeah. I had a Polaroid camera—'

'That sounds like quite an investment back then,' Talantire said. 'Why not an ordinary camera?'

Keane smiled ruefully. 'I'd saved up for it, to take candid pictures—'

'You mean nude, or was it pornographic?' Nuttall asked.

Keane shrugged. 'I'd had a few adventurous girlfriends who didn't mind, so… Anyway, I took a few ordinary snaps of all of us, just sitting together shivering at the seafront. There was one of Ruth with her arms draped round Neal and Jamie, but it was Neal she was giving an adoring look to.'

'Do those pictures survive?' Talantire asked.

'Most of them, yes. I had the ones I needed, but you won't find them.'

Talantire knew that a search was currently under way at Keane's home and office. 'Why not tell us where they are and save us some time?'

'I'll think about it. Anyway, a week later I saw Jamie in the house, and he looked downcast. I guessed what had happened, and he confirmed it. Said Ruth had dumped him for Neal. I knew he was pretty innocent for nineteen, but he seemed totally smitten and angry with Neal for "stealing his girlfriend" as he put it. I guessed this was one of the reasons the band broke up. Victoria had gone off in a huff too.' Keane looked at Talantire. 'It all sounds like a storm in a teacup, doesn't it?'

'People have been stabbed for less,' Talantire muttered.

Keane resumed his tale: 'The next Saturday, Victoria, who had dropped out of college in the first year, drove over to see me, in her father's XJ12 Jaguar no less. It was only a week or so after Ruth had dumped Jamie. She told me that Ruth was getting to be a problem, now pursuing Neal and making it obvious. She was angry about it, especially when she heard that Neal had come back to Ilfracombe to see the girl, and had her phone number. Victoria said she knew of my reputation with women, via Neal, and asked me to try to prise Ruth away from Neal. She had it all worked out. She knew where Ruth lived, the pubs she visited, and suggested that I help her.'

'So to be clear,' Talantire said. 'Victoria Carnegie commissioned you for what turned out to be a murder?'

'Whoa, no! She wanted me to seduce her, take her out, go to the cinema, that's all.'

'But how would that work? Ruth presumably preferred Neal to you?' Nuttall asked.

'Yes, but I could slip into the conversation some stories that would put her off Neal.'

'Such as?'

'A few lies. Victoria suggested I say that Neal had VD, as they called it then, or had got a girl pregnant and abandoned her.'

'So you went ahead with this?'

'Yes, but I had my own motives. Having heard from Jamie about sex on the altar, I thought I'd get some of that.' Seeing the look on Talantire's face he said, 'Look, I was twenty-one, for God's sake. Which young man wouldn't be tempted?'

'Go on,' she said.

'The following Wednesday, I rang Ruth at home and said Neal and I were coming to Ilfracombe for an evening out, but could meet her after the pubs closed—'

'So that was three days before she died?'

'Yes. I suggested at the disused chapel. "How do you know about that?" she asked. I told her that we'd heard it would make a great place to record a song, with the echo acoustics, and asked if we could get the keys. She was quite enthusiastic, and told me she had a spare key. She even wanted to sing along with us, so I said yes.'

'You lied to her, didn't you?'

Keane shrugged. 'We all did, didn't we? Victoria, Neal, me. Only Jamie was true to her, and she didn't want him, poor sod. He was all doe-eyed, radiating desperation. Victoria had given me a lift into town, but then made herself scarce. When I arrived, I saw Ruth. She showed me into the chapel, but wanted to know where Neal was, so I said he'd be a bit late as he was breaking up with Victoria. I told her he was doing it so he could be with her. She fell for this hook, line and sinker, and seemed enthusiastic. I brought out three cans of cider that I had with me. Once she'd had the first can I started on about the way Neal treated women, and that she could do better. She didn't say much, but she was up for the next can, though she kept asking when Neal was coming. When she wasn't looking I dropped half a tab of powdered Mandrax into her can and took a few amphetamines myself.'

'Mandrax was a date rape drug, wasn't it?' Talantire asked.

'Well, it's a central nervous depressant and hypnotic, so yes. You can use it for calming someone down. Anyway, we discussed the general failings of men while I waited for it to take effect. "Has Jamie been talking about what we did?" she asked. I said he hadn't. Anyway, after a while I started holding her and then we kissed. I know how to arouse a woman, and then after a while she unzipped me, and one thing led to another.'

'Let's be clear, Mr Keane,' Talantire said. 'You drugged her and got her to perform oral sex on you?'

'She wanted to.'

Talantire pointed her pen at him, which made her bruised forearm hurt. 'I would suggest that a drugged girl, barely of age, cannot give consent. You committed a sexual assault.'

'You weren't there. She was up for it. When I brought out the camera, she didn't mind at all.'

'You have a Polaroid of this?'

'Several. I gave one to her, and kept the rest. I don't recall exactly how the evening ended, but Victoria picked me up at eleven, so she later told me.'

'So you drugged this young woman, raped her and left her to find her own way home.'

'It wasn't rape!'

'She couldn't give consent, so I suggest it was,' Talantire said.

'How could it be? I rang her the next day, and she was happy to come back on Saturday for more.'

'Mr Keane, you of all people should be aware of the law on consent,' Talantire said.

'I wasn't a lawyer then, was I?'

'So she came back on Saturday,' Talantire said.

'And that was the day she died,' Nuttall interjected.

'Yes. But it was an accident.'

Talantire and Nuttall exchanged a glance.

'So what exactly happened?' Nuttall asked. 'Witness statements of the time said she stood outside the chapel at around eleven p.m., smoking, as if waiting.'

'Yes, that's right. I'd brought drinks, had already dropped a tab of hydrocodone, and it seemed she'd already had a couple of drinks – I could taste cider when I kissed her. It went on as before, we had sex on and around the altar, and I took a couple more photos. Then I found some old vestments and put them on. Ruth and I were playing around, being vampires. She said she wanted to be in a horror film, and I pretended to bite her neck, while she was on the altar, giggling away. Then we heard this noise, and saw that this gawky lad had been watching us. "What are you doing here, Gawain?" she asked. It was clear she

284

knew him. Turned out he was the son of the caretaker, and had provided Ruth with the keys. He was horrified as to what was going on, but he was clearly terrified of me, seeing me with my shoulder-length hair, black nails – and, with what I'd been taking, pinhole eyes. I think he thought I was some kind of priest. I told him I was the Dark Angel, come to take revenge on a Peeping Tom. I suppose I must have been an imposing figure, because I grabbed this old crucifix from the pillar above the altar, and told the boy to come to me. He was absolutely terrified, and I dragged him up to where Ruth was writhing on the slab, pretty much naked, pretending to be scared of the cross. I forced his hands onto it, and brought him over to her. He was terrified of her nakedness, but then I pressed the point of the cross against her body and took a photo or two. "No, look, you've got to kill the vampire by stabbing it with a stake through the heart." He didn't want any part of it, and with my hands on his we wrestled with the cross. Then, somehow, he stopped pulling away, and the crucifix with both our hands on it went down into her chest like a knife into butter. She stopped moving instantly – her eyes were still open, but she was definitely dead. I pulled away, but he didn't. He froze, and got covered in blood as it spurted out. "You did this, you idiot," I shouted at him. "And you will be punished by the Lord." I grabbed the Polaroids, those I could find, and fled.'

Talantire had been cross-checking the notes they had for the 1973 investigation. 'I'm surprised that, given the number of witnesses, you student band members weren't called in for questioning.'

'Oh, we were,' Keane said. 'Neal particularly, because they found something Ruth had written about him. But we stuck together, said we didn't know her well. Which in truth we didn't. With Gawain's prints on the murder weapon there was no need to look any further.'

'But we haven't found any record of those interviews,' Nuttall said.

Keane laughed. 'Victoria's dad the coroner saw to that. After a few years, Hogley let it be known that the interview records had been "lost". That's what she told me. The message that came back via her dad was that it was just student high spirits, nothing to hang over us for the rest of our lives.'

'So that's why the picture you have of Ruth Lyle gazing adoringly at Neal remained so powerful,' Talantire said. 'It contradicted his statement.'

'Got it in one. He knew to keep his mouth shut.'

'You're a blackmailer,' Nuttall said.

He shrugged. 'We all have our crosses to bear. I had enough on all the others, on Jamie and Victoria, to make sure no one ever breathed a word.'

'So then what happened?'

'It was a wake-up call, honestly. Over the following fifteen years, I got my act together. I gave up the dealing and using, scraped a law degree at a polytechnic and found myself a junior position at a conveyancing firm in Bedford.'

'And you changed your name, didn't you?' Nuttall asked.

'Yeah. It had been Grosvenor, and everyone called me Groz. So I changed it to my mother's maiden name, Keane. I worked my way up, and then in 1988 I read about the first DNA test used for a conviction in Leicestershire, and I thought, "Shit, my DNA is bound to be on the cross." I had to do something. I tracked down Victoria, then sent her a letter, with cuttings from the Leicestershire trial. I enclosed a photocopy of a Polaroid with her and Ruth in it. I made it clear that the advent of DNA would change everything. If I went down, everybody would go down. She told me not to worry, because Entwistle wasn't likely to appeal, but she was clearly worried.'

'So how did you retrieve the crucifix from police custody?' Talantire asked.

'Victoria said her father had mentioned DCS Hogley was rumoured to have kept mementos of the crime, something the coroner took a dim view of. By this time I'd taken a job at Harbyttle & Co in Barnstaple as a senior conveyancer, and bought a house in Westward Ho! So I found where Hogley lived, and was able to keep an eye on the place. When his caravan disappeared from his drive one summer's day, I broke in round the back.'

'Drugs, dealing, blackmailing, murder and now burglary skills too,' Nuttall said.

'No, not at all. The house seemed secure, but I forced the back door into the garage, any halfwit could have done it. I was intending to go through the internal door into the house, which turned out to be bolted from the inside. But I immediately recognised a police evidence bag on a shelf. In fact there was a big box of stuff. Not only the crucifix, but a labelled evidence bag containing Entwistle's bloodstained shoes, and his shirt. I took the lot.'

'Knowing Hogley could hardly have claimed to have lost it,' Talantire said.

Keane grinned, clearly still pleased with himself. 'That's it. Even better, a few weeks later he ended up dying after falling off a ladder trying to install a burglar alarm.'

'You think that's funny?' Talantire asked.

'Well, you have to admit there's a certain irony to it.'

Talantire looked down at the earlier statement. 'Let's fast-forward to the murder of Mrs Ruth Lyle.'

'Ah, but before that, five years previously, in 2018, I heard from Alan Lyle, an estate agent I worked with sometimes, that someone was trying to impersonate his dead sister. He said that his mother, Gwen, was completely taken in. He told me he had taken her to speak to the rector of Pip and Jim's to have this nonsense knocked out of her.'

'The rector being Neal Vaizey.'

'Yes. He listened to the full story, a woman who looked just like Ruth appearing out of the blue. Vaizey said that no one but Jesus could come back from the dead. He tried to reassure her that it really wasn't possible. It was a relief to hear from Alan that the police hadn't taken it seriously. None of us knew who this impostor could be, but it was stirring up old memories, that was for sure. And that in itself was dangerous.'

'So when did you actually meet Mrs Lyle?' Talantire asked.

'Well, I saw the rental agreement for Bluebird Cottage that a colleague had prepared for Mrs Lee, and did wonder that a Mrs Susan Lyle, as she described herself, would live there. Victoria leafleted the place, and got invited in. She recognised Jamie's features, and got to hear the full story.'

'Which was?'

Keane blew out a sigh, and cupped his arms behind his head. 'Well, it had its own logic. Back in 1973, Jamie was really smitten with Ruth, I mean he absolutely adored her, we all knew that. He had been shocked to the core by her death, and described how he had made a shrine to her. He hated me, that became clear. We already knew he'd had a breakdown, lost touch with everyone, never finished his degree, and dropped out. I didn't find out until later that he'd managed to finagle his way into a geology master's at some Scottish university, pretending he'd finished his bachelor's. And that wasn't the only thing. He'd stolen a load of paperwork from Victoria that she had pinched from her father.

'You mean official documents from the coroner's office?'

'Yes. She'd fallen out with her father, and hidden a load of paperwork from the inquest at Jamie's now-vacant flat in Cranmer Road. But Jamie apparently came back to get some stuff, and must have taken it.'

'The birth certificate and dental records from young Ruth?'

'Yes, and copies of her National Insurance registration, which had only just come through on her sixteenth birthday. Anyway, he told Victoria he'd done some travelling to India, and got into reincarnation. So he thought that a life as promising as Ruth's shouldn't be cut short, but recreated, corrected and put back on the path it should always have had. Something about two souls being unified in life, rather than death.' Keane laughed, and rolled his eyes. 'It suited him anyway, because he'd never liked himself, so to be her instead of himself was a release. With the dental records, he was able to have his teeth done like hers had been, and he'd had cosmetic surgery for dimples like hers as well as the gender reassignment. That's what he, or I suppose by then she, told Victoria. Mrs Lyle rang me up at work, and said Victoria had mentioned that I lived locally, and had even given her my new name. Mrs Lyle wanted to berate me about the past, and what I'd done. I was alarmed, and didn't want to be associated with her.'

'So why not live and let live?' Talantire asked.

'Because she was stirring things up!' There was a flash of anger. 'There she was, going to the graveyard, hanging around the school where Ruth had gone. She was obsessed. It had to end. After the first conversation, I didn't return her calls, but she left messages for me, and came to visit the office one time. I'd have preferred if we could just scare her away but Victoria, having talked to her, said it wouldn't work.'

'So you decided to kill her?' Nuttall asked.

'I didn't, Victoria did.'

'But you carried it out?' Nuttall asked.

'She'd had a brilliant idea. Once she suspected that Entwistle had been released, she thought it was plausible that he'd come back to the scene of the crime. She suggested I could smear his DNA around, from the items I'd found in Hogley's garage.'

'So you doctored the cross?' Talantire.

'Yes. When I found it in Hogley's garage there was still dried blood at the sharp end from the original murder, so I held it in plastic gloves at that end, while I smeared it in bleach to get any of my DNA off where I'd held it higher up. Of course that would remove most of Entwistle's original trace too, so after I rinsed it I then re-contaminated it, using a swab I'd taken from the inside of his shoes.'

'So what happened then?' Talantire prompted.

'I rang Mrs Lyle, and she asked me to come round on April the first, as a commemoration of the fiftieth anniversary of the girl's death. I suppose she expected me to apologise. Even then, I still hoped that somehow I could persuade her not to relive Ruth's life. But she wouldn't listen. I urged her to give up the idea because it would endanger everyone else. The reply was, "Well, it was you who ended her life. I'm here to resurrect it." We argued, and then I brought out the crucifix. I had plastic gloves, but I didn't get the chance to put them on, because things got out of hand very quickly. I held her down on the kitchen table, and she screamed blue murder, so I stabbed her. And I have to say, that cross, maybe a thousand years old, is still as sharp as a tack. It went straight in. I then gagged her with her tights, as if it was a robbery. I used some surgical spirit on the shaft of the crucifix to get my DNA off, then after wiping it again I took the swab that I'd already rubbed around the inside of Entwistle's shoes and rubbed it on the crucifix, so that his DNA would definitely be on it.'

'But actually your DNA still was on it, as well as his,' Talantire said.

'So you say. I obviously wasn't thorough enough.'

'What time was that?' Talantire asked.

'About three in the afternoon. I was wearing a hoody and a baseball cap, but I don't think anyone saw me.'

'No, the neighbour didn't phone it in until a day later,' Nuttall said.

'I left down the Wilder Road end, because I knew there was a camera on the High Street. Then I had to think up a reason for all the phone calls, so I invented this property search idea.'

'So Mrs Lyle wasn't looking to buy Ruth's childhood home?' Talantire asked.

'No, I just needed a bone to throw you.'

'So why did you kill Neal Vaizey?'

He sighed. 'I really hadn't wanted to. But he was going to confess, I could feel it. So could Victoria. I think he felt so guilty about Entwistle, and especially after he had given him a place to stay.'

'So you lured him up to the clifftop, but how?'

'I said I'd finally return the Polaroids. He was keen to get them destroyed. But I also think he suspected I'd never release them. With you having worked out his connection to Ruth, I think he was going to crack. Victoria certainly felt so.'

'What about the suicide note?'

'Well, that was quite clever, if I say so myself. I needed to be able to use his phone, and it needed to be unlocked, so I got him to use it to check whether he'd been messaged. Then I hit him straight afterwards.'

'With the hammer?' Nuttall asked.

'The same one you used on PC Compton and on me,' Talantire added.

He shrugged.

'Did you write the suicide note yourself?' Talantire asked, as insouciantly as possible. If he implicated the MP, then together with the electronic phone records that would be all they would need.

'I did, but Victoria rewrote and edited it.'

Talantire and Nuttall looked at each other, trying not to grin. This deadly conspiracy was unravelling.

Chapter 30

As soon as they'd finished with Keane, Talantire and Nuttall brought Victoria Carnegie back. They knew they didn't have too long before the police heavyweights intervened, so they'd have to work fast. The top London lawyer sat with Victoria, and interrupted almost every question they asked. For half an hour, Victoria denied everything, expressing outrage that something as criminal as this could be laid at her door, and denying that she had had any dealings with Keane.

'We have solid electronic evidence and witness testimony that you helped write Reverend Neal Vaizey's suicide note,' Talantire said.

'Witness? What witness?' she replied.

'We are not at liberty to disclose that at this stage,' Talantire said.

'You will have to let the defence know, as I'm sure you're aware,' the brief said, all smooth public-school tones. He then looked down at his phone and, grim-faced, asked for a suspension to the interview for five minutes while he consulted his client. Talantire and Nuttall agreed to the request and stepped into the corridor, hoping to get a coffee. Almost immediately, Talantire got the long-dreaded phone call from her boss. But this wasn't the direct order to charge Gawain Entwistle. Detective Superintendent Wells simply said: 'I've been speaking to the commissioner and the assistant chief constable this morning. In light of the impressive new evidence you have uncovered, you have our full backing to pursue the case against both Roger Keane and Victoria Carnegie. I've already spoken to the CPS, who eagerly anticipate a case conference later today.'

'I'm delighted to hear that news, sir,' she said.

'Actually I'm very impressed with your determination, and I apologise for doubting you, and for trying to railroad the investigation. That tracing of the MP's burner phone was a superb piece of detective work.'

'Our new digital evidence officer DC Chen deserves the praise for that. I'll pass on your congratulations.'

'Good. I think you'll be seeing a radically different approach from the Honourable Lionel in future.'

'The newspapers seem to have been raising the issue of a property development between the commissioner and our suspect Mrs Carnegie, involving the redevelopment of our crime scene,' she said.

Wells smiled, now fully back to avuncular mode. 'Don't quote me on this but I think we can safely assume that that is not going to go ahead, and I understand that the commissioner will be severing all links to her forthwith.'

After the call ended, Talantire updated Nuttall and marched back into the interview room, where the change in Victoria Carnegie's countenance was extraordinary. She had clearly been in tears. She must have heard that her ally the commissioner had cut her adrift.

'I think my client is prepared to plead guilty at this stage,' the brief said.

–

It was several hours before Talantire and Maddy were able to spare the time to visit Gawain Entwistle. He had been installed temporarily in a warden-supervised social services flat, with a family liaison officer in attendance. When the two detectives walked in they saw a dejected man, his face drained of colour, no doubt expecting to be charged with the murder of Mrs Ruth Lyle.

'We've got some good news, Gawain,' Talantire said, and sat down to explain what had happened. As she did so, tears began to roll down the craggy features of this wronged man.

'Thank you, thank you so much,' he said, rocking backwards and forwards.

'No doubt in due course you will be formally pardoned,' she said. 'But I'd just like to say on behalf of the police service, and going back fifty years, that I apologise to you for all the mistakes that were made, and the ruination of your life. I just hope that you will be able to resume your new identity, undisturbed, and perhaps enjoy all the years of freedom that you have left.' She stood up and leaned forward to shake his hand. 'I will do everything in my power to make that happen.'

Epilogue

Though the case took two years to come to trial, Roger Keane and Victoria Carnegie were both sentenced to life, each for a minimum of twenty years for each of the counts of murder, conspiracy to murder and attempted murder. Sitting in the public gallery with Talantire was former PC Ian Compton, who had made a partial recovery from the head injuries inflicted by Keane's hammer but, with his fitness compromised, had retired from the police on medical grounds. He nodded with satisfaction as the verdicts were announced.

After sentencing, the judge, Lord Justice Leadbetter, said: 'What the court has heard over the course of these past few weeks has been shocking, a litany of lies and deceit going back half a century, and which cost an innocent and vulnerable man a lifetime of liberty. It was, moreover, a cruel blow to the conceit that those who seek the highest public office somehow have a higher moral standing than the rest of us. You, Mrs Carnegie, have used every tendril of your web of political connections, every ounce of your undoubted energy, and strained every sinew to pervert the course of justice. You have brought your elected position and the House of Commons into disrepute. Others will have to take the consequences for having believed you, and being taken in by your wiles. I had the honour of having trained with your late father at Lincoln's Inn in London. May I take this opportunity to say that he was an honourable man, and would have been utterly ashamed of the conduct of you, his daughter. Take her down.'

The trial took place without the crucifix being presented as an exhibit to the jury. The courier's van taking it and other evidence to the Central Criminal Court was involved in a collision with an articulated lorry on the M25. Though the driver survived, and most of the physical evidence was recovered, there was no trace of the cross, only the shattered plastic container in which it had been kept.

–

Four weeks later, on a breezy June day, Alan Lyle stood at the side of an open grave at Marlborough Road Cemetery, while the coffin of his mother Gwen was gently lowered into the ground. The new rector of Pip and Jim's, a sandy-haired youngster recently appointed, read from the Good Book, whose silver-edged leaves fluttered in the breeze that blew in from the sea. At his mother's grave, at the verse of 'ashes to ashes, dust to dust', he thought about the now-burnt fragments of a Polaroid photograph he had destroyed a week ago. The photograph, a gift to Ruth, that he had stolen from his sister's vanity case in 1973. It portrayed a shocking act that he had now convinced himself had never existed. He looked away from his mother's open grave and at the headstone of the adjoining plot, that of his big sister, snatched from life at the age of sixteen. A girl who had never lived long enough to go to university, to marry, to have children, and to see those children grow and fulfil their own lives. Alan Lyle put an arm round his own daughter, and the other round his wife, who was holding their son by the hand. He rejoiced somewhat guiltily in the family life he would live on Ruth's behalf, her now-unblemished memory preserved in death and carried forth by others.

He wasn't the first to have done so.

Afterword

I spent quite a few days in Ilfracombe looking for the ideal crime scene for this book, and was helped by local historian Kelvin Farndell, by Jean and Stephen Baker, Frances Down and bookshop owner Paul Hewitt. Thanks are also due to my long-time sources Dr Stuart Hamilton and Kim Booth, and my beta readers Jo Joseph, Valerie Richardson, Tim Cary and John Selfe. Assistance was also given by Klaudia at Wilson's car sales, while I was given much good advice and hospitality by Julie Tripp, Sarah Bennett, Helen Jennings, Murray and Dani Sharpe, plus Bill and Sarah Allen. Clive Gilbert of English Heritage, and Stephanie Gilroy, deputy registrar at Oxfordshire County Council, gave me expert advice in their respective fields.

The Canelo team under Michael Bhaskar, and editor Sian Heap, provided invaluable advice. Craig Thomson and Julian Holmes at W. F. Howes were as always supportive. Jacqui Lewis did an excellent job on the copy-editing. All remaining mistakes are my own. Last but not least, I'd like to thank my wife Louise, for her boundless patience and support during the gestation of each and every book.

Do you love crime fiction and are always on the lookout for brilliant authors?

Canelo Crime is home to some of the most exciting novels around. Thousands of readers are already enjoying our compulsive stories. Are you ready to find your new favourite writer?

Find out more and sign up to our newsletter at
canelocrime.com